CALIA'S

A tale from The Book of Roses

Kelly River

Copyright © 2024 Kelly River

All rights reserved.

ISBN 9798338020814

For Ari

Many things helped me on this journey, but none more than having a friend who was always there to talk.

CONTENTS

Chapter 1	7
Chapter 2	16
Chapter 3	28
Chapter 4	40
Chapter 5	52
Chapter 6	64
Chapter 7	74
Chapter 8	85
Chapter 9	101
Chapter 10	111
Chapter 11	123
Chapter 12	135
Chapter 13	149
Chapter 14	158
Chapter 15	168
Chapter 16	182
Chapter 17	196
Chapter 18	209

Chapter 19	224
Chapter 20	237
Chapter 21	252
Chapter 22	262
Chapter 23	271
Chapter 24	283
Epilogue	292

CHAPTER 1

The first time Calia had tried to sew on horseback, she'd put the needle halfway through her finger. Even now, at the age of twenty, her mother was still scolding her to put away her sewing and focus on the road. But her horse knew where she was going, and there was little danger to be found on the path to Tannersfield. Why waste precious hours fidgeting with her reins when she could be mending a stitch in her gloves or re-hemming an old travelling dress? It wasn't quality work, but she'd learned how to handle her needle in time with the motion of the saddle, and she had thimbles to protect her fingers this time.

Her sister, Livy, was the real distraction, having spent most of the journey lamenting how she'd been unable to bring her current boyfriend along. Livy had been falling in and out of love every year since she was fifteen. It must be easy, Calia supposed, when you were pretty and sharp-witted like her. Calia echoed nothing of her sister's golden-haired beauty. She was a short, squirrelly girl with chestnut hair and comfortably homely features, the sort who turned no heads but invited no envy either. Her passions lay in threadwork, not romance. When it became clear that she had no appetite for marriage, several people had suggested that she might become a nun. The thought was not unappealing to Calia. She suspected she might have enjoyed the peace of a convent, but in all likelihood the rigour of monastic life would've driven her mad in the end. Calia preferred doing things her own way.

"Mother's about to tell you to put that needle away again," Livy said under her breath. Calia looked up and saw that they were leaving the forest path. The walls of Tannersfield town rose in front of them, a fat stone crown straddling the river that tumbled down from the northern hills.

"I want to go to the market after we meet Wolfram," Calia said. "Do you think they'll have lots of wool for sale?"

"Of course they will. It's the biggest market in the county."

Calia smiled. "Good. I want as many different shades of blue as they have."

"What for?"

"My tapestry."

"Why do you need that many?"

"Look at the sky." Calia pointed up. "It's not all one shade, is it? See those bits of cloud over there? They make it look much paler."

Livy shook her head. "You have such an eye for these things."

Calia always felt a swell of happiness when her siblings praised her. They were very different from one another, but she loved them dearly. Livy had a good head for numbers and knew how to handle people, so she'd been the one who followed their mother into the merchant trade. Their brother Wolfram had been a squire for the past seven years and was about to be knighted. That was their reason for visiting Tannersfield; a great tournament was about to be held here in the heart of the county, and a handful of young men like Wolfram would be receiving their knighthoods as part of the festivities. The king and queen themselves would be in attendance. Across the meadows, Calia could already see tents, stalls, stages, and shanty-town dwellings popping up like petals in a bright garden.

"Come up here, girls," Calia's father called. "There are always idle hands in Tannersfield."

"Really, Father, it's not as bad as it was when you lived here," Livy said, but she kicked her horse forward all the same. Calia put her sewing away and followed. James, their escort, straightened his sword belt and rode ahead to clear the path.

"We make quite a distinguished party, the five of us," Calia's mother said cheerfully.

"More's the pity," Papa said under his breath.

"Would you cheer up? Your son's about to be knighted."

"I'd rather he was coming home to mind the horses with me."

"But it's what he wants, Papa," Calia said.

"I know, I know." Papa sighed. "I'm happy if he's happy."

Mama squeezed his arm. "Then at least try to look it."

Their progress slowed as they approached the town gates. The road ahead was packed with travellers streaming in from the surrounding villages. Hawkers congregated on the sidelines trying to press their wares upon the endless tide of visitors. Wealthy families like Calia's drew the most attention, for their fine horses and colourful clothing marked them out as keen pickings for merchants and pickpockets alike. That was why they had James with them. The man-at-arms glared at everyone in his path as he urged his horse forward, keeping one hand on his sword to forestall the courage of any light-fingered bystanders.

Mama and Livy, the merchants of the family, were used to travelling in such company, but it always made Calia's father uncomfortable. Papa came from noble blood. His father had been a great duke, and his sister—Calia's aunt—was married to the count of Tannersfield. If anything, they should have been travelling with a far grander entourage. But from as early as she could remember, Calia and her siblings had always been discouraged from acknowledging their noble roots. They were just common folk now, Papa said, and they were never to curry favour or seek influence with their noble relatives. That was why he was upset about Wolfram's impending knighthood. Calia didn't know the specifics, but there had been a great deal of bad blood between Papa and his family. The idea that his son would now be stepping back into the ranks of the nobility clearly bothered him. He was a man who saw great virtue in living plainly and simply. Unlike most people, he put no faith in the religious and aristocratic traditions that governed the kingdom, believing instead that personal freedom was more precious.

In an effort to take Papa's mind off things, Calia rode up beside him and opened her saddlebag. Alongside her sewing kit and travelling clothes, she had a hand loom: a flat piece of wood shaped like an hourglass so that it could be gripped in the middle. It had evenly spaced nails in either end between which the warp threads of a small tapestry could be stretched. The warp was the backbone of a tapestry, consisting of strong, plain wool, while the ribs were the coloured threads of weft you wove across the warp to create a picture. Calia's hand loom held a piece she'd been working on for a couple of weeks. The design had to be abstract, for it was impossible to weave a realistic picture across such a small warp, but her father recognised it immediately. A smile spread across his face.

"It's Damson, isn't it?" he said, patting his horse's neck. "Look, girl. Calia's woven a portrait of you."

"I'm glad you recognised it. I always worry when I stare at these things for too long."

"You've nothing to worry about. Any lord would be glad to have one of your tapestries in his hall. I'd say you have an even better eye for it than your sewing."

"I'm going to make one for Wolfram while we're here. I want to depict him being knighted."

"That sounds like a lovely gift."

"Why don't you sell any of your tapestries?" Livy asked, ever the merchant.

The crowd tightened around them as they made their way through the town gates, and Calia had to raise her voice to be heard over the clamour. "The weavers' guild wouldn't like that."

"You should get them to admit you. You did as much weaving as sewing during your apprenticeship."

"I wouldn't want to cause a fuss."

They had to break off their conversation at that point, for the roar of the crowd was growing so loud that they struggled to hear each other. The street was packed, and they were forced to stretch out in single file behind James as he cleared the way.

Calia was talented at both weaving and sewing, it was true. She'd apprenticed for seven years under a seasoned old tailor named Milly who'd taught her as much about working a bobbin as she had a needle. But Milly had been a master of the tailors' guild, not the weavers'. Trade guilds policed the business of craftwork in the kingdom. To be recognised as a qualified craftsperson, you had to complete a lengthy apprenticeship under a master who belonged to one of those guilds. Those who did not faced fines, professional ostracism, and a constant uphill battle to find work. So while Calia was recognised as a tailor by Milly's guild, her weaving had to remain little more than a hobby. Guilds could be insular and incestuous organisations, and she didn't fancy her chances of convincing the weavers that she was worthy of recognition. She wasn't a confrontational person by nature.

The further they got into town, the worse the crowds became. They were heading for the count's castle, which sat just opposite the marketplace in the centre of Tannersfield. Everyone would be congregating there on a day like this. Calia clutched her saddlebag and tried to stay close to Livy's horse. The noise and the crowds frightened her. It wasn't anything like the quiet village she was used to. By contrast, Livy seemed to be in her element, sitting up straight in the saddle and waving to people she recognised. Calia just wanted to sit down somewhere cool and quiet and drink a nice cup of ale.

Upon reaching the marketplace, it became clear that the source of the clamour was twofold; the town gallows had been appropriated by a group of knights who appeared to be putting on an impromptu show. The tournament wasn't due to start until tomorrow, but that hadn't stopped this particular group of young men from donning armour and crossing swords in front of a baying crowd. They danced back and forth across the gallows, the precarious wooden platform adding an extra layer of drama to the spectacle as their blunt practice blades clacked and crashed amidst the cheers of the onlookers. Calia only stopped to stare for a moment, but when she turned back around, Livy's horse had already drawn ahead and people were pushing into the space between them.

"Excuse me!" Calia called, trying to urge her mare forward. A boy ran in front of her and she had to squeeze the reins suddenly to bring herself to a halt. The motion of the crowd was carrying her away from her family. People pushed on her horse's flank, trying to urge it out of the way so they could get a better look at the duelling knights. Someone cried out in front of her, and Calia realised she wasn't the only person in difficulty. The people at the back of the crowd were pushing forward, not realising that those nearest the gallows were being tripped up. If they kept on like this, someone would be trampled.

"Stop pushing!" she called.

A young farmer looked up at her with a scowl. He probably saw a haughty noblewoman out to spoil everyone's fun. He gave her horse a slap on the flank, and the mare lurched forward with a whinny. Half a dozen people in front of Calia toppled over as the horse bulled them aside. She stared down in a panic, frantically squeezing the reins to try and wrest her mare under control. At any moment, one of the horse's hooves might stamp on someone. People were shouting, their voices crashing against her ears like the clash of the knights' swords. A surge of bodies shifted the momentum away from the gallows, and people started pushing in all directions at once.

Calia frantically scanned the marketplace for her family, but they were nowhere to be seen. A mounting sense of terror clutched at her chest. She had to get free of the commotion before her horse injured someone or threw her off. The only hint of calm lay at the eastern end of the gallows, where some merchants seemed to be trying to quell the chaos before it spilt over into their stalls. That looked like the safest place to be right now, so Calia tried to guide her horse in that direction. The mare stumbled and whinnied as people pushed against her, snorting nervous breaths through her nostrils. Twice Calia felt her front hooves leave the ground as she threatened to rear. She pushed her weight down against the saddle as hard as she could, squeezing the reins with one hand and stroking her horse's neck with the other. There was a tailor's stall behind the merchants, and its colourful bales of cloth called out to Calia like a beacon. Her panic began to steady as the rowdy crowd thinned out.

"Come over here, miss!" a female voice called. Calia saw a neatly-dressed woman in her twenties motioning her over. She had a long linen bag draped over one arm of the sort that was often used to carry particularly expensive or delicate articles of clothing.

Calia was almost free of the crowd when someone gave her horse's tail a sharp yank. The mare whinnied and bolted forward, cannoning straight into the woman with the bag. Calia's heart leapt as she desperately squeezed the reins, but she pulled too hard, and her horse reared. She fell out of the saddle, remembering at the last second to tug her feet free from the stirrups before she twisted her ankle. The woman with the bag tried to catch her, but she fumbled and the pair of them crashed to the ground in a bruising twist of knees and elbows.

Calia groaned as she picked herself up, offering the other woman her hand. The pair of them were muddy, and they would probably have a few bruises by the evening, but it wasn't her safety the other woman was concerned with. Scrambling to her knees, she gathered up her linen bag with the delicacy of a mother handling a newborn infant. Calia helped her to her feet. A merchant at the tailor's stall managed to corral Calia's horse and calm her down. He led the mare back over and handed Calia the bridle.

"Are you ladies alright?"

Calia nodded her gratitude. "I think so. Thank you, sir."

"It's those bloody fool knights. There's a reason we hold tournaments outside the town walls."

The momentary ruckus was quickly settling. When people started falling over, the surge of bodies had loosened up and the knights on the gallows paused their performance to make sure no one got hurt. Bloody fools or not, at least they had the sense to keep the safety of their audience in mind.

The woman with the linen bag looked mortified as she laid it out on the merchant's bales and brushed off the mud. There was a rip in the bottom alongside a dirty bootprint. Calia immediately felt guilty. If she'd ruined this poor woman's purchase, she would have to compensate her. When the bag came open, she gasped.

The garment inside wasn't a dress; it was a masterpiece. Luminous blue and white silk had been sewn together to create a pattern of colour that reminded Calia of a river flashing in the summer sun. Trimmings of golden yellow accented the shoulders and flowed down the sleeves, complemented by silver and gold thread that sparkled even more brightly than the silk. Every hem boasted embroidery almost as elaborate as the tapestry on Calia's loom. It was broken only in one spot where an ugly rip had opened up a seam near the ankle. The priceless gold thread had twisted and snapped, marring the work of art with a horrible blemish. Calia didn't need to ask how much it cost; she knew she couldn't afford to pay for it.

The other woman stared at the ripped dress as if mourning the death of a lover.

"I'm so sorry!" Calia stumbled over her apologies. "This is all my fault! If I hadn't run into you, this never would've happened."

The other woman blinked, snapping out of her daze. She shook her head distractedly. "Oh, you're not to blame." The dismal tone of her voice only made Calia feel worse.

"I'll help you mend it. I'm a tailor. I don't think I can afford any gold thread, but I'm sure we can do something."

"We couldn't get any, anyway. The man who made this used up the last he had."

"Well, I still want to make amends."

The woman nodded and took a deep breath. "My name's Lucy. I'm a tailor, too."

Calia smiled at her. She hadn't met many tailors who weren't part of her guild. "I'm Calia. Between the two of us, we'll make this dress good as new." She looked at the wonderful garment again, taking a moment to admire its beauty. "It's marvellous work. It looks like something you'd see at the queen's court."

"It is," Lucy said. "I'm part of Queen Meredith's entourage. She's supposed to be wearing it to the banquet tonight."

CHAPTER 2

There was no question of having the dress properly restored in time for the banquet. Even if they could have returned it to the original tailor, procured more gold thread, and paid for it all, the embroidery was simply too intricate to replicate at short notice. It was already well into the afternoon, and the banquet at the castle was due to start within a few hours. Calia negotiated her way through the marketplace crowd with Lucy in tow. She found her family waiting outside the castle gates. Her parents looked relieved to see her.

"I thought we'd lost you in the market," Papa said.

Calia passed her horse's bridle to Livy and hurried on by. "Tell Wolfram I'm sorry I missed him! I'll see you all at the banquet later!" There was no time for her to explain. If there was any hope of salvaging the dress and keeping Lucy out of trouble, they had to get to work right away. Calia felt personally responsible for what had happened. She didn't know what kind of woman Queen Meredith was, but she'd heard all sorts of grisly tales about the punishments inflicted on royal servants who displeased their monarchs.

Lucy was recognised by the castle guards and they were let through the gate without delay. Tannersfield Castle bustled with noble guests. Colourful dresses and surcoats bloomed all around them, a stark contrast to the brown and grey homespun that blanketed the marketplace. As relatives of the countess, Calia's family would be attending the banquet as well, though they would probably be seated at one of the low tables far away from the royals. Had she not been in such a rush, Calia would have stopped to stare at the noblewomen in their striking dresses, the knights with gilded buckles on their belts, the bishop and his deacons huddled in a cabal of black robes, and the minstrel setting up an instrument that looked like a fretted loom played with tiny hammers.

Lucy led the way into the keep, across the great hall, through another door, and up a flight of stairs to a solar. It was a large living space with private rooms used by the count of Tannersfield and his family, but today it would doubtless be housing the royals. Lucy took them into one of the side chambers and closed the door behind them. She unshuttered a pair of large windows to illuminate a long table laid with several dresses, most of which looked almost as expensive as the damaged one. Calia would have given anything to spend all afternoon admiring these treasures. She loved studying other people's work. Everyone did things slightly differently. Whenever she saw a new type of stitch or seam, she wanted to understand why the tailor had chosen that particular technique and reflect on whether she would have made the same choice. Old Milly had always said a craftswoman's training didn't stop when she finished her apprenticeship; it was a lifelong process. Innovation kept the craft fresh, and those who didn't adapt to new techniques ended up stagnating.

"I think I can repair the rip in time," Lucy said breathlessly. She no longer sounded bleak, but there was an undercurrent of panic in her voice that impressed upon Calia the urgency of their task. "I don't know what to do about the embroidery, though."

"What sort of thread do you have?" Calia asked.

"No gold."

"It doesn't have to be. Just a yellow that matches the hem patterns."

Lucy shook her head with a pained look. "It won't work. Even if we can cover up the damage, it won't match the other side. It all has to be symmetrical."

She was right. The left side of the dress perfectly mirrored its counterpart. Any improvised pattern would stand out like a scar; an ugly crease in the harmony of the garment. Calia continued to think as she searched Lucy's thread box for a colour that matched the golden yellow of the embroidery. To her relief, there was one spool that held almost the same shade. The difference would be noticeable up close, but not under the firelight of an evening banquet. Hopefully tomorrow Lucy would have time to take the dress back to the original tailor and get it mended properly.

"I've got an idea," Calia said as Lucy set to work repairing the torn seam. "We can't both sew the same part at once. What if I embroider a new pattern on the right side, in the same place the tear is on the left, then we copy it over onto the left side after you've mended the seam? That way, everything will match."

"Are you good with embroidery?"

"I've been sewing since I was eleven."

"I started when I was thirteen."

Hearing no objection, Calia sat down on the opposite side of the table and smoothed out the area of the dress she would be working on. "You look older than me, though."

"I'm twenty-seven."

"Have you served the queen long?"

Lucy shook her head. The conversation seemed to be helping with her nerves. She was a tall, broad-shouldered woman with curly brown hair and a gentle voice, sporting a complexion that indicated she spent most of her time indoors.

"No, I'm not part of the royal household. I work at the

queen's manor house in Farrenwold. She only visits when she's away from the capital. Her personal tailor took ill on the way here, so I had to take her place."

Lucy's panic made even more sense now. If this was only a temporary duty, it would reflect especially poorly on her if she made a fool of herself. Calia had brought her saddlebag in with her, and she set it down on the table to take out her sewing box. It had fallen to the bottom beneath everything else. She lifted out her hand loom, then opened the box and retrieved the folded leather pocket that held her needles. She felt the material of the queen's dress between her fingers, getting a sense of its texture and thickness. Silk was a delicate and slippery fabric. She sometimes used a bone needle when working with silk thread, but fabric was different. The yellow thread was quite coarse, and she was afraid that her thick bone needles might tear the fabric if she wasn't careful. A thin metal needle was best for delicate embroidery like this.

As she prepared her thread, she noticed Lucy staring at the tapestry on her hand loom.

"Sorry, that's just a hobby of mine," Calia said, hastily moving it out of the way.

"It's wonderful. Who taught you?"

"My master, Milly. She was a good weaver."

"If you can embroider half as well as you weave, I think we might just save this dress after all."

Calia smiled. She was starting to like Lucy. The other tailor could've easily been angry or impatient at a time like this—Calia certainly felt like she deserved it—but the compliment lifted her spirits and rekindled her determination. She'd always wondered whether her friends and family were just humouring her when they praised her weaving. Having never been able to sell it to anyone with an artistic eye, she was only half-sure she was any good. But to have a fellow tailor acknowledge her skill was a validation she hadn't known she needed. Perhaps, when she got home, she would pursue recognition from the weavers' guild after all.

The pair of them worked tirelessly on the queen's dress for the better part of three hours. Several servants came and went, but none of them interrupted. At first Calia was worried it would be impossible to add anything to the complex embroidery without making her side look ugly. Whoever had made the dress was a master beyond compare. She felt like a child daubing finger paints over someone's grand mural. But when she studied the embroidery closely, she noticed that there were thicker patterns of golden-yellow thread in certain places. They'd been used to cover up a few particularly difficult seams in the numerous layers of blue, white, and gold. Most of them were shaped in a repeating hourglass pattern, which was easy enough to replicate. A tailor would know they were only supposed to appear along specific seams, but the queen and her vassals wouldn't.

"Let's use this pattern." She pointed it out to Lucy. "It'll look like it matches the rest of the dress."

Lucy nodded, her eyes lighting up. "That could work."

Calia embroidered as fast as she dared. Her stitches weren't as tight as she would've liked, and the pattern would be loose as a result, but it only had to last one evening. She spent most of the afternoon ensuring that the parts connecting to the original pattern matched evenly. Lucy worked faster than her and soon had the rip mended. It was a good thing they'd divided the work as they did, for despite having more sewing to do, Lucy managed to complete her section of embroidery at the same time as Calia.

"You're very good," Calia said once they were done. "No wonder you work for the queen."

"I still couldn't have done it without you. I expect Her Majesty will be up here to change any moment now."

"I should go, then. My family will be wondering where I am."

"Won't you stay? We could present the dress to her together."

Calia flushed and shook her head. "Oh, no. I couldn't. Besides, she might ask what happened."

"I have to repay you somehow."

"I should be the one repaying you! It was my horse that caused all this trouble."

Lucy tutted. Now that she'd calmed down, she had the air of an older sister about her. "That was an accident, and not many people would've given up their afternoon to set it right."

Calia shrugged, still feeling uncomfortable. People always told her she was shy and should take more credit for herself. Perhaps they were right, but she didn't view it that way. She just didn't see the need to make a spectacle of something that came naturally to her. She mended clothes every day. An audience with the queen seemed an absurd reward for a few hours of embroidery.

Lucy pursed her lips sternly, but she relented when she saw that Calia wasn't going to change her mind.

"Alright, then. But I'm going to make it up to you one way or another. Are you staying here at the castle?"

Calia nodded. "We'll be at the banquet. Perhaps I'll see you there?"

"I expect so. Thank you again. I'd give anything to have an assistant like you at home."

Not wanting Lucy to see her blush, Calia picked up her saddlebag and hurried to the door. She felt like she'd made a friend that afternoon.

When she got downstairs, the great hall was in the process of being set for the banquet. Tables that had been pushed against the walls when she came in were now lined up in tiered rows. Most of the guests had cleared out, and the servants were bringing in casks of wine and stacks of tableware. Through the high windows, Calia could see the sky turning sunset orange.

She found her family outside by the stables. Her mother

and Livy were sitting on a bench talking to a pretty young noblewoman while Papa and her brother Wolfram fawned over the horses. Papa's spirits looked much improved by the change in scenery. Horses were his passion, and there were few things he enjoyed more than bonding with his son over stable talk. When Wolfram saw Calia, he ran over with a grin and lifted her into a big hug. He was tall and handsome, with the same fair hair as Livy, and years of training as a squire had given him hard muscles that squeezed the breath from her lungs. She was always pleased to see her brother. As children, Calia and Livy had bonded naturally as the two girls of the trio, but in terms of personality, Calia had always felt closer to Wolfram. His heart was an open book, while Livy tangled hers up in work and whimsy.

They talked until the light faded, catching up on news of the past few months before going inside to join the banquet. Papa made a point of picking seats far away from the nobles at a table occupied by the bishop's deacons and a few squires. The pretty girl Livy had been talking to earlier joined them. As the food and drink were served, Calia noticed that her sister had stopped talking about the boy who'd been on her mind since they left home. Now she seemed far more interested in laughing at her new friend's jokes and touching her hand beneath the table.

Calia held her breath when the royals were announced. They came in through the door leading to the solar. King Fendrel took the lead. He was slightly younger than Calia's parents, though his hair was mostly grey despite only being in his early forties. He'd been on the throne for twenty-eight years, during which time he'd been locked in a seemingly endless power struggle between his vassals and the church. People called him King Fendrel the Pious because of how consistently he favoured the clergy. Bishops loved him and barons resented him, but his faith was a shield that had kept the land largely at peace during his reign. He was broadly considered to be a saintly figure, and it was difficult for anyone to challenge such a man without inviting the ire of the kingdom at large. An attack on the king was an attack on God, and Fendrel stood closer to Him than any of his forebears in living memory.

Queen Meredith entered next. She was an unassuming woman, plain in appearance and perhaps a decade her husband's junior, but her high cheekbones and pinned buns of hair conveyed a look of absolute confidence and authority. The blue and white dress Calia had spent the afternoon mending fit her figure perfectly. Every time she moved, the silver and gold thread caught the light, making her sparkle and shimmer like a nymph crossing a mirrored pond. No one in the room could have ignored her even if they tried. It was hard to tell from a distance, but when Calia caught sight of the spot that had been torn, it seemed as good as new. Lucy came in with the queen's other retainers and caught her eye, flashing a smile before taking a seat at one of the lower tables. It brought Calia a warm sense of accomplishment to know that she'd been involved in preserving a small piece of tonight's spectacle, even if no one would ever know it.

As the wine began to flow, the festivities opened in earnest. Along with fine food and drink, entertainers were brought in to perform throughout the night. Minstrels played music and sang songs, jesters tumbled and juggled, knights recited poetry, and at one point a monstrous beast from a foreign land was put on display in the centre of the hall. It looked like a domestic cat, but it was as big as a hunting hound, and when the handlers pulled back its paw pads, claws the size of knives slipped out. Wolfram looked fascinated by the beast, but Calia was terrified, and she was relieved when the handlers took it back outside.

Noticing her distress, Papa asked if she would show Wolfram the tapestry she'd been weaving. Calia was glad for the distraction. She reached into her saddlebag beneath the table and felt around for the hand loom, but it wasn't there. With a swell of dismay, she realised she must have left it in the solar. She'd moved it aside when Lucy asked about it, and in her hurry to leave she hadn't remembered to pick it back up. She hoped it hadn't been tidied away somewhere by a servant.

She explained what had happened and pointed Lucy out to her family.

"Go and ask her where it went," Livy said, giving her a nudge.

"I don't want to go up there on my own."

"Oh, come on, Calia. You're the countess's niece. It isn't as if you're asking for a sip from the queen's goblet."

Livy's new friend giggled.

"I believe in you," Wolfram said encouragingly.

"Alright. Give me some courage. I'll take a sip of your wine instead of the queen's."

Wolfram passed her his cup. Calia swallowed a third of its contents in one go. The wine was much stronger than her ale. Feigning confidence, she stood up and approached Lucy's table near the end of the hall. Lots of other people were milling about by now, but she still felt painfully conspicuous as she drew closer to the king and queen. They were seated at the high table next to the count of Tannersfield and Calia's aunt. She prayed she wouldn't be noticed and called over. She angled away from the high table when she reached the end of the room and bent down to pluck at Lucy's shoulder.

"I'm sorry to bother you, Lucy, but do you know what happened to my little loom? I think I left it upstairs earlier."

Lucy beamed the smile of a woman who was enjoying her wine a little too much. "Of course! Come with me, I'll show you."

Calia's shoulders sagged with relief. "Thank you. I would've been so upset if I lost it."

Lucy got up and took Calia's hand, leading her around the edge of the steps that surrounded the high table. They made for the door at the back of the room, but to Calia's dismay, Lucy turned before they reached it and ascended the steps toward the royals.

"Lucy!" Calia hissed under her breath. "Where are you going?"

"Shh, I told you I'd think of something to repay you. Come on, your loom's right here."

Calia tried to resist the tug on her hand, but Lucy was insistent. She took her behind the high table, past the count and countess, and came to a halt directly beside Queen Meredith's chair. Calia's heart pounded like a drum. She was certain every eye in the room must be on her as she stood there waiting to be acknowledged. Once the queen had finished an exchange with the bishop seated opposite her, she turned towards them. Lucy curtseyed, and Calia quickly copied her. Queen Meredith appraised them with a curious eye.

"Is this our weaver?" Her voice was sharp and strong, somehow reminiscent of the taste of Wolfram's wine.

"Yes, Your Majesty," Lucy said. "This is Calia Tailor, from Kingalen."

"You've come a long way for the tournament."

Calia didn't know how to respond, so she just said: "Yes, Your Majesty."

Queen Meredith moved her hand and picked up something that had been sitting on the table just out of view. Calia's heart skipped a beat when she recognised her hand loom.

"So, Kingalen is where all the talented young weavers hide, is it?"

"I wouldn't know, Your Majesty."

"Don't be modest. Your work is excellent. Lucy knows I've been searching for skilled weavers. Are you commissioned at a master's rate?"

Calia tried to explain that she wasn't a formally qualified weaver, but she tried to say two things at once and stumbled over her words.

The queen waved a hand to quiet her and went on: "I will

pay you twice that much if you come and work for me at my Farrenwold manor. I'll need you till at least the end of the year, perhaps longer."

Calia was dumbstruck. A master tapestry weaver's rate was often in excess of twenty silver shillings a month, a small fortune compared to the two or three silver shillings most decently-paid jobs provided. A year of work at that rate would make her wealthy, to say nothing of the prestige it would bring.

Queen Meredith seemed amused by her reaction. "Think it over if you would like, but I expect an answer by the time I depart. You can join my entourage and we'll deliver you straight to the manor."

"Thank you, Your Majesty. May I ask what the work would entail?" Calia still had no idea whether she could accept such a job. It would mean leaving home and striking out by herself. She wasn't sure if she was ready for that, let alone in a position that put her at the disposal of the queen herself.

Meredith admired the weaving on Calia's loom one more time before handing it back to her. "Are you familiar with a tapestry called the Farren Vale?"

"Passingly, Your Majesty. It's very famous, is it not?"

"Only among those with an interest in art." Meredith shot a pointed look in her husband's direction, but he was talking to the bishop and seemed not to notice. "It's rather a legend; one of the largest tapestries ever woven, and reputedly with a skill never since replicated in this kingdom. Foreign tapestries put ours to shame these days, but I've taken it upon myself to change that."

"By recreating the Farren Vale?"

Queen Meredith nodded. She seemed to enjoy discussing her idea with someone who could appreciate it. She struck Calia as an eccentric woman who didn't get the chance to indulge her passions very often.

"The original was destroyed when Castle Ashmount was

razed some eighty-seven years ago, but sketches of much of the design survive. I've been collecting talented artisans like yourself in an effort to recreate it. You'll be able to visit the castle ruins and see where the original once hung for yourself. My manor is only a short distance down the hill."

Calia noticed that the queen was speaking as if she'd already accepted the job. She probably wasn't used to having her offers rejected. Did Calia even have a choice? As far as she understood, weavers were usually commissioned through their guilds, who negotiated fees and wages, but it stood to reason that the queen had the power to circumvent that.

When Calia remained silent, Meredith abruptly turned around and waved her away. "You may go to Lucy if you need help organising your personal affairs. We leave the day after the tournament concludes."

Lucy curtseyed even though the queen was no longer looking at them. Once again, Calia copied her. The pair of them made their way down from the high table, whereupon Calia immediately pinched Lucy's arm.

"Why did you have to show her?"

"I thought you'd be pleased! It'll be the making of your career."

Calia chewed her lip nervously. "I know, but it's so much. Am I even allowed to say no?"

"If you really don't want to go, it's best you don't say anything at all. The queen will be too busy to chase you down before she leaves. But please think it over. I meant what I said earlier about wanting an assistant like you at the manor."

The thought of accompanying Lucy made it seem a little more palatable. At least she would have someone friendly to help her settle in. All the same, it was too much for her to decide right away.

The tournament was set to last for the next four days. She had that long to decide whether she wanted to remain a humble tailor, or pledge herself to the queen's service.

CHAPTER 3

Wolfram was knighted on the first day of the tournament. Calia sketched the ceremony in charcoal on a vellum square. She wasn't an exceptionally good artist, but that didn't matter. Once she had a reference for her weaving, coloured thread would bring her simple black-and-white sketch to life. It was Wolfram's day, so she didn't steal his thunder by bringing up the queen's offer. When her family asked what had happened at the high table, she only said that Lucy had introduced her to the royals as a thank-you for the work she'd done.

She spent most of the day with Wolfram and Livy picking out thread for her new tapestry at market. Her brother was in high spirits, thrilled that he'd finally achieved his life's ambition of becoming a knight. There was a girl back at his lord's manor he'd fallen in love with, and now that he had his title, he was going to marry her. He would save his money and build them a fine house, then everyone would be invited to a wedding celebration when they moved in. Calia was happy for him. Both her siblings seemed to be striding headlong into bold and ambitious new lives. Livy negotiated the marketplace with supreme confidence, pointing out which merchants were trustworthy and which were not, exchanging sharp, witty banter with the locals, and flirting with a couple of the sellers to invite discounts.

Calia had never felt like she was destined for the rich and glamorous lives of her siblings. To her, a good life would be one like her father's, full of honest, satisfying work, loving people, and financial security to carry her through the hard times.

But, if she wanted, she *could* lead a life of wealth and prestige. The opportunity had been laid before her. All she had to do was reach out and take it.

Instead of thinking about what she was going to do, she spent most of the tournament working on Wolfram's tapestry. She kept her thread in her bag and her loom in her lap as she sat in the stalls watching the grand melee on the second day. The men of Tannersfield County were fighting the men of Farrenwold. Wolfram participated on the Tannersfield side. Clubs thudded into shields and greathelms rattled as both groups tried to beat each other into submission. It was a mock battle, but just like in real war, the victors had the right to ransom any captured opponents back to their families. The men of Farrenwold won in the end, but Wolfram distinguished himself by managing to avoid capture.

On the third day, contests of archery and wrestling were held. These were considered the peasant sports in which anyone was free to participate. Calia applauded when a gap-toothed woodsman's son claimed the foremost archery prize of two dozen silver shillings and a longbow made by one of the finest bowyers in the county. Her tapestry was coming along well, but there was no chance of finishing it before the tournament was over. She would have to arrange for it to be sent on to Wolfram at a later date.

And she was still no closer to making her decision.

The final day of the tournament dawned with a queasy feeling in Calia's stomach. She couldn't concentrate on her tapestry, nor could she focus on Wolfram's explanation of the main event that day, the joust, which was a new trend of mounted knights attempting to knock one another off horses. Her brother was saying something about how the rising popularity of plated armour had turned cavalry training like this into a thrilling contest, but it went in one ear and out the other. She couldn't stop looking at the king and queen's stage on the opposite side of the tournament grounds. She spotted Lucy there amongst the crowd and fancied she was looking back at her.

Knowing that she would never decide on her own, she finally confessed her turmoil to her parents during a lull in the festivities. Livy and Wolfram were off enjoying the tournament stalls while Mama and Papa sat beneath a shaded tree at the edge of a meadow.

"I have to decide today," Calia concluded, twisting a stalk of grass about her fingers. "The queen will be leaving tomorrow."

Papa rested a hand on her shoulder. "It's your choice, Calia. You're a grown woman. If you think this is what you want, you should do it. And if you feel you'd be happier at home, we'll always be there for you."

Despite Papa's reassuring tone, it wasn't what Calia needed to hear right now. He valued freedom to a fault, so much so that he wouldn't push her one way or another. But she wanted to be pushed. She needed a reason to stay or go. She looked to her mother instead. Mama's expression was pained but firm.

"You'll never get an opportunity like this again. Whether you think it's right for you or not, it's something special. You'll learn things you never could at home. And the money won't hurt, either."

"So you think I should do it?"

"Yes."

"Only if you want to," Papa added.

"Then I think I will," Calia said, feeling her anxiety rush out of her as it gave way to excitement. "The queen's supposed to be getting lots of good weavers together. Milly always said you don't stop learning just because your apprenticeship's over."

"Quite right," Mama said. "You'll be able to learn from the best in the land. Let's see the weavers' guild try and reject you after you've worked on a tapestry for the queen! Speaking of which, I wouldn't mention that you haven't been recognised by a guild. Folk of privileged birth are always looking for ways to exclude those who don't live up to their standards. Don't give them any reason to think you're not every bit as good as them. Let your work speak for itself."

Calia nodded. "Alright. I'll do it. I'll find Lucy and tell her I want to work on the queen's tapestry."

Mama pulled her into a big hug. Her brusque confidence was exactly what she'd needed. Mama was a tough woman. She'd been born poor and built her fortune while bringing up three children. When she made decisions, Calia knew there was good sense behind them.

She found Lucy at the castle that afternoon and gave her her answer.

"I'm so glad you said yes! Ashmount House is a wonderful place. We'll get you settled in before you know it. Have you got everything you need for the journey?"

"I think so. But if I'm to move permanently, I'll need my things from home. Clothes and bags and my full-sized loom."

"Oh, don't worry about that. You'll have a loom of your own at Ashmount House. We can have everything else sent for."

"I suppose I'll be able to afford it."

"You'll be able to afford a dress like the queen's before long."

Calia gave her a wry smile. "Don't be silly. I wouldn't look good in something like that."

"Everyone looks good in something. I think green would suit you. If you commission me, I'll make sure you get a discount."

"Maybe one day. Thank you. I'm sorry I was short with you at the banquet. It was just very overwhelming."

Lucy brushed off the apology with a shake of her head. "I was a bit drunk. I should've asked you first."

"If you had, I probably would've said no."

"We'll need to work on your confidence. You impressed the queen! Not many women can say that."

"I'll try my best."

"You'll *do* your best," Lucy insisted. "Come on, let's make sure we have everything packed for tomorrow. The king likes to leave early."

Calia bade an emotional farewell to her family outside the castle stables the following morning. It was barely light, the sky still mauve with waning darkness. Hooves clopped down the castle path in procession as knights and servants of the royal entourage led their horses out one at a time. Soon Calia would fall in behind them. She shouldn't be too sad, she told herself. Ashmount was only about two days' ride from the little village of Kingalen she called home. That was closer than Tannersfield town, but it was also across the county border in neighbouring Farrenwold. That made it seem farther away somehow. People said Farrenwold was a wild and windy part of the kingdom, covered in lonely moors and weathered farmsteads, quite unlike the sunny hills she was used to.

Calia hugged her siblings and parents one last time, then mounted up and waved goodbye. They promised to visit her as soon as she was settled. As the royal procession moved off, Wolfram called after her, saying she had better find time to make his fiancée a dress for their wedding. That made Calia look back with a grin. It was a happy end to the parting.

The journey to Farrenwold took five days, with a few stops and starts along the way as the royal entourage shed followers and gained new ones. Calia rode near the back of the group with Lucy and some of the queen's other servants. She had no opportunity to interact with the royals again. During the day, Queen Meredith and King Fendrel rode far ahead surrounded by knights and nobles, and at night they lodged at their subjects' manor houses while Calia and the others slept at inns or on church floors.

It was a warm spring and the weather was fair for riding, but Calia had never endured travel particularly well. By the time they arrived at their destination, she was worn out, her thighs so sore she could barely climb out of the saddle. Ashmount was a small but prosperous town, lacking much cultivable land but boasting a working gold mine to make up for it. The town sat on a hill at the crest of a rocky valley that shot out from the forest to split open the endless moors beyond. The mine was somewhere down below, far enough away that the noise of hammers and the smoke of smithies didn't bother the rich folk who profited from them. There seemed to be a lot of jewellers and merchants in town, and Calia made a mental note to tell Livy about it when they next spoke. Livy had always loved fine jewellery.

Two structures crowned the hill overlooking the valley: the ruins of the old castle and the queen's manor house. Castle Ashmount stood at the top, one wall reduced to rubble and the rest gapped like broken teeth. The keep roof was missing, and Calia assumed the interior was similarly gutted. Lucy said the town had been razed in war almost a century ago, the castle burnt out and its famous tapestry destroyed. Even in times of peace, martially-minded noblemen still favoured stone castles as symbols of might and prestige, but there was a growing trend of lords and ladies living in comfortable manor houses like the ones enjoyed by the merchant class. Ashmount Manor was just such a house. It sat on the edge of the town proper a few hundred yards down the hill from the castle. It was one of the biggest buildings Calia had ever seen. Like a convent, it had a square outer wall enclosing a courtyard with stables and kitchen buildings on either side. The manor itself had three vaulted rooftops, a large one in the centre and two smaller ones abutting it at right angles. The central part probably housed the great hall. It was two storeys high, the lower course built of stone while the upper was timber. A hundred people could have comfortably lived there, and the great hall was probably big enough to seat many times that number.

"Home at last," Lucy said as she dismounted with a satisfied groan. Calia followed her to the stables where they waited their turn to hand over their horses. Most of the royal entourage had broken off to find lodgings in town, leaving only the nobles and their servants with the main party.

"Will the queen want to speak with me now that we're here?" Calia asked.

"She's probably too tired. They'll be heading back to the capital in a day or two. Things will be nice and quiet again once they've gone." Lucy looked relieved that her stint as the queen's personal tailor was coming to an end.

"Does she visit Ashmount House often?"

"Only in the summer or when she's travelling, but she's been here a few times since work on the tapestry began."

"Who's the lord when the royals are away?"

Lucy pointed out a man who stood waiting to welcome the king and queen at the manor doors. He looked like he could have been thirty or forty, with a head of short, prickly hair that matched his short, prickly stature.

"That's him. Oswin Kendrick. He's the royal bailiff here. He takes care of the house and presides over the manorial court."

"What's he like?" Calia asked curiously.

"A stuffy sort, but he's not that bad. Just mind your manners and don't get under his feet. It's Ana you need to worry about." Lucy guided Calia's attention to another face in the crowd. Slightly apart from Lord Oswin stood a tall young woman with sharp, hawkish features and copper-coloured hair that fell to her waist. Her clothing looked expensive, but not ostentatious. A dark red dress complemented the lighter colour of her hair, contrasting with a green shawl about her shoulders that could have looked rustic on a peasant, but somehow conveyed a sense of dignity on her. At her side stood two other women who shared her hair colour, one older and greying, the other a child clutching a doll. Perhaps her mother and daughter, or a young sibling.

"She looks quite severe," Calia said.

"She acts it, too. That's Anastasia Fiala, your mistress. She's the painter who designed the new tapestry. When the queen saw her work, she put her in charge of the whole project."

The name sounded foreign to Calia. She'd never heard of anyone called Anastasia before, and the surname Fiala was unusual too. Perhaps it meant "painter" in another language.

"Isn't the new tapestry based on the old design?"

"Mostly," Lucy said, "but we only have sketches, like that charcoal one you've been working from for your tapestry. The Farren Vale was made up of forty-eight different squares, each with its own corresponding sketch. They're very old, so some of them have been lost or damaged. The queen commissioned Ana to paint forty-eight new cartoons based on those sketches. She had to come up with completely new designs for the ones that were missing."

Calia nodded, fascinated by the scope of the project. A cartoon was a detailed painting used as a reference for high-quality tapestries. It was the job of the weaver to translate the lines and colours of the cartoon into a weft that captured the essence of the artist's design. It sounded like Anastasia Fiala had not just brought the Farren Vale back to life, but improved upon it enough to win the queen's favour. Despite Lucy's warning, Calia was eager to meet the woman.

Once their horses were settled, they got themselves some food from the kitchen and found seats in the great hall. It wasn't as lavish as Calia had expected. In her mind's eye, she'd pictured the king and queen living in houses covered in golden columns and rich tapestries, with colourful rugs underfoot and sweet incense burning in every corner. The hall of Ashmount House was exceptionally neat and tidy, but not lavish. Everything from the furniture to the rush mats was clean and well-kept. Calia felt guilty every time a crumb fell from her bread trencher to the table.

She realised halfway through supper why the hall seemed so unassuming; it wasn't that it was completely barren of decoration, but because the wall she was facing had been left conspicuously bare. Bare save for the lines of tapestry hooks from which an enormous piece of art would one day hang.

Lucy and the other women at their table were chatting about the tournament in Tannersfield, but Calia was entranced by the bare wall. She tried to imagine the finished Farren Vale hanging there. Lucy said it was made up of forty-eight squares. As an educated woman, Calia was both literate and numerate, yet it still took her a while to count all the hooks and deduce how large each square would have to be to fit them. In the end, she concluded that each piece would be about a yard across, hanging six vertical and eight horizontal. The finished tapestry would be eight yards wide and six tall, dominating the back wall of the room. It would be the first thing anyone saw when they came in.

Calia wondered whether she would be weaving a single square, or if she would have to do several in her time here. A yard-square tapestry could be completed in a month or two, but complex designs that integrated many different colours and types of thread took longer. The queen's estimate of a year or more seemed reasonable if she had at least a dozen weavers working for her.

Calia was introduced to some of the other weavers as they finished their meal. Most were surprisingly young, though at twenty she was still the most junior among them. She tried not to feel too intimidated, remembering what her mother had told her: *Let your work speak for itself.*

To her relief, many of the young weavers were welcoming. They praised the small tapestry she'd been making for Wolfram, commenting that she had a good eye for colour and texture. The older weavers, clearly the seasoned masters of the group, offered no more than the necessary courtesies.

"The queen's very wilful about what she wants," Lucy explained as the servants cleaned up. "She hand-picked every weaver here. But not all of them are masters, and not everyone's happy about that. It isn't the usual way of doing things."

"There aren't any men, either," Calia observed. Weaving, much like tailoring, was a far more female-dominated profession than most, one of the rare industries in which women were able to exercise a large degree of autonomy and independence. But there were many skilled male weavers as well, and it seemed strange that none had been selected to work on the Farren Vale.

"The queen is a woman of particular temperaments," Anastasia Fiala said as she walked by. Her voice was every bit as cutting as her features, and the sound of it made Calia flinch involuntarily. "She is keen that the tapestry be made exactly to her tastes."

Calia dipped her chin politely. "Milady. I'm Calia Tailor, from Kingalen."

"Tailor?" Anastasia's voice probed like a needle trying to work its way beneath her skin. A trace of an accent fringed her words, but it was barely noticeable, as if she'd spent many years fighting to suppress it.

"She's known for her tailoring work as well as her weaving," Lucy answered when Calia became tongue-tied. "She helped me with the queen's wardrobe in Tannersfield."

"It is a fine thing to have more than one talent fit for a queen's service," Anastasia observed in a tone that implied she was referring to herself moreso than Calia. Perhaps she was one of those people who struggled to give compliments. Calia hoped it was just awkwardness and not genuine hostility.

Thankfully she was spared any further interrogation when Anastasia moved on to the other end of the hall and disappeared through the door leading to the royal chambers.

"I see what you mean about her," Calia said under her breath.

"Luckily for us, she lives at the other end of the manor. Come on, I'll show you our place."

Calia was glad to be out of the noise and bustle of the great hall. She'd been worried she would have to sleep there, as many servants did in such large households, but a lucky few always managed to keep beds elsewhere. Lucy led her into the southern wing of the manor, which appeared to be a work area. It was its own hall, though smaller than the main one, and instead of comfortable furnishings, the place was lined with buckets, barrels, baskets of linens, scrubbing brushes, stacks of firewood, dirty tableware, and numerous other items waiting to be cleaned or repaired. It looked like this was where the servants kept the household running. The far end of the hall was segmented off into a store room, and a flight of stone steps led up to the second floor.

Lucy took Calia upstairs. They had taken a candle from the workroom, and several doors were visible by its dim light running the length of a landing. This part of the manor was probably cordoned off into individual chambers so the specialised servants like Lucy could keep workshops for their tools and materials.

"Through here," Lucy said, drawing a curtain aside from the largest doorway. It led into a spacious room directly above the great hall. An empty loom and a table littered with thread spools occupied one corner, but it didn't appear to be the main weaving area. Instead, covering almost the entirety of one wall, Anastasia Fiala's painting of the Farren Vale hung like a window into another world. Calia took the candle from Lucy and stepped toward it, her eyes wide.

"Isn't it incredible?"

Calia could only nod. The painting went all the way up to

the vaulted ceiling. Like the tapestry itself, it was made of discreet segments, each a yard across, painted upon wooden panels hanging from hooks. There were two stepladders on either side so that the higher ones could be lifted down. The instant Calia saw the design, she recognised it as a view of the valley outside town, but this was more than just a common landscape. Anastasia had glorified the greens and browns of the Farrenwold moors with explosions of red, gold, orange, and yellow, depicting an evening sky with the sunset blazing at its centre. In the stylised rays of light swirling through the clouds, depictions of saints and angels could be seen, while down below peasants toiled in the fields and a king with a golden crown rode with a host of knights on horseback. There were a thousand tiny details, each of them so intricate that Calia felt she could have stared at the painting for days without finding them all.

"Which are the new parts?" she asked.

"Across the top and at the left. The first nine panels were missing from the original sketches."

"I can't tell at all. It looks like it goes so well together."

Yet as she stared, Calia did feel like there was a difference in the uppermost part of the painting. It had been done subtly, so as to reflect a natural escalation of the mundaneness of earth to the glory of heaven. Calia couldn't quite put it into words, but something about the blazing golds and oranges in the topmost row of panels made her question Anastasia's composition. It was as if her eyes were constantly being dragged upwards, when the focal point should have been the glorious sunset at the tapestry's centre.

"Come on," Lucy said. "It's getting late. You'll be able to look at it properly tomorrow."

Calia nodded, but she kept staring at the Farren Vale on her way out of the room. It had already captured her imagination.

It was magnificent. But it was not the design she would have chosen.

CHAPTER 4

The largest obstacle to Anastasia Fiala's work, both she and her mother agreed, was the queen herself. It had been aggravating but not unsurprising when she returned to the manor with yet another unknown and inexperienced weaver in tow.

"It's the way with all monarchs," her mother, Vesna, said. She was sitting behind Ana in their room in the royal chambers, peering over her shoulder as she worked. To Ana's left stood one of her square panels of the Farren Vale. A fresh panel mirrored it on an easel to the right. She was translating the design into a simpler, less expensive copy that could be kept as an additional reference. What had been lost once could be lost again, and these were brushstrokes worth recording. One copy would probably go back to the capital where it could be shown off to the royal court while the other remained here in Ashmount.

"They want much and understand little," Vesna continued, pinching Ana's arm when she put down her brush to swap it for another. "Keep using that one."

"This copy doesn't have to be as fine as the first painting."

"Are you happy setting down a sloppy legacy?"

"...No." Anastasia picked up the finer brush again and resumed her work. Her eyes followed each stroke meticulously, mindful of the tiniest mistake that might earn her another pinch.

"We'll have to find a way to get rid of some of these weavers. They aren't good enough for you."

"I know," Ana replied irritably. She'd tried her hardest to make the queen hire weavers of her choosing, but it was like drawing teeth. A few months ago, she'd dismissed two whose work she hadn't liked. Queen Meredith had been livid when she found out, threatening to take the entire project away from her if she undermined her again. The shame and guilt of that moment still weighed on Anastasia like an iron mantle. She couldn't bear the thought of ruining everything for her mother after all she'd done for them. Ana had learned to tread carefully around the queen ever since.

"Well, what are you going to do about it?" Vesna demanded.

"There has to be a good reason to dismiss them. The queen needs to make the decision for herself. I just need to coax her into thinking it's the right idea."

Vesna nodded approvingly. "Find out more about the new weavers. Perhaps some of them come from disgraced families."

"The queen isn't likely to care about that. If they were heathens, on the other hand..."

Vesna smiled. "She's as pious as her husband, isn't she?"

"Exactly."

"You're a brilliant woman, Nastya, just like your mother. You make me proud."

Ana instinctively pulled her brush back as Vesna squeezed her arm, anticipating another pinch, but it was only a gesture of affection. Such attempts annoyed Ana. She hated the nickname Nastya as well. It was a reminder that they were outsiders, refugees from across the ocean who had barely escaped a crumbling royal court before it collapsed beneath the ravages of war. Vesna had served that court as the king's painter. When Ana was old enough to hold a brush, she'd become her apprentice. Here, in this new country, they had eventually parleyed their former prestige into favour with Queen Meredith. This tapestry, Vesna said, was their chance to rebuild their legacy.

But Vesna was starting to get old. Though only fifty, her hands had developed a persistent tremor that impacted her painting. She showed no other signs of declining health–if anything, her spirit was fiercer than ever–but the tremor had only grown worse, and a master painter could not work without her hands. So Anastasia had stepped into her shoes. Now, the legacy of the Fiala name was hers to bear.

"A pity she didn't let you redesign the whole tapestry," Vesna said. "The only artists in this country are old men who don't care to paint anything but the saints. You could have done so much more."

"I will," Ana replied. "One day."

"But not before you create the greatest tapestry this kingdom has ever seen."

"For that, I need the queen to let me work with weavers of my choice. You needn't worry, Mother." She raised a hand to silence the heated comment she knew was coming. "I'll take care of it."

There was no false confidence in Anastasia's words. She was certain she could find a way to have the tapestry made to her specifications. It was just a question of time and patience. What did it matter if work on the project had to be scrapped and restarted? The queen had the money for it. Ana's design was what mattered most. She knew she was special. Vesna had always told her so. She was talented, intelligent, and most importantly, she had the ruthless drive to exploit those attributes. When she set her heart on something, she got it.

Her fierce concentration was only broken when her little sister, Karaline, hopped down from her window seat to watch her work. She was nine years old, born just a few months after they came overseas. Unlike Ana, she'd inherited none of their mother's aptitude for painting. She was a quiet girl whose closest friend was the wood-and-cloth doll she always carried with her. When she reached for one of Ana's paint brushes, Vesna leaned over and plucked it from her hand.

"What have I told you about interfering with your sister's work?"

Karaline shied away and lowered her head, hiding behind her hair.

"Let her be," Ana said. For an instant, Vesna met her with a challenging glare, and a part of Ana wanted to curl up and hide like Karaline, fearful of those pinching fingers that had nipped her a thousand times, leaving red marks up and down her arm for every mistake she made. But Ana wasn't a child anymore, and when Vesna saw the look on her face, she backed down. This was the one issue she'd learned not to fight her daughter on.

Ana loved Karaline. She was the only person in the world she did love. The bond she shared with Vesna was not that of mother and daughter, but master and apprentice. It was built on respect, obedience, and a shared passion for their craft. But it wasn't love.

"Here, have this one," Ana said, taking one of her spare brushes from a cup and handing it to her little sister. Karaline grasped it tightly and smiled her thanks before running back to her window seat, where she pretended to make her doll paint patterns on the sill using rainwater.

"She's too old to still be playing with that thing," Vesna said.

"There's no harm in it."

"And she'll ruin a good brush, scrubbing it around on the stone like that."

"I can buy more."

Vesna clicked her tongue reproachfully and returned to her perch behind Anastasia, stooping like an old raven as she appraised her daughter's work.

When the light grew too dim to continue, Ana put down her brushes and got up, stretching her aching back. Vesna took Karaline down for supper, but Ana remained upstairs. She liked to check on the weavers at the end of the day to see how their work was progressing. It was a welcome respite from her mother's company. Instead of feeling like the novice working under her master's nose, she got to make others feel that way. She glanced into the mirror before leaving the room, taking her hair out of its tie and brushing it straight so that she looked like a noble mistress instead of a common labourer. She put on her green shawl and adjusted it around her neck, then went out through the solar.

Most of the time, only her family and Lord Oswin lived in this part of the house. Esteemed guests sometimes came and went, and when the royals visited they took the finest rooms for themselves, but otherwise Anastasia had come to think of the solar as her own. This wing of the manor had its own chapel, garderobe, dining room, and bathing area complete with a heatable water cistern. It was completely separate from the rest of the house save for the door leading to the great hall and a locked servant's passage upstairs. Only the senior servants held keys to that door, but Anastasia had bullied the head laundress into giving her one. Even though Ana only technically had authority over the weavers, she found it easy enough to make the servants do what she wanted. Lord Oswin was a stickler for efficiency, pedantically dedicated to keeping the estate pristine for his royal masters. All it took was a word from Ana about how her bed linens hadn't been changed, her food was cold, or her horse hadn't been brushed, and the bailiff's hackles would immediately rise. The servants responsible became much more compliant with her requests after she dropped a few comments like that.

She unlocked the door leading out of the north wing and headed through the rooms above the great hall into the weaving area. It was comprised of three chambers, one in which the cartoon of the Farren Vale hung, and another two for weaving. The weaving rooms had been set up at the front of the manor where there were lots of windows. The first room, which had been in use the longest, held eight looms, while the second currently had three, one freshly brought in that morning. That was where Calia Tailor sat now. A piece of the Farren Vale cartoon was propped up on a stand behind her, its details reflected in a large copper mirror that stood in front of the loom. Weavers made tapestries from the back side, working on the reverse of the warp threads. If they put the cartoon in front of them and copied it directly, they would end up creating a flipped version of the image. But by placing the cartoon behind them and reflecting it in a carefully-aligned mirror, the tapestry would end up the right way around. It was an elaborate and costly setup, but no expense was too great for the queen.

Anastasia's soft felt slippers made no sound as she entered, and none of the weavers noticed her arrival. She stood in the shadow of the doorway watching them. Ana liked to watch and listen. It was what gave her an artistic eye, Vesna said. Most people looked at a meadow and saw only a sea of green. Ana saw every blade of grass and patch of clover. Now she looked at Calia the same way, trying to discern the details from the broader picture.

She was a small, unremarkable sort. When Ana met her in the hall yesterday, she'd reminded her of a frightened little bird. But now that she was working at her loom, there was a quick efficiency to her movements. The little bird looked like she was building a nest, snatching lengths of wool from her lap to measure up against the warp, comparing them first with the reflection in the mirror and then the paint on the cartoon. Those that she deemed suitable were attached to a bobbin and set aside, whereupon she began the process all over again. Ana was almost impressed until she realised that after a full day's work, Calia still hadn't woven a single thread across her warp. She stepped forward, startling the three weavers as she made for Calia's loom.

"Why haven't you started yet?"

Despite her alarm, Calia responded evenly, perhaps feeling more confident now that she was in a work setting.

"I've been picking out my thread."

"All day?"

"Yes. I had to organise my work area, then I spoke to the other weavers and asked for their advice. We have to coordinate which thread we're going to use so that the edges of our squares match."

Ana looked up at the cartoon panel behind Calia. It was one of her original designs, second from the left in the topmost row of squares. One of the dismissed weavers had been working on it before her work was scrapped.

"It still doesn't look like you've made much progress."

"It's important to get all of my shades right before I start. There are so many different colours in this piece, and they blend into one another very evenly. I was thinking of using silk for this part here." She pointed to a section of Ana's painting that depicted two angelic women fighting for possession of a shiny horn.

"Use silver thread for the horn."

"I don't think that would be best."

Ana glared at her, instinctively preparing a reprimand, but she thought better of it. She still didn't know much about Calia Tailor. For now, she would watch and listen.

"Why?"

Calia flashed a nervous smile. "Well, the others are using silver and gold thread for the centre of the tapestry to make it look like the sun is really shining."

"That horn is supposed to shine, too."

"We can achieve that effect with white silk. It'll catch the light better than the wool around it. The horn will still stand out without being conspicuous."

Anastasia was impressed with the girl's eye for detail. Texture and luminosity were important considerations in tapestry making, ones that she tended to defer to the master weavers. Calia was no novice, that much was clear, but her suggestion still irked Ana. She wanted her new designs to be the most prominent parts of the tapestry. That was where people should be looking, admiring *her* work, not the parts she'd copied from the old sketches.

"Use silver thread."

Calia bowed her head. "If you think that's best."

Ana moved behind Calia, watching her as she went back to work. She had a bronze sewing needle tucked into her hand that she controlled deftly, using it almost like an extra finger to tease out wool from spools, scratch notes into a wax tablet, and pin short lengths of thread together as a means of organising them. A tailor's quirk, Ana surmised.

Before long, her thoughts returned to their original purpose. Whether Calia had an eye for detail or not, her youth was a mark against her, and Ana doubted she would be a worthwhile addition to the project. Her insistence on silk thread instead of silver was already proof that she was going to be difficult. She needed to find some weakness in the girl, some flaw she could present to the queen if she decided to get rid of her. The sewing needle was a strange preference. Perhaps she was more tailor than weaver? But the queen probably knew that already based on Calia's surname, so Ana dismissed it for now. A far better tactic would be to suggest that she was impious; that she shunned churchgoing and favoured heathen beliefs. Perhaps if Calia was observed not to attend church as often as others, if she depicted the tapestry's angels and saints in a manner that could be construed as disrespectful, or if she visited the town's wise women instead of praying for relief from her ailments, those dalliances could be composed like brushstrokes into an unflattering picture.

There were things Ana could do to ease such a narrative along: set chores that kept Calia busy on church days, send her to fetch remedies from the wise women every month, make up rumours about how the thread she used was dyed using the urine of whores and the blood of pigs...

This was how Ana usually got what she wanted. All her life, she'd been frustrated that people failed to recognise her talent. Even the queen thought she knew better than her which weavers to commission despite being blind as a bat when it came to artistic appraisal. Relying on one's own skill was not enough; you had to stand out from the crowd. Women and foreigners faced natural hurdles in that regard. Ana had lost count of the times she'd presented her work to the royal court only for the king to commission a less gifted male painter to design his frescoes and beautify his chapels. It wasn't enough to be the best when everyone else stood taller than you. You had to push them down so that you could rise up. Sometimes it was as simple as bribing a cook to slip something into a rival's food so they would miss an important appointment. Other times you had to work harder, collecting unsavoury rumours about them over the course of months until their reputation became tarnished.

Ana was already concocting a handful of such schemes for the weavers, hoarding their dirty secrets like jewels. There was a page called Sigrad who would gladly repeat anything he overheard in the servants' wing for a few pennies. He said one of the weavers had been seen kissing a married silver merchant in a public house. Another was purported to be sneaking wine out of the storeroom. Some had made comments that were derogatory to the queen and Lord Oswin, while others slipped away from work early and started late. Ana had a dozen such gems tucked away in the back of her mind. None of them were substantial enough to do anything with—not yet, at least—but later, in conjunction with other tidbits, they could be worth something. Not even the senior weavers were immune from Ana's schemes, for she would not have any of them upstaging her when the tapestry was done. She'd been the one who created the design. It was hers to take the glory for.

She would have liked to watch Calia for longer, but supper

was being served downstairs, and soon the weavers stopped work for the day. Ana waited for them to leave, lingering at the rear as they filed downstairs into the servants' hall. Rather than following, she headed across the landing to Lucy Tailor's workroom. Though Lucy wasn't directly involved with the tapestry, Ana consulted her regularly. As the resident tailor, she knew more about the local dyeing and thread-making business than anyone, and she helped the weavers source many of their materials.

Ana stopped at Lucy's door and knocked. No one answered. She checked behind her to make sure no one was watching, then slipped inside. The tailoring workshop was a haphazard nest of spools and stands, snips and shears, pins and fabrics, and a dozen articles of half-mended clothing. Some of the servants' stockings were laid out on a work table, while one of Lord Oswin's fine black surcoats hung on a stand near a window filled with a lattice of expensive translucent glass.

Ana ignored the usual tailoring clutter. She'd been in here before and determined that there was nothing noteworthy to be found in Lucy's belongings. It was the straw mattress beneath the work table that she was interested in. Lucy seemed to have taken a shine to Calia, and she often let her friends sleep in her room. Just as Ana had suspected, there was a travelling cloak bundled up on the mattress next to a saddlebag. She bent down and opened the bag. Inside was a sewing box containing needles, thimbles, pins, and thread. An insignia had been burned into the lid, probably the mark of a regional tailoring guild, but Ana wasn't familiar enough with the guilds in this part of the kingdom to recognise it. Finding nothing of interest in the box, she closed it and set it aside.

Besides clothes and some leftover travelling food, there was nothing else in the saddlebag except a small hand loom. It had been bundled up in cloth to protect the design. When Ana unwrapped it, she was momentarily taken aback by what she saw. The little tapestry was only half finished, but already she could tell that it depicted a man kneeling before a crowd in some sort of ceremony. The picture itself was unremarkable, but the way it had been composed struck Ana as nothing short of inspired. She'd never seen a weaver convey such a vivid image on such a small warp before. The effect had been accomplished not by portraying every figure realistically, but by making them distinctly abstract. At a close glance, the horizontal lines of thread were just streaks of green, yellow, blue and cream, but like an image reflected in the ripples of a pond, there was a pattern to them that made it obvious they were figures in a crowd when you took in the picture from afar.

Ana knelt on the floor admiring Calia's work for several minutes. She was no longer afraid the girl would prove a liability. No, if anything she was *too* good. If she could apply this striking style to the fine details of the Farren Vale, she might become a rising star among the weavers. It was a good thing she was working on one of the brand-new panels. That way, her skill would serve to enhance Ana's original creation rather than making it look dull in comparison to the old tapestry.

The sound of footsteps on the landing made her freeze. Her first thought was to leave immediately and make it look like she'd only ducked in momentarily looking for Lucy. But then she heard voices, Lucy and Calia's, and they were coming her way. If they saw the contents of the saddlebag on the floor, they'd know she'd been rummaging. Without panicking, Ana quickly put everything back where she'd found it, then picked up a spool of thread and held it up to the window, pretending to examine its colour in the fading light.

"I think I should just tell them," she heard Calia say outside the door.

"Tell them later, once you've settled in," Lucy replied. "Those old hags are just fishing for a reason to look down their noses at you."

Ana's curiosity was piqued. She hesitated for a moment,

then backed away from the window and stood next to the door. Her slippers were silent on the floorboards. When the door opened, Ana was standing behind it, and the shadow that fell over her plunged her corner of the room into darkness. She held her breath, careful not to make a sound. Someone entered and began rummaging under the table.

"But they keep prying for details," Calia said. "It's as if they know."

"Make something up. Or just tell them about your tailoring guild instead. None of them are from Tannersfield, so it's not as if they'll know the difference."

"I don't like being dishonest."

"Calia, you little goose, you've no obligation to be honest with people who don't have your best interests at heart."

"I suppose not."

"Besides, a year from now you can show off your work to every weavers' guild in the kingdom. They'll all be champing at the bit to accept you."

Around the edge of the door, Ana saw Calia's hand clutching her little loom with its half-finished tapestry.

"If this persuades everyone downstairs that I'm not a fraud, then I'll believe you."

Lucy laughed, and the pair departed, closing the door behind them. Ana waited until she could no longer hear their footsteps before slipping out and making her way back to the northern wing. She wore a smile the whole way. She couldn't be certain, but it had sounded like Calia Tailor wasn't a formally recognised member of a weavers' guild.

That was a gem worth hoarding indeed.

CHAPTER 5

Life in Ashmount Manor slowed down after the royal entourage returned to the capital. The bustling house became a vacant convent, the creaks of its floorboards and the crackling of its fires growing ever more conspicuous as the fog of noise dissipated. It felt almost too big now. With most of the tables in the great hall going unused, the room became chilly without a constant current of bodies warming it. For some, it might have been a dour change of atmosphere, but Calia quite liked it. The spring weather was only growing finer, and she spent most of her days in the comfort of the weaving rooms away from the draughty hall. She'd grown up at her mother's inn, where noise was constant and privacy scarce. To be living in a grand house with private rooms and work areas was a luxury she was unaccustomed to. When her mind wandered, she caught herself daydreaming about the future, imagining a house with a workshop where she could weave and sew all day long, taking commissions from wealthy clients and entertaining a few close friends in a comfortable little hall. With the wage she was earning, she could make it happen if she wanted.

As she began to work on her section of the tapestry in

earnest, the first hints of Anastasia's design started to take shape. Calia's loom was of excellent quality. Its large vertical frame bore a line of nails at the top, just like her hand loom. The horizontal warp threads stretched down from those nails to a tensioned bar at the bottom, each one so close to the next that it was difficult to slip a bobbin between them. Such a tight alignment was necessary to produce the detail required in a tapestry like this. That was why the loom had a heddle: a bar hanging over Calia's head that was attached to the upper part of the warp by strings. By pulling on those strings, the weaver could raise individual warp threads as if they were drawing back a bowstring, opening up gaps through which the bobbin could slip with ease. Though not intensely physical work, the constant reaching up left Calia's arms sore by the end of each day.

She had a dozen bobbins on a work table next to her, each wrapped with a different colour of thread, while several more hung from the back of the tapestry waiting to be used again later. Each time Calia wove her thread through the warp, she would tamp it down with the pointed end of her bobbin, making sure it was evenly compacted. There was an art to this that she'd learned through trial and error. Thick, voluminous wool took up more space than fine silk. Even if the difference was almost imperceptible at a glance, hundreds upon hundreds of wefts stacked atop one another would magnify those differences. The finest thread had to be woven tighter, tamped down harder, to avoid exposing the white warp underneath.

It was easy to feel overwhelmed when Calia considered the sheer size of her yard-square segment of the tapestry. A mistake early on could throw off the entire piece, and such mistakes were not easily remedied. Each length of thread was precious, every hour valuable. But moment to moment, weave by weave, the work was both engrossing and rewarding. At the end of each day, Calia looked at the small amount of progress she'd made and saw more of Anastasia's design resolving along the stark warp. She enjoyed her work, and the two other weavers sharing her room—Rovena and Goldie—were pleasant company. They were young like her, one local and the other from the capital. Rovena had a studious mind that adored the technical aspect of weaving, while Goldie spent as much time gazing wistfully out the window as she did tending her loom. Her husband was also a weaver and a favourite of the royal court, but he'd been commissioned overseas and she hadn't seen him for almost two years. Their two young children lived at the manor with Goldie, tended by the servants while she worked during the day.

"Do they play with Anastasia's little sister?" Calia asked her.

"No. That Karaline's a quiet girl. She keeps to herself mostly."

Calia had only seen Karaline a few times. She sometimes came in to watch them work, though she never spoke to anyone. She would find a corner at the back and sit down with her doll, whispering it secrets and pretending not to hear whenever someone tried to address her. Calia felt sorry for the girl. She didn't seem to have any friends, and her mother, Vesna, was always impatient with her. Karaline was warm towards her older sister, though Calia couldn't imagine why. Ana struck her as a bully. The initial respect she'd held for the painter had quickly faded during their subsequent interactions. Ana liked to peer over her shoulder, always admonishing her for what she was doing wrong, never praising her for what she was doing right. She was cold and aloof with the weavers, and there was a tension between them that implied their relationship was competitive rather than collaborative.

Fortunately, Ana didn't interact with the weavers very often. Some evenings she would come in for an hour or two to appraise their looms, but otherwise, she left them alone. Calia mostly saw her elsewhere in the manor, holding quiet conversations in the great hall or talking to visitors out in the courtyard, conducting a dozen private lives in between work hours.

It was a little after noon, and Calia and the others had just come up after their midday meal. She could still hear the distant thrum of conversation in the great hall below as the servants finished eating. Karaline came into the weaving room with two apples in hand—one for her, one for her doll—and sat down by the window behind Calia. In the polished copper mirror, her reflection started to nibble at the fruit, taking small, quick bites like a squirrel. Calia watched her while she wound some leftover thread onto a bobbin, smiling as she remembered the games she'd used to play with Livy and Wolfram when they were little. They'd used to scoop sticky, clay-heavy mud out of the stream behind the inn and build castles with it. Calia's had always been the best.

Once Karaline had finished her apple, she crept over to the stand bearing the cartoon Calia was working from, oblivious to the fact that her reflection was visible in the mirror. Vesna would have scolded her for interfering with the weavers' work, but Calia didn't mind. She watched as Karaline stared up at her sister's painting, picking at a splinter of wood that had come loose from the side of the panel. The girl gasped suddenly, pulling her finger away and sticking it into her mouth.

Calia turned around on her stool. "Did you give yourself a splinter?"

Karaline shook her head vigorously, but there were already tears brimming in her eyes.

"Let me have a look." Calia motioned for her to come over. The poor girl looked equal parts pained and terrified, as tormented by the thought of getting in trouble as she was by the pain of the splinter. Calia rose from her seat and went to her, tugging on her wrist gently until she took her finger out of her mouth. A sob left Karaline's lips as she saw blood welling up around the long sliver of wood that had gone in beneath her fingernail. Calia winced at the sight of it.

"That must really sting. Here, I think I can get it out for you." Calia took out her sewing needle. Karaline immediately shied away. "Don't worry, I'm not going to stab you. I just need to pinch that little bit of wood against your fingernail so that I can tug it out."

"No, don't!"

Calia gave her a patient smile and rubbed the back of her hand. "You need to be brave. It'll stop hurting after we take it out. Do you want to know a special secret my nana told me? She was a wise old lady. Whenever I hurt myself, she always said that looking at it only made it worse. Why don't you look at your doll? I think she's enjoying that apple."

Karaline was still tugging weakly against Calia's grip, but she did as she was told. Calia felt the girl's resistance slacken. Quickly, she held Karaline's finger beneath the top joint, slid the tip of her needle into the tiny scrap of wood protruding from beneath the nail, and drew it out. Her distracting tactic worked. Karaline only flinched a little as the splinter came free, staring back wide-eyed at the tip of her finger as if amazed that it had been over so quickly.

"There you go," Calia said. "Why don't you come downstairs with me so we can get that cleaned and wrapped up?"

Karaline stuck her finger back into her mouth and ran to the window. Calia feared she might not return, but she'd only been going to collect her doll. Calia guided her downstairs into the servants' hall, where she found some strips of clean linen to bind the wound. She made Karaline soak her finger in a cup of strong wine beforehand, then gave her a few sips as a reward for being brave. Calia's nana had always sworn by wine as a preventative measure to stop wounds from festering. It wasn't the first time she'd had to bind a cut or draw out a splinter. Parents had often left their children at her mother's inn during the day, and since Calia spent most of her time sitting at a loom or sewing at a work table, she'd been a convenient pair of eyes to deposit youngsters in front of.

"There, all better," Calia said once she was done. "I'm sure it's already stopped hurting, hasn't it?"

Karaline nodded, but she still looked miserable.

"What's the matter?"

"Mother will be cross."

"I won't tell her you were fiddling with your sister's paintings."

Karaline frowned and looked away. It was a reaction Calia had become accustomed to when youngsters felt that adults didn't understand them.

"Does Vesna get cross with you often?"

"Yes."

"Do you think she'll be cross because you hurt yourself?"

Karaline nodded. Calia pursed her lips, feeling a flash of resentment towards the girl's mother. It was little wonder Kara was so shy and anxious if she got in trouble just for doing the same things all children did.

"I want Ana," Kara said tearfully.

"Shall we go and find her?"

The girl shook her head. "She's painting with Mother."

Calia sighed, unsure of what to do. She had to get back to work, but she didn't want to leave a distraught child on her own. "What do you usually do with Ana when you're upset?"

"We go away on our own. She was going to take me to see the castle, but she's always busy."

Calia wasn't a rebellious woman by nature, which made her next impulse all the more unexpected.

"Would you like to go with me? I haven't been up there yet either." She knew she had work to do, but her sympathy for Karaline and her frustrations with Ana and Vesna momentarily overwhelmed her timidity. Making an upset little girl happy, she thought, was surely worth an afternoon of missed work. Besides, if she got back before Ana came to check on her that evening, her absence would probably go unnoticed. Rovena and Goldie wouldn't say anything.

Karaline swallowed her tears, squeezed her doll tight with her uninjured hand, and nodded.

"Come on, then. It's just a little trek up the hill. Have you got walking shoes on?"

She did. Calia hurried up to Lucy's room to put on her boots, then they slipped out through the servants' hall. Ashmount Manor wasn't a secure fortress like a castle, and a side gate allowed them to exit onto the hillside without making their departure conspicuous. The weather was warm and breezy, tickling the treetops into a dancing line beyond the stream that circled the base of the hill. Karaline clutched her doll beneath her elbow as she held on to Calia's hand. She seemed paradoxically more independent and yet more childlike than most girls her age. Her upbringing obviously hadn't been a conventional one. As they walked the few hundred yards up the hillside toward the ruined walls of Castle Ashmount, Kara began to open up a little, talking more freely and even starting to make eye contact when they spoke.

"This is where the old tapestry came from."

"That's right," Calia said. "I wonder if we can see where it used to hang? There must be a big hall in the keep somewhere."

"I bet it's not as big as the king's castle."

"Have you been there?"

Kara nodded.

"Wow. I've never visited a king's castle. You must be very important to have been given an invitation."

"Mother and Ana are."

"Are you going to be a painter like them when you're older?"

"No. I'm bad at it."

"Maybe you could be a weaver like me."

Kara just shrugged. It didn't seem like she was being

groomed for any particular vocation, given how often Calia saw her wandering the manor with nothing to do. By her age, most children were already preparing for the life of work ahead of them, either by helping their parents, eyeing an apprenticeship, or receiving an education if their family could afford it.

They soon reached the castle wall. Rather than clambering over the fallen stones, they made their way around until they found the main gate. A worn path that might have been a road in another age snaked through into the courtyard. The only part of the castle that still appeared to be maintained was the gatehouse. While the gates themselves were long gone, the fortified building next to them had a roof of shingles and a painted door. Several people could probably have lived inside, but when the door opened, only a single old man came out. He must have heard their voices as they approached.

"Afternoon, ladies," he said, touching the brim of his wool cap respectfully. He had a weary voice that matched the lines on his face, but there was a warmth to his weathered tone that Calia saw reflected in the man's eyes. "What brings you up here?"

"We came to see the castle. I'm Calia Tailor, and this is Karaline Fiala."

"Up from the manor?"

"How did you guess?"

"You look like fine folk. I'm Huwel Ward. The crown pays me to keep an eye on this old castle. Can't have young'uns playing around up here, climbing the towers and falling to their deaths. Mind you, it's the older ones who're more of a problem. Some of 'em see a wall still standing and think it's their god-given duty to make sure it falls down. I've told the bailiff we need a fence up here and a night watchman, but..." He trailed off with an exasperated breath. "Would you like me to show you around?"

Guessing that he would be disappointed if she declined,

Calia said yes. Huwel probably didn't get many visitors up here. He showed them across what had once been the courtyard, now an overgrown meadow, pointing out the stone shells of the surrounding buildings as they went.

"That there would've been the stables. Big ones, 'specially for the time. I reckon there must've been space for fifty horses inside. And just at the end there you've got the steps going up to the wall. I wouldn't do any climbing if I were you. It's not safe to walk about up there."

Karaline kept a tight hold of Calia's hand, clutching her doll close as she listened with rapt attention.

"Can we see where the Farren Vale used to hang?" Calia asked.

"Of course. Right this way." Huwel led them into the ruined keep, the only structure of the castle that was still recognisable. It stood against the back wall, larger than all the other buildings, with two smaller structures attached to either side. The stonework was largely unscathed except for some ragged holes at the top. The roof was completely gone, leaving the old flagstones bare to the sunlight. There had been ruined buildings around Calia's village, but nothing as big as this. Lichen covered the columns and crept across the surviving stonework overhead, curling into the cracks like a living rug. Most of the flagstones had broken apart, giving way to colonies of moss and inquisitive weeds.

"There are lots of holes," Karaline observed as she craned her neck upwards.

"That there are," Huwel said, bending down and pointing so that Kara could follow his finger. "The beams that supported the upper floors would've gone through those ones there. Of course, those all burnt away a long time ago, so only the holes are left now. There's a cellar beneath us, too." He tapped his foot on a broken flagstone.

"Can we see?"

"Not unless you've got a shovel I'm afraid young lady. It's all caved in and blocked up from when the place burned down. But your tapestry, now," he moved his finger to point at the wall directly in front of them. "It would've hung right there behind the high table."

The end of the great hall was slightly elevated, as was often the case to emphasise the status of the lord's table. While the wall behind it was tall and wide, it seemed a poor place to have hung a tapestry the size of the Farren Vale.

"It looks like it would've barely fit," Calia said.

"Aye, well these old castles were built for strength, not style."

"Is there anyone still alive that remembers the castle before it burned down?"

Huwel shook his head. "That was almost ninety years ago. Even the oldest man in the county would've been a babe when it happened. Not many stories passed down, either. The whole town burned along with the castle. Almost everyone who lives here now traces their lineage back to someplace else."

"But the tapestry cartoons survived," Karaline said knowledgeably. "And the steward's journals."

"You're a bright young miss, aren't you? Yes, they say the steward packed up all the valuables he could carry and ran off before the castle was attacked. Not very courageous of him, but I suppose he did keep that tapestry alive for future generations."

Karaline let go of Calia's hand and ran off to explore the great hall. Calia followed at a distance with Huwel, telling the old man about how she was working on the recreation of the Farren Vale. He was an amicable sort, as eager to listen as he was to speak, and she quickly warmed to him. She could survive the Anastasias of the world as long as there were two Lucys or Huwels for every one of her.

It was a pleasant walk around the ruins as they looked at the carvings that survived in the old chapel, the blocked cellar passageway, the empty shells of kitchen ovens, and the eerie towertop windows that looked in on rooms no one had entered in decades. They remained on the ground floor, for even the accessible parts of the upper areas were dangerous according to Huwel. Karaline's glum mood had evaporated by the time they'd seen everything. She'd been having fun playing imaginary games with her doll as they explored the castle together. If only she had activities like this to occupy her every day, Calia thought, perhaps she wouldn't be so withdrawn.

They ended their tour back in the castle keep, and once again Calia found herself staring at the spot where the Farren Vale used to hang. She still couldn't picture it. It just didn't seem right to her. The hall was so long and narrow, and if the tables were arranged along the length of the room, most guests would have sat facing bare walls instead of the tapestry, which itself would have been half-obscured by the high table. All of Calia's artistic sensibilities told her that the end of the room would have been an awful place to mount such a work of art. She looked for anywhere else it might have hung, but all the other walls were broken up by doorways and windows. She had to concede that Huwel was right. The former lord of Castle Ashmount must have prized strength over style. Nobles were not artists, after all.

With a promise to come and visit again soon, they said farewell to the old warden and made their way back down the hill to the manor house. They'd only been gone a couple of hours, so there was plenty of time for Calia to get back to work before she was missed. She felt both guilty and invigorated at having shirked her duties to go off gallivanting on an impromptu adventure. But it had been worth it. She felt like she'd made a new friend in Huwel, and perhaps in Karaline, too. When they got back to the manor, the girl no longer seemed worried about confronting Vesna.

"I'll tell Ana it was one of the servants who took me to see the castle. I know you'd get in trouble if I said it was you."

Calia smiled. "Thank you. We can go again another day,

though perhaps not when I'm working."

Kara nodded, the head of her doll bouncing in unwitting mimicry. She turned to leave but hesitated for a moment. "I liked that secret you told me about my finger only hurting if I looked at it."

"I've plenty more secrets like that from my nana."

"Can I share one, too?"

"Of course."

Kara came close to Calia and whispered: "My sister said she's inviting the alderman of the weavers' guild to supper tomorrow. She said they were going to make things uncomfortable for you."

A tense knot formed in Calia's stomach. "Why would she do that?"

"She doesn't like you. Ana doesn't like most people. But I think you're nice."

Calia nodded, wondering whether Anastasia had somehow found out the truth about her not being in a guild. If anyone could put her on the spot about something like that, it was an alderman.

"Thank you for telling me."

Kara smiled and hurried off in the direction of the royal chambers.

The knot in Calia's stomach remained long after she returned to her weaving. Anastasia Fiala's opinion of her was obviously worse than she'd thought. If she didn't tread carefully, she would have the weavers' guild breathing down her neck tomorrow evening.

At least, thanks to Karaline, she now had a chance to prepare.

CHAPTER 6

"This is just like her," Lucy told Calia when she broke the news about the alderman's visit the next day. "Ana got in trouble the last time she dismissed some of the queen's weavers. She won't try it again unless she can come up with a good reason. But she doesn't want the queen thinking she's being vindictive, either. If the alderman presses you and finds out you're not part of a guild, it'll look like he's the one making the accusations. Then Ana can pretend she had nothing to do with it when the queen finds out."

"But why?" Calia fretted. "I haven't done anything to spite her."

"Some people don't need a reason. She's a stuck-up bitch."

"I wish you wouldn't say things like that."

"Well if you won't, someone has to. You need to stand up for yourself, Calia, or she's going to walk all over you."

Calia threw her hands in the air. "What am I supposed to do? Lie to the alderman in front of everyone?"

"I would."

"I don't think that's going to help. If Ana knows the truth, she'll expose me sooner or later, and it'll look much worse if I've been lying about it. I should just be honest."

Lucy tutted and shook her head. It was midday, and they were sharing a meal in Lucy's room while they worked on hemming an old tunic of Lord Oswin's. Calia often helped her friend with simple sewing chores. It was the least she could do as thanks for sharing her room.

"Maybe you'll have to tell the truth eventually, but now's not the time. You've barely started with the tapestry. Wait till the other weavers are on your side, then they'll stand up for you if Ana tries to get you dismissed."

Calia put down her needle and took a huffy bite from a piece of cheese. "Well, there's nothing else for it. I'll have to skip supper this evening. If Ana's going to dance around the topic, I can too."

"Good idea. I'll skip it with you. We can go to a public house and buy a jug of wine to share."

Calia didn't think it would do anything to improve her standing if she was seen skipping supper to get drunk at local alehouses.

"Perhaps we can buy a jug of wine from the cellar and take it up to the gatehouse at the castle instead? The warden asked me to visit again. He seemed like a nice man."

"Oh, old Huw? He's a darling. Alright, we'll get some wine and a pot of stew to share with him. I wish I could see the look on Ana's face when she realises we've gone out."

Calia just hoped she wouldn't provoke Anastasia's ire any further by dodging the alderman. She finished up her weaving early that afternoon and went downstairs with Lucy to buy a jug of good wine from the pantry. They filled a lidded pot with thick, oaty stew in the kitchen and carried it up the hill to the castle gatehouse. Huwel Ward was glad to have them. He lit some extra candles and drew up chairs for them at his table, where they enjoyed the warm, tongue-loosening taste of wine alongside their supper. Before long, Calia and Lucy had divulged the real reason for their visit, and the topic of conversation turned towards Anastasia.

"I think Lucy's right, Miss Calia," Huw said. "You need to stand up to people like her. She's no noblewoman, and you don't have to treat her as such. Now, that doesn't mean you have to antagonise her, mind; there's a difference between standing your ground and pushing back. Bullies always look for weak targets, and the ones who squirm tend to be their favourites. Just stay stoic. Show her you're more trouble than you're worth, and I expect she'll leave you be."

"I've never really had to deal with anything like this on my own before. My brother and sister always took care of me."

"Well, now you have us!" Lucy clapped her on the thigh. Her taste for wine had reared its head again that evening, and she was making the most of it.

"I don't want my name getting dragged into anything," Huw said. "But if you ever need a break from your mistress, you're always welcome here. I like having guests at supper. Just bring us another jug of that wine, eh?"

They shared a chuckle, and Calia felt better. The money and prestige that came from working on the queen's tapestry was one thing, but striking out on her own and making new friends was an equally rewarding part of this journey. She wondered whether that was why her mother had urged her to accept the position. It was teaching her independence, something she'd enjoyed precious little of at home.

They waited until after dusk before heading back to the manor. By now, the alderman would surely have gone home. Calia didn't trust the tipsy Lucy to pick her way down the hillside in the dark, so they took the longer walk through town before circling back around to Ashmount House. It was unnerving to walk the streets after dark, but Lucy assured her that Ashmount was a safe place. Lord Oswin took a keen interest in keeping the town free of crime, as did the wealthy merchants and jewellers who lived here. The only people they passed in the street were a few harmless drunks filtering out of the public houses.

The next morning, Calia found Anastasia waiting for her in the weaving room. The painter had her arms folded, a look of composed indignation on her face as she appraised Calia's loom.

"We missed you at supper last night." Her voice cut like the snip of a scissor.

Remembering what Lucy and Huwel had told her, Calia summoned her courage and stepped forward nonchalantly, taking her seat behind the loom as if nothing was amiss.

"Oh, I was visiting a new friend with Lucy."

"You missed the alderman of the weavers' guild."

Calia feigned surprise. "No one told me he was coming."

"It was a surprise to all of us," Goldie said from behind her loom.

Ana shot the other weaver an annoyed look, but she could offer no rebuttal. Obviously the whole point of her scheme had been to catch Calia off guard. She couldn't very well reprimand her for dodging a meeting she'd purposefully kept quiet about. The secrecy of her plan had been its own undoing.

"Well, your absence was unfortunately timed," Ana said after a moment. "Tell me beforehand when you're going out again."

Calia knew she had no obligation to do that. Ana might have been in charge of the tapestry, but she wasn't entitled to control what the weavers did outside of work. This was a subtle test of her power; an attempt to see whether Calia would resist or submit. Once again, Calia recalled what Huwel had told her. She should stand her ground, but not push back.

She said nothing, picking up one of her bobbins and immediately getting to work. The back of her neck prickled with warmth as she felt Anastasia's gaze lingering on her. For an awful moment, she feared she'd gone too far, and she felt the urge to apologise and insist that yes, she would ask for permission before she went out again. But she held her tongue, waiting out Ana's awful stare until it finally broke. The painter turned away and swept out of the room, her soft slippers hitting the boards with an audible thud.

"She wasn't happy about that," Goldie said under her breath.

"We're not nuns under an abbess," said Rovena.

"Don't let her know that, or she'll have you doing penance in the chapel."

Calia let out a breath. For now, it seemed like Anastasia had been de-clawed. As long as she kept her head down and ingratiated herself with the other weavers, perhaps she could endure the painter's vindictive streak. All she had to do was prove herself worthy of their respect.

Anastasia made no more attempts to sabotage Calia in the days that followed, but there was a lingering hostility between them now that was apparent in every conversation. Calia began to dread the end of the day, knowing that Ana would find some new reason to criticise her choice of thread, the tidiness of her work area, the speed at which she was weaving, or the way she looked. She seemed intent on putting her down, making her feel inadequate and humble in front of the others. Fortunately, Rovena and Goldie saw right through her. They weren't immune to Ana's critiques either, and the three of them soon became united in solidarity against their overbearing mistress.

They formed a friendly social group with Lucy, taking supper and visiting the town market together on their days off. By the end of her first month at Ashmount House, Calia had a purse brimming with silver shillings and pennies. It was more money than she knew what to do with. When her parents came to visit, she gave them most of her silver to take home for safekeeping, but the rest she kept in a secret compartment at the base of Livy's cloth trunk. On market days, they would take out some of their money, head into town, and peruse the fine wares of the local merchants. Calia didn't spend large amounts of money very often. Her mother, who had grown up poor, had instilled in her the virtue of living frugally despite their relative wealth. Calia enjoyed looking at the beautiful golden rings, necklaces, pins, buckles, brooches, clasps, and other adornments sold by the jewellers, but she rarely bought any.

There was fine clothing on sale, too, some of it almost as magnificent as the dress the queen had worn in Tannersfield. Even with her new wages, Calia couldn't afford anything like that, but she did treat herself to a dark green dress embroidered with pale, silvery silk and sporting wide sleeves that trailed halfway to the ground. Such open sleeves had been in style for a long time, and Calia was particularly fond of them. When she wore her new dress outside, she even received a couple of compliments from men. She knew she wasn't pretty, but she obviously looked distinguished enough to seem like a decent catch for some of the young merchants in town. Flattering though the compliments were, Calia could have done without them. She was no more interested in romance now than she'd ever been. It was her friendships and her work that stirred her passions, and she didn't feel like she would've had the energy for courtship even if she'd wanted it.

As spring crept toward summer, Calia's segment of the tapestry began taking shape. She took her time with it, focusing on detail rather than speed. It was a very complex design, with a high warp count and numerous types of thread. Despite Ana's observations that Calia didn't work as fast as the others, she reasoned that a few extra weeks now were a small price to pay for work that might hang in Ashmount House for a hundred years. The more hardened she became to Ana's critiques, the more trusting she became of her own judgement. While Ana had a great many opinions on how the tapestry should be made, her technical expertise was lacking. She understood paint, not thread. After asking for a different colour to be used here or a finer type of thread there, she only sometimes noticed when her instructions were ignored. Calia wondered whether she was genuinely oblivious, or simply feigning ignorance to save face. Ana didn't seem like a woman who missed much.

There was a closeness between a weaver and her weaving that embraced Calia more tightly with each thread she twined into her warp. The more progress she made, the more the tapestry began to feel like hers. Ana's design could only be translated so accurately from paint into wool. There would always be minor variations in shape, texture, and colour. Those small differences were Calia's. When she stood in front of her loom to compare her design to the cartoon behind it, she felt proud of what she'd accomplished. Recently, she'd been working on the part depicting the two angels fighting over their silver horn. In Ana's painting, the pair looked combative, their faces lined and their eyes narrowed. Calia knew it would be difficult to reproduce those expressions in woollen thread, so she took a risk. The two angels did not have to be combative. The tiny wefts depicting their eyes could be wider, the corners of their mouths slightly upturned. In Calia's mind, she saw the angels as a playful pair. When it came time to choose her thread for the horn, she went with white silk rather than the silver thread Ana had suggested. By the time the two angels were finished, they looked subtly different from the pair in the cartoon. It wasn't obvious at a glance; Ana herself didn't even appear to notice at first. But they were Calia's angels, playfully harmonious, their silver horn humble and their expressions warm. It was a small detail that bore her unique influence as the weaver, like a lord's seal on the corner of a town charter.

After Ana departed that day, Calia noticed that Goldie was still sitting at her loom. Rovena had already gone downstairs for supper, leaving the pair of them alone together. Goldie had been distant like this for a few days now. Something was bothering her, but she didn't seem interested in talking about it. In an effort to cheer her up, Calia called her over to look at the pair of angels.

"Ana might be upset with me when she notices the difference," she said in a playful whisper. "But by then it'll be too late to change anything."

To her shock, Goldie clasped a hand to her mouth and started crying.

"You're so good at this, Calia."

"So are you," Calia said encouragingly, taking the other woman's arm and rubbing her back. "What's wrong?"

"My work isn't good enough. Ever since you outsmarted Ana, she's had her eye on me instead. I've been trying to shrug it off, but I don't think I can anymore."

"Of course you can. We're all here for you. Ana's just being a bully. You've got us and your family, and your work is more than good enough."

Goldie shook her head. "I *don't* have my family. I don't like being a mother. I'm glad I can get away from the children up here. It was always too much for me. But I stuck at it, for Tom's sake. It's been half a year since I heard from him. He should've been on his way home by now. All I hear are rumours from the merchants who deal with sailors up north. The other day Sigrad said–" She had to swallow as her voice cracked. "He said my Tom had married some other woman. That he wasn't coming home."

Calia's heart went out to her. "Don't listen to Sigrad. That boy repeats anything he thinks will get a rise out of people. Why don't you ask the merchants yourself? Plenty of them have partners overseas. I'm sure someone can find out what's happening with your husband."

"But what if it's true? I'll be stuck on my own with the children forever."

"You'll still have us. And you'll have your work. You won't want for money." She knew her words were probably small comfort to a woman whose heart was breaking, but small comforts were all she could offer.

"I'm drinking half a jug of wine just so I can face getting up in the morning. And it's making my weaving worse."

"Why don't you come and stay with Lucy and me? You can share one of our beds. No wine in the mornings. We'll make sure you can face the day without it."

"The children will wonder where I am."

"Just for a day or two. Then maybe I can move downstairs with you. I'll help get the children up so it isn't as much of a hassle."

Lucy finally managed a smile through her tears. "You're a saint, Calia. No wonder you weave such beautiful angels."

Life became far more exhausting after Calia moved into the great hall with Goldie and the children. The little boy and girl weren't too much of a handful, but combined with the constant noise and bustle, she found herself waking up in the night and rising early. Goldie continued to worry her. She kept a close eye on her friend to make sure she didn't slip off and drown her sorrows in wine when no one was looking. Lucy volunteered to sit with her in the evenings so she always had someone to talk to.

"My father was a brewer," Lucy told Calia one evening. "He showed me how to enjoy a good drink, but seeing what it did to him taught me to mind my limits. Ale was all he'd ever have, morning, noon, and night. It got to the point where he couldn't get through the day without a tankard in his hand. He said he got headaches without it. Whenever he was sober, he was in a foul temper. He wasn't fifty before he dropped dead one day in the middle of work. We can't have Goldie going that way."

Calia nodded along. Priests often warned against the corrupting nature of drink, wealth, fine food, extra-marital relations, and similar indulgences. Some of their sermons seemed far-fetched to Calia, but common wisdom supported the idea that there was something insidiously habit-forming about drink, and she didn't want Goldie falling prey to that temptation. If Anastasia found out, she would surely use it as justification to dismiss her. Then Goldie would be on her own, without work and with two young children to raise by herself. She could get back on her feet with the money she'd saved, but Calia feared the woman's worries over her husband would drive her to drink it all away. They had to make sure Goldie got her vices under control before Ana noticed anything amiss.

CHAPTER 7

For as much as Anastasia despised the page boy Sigrad, Vesna had impressed upon her the usefulness of keeping someone like him around. He did as he was told, kept his mouth shut, and had no scruples when it came to handling secrets and lies. Pages were noble servants, apprentices who hoped to become squires or men of court someday, and as such they were paid no formal wage. Like many young men in his position, Sigrad was hungry for every penny he could get his hands on. He was fifteen, old for a page, and resentful of the fact that some of his peers were able to throw their money around while he only had the prestige of his position in Ashmount House. But the Fialas had relieved him of that particular burden. As long as Ana and Vesna kept slipping him silver pennies, he was more their servant than Lord Oswin's. He came to their room once or twice a week, always under the pretext of some errand, and divulged all the gossip that had run its circuits around town before trickling into the servants' hall. It was through him that they'd learned about Goldie Weaver's drinking habit.

After the ill-fated ploy with the alderman of the weavers' guild, Anastasia had decided to bide her time with Calia. The alderman was difficult to work with, strong-willed and highly particular, and despite her attempts to coax him back to the manor, he had thus far declined her invitations. Ashmount was home to several excellent weavers, only a few of whom had been selected to work on the queen's tapestry, and the alderman resented the fact that he wasn't involved.

Ana would have been willing to forget about him and tackle Calia some other way, but the woman was infuriatingly difficult to deal with. Because she slept upstairs with Lucy Tailor, Sigrad rarely heard any gossip about her. Beyond the fact that she wasn't part of a weavers' guild, there didn't seem to be any easily exploitable weakness in her character that Ana could pick at. Week by week, her square of the tapestry took shape, and it was just as Ana had feared; Calia was one of the best weavers in the household. Insidious worries needled at her daily. What if she was no longer the queen's rising star? What if the royal court started talking about Calia Tailor, not Anastasia Fiala, as the brilliant young artisan bringing the Farren Vale back to life?

She told herself she was overreacting. One lone weaver could not upstage her. But she'd worked so hard for this, overcome so many rejections, and if this project was anything less than a glorious triumph—*her* glorious triumph—then she would be relegated to the refuse heap of failed artists whose frescoes would be painted over and their panels left to rot in cellars, their work disregarded and their names forgotten.

"It's too late for me, Nastya," Vesna would tell her, "But you still have the hands of a master. These years are precious. Don't squander a single day until you have everything you deserve."

And so, after her efforts with the alderman stalled, Ana focused her attention on the other weavers. If Calia couldn't be dealt with directly, it might be possible to tarnish her reputation by association instead. Goldie Weaver was adequately skilled, but by no means up to the standards of some of the others. Everyone knew that she, Calia, Rovena, and Lucy were part of the same clique. They were young, most of them new to the household, and if one could be made to look bad then the others would be dragged down along with her.

The rumour about Goldie's estranged husband having remarried was a vague one, something Sigrad had picked up in a public house from one of the merchants. It might be true, or it might just be mean-spirited gossip. The page himself had thought nothing of it, but, at Vesna's insistence, Ana had given him a silver penny to repeat it at supper time. Now it was all over the manor. Calia had even moved downstairs into the great hall, highlighting the fact that her friend was struggling. It was early days still, but Ana felt confident that she could paint Calia's social group as volatile, immature, and unreliable the next time the queen visited.

The only problem was the quality of their work. Ana found herself staring at it longer than usual these days. She stood in the weaving room one evening pacing back and forth in front of the weavers as she appraised their progress. For all of her desire to undermine these three women, the artist in her could not deny the beauty of their work. Rovena's wefts were painstakingly tight and even, the picture betraying no hint of distortion when she switched between different parts of the design. Goldie's loom, while less impressive than the others, nevertheless captured the image of Anastasia's cartoon with stark accuracy. There was none of the improvisation or deviation that some weavers insisted was necessary to bring the design to life.

Calia's tapestry was the most striking of all, and it seized Ana with a maddening clash of fascination and jealousy. She came to a halt in front of it, staring intently at the double-woven wefts. It frustrated her because it was different from her design. Some of the colours were distinctly off. The spacing and alignment of certain elements had shifted. Yet the piece had not suffered for it. When Ana looked at Calia's loom, she felt like a novice being reprimanded by her master again, Vesna's sharp pinches digging into her arm as she corrected her work, tweaking it, altering it, demonstrating how it could be done better.

The longer she stared, the more differences she noticed. Her eyes flitted between the loom and the cartoon standing behind it. Hadn't she told Calia to weave that horn in silver instead of silk? Her indignation at being ignored rose like fire in her belly. She leaned in closer, studying the pair of angels, then approached the cartoon to compare them to the original design.

"Why didn't you copy my angels properly?" she snapped.

Calia tucked her bobbin into a hanging loop of thread and turned around. "I haven't spoilt it, have I?"

Ana compressed her lips. Calia always had a way of phrasing things with such frustrating innocence.

"Yes, you have. Look at my angels. Now look at yours."

"Mine look a little happier."

"And why did you use silk for the horn? I specifically told you that I wanted silver thread."

"I'm sorry if you don't like it. Silver thread is so expensive and time-consuming to make. But the silk captures the same effect, doesn't it? You didn't even notice until now."

"The silk is nice and subtle," Rovena said.

Ana rounded on her in frustration. "It is not *supposed* to be subtle! Do none of you know the parable of Tayle and Myra?" She received only blank looks. "No, of course you don't. They were two angels, sisters of the heavenly chorus who heralded God with their horns. Each of them wished to have her music ring loudest, her horn shine brightest, so they fought over the most glorious instrument in all of heaven. Why would Tayle and Myra fight over a plain horn like that?" She motioned to Calia's tapestry. "They barely even look like they're fighting! The comparison has been completely lost."

Calia averted her eyes, finally looking guilty.

"I don't think the queen would want angels fighting on her tapestry," Rovena said.

Anastasia was about to say: "It's not about what she wants," but caught herself just in time. She bit the inside of her lip and glared down at Calia.

"No more changes like this. I want you to copy my design exactly as it is depicted. Do you understand?"

Calia nodded, but Ana had a feeling the girl's deviant streak would endure. She'd almost finished this square of the tapestry, and it was too late to change it. Angrier than ever, Ana stormed out of the room and went back to the royal solar.

Her temper cooled slightly when she found her sister alone in the hall. Karaline was sitting on a rug playing a board game against Tappy, her doll.

If only my weavers were so obedient, Ana thought. Dolls never answered back or made decisions on their own. How long had Kara had Tappy now? It must have been four years, ever since she was five. The doll had been called something else originally, but Kara soon changed her name because of the sound her wooden legs made when she pretended to walk her along the floorboards. Ana tried to recall the doll's first name, but she was too frustrated. When she'd been Kara's age, she'd run off to cry when she felt like this. She'd always had to find a cupboard or a trunk to hide in, because crying in front of Vesna only earned her more pinches and swats of her mother's hand.

Karaline looked up and saw the distraught look on her face. Ana felt like she had to say something, anything, to take the edge off her temper.

"Where's Mother?"

Kara pointed in the direction of the small dining hall attached to the royal chambers. Vesna must have been having supper in there with Lord Oswin. They probably expected Ana to join them, but she couldn't stomach it. She reached out to her little sister and beckoned her over. Kara picked up Tappy, the board game forgotten, and took her hand.

"Have you had supper yet?" Ana asked.

"No."

"Come on, then. We can eat outside." Ana wanted to get away from her mother and the weavers and everyone else in the house. She was in too foul a mood to tolerate anyone but her sister that evening.

Kara looked out through one of the glazed windows as they made their way downstairs. "It's going to be sunset."

"Yes, within the hour. We can watch it together."

"Huw Ward says you have the best view from the old castle wall."

"Who's Huw Ward?"

"He's the old man who lives at the castle."

"Oh, the caretaker." Anastasia frowned. "When did you go up there?"

Kara didn't answer. She'd probably slipped out on her own when Ana and Vesna were busy. Ana knew she should have reprimanded her—she was certainly annoyed enough to consider it—but Karaline already received more than her fair share of scoldings, so she let it drop.

"We'll go to the castle, then. The caretaker's right. The view of the moors is beautiful up there."

Ana went to the kitchen and hollowed herself out a loaf to use as a bread trencher, filling it with meat and vegetables before making up a smaller one for Karaline. She put their food in a satchel along with a big flask of sage water, then they headed up the hill to the castle.

The fresh air helped cool Ana's temper. She felt angry every time she thought about what was going on at the manor, so she tried to put it out of her mind. For an hour before sundown, she could step away from all of that.

"Are you upset?" Kara asked as they picked their way over the fallen stones around the castle's perimeter.

"No. Not with you. I'll feel better soon."

Ana returned the smile her sister gave her. She found these moments very peaceful. At Karaline's age, Ana had been painting every day under Vesna's watchful eye. There had rarely been time for her to relax. As she got older, life only became more stressful, winding tight like thread about a hard spool. She felt stretched and exhausted. Exhausted by the queen. Exhausted by the weavers. Exhausted by her mother and Lord Oswin. Exhausted by the constant plans she had to make. She didn't know any other way of being–except for when she was alone with Karaline. Her sister's life was simple and straightforward. For a few hours every now and again, Ana liked to share in that simplicity.

They avoided the warden's gatehouse and crossed the courtyard, making their way to a safe part of a tumbled-down wall on the other side. They sat on a mossy stone overlooking the valley beyond. From the top of the hill, they could see for miles across the moors.

"I did some of my first sketches up here," Ana said as she passed Kara her loaf. "On days just like this. Do you recognise the view?"

Kara nodded through a mouthful of food. "It's the one in your painting."

Ana gazed out over the valley, watching the way the setting sun cast one side into shadow while the other glowed gold. The sun would never set over the centre of the vale the way it did in her painting, nor were there any angels dancing in the sky, but it was a stunning view nevertheless. She could see why the original artist had chosen it. It was a little slice of the kingdom's beauty embellished into something magnificent. That blending of the mundane and the fantastic had always captured Ana's imagination. She wondered what the missing panels of the original Farren Vale had looked like. Had the painter filled the sky with scenes from the scriptures like she had, or had they chosen something else? The mystery of it fascinated her.

"Do you know Calia Tailor?" Karaline asked.

Ana frowned, unhappy to be reminded of work. "Yes."

"She's nice."

"Well, don't get too attached to her. She might not be here

forever."

"Why not?"

Ana took a bite of her food so she didn't have to answer.

"Are you going to scare her away?" Kara asked.

"Maybe."

"Why?"

"Because she's not right for this tapestry. She doesn't copy my design the way I want. I won't have her competing with me."

"But I like her."

Ana felt a twinge of guilt. She never enjoyed doing anything that upset Kara. She tucked a stray tangle of her sister's hair behind her ear when a gust of wind blew it into her mouth.

"You can like whoever you want, Kara, but not all of us are so lucky. I'm vying for the queen's favour, and so is she."

"Is she?"

"Of course. All of us are. So I'm going to do what I must to make sure I keep it and she doesn't."

Karaline's expression fell. She worried a piece of bread from the edge of her loaf and tossed it into the grass. A bird hopped down from the castle wall to snatch it up. The guilty knot in Ana's stomach tightened. There was part of her that wished she could set this friction between herself and the weavers aside, forget about competition and simply focus on the work she was passionate about. But years upon compounding years of Vesna's tutelage had crushed that desire beneath the urgent need to always be one step ahead. To always stand out. To keep her peers down so that she could rise up.

She heard the sound of voices behind them and looked over her shoulder to see a group of adolescent boys coming up the path from the town. They gave the gatehouse a wide berth, collecting rocks to throw at the birds perching in the castle windows. A distasteful scowl pinched Ana's face, but she ignored them and went back to her meal. Hopefully the warden would hear the boys and shoo them away.

Kara finished her food and began picking daisies to weave into a chain. She made them into a little necklace for Tappy, then a crown. It was already sunset, but Ana didn't feel like returning to the manor and dealing with her mother. They could stay out here a while longer. Kara ran about collecting more daisies so that her sister could try her hand at making chains, too. It wasn't something Ana had ever done before. She hadn't had time to make daisy chains when she was little. Kara showed her how to push her fingernail through the stem to create a gap through which another daisy's stem could be secured. Ana tried her best, but her fingers were larger than Kara's, and she kept her nails clipped flat and short. More often than not, she ended up mangling the stems and breaking the chain. She resented her lack of aptitude for the childish game. It was so simple, yet she was struggling with it. Why was she so clumsy? Her arm itched with the anticipation of phantom pinches.

Kara giggled as another daisy dropped through a broken stem. Ana frowned, hurt by her sister's mockery, but when she looked up she saw no scorn on the girl's face. Her frown melted into a smile, the tension running out of her. This wasn't painting. It wasn't the end of the world to be bad at making daisy chains.

Ana jumped suddenly as a fist-sized rock cracked off the ruined wall next to her, bouncing upwards and spinning over Karaline's head. She was on her feet in an instant, the daisies forgotten. The group of youths stood behind them, their laughter echoing off the castle walls as they tossed their stones about carelessly.

"Stop that!" Ana shouted. "You almost hit us!"

"What are you going to do about it?" one of them jeered back.

"I'll fetch the warden."

"He's not here."

"Lord Oswin will hear of this!"

The boys chorused a mocking "ooh" back at her, and one of them lifted the front of his long tunic to expose his genitals. Another threw a stone that thudded into the grass near her foot. Ana's indignation simmered beneath her skin. Had she been on her own, she might have ignored them and simply left, but the thought of them spoiling Karaline's evening enraged her. She strode forward, her eyes fixed on the boy who'd lifted his tunic. He came to meet her with a cocky grin.

"Want another look?"

His bravado faltered when he saw the look in her eyes. At the last moment, he threw his arms up to try and push her away, but she was taller than him, and he was the one who ended up stumbling backwards. She grabbed the front of the tunic. His friends came forward, but Ana's free hand was already on the handle of the knife in her satchel. The blade flashed in the setting sun. When the boys saw it, they immediately backed off. Ana felt a smug sense of satisfaction. Little thugs like them were all talk. She pressed the blade to the boy's cheek. A bead of terrified sweat stood out on his brow.

"The next time you flash your little prick around, I'm going to cut it off."

The boy said nothing. Judging by the look on his face, he believed her. She let go of his tunic and shoved him away. The other boys had already made themselves scarce, hurrying off behind the gatehouse the second they saw the knife. Ana watched the last lad go with a scowl. This was exactly why you had to stand up for yourself. If you didn't, idiots like them would try to walk all over you. She put her knife away and went to fetch Kara. Neither of them spoke on the walk back to the manor. The peace of the evening had soured, bringing Ana's bad mood back to the surface.

Vesna was waiting for them in the royal solar. She put Karaline to bed before coming to stand with Ana by the fireplace. Dusk had fallen, and the crackling hearth was the only light source in the room.

"You're in a mood, Nastya."

"Shut up, Mother. You know I hate it when you call me that."

Vesna's sharp fingernails dug into her arm, so painful and abrupt that Ana cried out and shied away, cowering.

"I call you that to remind you of your heritage," Vesna said in their native tongue. "You're not one of these people, Nastya. You never will be. You're better than them. I didn't raise you to be ashamed of who you are."

Ana rubbed her arm, tears of anger beading in her eyes as her mother's scorn bore down on her.

Vesna let the feeling endure for an unbearably long moment before her demeanour abruptly changed. "I've some good news for us."

"What?" Ana asked, trying to swallow her tears.

"The queen will be visiting again next month. Oswin told me over supper."

For an instant, Ana was afraid. There wasn't enough time. Calia and the others would outshine her. The queen would be disappointed. She would be dismissed from the project.

Then her resolve hardened, winding tight once more as fear succumbed to determination.

"Good. I'll be able to show her what happens when she picks nobodies to do her weaving."

"You have a plan, then?" Vesna asked.

"Oh, yes. I'm ready for her."

CHAPTER 8

Calia put the finishing touches on her first tapestry square just in time for Queen Meredith's visit that summer. All told, eighteen of the Farren Vale's forty-eight pieces were now complete. They were to be presented to the monarch in the great hall, hung upon the tapestry hooks that would eventually hold the finished piece with Anastasia's painted panels substituting for the missing parts.

An air of apprehension chilled the mood amongst the weavers. Goldie was particularly on edge. She'd still not heard any news of her husband and was terrified that the queen would find fault with her work and dismiss her. Anastasia would undoubtedly try to paint her in a negative light. But the bonds of solidarity between the weavers had only strengthened with time, and most were prepared to stand up to Ana if she forced them. Only a few of the old masters still harboured a lingering hostility toward the newcomers.

The entire household assembled to welcome the royal entourage in the great hall. The weavers lined up with the servants. Calia was wearing her nice green dress for the occasion, and Lucy had braided her hair into a neat plait. Anastasia and her family stood opposite them, close to Lord

Oswin. The royal bailiff wore a smart black tunic with silver fastenings, a stark contrast to the colourful orange dress Ana had chosen. The painter was by far the most striking figure in the hall. She wore gold rings on her fingers and a heavy necklace with a sparkling blue gemstone at the centre. Blue highlights accented her entire outfit, a contrast that naturally drew the eye without relying on explosive gaudiness. She'd gone out of her way to ensure she was the first person the queen noticed.

Sure enough, Queen Meredith turned immediately to Anastasia when she entered the hall. The pair walked to the tapestry with a halo of followers in tow. The weavers strained their ears to hear what was being said, but the polite silence that had welcomed the queen was quickly dissolving into noise.

Calia and Lucy edged closer with Goldie behind them. They approached as far as they dared before stopping to listen. The queen was standing directly in front of the partially-assembled tapestry, nodding along as Ana pointed out the details to her.

"I would like to get a closer look," Meredith said. "One square at a time. I can't take in all these wonderful details when the best parts are near the ceiling."

"Of course, Your Majesty," Ana said. "I'll have the pieces taken down and moved back upstairs. They'll be ready for you tomorrow morning."

"Wonderful. I'm pleased with the progress you're making."

Ana voiced an audible sigh of relief, so loud and obvious that the queen turned on her with a frown.

"Forgive me, Your Majesty," the painter excused herself. "I'm glad everything is to your taste."

"Is there any reason it shouldn't be?"

"Oh, not that you need trouble yourself with. Such problems are for your servants to worry over."

The queen looked back at the tapestry, still frowning.

"She's up to something," Lucy said under her breath.

Calia nodded in agreement. Ana was being far too overt. If there was a genuine problem, she wouldn't have let it slip out so carelessly. She never liked anything to reflect badly on her.

"She wants the queen to think there's trouble afoot," Calia said.

"Without coming out and accusing anyone," Lucy added with a scowl. "We'd better tell the others. You've got to show a united front if you want the queen to take your side over hers."

"I can't stand this," said Goldie.

Calia rubbed her arm. "It'll be alright. Come on, let's go and have a word with everyone upstairs." She turned around and almost bumped into Sigrad. The page had been hovering uncomfortably close behind her. "What are you doing there, Sigrad?"

"Nothing, mistress," he replied placidly. Calia didn't like to judge a book by its cover, but there was something unnerving about Sigrad. He was wiry for his age, like a tough little ferret. His cheeks bore a light scattering of acne scars, and his eyes darted about with an oily certainty that reminded Calia of a fox eyeing chickens. He was always gossiping, and the gossip he indulged in was rarely the harmless kind.

Calia hurried past him and went upstairs with the others. They got the weavers together in one of the workrooms and outlined their worries.

"We're all in agreement, then?" Rovena said. "We don't break ranks. If Ana singles one of us out, the others will back her up. If anyone's going to come out of this looking bad, it'll be her, not us."

There was a general murmur of assent from the weavers. Only two of them raised their voices in objection.

"If Mistress Ana takes issue with anyone's work, I'll make up my own mind about it," said Elaine, one of the middle-aged masters.

"It's not our place to second-guess our betters," added

Bess, an older woman with grey in her hair. "A serf pushes the plough in his master's field, and a weaver works the loom for her commissioner. You'll invite nothing but trouble by getting above your station, especially you young folk." She gave Calia's group a pointed look.

"Of course you'd say that," Lucy retorted. "You're not the ones Ana's picking on."

"And you're not even part of this project. Why don't you go back to your sewing?"

Calia felt the tension in the air, sensing the group's harmony on the verge of fraying as more people raised their voices in argument. She desperately wanted to say something that would calm them down, but everyone was being so loud, their voices cluttering up the room like a swarm of hornets. She shut her eyes tight. It was all getting too much for her.

"Are you alright?" Lucy's voice cut through the buzz. "Shut up, all of you! Poor Calia looks like she's about to have a turn."

"I'm fine," Calia insisted, her face warming with embarrassment when Lucy clutched her shoulders.

"You see?" Old Bess said. "This is no good for any of us."

Calia felt foolish for being so sensitive. She didn't like the way she clammed up when situations became heated and boisterous. She'd been trying to assert herself and show greater confidence, but she obviously still had a long way to go. Perhaps with a hardier disposition, she would have been able to defuse the situation before it escalated.

The weavers slowly trickled back downstairs, their resolve fractured. Calia hoped their mutual understanding would endure tomorrow morning, but with Elaine and Bess dissenting, it was no longer a sure thing.

Calia and Goldie were woken early the next day. For once it wasn't Goldie's children who roused them, for they had tired themselves out the night before amidst the excitement of the royal visit. Ever-weary in the clamour of the great hall, Calia usually dozed through the early part of the morning until breakfast began. That day, the servants hadn't even started preparing the tables when Sigrad woke her with a rough shake of the shoulder. She sat up blinking as Goldie suffered a similarly brusque awakening.

"You're wanted upstairs," the page said.

"What for?" Calia asked, rubbing the sleep from her eyes.

Sigrad shrugged, but the barely-suppressed smile on his lips suggested he knew more than he was letting on. An uneasy feeling turned over in Calia's stomach.

They got up and fetched Lucy to keep an eye on the children, then tidied themselves up as best they could and followed Sigrad upstairs. He took them to the chamber adjacent to the weaving rooms where the tapestry cartoons were kept. They'd been returned to their original places since yesterday, and the finished squares of the Farren Vale were displayed on stands before them. Calia's queasiness intensified as she took in the room's occupants. Three of the other weavers were already present: Rovena, Elaine, and Bess. They stood in a line at one end of the room while Anastasia and Vesna attended Queen Meredith by the tapestry. Ana looked as if she'd already been up for hours, her hair brushed and her dress immaculate. Elaine and Bess, too, seemed to have been given time to prepare. The only other person in the room was a man Calia didn't recognise. Tall and pale, he was richly dressed and clean-shaven, with long ash-blonde hair that lent him an air of fey dignity. Sigrad went to stand by the man while Calia and Goldie joined the other weavers. Calia desperately wanted to ask what was going on, but she dared not speak in front of the queen. A few things were obvious enough: Anastasia had arranged this impromptu meeting, forewarning her allies in advance so that only Calia and her friends would be dishevelled and sleepy when they arrived.

None of the other weavers came in to join them. The queen walked from tapestry square to tapestry square, examining each one in detail before turning to acknowledge the young weavers.

"I have been made aware of some concerns regarding you three."

Calia heard a barely-audible groan slip through Goldie's lips.

"Your Majesty–" Ana began, but Queen Meredith held up a hand to silence her.

"That will be enough. My mind is set." She addressed the weavers again. "Your mistress believes that I should leave the handling of this matter to her. But this is my project. I appointed you, and if my faith was poorly placed then I shall not be coddled out of acknowledging it. Clearly I need to take an active interest in this tapestry if it is to be handled in accordance with my wishes." There was a frostiness to her that Calia hadn't seen before. Queen Meredith was known for her eccentricities and her temper. This was a dangerous moment for all of them. "There have been accusations," she continued, staring at Calia and her friends, "that the three of you are not conducting yourselves in a manner befitting your station. What do you have to say for yourselves?"

Calia's tongue felt like it was stuck to the roof of her mouth. Her head was still foggy with sleep, and the inquisition of Anastasia, Vesna, and the queen was too much for her. She tried to think rationally. They had to piece together a defence and show themselves in a good light if they wanted to get out of this. It wasn't technically a trial, but Calia had a feeling the distinction was nebulous at this point. The queen was one of the highest authorities in the land. If she wanted to punish them, they would be punished.

Rovena found the courage to speak first.

"If we are being accused of something, might our fellows be allowed to speak up on our behalf?"

Meredith gestured at Bess and Elaine impatiently. "Are two of your most senior weavers insufficient?"

"They do not work closely with us, Your Majesty." Rovena

was trying her best to be polite and tactful, but Calia could hear the thread of indignation coiling through her words. "We might be able to paint you a better picture of the situation if the others were here also."

"That won't be possible," Anastasia said. "They're indisposed right now."

"Indisposed with what?" Rovena retorted, unable to maintain her cordial tone when she addressed Ana. "It's not even past breakfast."

Ana didn't let Rovena ruffle her feathers. She was presenting herself as the level-headed one, and, to Calia's dismay, it seemed to be working.

"You know I always send a group of you to put in orders with the dyers every other market day."

"One or two of us, yes, not half a dozen! And it isn't even market day!"

"Lord Oswin declared the market should open a day early this week to coincide with the royal visit. The town aldermen insist these are good business days."

Calia wondered whether Ana had persuaded the bailiff to open the market early, or if she'd just taken advantage of a favourable situation. Either way, it didn't seem like they would be getting any help from the others. She'd successfully divided them.

"Might I ask what we have been accused of?" Calia asked. Her voice sounded scratchy and weak. She hoped the queen didn't interpret her tone as one of guilt.

Meredith turned to Rovena, apparently ignoring Calia's question. "Rovena, yes?"

"Yes, Your Majesty."

"The quality of your work is very fine. I would like to retain your services. But I have some concerns. Is it true what I hear about you leaving the manor late some evenings and crossing the stream to visit the home of a heathen woman?"

Elaine spoke up for the first time: "I've seen her coming and going. She tries to be quiet about it. Doesn't come home until after dark sometimes. And she won't speak a word to anyone when we ask her."

Rovena shot the other woman a filthy look. "What are you accusing me of? Visiting someone's house in my own time?"

"Don't be flippant," Queen Meredith snapped. "Answer the question."

Rovena bit her tongue. "Yes."

"And is it also true that this woman whose company you frequent has not been seen attending church in over a year? That she is accused of witchcraft and speaks in tongues to those who visit her?"

Rovena was trembling now, though not in fear. It seemed to be taking all of her composure to keep an even tone when she spoke. "She has not attended church lately, no, Your Majesty. The journey is too difficult for her, and she gets confused when she's away from home for too long. If anyone has accused her of witchcraft then it is nothing but mean-spirited gossip. She has never been prosecuted by an ecclesiastical court. As for her speaking in tongues, her mind is not what it used to be. I'm sure you've seen elders say and do things that seem nonsensical when their faculties start to fail them. I visit her house in the evenings because she needs someone to look in on her. She's my great-aunt." Her spiteful gaze turned on Elaine again. "Anyone who'd lived here more than a few months would know that."

Elaine had the decency to look ashamed. Anastasia's brow furrowed slightly, but she remained silent. The queen, too, seemed to have been taken off guard by Rovena's impassioned defence.

"Can this be confirmed by anyone else?" Meredith asked.

The long-haired man stepped forward to speak. "It's true. I've known Rovena since her days as an apprentice." He sounded impatient, as though he would rather be anywhere else right now. Calia wondered again who he was and why he'd been summoned. He wasn't a member of the household.

"Very well," Meredith went on, quickly putting the matter

behind her. "Now you, Goldie Weaver." She turned to regard Goldie's square of the tapestry before continuing. "Your work is not up to the standard I expect. Certainly not the standard of your husband."

Once again Goldie made a wordless sound of anguish. She was in a worse state than any of them.

"I'm sorry, Your Majesty! I'll do better."

"Will you? Page, would you bring her belongings."

Like a stagehand waiting for his cue, Sigrad scampered forward dragging a small chest behind him. Several of the weavers had boxes where they kept valuable belongings. Most of the time they were locked, but this one had been opened. Goldie stared in horror as Sigrad turned out her possessions onto the floor: A fine leather travelling bag, a box of jewellery, a richly embroidered blanket, two fine dresses, and beneath them a porcelain jug with a wax-sealed stopper. Calia's heart sank as Sigrad took out a knife and cut the seal open, taking a long sniff of the contents and wrinkling his nose at the smell.

"Wine, Your Majesty. Very strong. I'd be drunk on a single cup."

Goldie stammered over her words as she tried to explain herself. "Can I not have just– It's only a little wine! A travelling gift. Why have you been going through my things?!" Her shrill, defensive tone was doing her no favours. She sounded like a guilty woman outraged at being caught.

Queen Meredith's expression darkened. "Are you telling me that hoarding wine is not something you indulge in regularly?"

Goldie opened her mouth, shaking her head with tears in her eyes.

"She's always sneaking it out of the cellar," Sigrad said. "Half the servants have seen her."

"As have I," Vesna confirmed.

"And me," said Bess.

Goldie was sobbing now. "I haven't! Not recently! Calia

can tell you."

"It's true," Calia said, her voice hardening now that she had someone else to defend. "She had a difficult time, but she's on the mend now. I haven't seen her drinking in days, let alone sneaking wine."

To her dismay, Queen Meredith didn't look impressed.

"Refuge in drink is the vice of peasants and merchants; men who beat their wives and women who neglect their children. I am ashamed to have this behaviour under my roof."

Calia could have told the queen about a dozen other servants who were overly fond of drink, but she doubted that would help right now.

"Your Majesty, we've been doing all we can to help Goldie. Her weaving is still of a fine standard, and we promise you, she shall never touch another drop until work on the tapestry is complete."

"It says much to me that she needs others to make excuses for her," the queen replied. "Look at her. She's a mess. Clearly whatever efforts you've been making are insufficient. This woman needs a convent, not a royal commission. Goldie Weaver, as of today your services are no longer required. You will be paid any outstanding wages before you leave."

Goldie's mouth dropped open. She looked like she'd been slapped in the face.

"Please, Your Majesty, let me stay!"

"Don't beg, it's beneath your dignity. Goodness, woman, what would your husband say?"

Goldie raised her shaking hands to her mouth, tears streaming down her cheeks as she crumpled to the floor in despair. "Where will I go?"

"Home. I assume you have one. You can return to the capital with my entourage if you wish."

"But my husband owns that house." She trailed off into more tears, unable to explain the horrible uncertainty that hung over her. Calia knelt and put her arms around her, trying to ease her back to her feet.

"As I said," the queen continued stiffly, "you might benefit from some time in a convent. Page, would you please take her outside."

Sigrad bounded forward and grabbed Goldie by the arm, helping her none-too-gently to her feet. Calia scowled at him. Anastasia had remained impassive throughout the exchange, but Sigrad looked like a boy squashing ants. Goldie's misery delighted him. He would have a first-hand account of her humiliation to spread about the servants' hall that afternoon.

It was seldom in Calia's nature to hate others, but in that moment she loathed Sigrad. They were in this together, weren't they? Him, Ana, and her spiteful crone of a mother. The group of them had plotted to ruin the livelihoods of three innocent people. In Goldie's case, she stood to lose even more. She would have money, yes, and the potential to return to work if she could outrun this scandal, but how would she look after the children, find new employment, and move past her drinking habit with no one to support her? Calia prayed the rumours about Goldie's husband were false and that he was waiting for her back at the capital. She dreaded to think what might become of her otherwise.

She wanted to stay with Goldie and console her when they went outside, but Sigrad dragged her back into the chamber and shut the door behind them, cutting off the distant sound of Goldie's sobs. Queen Meredith looked relieved that the spectacle was over and done with.

"Now, Calia Tailor," she put particular emphasis on the *Tailor* part, and Calia felt the back of her neck prickle. "Your work is quite impressive. I am willing to overlook any poor judgements you may have made in your choice of friends, but your mistress tells me there is another matter that has been concerning her."

Anastasia finally stepped forward. She beckoned the long-haired man to join her.

"Do you know who this is?" she asked Calia.

"No."

"And have you ever met this woman before, Leander?"

The long-haired man shook his head. "I have not. Nor have any of my counterparts in the area."

"Leander is the alderman of the weavers' guild here in Ashmount," Anastasia explained. "If neither he nor any of his peers know who Calia Tailor is, then..." She motioned for Leander to continue where she left off.

"Then clearly she is not a member of a guild. She has no right to take commissions for weaving in this town or any other. It is an outrage, Your Majesty, for this sort of thing to be going on in the royal household. I explicitly insisted on local weavers for this very reason."

At first it had seemed like their argument was working, but the alderman's abrupt shift into petulance struck a nerve with Queen Meredith. Calia sensed this was an argument they'd had before, perhaps one that was a lingering source of contention between the weavers' guild and the monarch.

"And yet she clearly displays the talents of a fully trained weaver," Meredith said.

"I was taught by an excellent master," said Calia. "It's true that I completed my apprenticeship in tailoring, but I learned just as much about weaving during those years."

Leander snorted derisively. "An apprentice can't master two skills at once. Tailoring and weaving are a world apart."

"No, they're not!" Calia said, surprising herself with her passion. "Both work with thread. Both teach you to train your eyes and fingers. A bobbin is just a big needle, and an eye for embroidery is an eye for weaving."

The queen seemed mildly amused by the argument, but there was nothing funny about it to Calia. She was fighting for her job, and perhaps her right to professionally weave ever again.

"As I said," Meredith reiterated, "her work is of excellent quality despite the circumstances of her training."

Leander turned to her with a look of indignation. "Your Majesty, the precedent of tradition is more important than the talents of one girl. What would happen if this were to become public knowledge? That the queen herself was hiring unguilded artisans to work for her? The integrity of our entire craft–of all crafts–would be undermined. When you commission a weaver from within a guild, it brings with it the assurance that they have been trained to the highest standard, that their work will be of sound quality, professionally conducted, and backed by an organisation with the power to resolve any disputes that arise. What if everyone started commissioning artisans with no formal recognition? One in a hundred might be lucky. The rest would be swindled. And the reputation of all artisans, guilded and unguilded alike, would fall into the mud."

Leander was short of breath by the time he finished, and the queen no longer looked quite so amused. The appeal to tradition seemed to have resonated with her. Calia hated to admit it, but Leander made a convincing argument. For all of their problems, guilds were an important institution for maintaining the standards and practices of skilled work. When you hired a carpenter, you needed to trust that the house he built wouldn't fall down on you in your sleep.

"I see your point," the queen said. "Yet surely there is a simple remedy to this: Calia Tailor must be acknowledged as a member of the Ashmount weavers' guild."

Calia's heart leapt. Could it really be that easy?

Leander shook his head. "Out of the question. She has not gone through the appropriate training."

"Does it really matter?" Calia asked. She needed to argue her side now. She was teetering on the brink, afraid that a single push would settle her fate. "Guilds often welcome new artisans if the masters agree that the newcomer's work is of sufficient quality."

Leander scowled. Perhaps he'd been hoping that Calia's youth would make her ignorant of such things. He couldn't very well appeal to one well-established tradition and then ignore another when it suited him.

"The question is whether Calia Tailor's work is of sufficient quality," he said.

"Your Majesty," said Calia, feeling salvation at the tips of her fingers. "Do you think the quality of my work is sufficient?"

Queen Meredith gave her a coy smile. She seemed to be enjoying herself again. Perhaps this process of accusations, refutations, drama, and rivalry interested her more than the tapestry. Calia wondered whether it was always like this at the royal court. It seemed bizarre to her that a person could take pleasure in treating other people's lives like roles in a farce.

"I certainly think so," the queen said.

"Might I invite you to take a closer look at her tapestry, Your Majesty?" Anastasia asked. "Sigrad, Leander, would you be so kind as to bring down my original painting so that we can compare the two?"

Calia's heart pattered in her chest as she watched the two men climb the step ladders and lower down the cartoon she'd been copying from.

"I can see the problem already," Leander said as he studied the painting. "Deviations in shape, colour, and especially the tone."

"What do you mean by that?" Meredith asked.

"The mood, Your Majesty. The overarching feeling conveyed by the piece."

Calia edged forward and said: "If there's anything in particular you take issue with, I would be happy to explain my choices." She remembered what her mother had told her; she had to let her work speak for itself, and she wouldn't let it be misrepresented by someone with a vendetta against her.

Leander ignored her. "This is exactly the problem with untrained weavers. Compare this to Rovena's work. Hers matches the cartoon exactly."

Anastasia nodded in agreement, pointing out the pair of

angels wrestling over the silver horn. "Take this part. Can you look at Calia's angels and say they accurately resemble mine?"

The queen turned to Calia with a cocked eyebrow. "Well? Do you think I can, Calia?"

"No, Your Majesty." There was a smug huff of satisfaction from Leander, but she ignored him. "I thought you might prefer two playful angels in harmony over two locked in conflict. And the silk I used, this one in particular," she pointed out the colour of the horn and several other embellished sun rays she'd woven using the same thread, "it is gentle, so as not to draw the eye away from the centre of the piece."

There was a long pause. Calia wrung her fingers together behind her back, her palms cold and clammy.

"I quite like your angels," Meredith said. "And I agree. They should be in harmony, not fighting."

"All the same," Anastasia cut in, "she has copied the cartoon inaccurately. How many more deviations will slip through if she continues working on this project? We are recreating a storied work of art, not experimenting with something new."

"Aren't your panels something new?" Calia retorted. "They were never part of the original."

Ana's cheeks flushed. "My point still stands."

"Again," Queen Meredith said, "I see a simple solution. I like Calia's work. If anything, I think she has improved upon your design, Ana. The two of you complement each other well. As long as Calia only works on your original squares, I see no reason why her style should not sit in harmony with the rest of the piece."

"But we cannot admit her to the guild!" Leander protested.

The queen's demeanour shifted in an instant. "Then make an exception. I want Calia Tailor admitted to your guild at the next meeting. You may present her work to the other masters and they will vote in favour of her admission."

There was no mistaking her tone; this was not a suggestion, it was a command. Calia didn't know whether the queen had the legal authority to impose her will on the weaver's guild, but it didn't seem to matter. The implication was clear. If Leander defied her, he would regret it.

With a stiff nod, the alderman averted his gaze and stepped back.

"Thank you, Your Majesty," Calia said, dipping a curtsey. She couldn't feel relieved, not after what had happened to Goldie, but the threat hanging over her had lifted. She was safe, for now.

Sigrad opened the door for the queen and followed her out. Leander went next, making a hurried exit before anyone could accost him. The uncomfortable silence that lingered in their wake was palpable. Calia took Rovena's arm and made for the door, her concern for Goldie undercut with bitterness. Up until now, she'd tolerated Anastasia. She'd been an unpleasant mistress, but nothing more. Today, that had changed. A bubble of resentment rose through Calia's anxiety, forcing her to turn and meet Anastasia's gaze before she left the room.

"How can you be so heartless?"

Ana seemed to stare right through her, dispassionately divorced from what had just happened. There was no regret in her expression, no anger, only a cold hardness.

It was Vesna who answered Calia's question.

"This is Ana's project, not yours, and you'd do well to remember it."

"I don't understand you."

"Then keep your simple mind where it belongs and don't question us again."

Calia walked out.

CHAPTER 9

That summer was a gloomy one for Calia. Goldie left with the queen's entourage when they departed, promising to send word once she was settled back at the capital. Calia hoped the promise would keep her focused on getting back on her feet, but as the weeks passed and she received no correspondence from her absent friend, her hope began to wane.

The weavers' guild summoned her to one of their meetings and voted on her admission, just as the queen had demanded. It turned out to be a painless process. Most of the weavers seemed level-headed sorts, and they immediately recognised the quality of Calia's work. Even Leander's opposition subsided. He was not a vindictive man, but a prideful one. His obstinance at the manor had been directed at his exclusion from the project, not Calia personally.

In the weeks that followed, Calia became a subject of gossip about the house. Many people seemed to think—no doubt encouraged by Sigrad—that she'd tricked her way into the queen's service under false pretences, only to be saved by the monarch's mercy when she was dramatically exposed in front of the other weavers. Everyone wanted to know what had gone on upstairs, and Calia found herself bombarded with he-said-she-said questions at meal times. With Goldie gone, she moved back into Lucy's room for some peace and quiet, and she started working longer hours to avoid the suppertime rush. When she did venture downstairs, she tried to keep her visits brief. If the weather was good, she took her food outside so she could eat on her own.

Worse than the gossip was the lack of passion Calia now felt for her work. She'd begun weaving a second square from the top row of the tapestry, but in defiance of her extra hours, it was taking much longer than the first. She couldn't shake the feeling that all her effort was for someone else's gain. Ana was determined to take credit for the collaboration, and anyone who lifted their head to stand out from the crowd was either stamped down or driven out. It wasn't that Calia yearned for recognition, but she didn't think Anastasia deserved to reap the rewards when she seemed to be doing all she could to sabotage the project. The painter wasn't stupid; Calia had spent enough time around her to understand that she was a fiercely intelligent woman, but her pride and ambition outstripped her passion for art. The tapestry was a means to an end for her. The prestige of the Fiala name mattered more than the beautiful piece of history that would hang in Ashmount House for years to come. It was almost sad, but Calia struggled to find pity for a woman who might well have ruined Goldie's life.

After a few weeks of moping, she started looking for ways to rekindle her enthusiasm for the project. It was bigger than just Anastasia, she told herself, and besides, if her work began to suffer then she might find herself next in line for dismissal.

The summer weather was exceptionally fine, full of clear skies and warm breezes, which gave her a good excuse to take her meals up the hill to Huw Ward's gatehouse. Learning more about the history of the old castle seemed like a good way to reignite her passion. Karaline Fiala joined them sometimes when her mother and sister were busy. The young girl was bright and inquisitive, no doubt possessed of the same intelligence as her sister, but terribly lonely and neglected. Now that Goldie's children were gone, she had no one her age to interact with even if she'd wanted to come out of her shell. Her doll Tappy was her only friend. Calia didn't think she'd seen Karaline apart from it a single time since she arrived at Ashmount House.

The pair of them were walking around the ruins with Huw one afternoon as he told them about the different lords who had ruled over Ashmount in the past. It was a religious holiday, so they had the whole day to themselves. The bishop had come to town to perform service that morning. After church, Anastasia and Vesna had gone to dine with him, and Karaline said they would be there all afternoon. Most of the townsfolk were playing games and relaxing out in the meadows. A few had come up to the castle to lounge on the walls, but the atmosphere was quiet and subdued. No youths dared disturb the peace with so many of their elders watching.

"There's something about that wall," Calia said to Huw as Karaline skipped ahead of them into the shade of the ruined keep. "I still can't picture the tapestry hanging there. It just seems unusual to me."

"Old buildings often feel that way once they have grass coming up through the cracks and moss growing on the mortar."

"I wouldn't put a tapestry there," Karaline said.

Calia was glad someone agreed with her. "I wish we had a sketch so we could see what it looked like when this room was in use."

"I don't recall ever seeing anything like that, but if it exists, it'd be in the old steward's journals. They're our main source of history for the castle. Been a few years since I looked at them myself."

"Where are they now?"

"At the manor. Locked up with all the charters, I expect.

Lord Oswin should let you look if you ask nicely."

Taking advantage of the light holiday atmosphere, Calia asked Lord Oswin about the journals that evening. He was reluctant at first. A neat and tidy man, he liked everyone to follow his example, and Calia's friendship with Goldie Weaver had been a messy association. Still, he had no real reason to object, and when she said she wanted to research the old tapestry he eventually relented.

The house clerk fetched the journals and allowed her to read them in the chapel where it was quiet. Calia enjoyed reading. It wasn't something she'd been able to indulge in often at home, for books were exceedingly expensive. Her mother kept written records of her business, but those had never interested Calia. Livy was the one who enjoyed pouring over ledgers full of lists and numbers. Most of Calia's reading had been done at a nunnery up the hill where she'd been schooled intermittently before her apprenticeship. The kindly prioress had let her read from a big tome called The Book of Roses, which was filled with parables from the old scriptures alongside modern theological discourse. The academic content of the book had largely gone over Calia's head, but the stories from the past had engrossed her. Learning about people and places from another time felt somehow magical. It was different from hearing a minstrel tell a story, because everyone knew those were all made up. When someone recorded history and wrote it down in a book, it felt like a window into the past. It was like staring at the old castle stones when Huw told stories about them.

To Calia's disappointment, the steward's journals were far from a rigorous historical record. Rambling and poorly worded, the spellings were confusing and inconsistent throughout. The two old books seemed to be the personal musings of a man named Haelcar of the Vale who had served as the castle's steward for nine years prior to its destruction. He was a self-aggrandising sort, spending more time writing about the greatness of his accomplishments and the failures of his rivals than anything substantial. Calia found her eyes glazing over as she scanned page after page of similarly trite commentary. There were some interesting details to pick out here and there, but they were few and far between. She suspected that a scholar could have condensed everything of historical note in the journals into a book less than one-quarter the length.

Nevertheless, she pressed on, enjoying the act of reading for its own sake. When the light began to fade, she lit candles and fetched a cup of warm wine. She wanted to find what she was looking for before she went to bed: a description or a sketch of the great hall. The latter seemed unlikely, for Haelcar was no artist, so she skimmed the pages for written descriptions instead. There were a handful throughout the journals, but they were all incidental to other anecdotes and of little use by themselves. Like a lot of writers, Haelcar took many assumptions for granted, including his readers' familiarity with the layout of Castle Ashmount. He'd probably assumed that anyone reading his journals would have done so inside the castle itself, not almost a century after it had burned down.

Calia had a small wax tablet with her, one her mother had brought from home the last time she visited. Mama was a great proponent of organisation, and no tool was more important to an organised woman than a tablet. Using the sewing needle she always carried, Calia scribed brief notes into the surface, placing leaves between the journal pages to mark the spots where a relevant passage occurred. She wasn't going to be the scholar who condensed the thing down in its entirety, but she could at least try and piece together a description of the great hall. She didn't really know why she was doing it. It was a curiosity, something that might help scratch an itch at the back of her mind. Perhaps it would get her invested in the tapestry again. If nothing else, she was sure Huw would enjoy hearing about it the next time they spoke.

There were three main segments that described the great hall in any manner of detail: one about decorations that had been put up prior to a royal visit, another about the difficulties of organising a lavish banquet, and a third focusing on the steward's outrage when a builder had attempted to overcharge him for repairs to the room. It was late by the time Calia had copied all the relevant details onto her tablet. She snuffed her candles and returned the journals, then crept upstairs and slipped into Lucy's room without waking her. Whether she was passionate about her tapestry work or not, at least she had another project to distract her now.

It began raining the next morning, so it was a few days before she managed to visit the castle again. When she did, Karaline joined her. They brought sage water and fresh bread from the manor, and Huw shared some of his bacon and a delicious goat's cheese from the town market. After supper, they strolled over to the great hall and Calia shared the notes she'd made on her tablet.

"They're not terribly comprehensive, unfortunately," she explained. "The steward talked about the tapestry, of course, and some wonderful cloth flowers a tailor made for a royal visit. Oh, and the chairs at the high table. Apparently they had very prickly decorations on the backs that resulted in a few injuries when people grabbed them carelessly."

Huw chuckled. "That steward always struck me as the type who'd have chairs too fancy for their own good."

"He blamed the carpenter, of course. And listen to this: when the great hall had a problem with damp, the builder making repairs told him it was twenty-two measures of his stick long and ten wide. But Haelcar knew it was only twenty measures long. He had the builder bring out his stick to prove it, then took him to court for attempting to overcharge for unnecessary work."

"Well, at least he wasn't a complete fool."

"How long is a measuring stick?" Karaline asked.

"One yard's the standard," Huw said, then took a careful step back and forward, showing Karaline the distance between his two footfalls. "About that much."

Karaline lined her feet up with Huw's and began walking backwards to the wall, counting out the yards as she went.

Calia smiled encouragingly. She enjoyed teaching youngsters useful new things in the guise of a game. "Let's see if the old steward was right. Twenty yards from the keep door all the way to the far wall."

Karaline miscalculated her steps several times, but quickly realised that she could use the cracked flagstones to help measure out each yard more accurately. After a few attempts, she had a consistent answer.

"It's twenty, or twenty-and-a-half."

"Sounds like old Haelcar was right," Huw said. "What about the width?"

Kara went back to pacing. A few widths later, she declared: "Almost eight yards."

"Well, he was wrong about that part."

Calia frowned. "By quite a lot. You don't mistake ten yards for less than eight."

Huw put his hands on his hips and looked from one side of the room to the other. "Truth be told, I've never thought to measure it myself. I don't suppose many folk would, except builders."

Calia realised then why she'd never been able to picture the Farren Vale hanging at the far end of the ruined hall. The room was too narrow. Each piece of the tapestry was a yard square, and it was eight squares wide. The final width might even be even greater, depending on how closely the tapestry hooks were spaced.

"If Kara's right then the tapestry never would have fit up there," Calia said. "If it did, it would've been completely flush with the walls. That would've looked terrible."

"I suppose so."

Calia shook her head, intensely curious now. "It *can't* have hung up there. The size of the original was very well documented, but not the size of the room it hung in. Haelcar's journals say this hall is supposed to be ten yards wide. That would've been enough. But Kara says it's less than eight."

"Why don't we get a measuring stick?" Kara said. "Then we can see who's right."

"You could ask Pete Builder for one," said Huw. "He lives just down the path on the left. Big house with a big yard. Tell him I sent you."

Calia and Karaline hurried down the castle path toward town. Pete Builder's house was hard to miss. It was on the very outskirts of Ashmount, and the yard housed a generous stockpile of construction materials. Several men were loading up a cart with stone when they arrived. Calia guessed Pete probably rented out his storage space to all the builders in town, given how full it was. After asking the carters for directions, they tracked down the owner, who was sitting atop a pile of timber calling instructions to an apprentice below.

Craftsmen were often protective of their tools, measuring sticks in particular. Calia had known builders who treated them like sacred relics; magical rods that held all the secrets to digging sturdy foundations and shaping strong archways. Thankfully, Pete Builder wasn't one of them. He was younger than Calia had expected, with a bright and carefree demeanour, and he had his apprentice fetch a rod for them when they said they were friends of Huw's. It was a long, heavy thing made of solid metal, dense enough that it wouldn't warp or break easily. Karaline and Calia took turns carrying it up the hill.

"There we are," Huw said when they came back into the great hall. "Put it against the wall and measure it end to end."

Kara was delighted to. She used Tappy's arm to point at where the stick's end had been every time she moved it, slowly dragging it length after length across the floor until they had an exact measurement.

"I was right!" she announced. "It's twenty yards long and a bit less than eight wide."

"Well well, you can't argue with a measuring stick. Old Haelcar must've been wrong."

"But the tapestry," Calia said, gesturing at the far wall again. "It wouldn't have fit in this room."

"It's possible they rebuilt it at some point. Didn't you say he wrote about having to make repairs?"

"That's true. Perhaps I should look again."

That evening, Calia went through Haelcar's journals once more. She found nothing about the great hall that she hadn't seen already, but upon re-reading the passage about the dishonest builder, she noticed a detail she'd previously dismissed as irrelevant. She went back to the castle the next evening to share it with Huw.

"Look here." Calia pointed at her tablet, the wax having been melted and smoothed over since yesterday so she could copy out new notes. "Haelcar says the builder recommended they move the great hall upstairs to solve the damp problem they were having."

Huw frowned, tilting his head skyward to study the burnt-out shell of the keep. "That would've been an odd choice. Mind you, I've seen odder. Noble folk get eccentric with their manor layouts."

Calia followed his gaze, but her heart sank as she realised what he was frowning at. The keep walls held exactly the same dimensions on the second floor as the first. Even if the great hall had been moved up there, the problematic width remained the same. Calia felt like she'd been on the cusp of unravelling a perplexing mystery only to hit a dead end.

"Of course, there's always the cellar," Huw said.

Calia stared at him for a moment, then hurried to the blocked passageway that led underground. Mud, stone, and fallen timbers had rendered it completely impassable, leaving only a jumble of weeds sprouting from a patch of earth where the stairs had once been.

"It probably would've been as long as the hall up here, wouldn't it?" Calia said. "But without the rooms on either side, it could've been wider. And cellars are always damp."

"I think you might be right. No wonder the builder recommended moving it upstairs. What sort of madman has his great hall underground?"

"Has it been blocked off ever since the castle burned down?"

Huw nodded. "As far as I know. Some folks tried lifting the flagstones to get in one time, but the vault underneath was so thick they couldn't break through. You'd need a full team of workmen to open it back up."

A spark of excitement danced in Calia's eyes. "And no one's ever bothered because they think it's just an old cellar full of broken barrels and stone dust."

Huw smiled at her enthusiasm. "Aye. I suppose there could be all sorts of treasures buried down there if it really was the great hall."

"And if the vault's as thick as you say, some parts might have escaped the fire."

"You're thinking of the old tapestry. You know, even if it did survive, it's probably all rotted away by now."

"I know," Calia said. "But what if it hasn't?"

CHAPTER 10

"Have you ever wondered if there's anything left of the old tapestry?" Lord Oswin asked Anastasia over supper one evening. She considered his question as she chewed a bite of gingered heron. It was a dry meat garnished liberally with butter and spices to suit noble tastes. Oswin took a sip from his goblet to moisten his mouthful. The light wooden drinking vessel was painted red and green, the design inset with gold leaf. A small fragment of it was breaking off near the rim, and every time Oswin put his cup down a slight frown creased his brow as his thumb brushed over the imperfection. They were eating alone in the royal solar that night. Vesna had taken to making excuses for herself when there were no other guests present, no doubt hoping that her daughter would be able to woo the royal bailiff and thus further secure their influence with him. Ana found that idea distasteful, but she preferred Oswin's company to her mother's, so she went along with it.

"It's moot speculation," she replied. "If there were any further records of the tapestry, they would have been found by now."

"Calia Tailor and Huwel Ward seem to think otherwise.

They came to me today with the proposition that I might finance an excavation of the castle cellar. Apparently they found something in the old steward's journals that suggests the great hall might have been down there, thus making it the final resting place of the original Farren Vale."

Ana raised her eyebrows, curious but unconvinced. "A great hall in a cellar? That seems far-fetched."

"Yes, I said the same thing. But they took some measurements that didn't match up with the records. Calia insists the tapestry would never have fit in the main hall."

"Why do they want to excavate it? Surely there's nothing salvageable down there."

"Indeed, indeed. It sounds like a waste of time and money to me, but I wanted to consult with you first. It does relate to your project, after all."

Ana took a sip of her wine as she mulled it over. She didn't doubt that Calia had evidence to back up her claims. The girl had an eye for such details, and Sigrad said she'd been borrowing old books from the clerk recently. Though reluctant to indulge her rival's interests, Ana was curious about the Farren Vale as well. If some part of it really had survived the fire, she wanted to see it for herself. It would be fascinating to see how far her new design had diverged from the original. Had it been humble? Magnificent? Had the topmost yard complemented the rest of the design or contrasted with it? What kind of thread had been used? Were the colours realistic, or abstract? The more she dwelt on it, the more the idea appealed to her.

Calia no longer seemed like much of a threat. The queen's decision to keep her on had been disappointing, but the girl's reputation had taken an undeniable blow when it came out that she wasn't part of a guild. Since then, she hadn't been working with the same fervour as before, blending comfortably into the background with the other weavers who did as they were told. Perhaps she'd been humbled enough for now.

"How much would it cost?" Ana asked.

"No less than two dozen silver shillings, I'd imagine. Perhaps as much as a gold crown. It can't be a simple job, or someone would have done it already. I shan't be paying for it, that's for sure."

Ana resisted the urge to wrinkle her nose in distaste. Had she expressed no interest in the project, she was certain Oswin would have offered to cover the cost, knowing full well she would turn him down. Vesna had taught her that such noncommittal endearments were a cunning way of building favour. It was easy to offer your neighbour a dozen horses when you knew their stables were already full.

"I believe we have in excess of a gold crown to spare in the tapestry fund."

Along with wages for weavers and money for tools and materials, the queen allocated a modest sum of cash to cover any unforeseen expenses. Ana was in charge of managing that fund, and this seemed like an appropriate use for it.

"I'm surprised. I didn't think you thought very highly of Calia Tailor." Oswin gave her a look that made her uncomfortable, as though he understood more about her relationship with the weavers than was polite to say out loud.

"Personal opinions shouldn't undermine the queen's project," Ana said crisply, hoping her decisiveness would set the bailiff's suspicions to rest. "If it helps us learn more about the original tapestry, I say we make the investment."

"Very well. I'll put Huwel Ward in charge and see that he gets your money tomorrow."

A sense of intrigue buoyed Ana's spirits as they finished supper. It had been a long time since she'd seen a beautiful piece of old art. Her favourite memories from her childhood, the few in which Vesna had felt like a mother instead of a master, were of visits to cathedrals whose walls had been painted with magnificent frescoes from centuries past. She'd seen the passionate side of her mother during those visits, and that passion had been infectious. It had made Ana want to paint frescoes like that herself one day.

With those fond memories in mind, she returned to their room to tell Vesna about her conversation with Oswin. It would be nice to discuss something light and optimistic for once, divorced from the constant stress and urgency of their usual exchanges.

It was not to be. Ana saw Vesna's expression darken when she recounted the details, and her excitement became a tight strain in her chest.

"You shouldn't have agreed to it," Vesna said. "What good do you think will come of this?"

"Don't you think the queen will be impressed if we can present her with fragments of the original Farren Vale?"

Vesna pinched her on the arm. "Who do you think will get the credit? Calia Tailor and the old warden, that's who."

Ana pulled away, rubbing her sleeve with a scowl. Vesna's disapproval hurt more than the pinch. "Oh, Mother. We've cowed her enough."

"The moment you start thinking like that is the moment you slip. You can't let your guard down, Nastya. Do you think Calia hasn't been looking for a way to get back at you after what we did? No, she wants to make herself the queen's golden child again. That's what this is all about. What if they do find pieces of the Farren Vale and the queen decides she likes them more than your new design, hm?"

The tight feeling closed in around Ana, filling her with guilt. She'd been stupid. How could she not have seen it? Her design was at risk. She'd let childish curiosity get the better of her. She felt lost until Vesna took her by the arm and led her to the door, away from the bed where Karaline was sleeping.

"You can still stop this from going ahead."

Ana nodded, getting a grip on herself. "Yes. Of course. I'll tell Lord Oswin I've changed my mind."

"No. Then you'll appear indecisive. Worse, he might guess what you're really up to. If we tread carefully, this might work out better for us in the long run."

"What do you mean?"

"Think. Oswin's been cold to us ever since the queen's visit. He thinks we're jostling too roughly for her favour." A sardonic note entered Vesna's voice. "If you would just sleep with him, we could stop worrying about that. But if you won't, we have to be more careful. You've already said you approve of Calia's plan. That should convince him that you don't bear a grudge against her. And if he thinks you have a genuine interest in the old Farren Vale, he won't suspect you're trying to keep it hidden so that your work can shine brighter."

Ana caught the thread of what her mother was saying now. Agreeing to something in public only to ensure it failed in private was an excellent way of throwing your enemies off the scent. The question was, how would she stop the excavation? She spent a moment thinking it over, then said: "Will you fetch Sigrad for me?"

Vesna gave her a look that held the faintest hint of approval, perhaps even pride. But it was buried beneath the frown of the overbearing master who would tolerate nothing less than perfection. Ana swallowed the shame that threatened to warm her cheeks and moisten her eyes. There was no time for self-pity. She needed to fix her mistake before Oswin handed over the money tomorrow morning.

A few minutes later, she met Sigrad downstairs in the royal chambers just outside the chapel. Few people came through this part of the manor in the evenings. Next to the chapel was a heavy iron-bound door that opened on a flight of steps leading underground. It wasn't the entrance to the cellar, but a second, more secure part of the manor that housed the treasury. At the foot of the stairs, there was a locked room containing chests of valuable documents, precious ornaments, and hidden vaults full of silver and gold. It wasn't quite the royal treasury, but Lord Oswin's riches would have been the envy of many a baron.

"Wait until the candle burns down to here," Ana said, notching a mark in the wax with her fingernail before passing it to Sigrad. "Then pretend to fall down the stairs. Snuff all the other lights up here so it looks like you tripped in the dark. And make it convincing."

Sigrad leaned forward and peered down the stairs. "That looks like it'll hurt."

"I'll pay for you to visit a physician. You'll get an extra silver shilling if you do well."

Sigrad nodded, the temptation of silver quashing his misgivings. Ana took a second candle and went down the stairs, turning once as the steps doubled back on themselves. The walls were tight and the air cold down here. She didn't know how the treasurer could possibly stand it, spending most of his life in this dungeon. But there were always an odd few who could tolerate the unusual jobs. The treasurer was a plump monk named Alan, careful and studious, and Ana knew she would slip nothing past him while they were alone together. That was why she needed Sigrad. If everything went to plan, there would be no money left in the tapestry fund for Oswin to give Huwel Ward tomorrow.

Getting caught stealing was not an issue; if Anastasia asked Alan for the money, he would simply give it to her. She could even say she was taking it to Oswin. That would be her cover if anything went wrong. But that wasn't the purpose of her visit. She needed to make it seem like the money had been spent weeks in advance. That way, she could put a stop to Calia's plan without Oswin suspecting anything. She needed to slip the money out quietly, without the treasurer noticing, then alter the records so that its absence would be accounted for.

There were other rooms in this subterranean passageway that Ana had never entered. She didn't know what they were used for, but they were all locked with the same heavy iron-bound doors, silent and imposing in the gloom. She approached the treasury door and knocked. A thin peephole slid open, revealing candlelight on the other side. Alan's beady eyes peered out at her. He opened the door without a word. She was a regular visitor. Barely a day passed without Ana coming down to collect money or account for her expenses.

"Ledger or silver?" Alan asked. His boots sounded unnaturally loud against the floor in the enclosed space. Beneath his robe, he wore a thick woollen shirt and leggings to stay warm in the chilly stone vault. Monks were popular as treasurers, for their vows of poverty theoretically made them immune to the temptations of wealth. The renowned piety of King Fendrel and his wife had drawn many such men into royal service. More often than not, they were gifts from priors and bishops who wanted to ingratiate themselves with their noble counterparts. Or spy on them.

"Just the ledger," Ana said.

Alan closed the door behind her and locked it. The treasury consisted of two rooms: a small office and the main vault behind it. Ana took a seat at a table strewn with writing supplies next to the door. Alan unlocked the vault and went in. He returned a moment later with the ledger in his hands. Ana breathed an internal sigh of relief when he left the vault open behind him. She opened the ledger and pretended to study the columns of expenditures the tapestry project had accrued over the last few months. There were dyers' fees for making thread, carpenters' fees for the looms, the weavers' wages, wool, bobbins, stools, mirrors, stands, hooks, scissors, and dozens of other costs that had trickled in over time. Several pages of the ledger were covered in notes tallying up the figures month by month. Ana pretended to be combing through each page, flipping back and forth to cross-reference some made-up problem. Alan allowed her to work without interruption, but she could feel his eyes on her back. There was no chance of her so much as picking up a quill, much less slipping into the vault, without him noticing. To pass the time while she waited for Sigrad, she pretended she was calculating the cost of remaking Calia's first tapestry square. She used an abacus on the desk to keep count, estimating how much thread Calia had used, in what colours, how efficiently, and over how many weeks. It was a lengthy process. She wanted to make sure her visit didn't coincide too conspicuously with Sigrad's distraction, so she'd allowed herself ample time with her mark on the candle.

After what felt like an hour, there was a noise outside. A distant rattle and a scrape. It was far fainter than Ana had hoped. To her annoyance, Alan didn't react. She looked up as if startled and rose from her stool.

"What was that?"

"Something outside," Alan said.

They stood in awkward silence for a moment, then a moan came down the passageway. Ana needed to get rid of the monk. He seemed painfully reluctant to investigate despite the obvious commotion. Perhaps he thought someone else would take care of it.

"What if it's someone trying to break in?" Ana said in a frightened whisper. She was a good actress, and her distress moved him to action.

"Wait in here. I'll have a look." He glanced through the peephole. Seeing no immediate danger, he took the candle Ana had brought in and unlocked the door.

If there really were thieves out there, you'd be playing right into their hands, Ana thought. The muffled sound of Sigrad's voice echoed down the passageway, and the light of Alan's candle slowly receded. Ana carefully pushed the heavy door shut behind him, then hurried into the vault. She took the ledger with her. If the treasurer came back, she would say she'd been returning it to its place. She'd seen Alan open the chest containing the tapestry fund dozens of times. It was a small wooden box on a shelf near the door, one of many lining the vault walls. He'd left it unlocked. Ana lifted the lid and peered inside. There were two compartments within. The one on the right held a collection of documents and space for the ledger, while the left one housed two wooden trays full of silver coins. Ana lifted the first tray out and set it aside. That was the money earmarked for wages. The second tray held the funds Ana was allowed to dip into. The number of silver coins was daunting, but she didn't need to take them all, only enough to prevent Huwel Ward from hiring his labourers. She started gathering up all the shillings, leaving the pennies behind. That would make it look like there was still a lot of money in the box at a casual glance.

She listened carefully for the sound of the door opening, fearing that her time was running out. Alan could come back at any moment. Handful by handful, she slipped the silver shillings into a bag on her belt, raking her fingers through the box to find as many of the large coins as she could. Ana counted every one that went into her bag. She needed to make sure the sum she took was accounted for when she changed the ledger.

When she was confident she'd picked out most of the shillings, she put the trays back where they belonged and shut the chest. She took the ledger out of the vault and sat back down at the writing table. There was still no sign of Alan. Opening an ink pot and dipping a quill, she started making the adjustments she'd planned in advance.

A spool of fine scarlet silk was worth exactly one silver shilling. She'd taken eighty-five shillings from the chest. With a careful stroke of her quill, she changed a three into an eight, making it look like five additional spools had been bought a few weeks ago. That was five shillings accounted for, eighty more to go. She was probably being overly cautious, but she wanted the records to look natural. Five extra spools of thread could easily be overlooked, but eighty would look strange. She made a dozen minor changes across the last page. One spare chair became four. Ten spools of wool became eighteen. She worked quickly and precisely, and the final stroke was finished by the time she heard Alan's boots knocking against the flagstones outside. She left her ledger open so the ink could dry and returned the quill and ink pot to their places.

"What was it?" she asked when the treasurer came back in.

"Sigrad. The silly boy fell downstairs in the dark. Did you leave the door open when you came down?"

"I can't remember. I suppose I must have."

"He was wandering around without a candle. Probably up to no good."

"He wasn't hurt, was he?"

Alan shook his head. "Just a little bump on the head. He perked back up after I helped him upstairs."

"That's fortunate."

"Mm." Alan sat back down in his chair. He was a difficult man to read, but any suspicions he harboured seemed to be focused on Sigrad, not Ana. She stayed at the table a while longer, pretending to be finishing up her imaginary calculations. Once the ink was dry, she closed the ledger and handed it back to him.

"I've finished for tonight."

He took the ledger and returned it to the vault. Ana could feel her pulse pounding in her heels all the way back up the stairs. Everything had gone to plan. There was a chance Alan might count the coins in the tray and notice some were missing, but the figures in the ledger would allay his suspicions.

"Did you do it?" a voice whispered from the chapel doorway.

Ana jumped, her candle guttering as Sigrad appeared.

"Yes," she snapped, channelling her fear into annoyance. She untied the bag from her belt and pressed it into Sigrad's hands. "Take one of those shillings for yourself and bury the rest outside somewhere." She immediately second-guessed her decision when the greedy page peered into the bag and saw its glittering contents. There was a small fortune in there.

"Why don't we keep them all?"

"Don't be stupid. I don't need the money, and if you're caught with that bag everyone will know you stole it."

She could see the wheels turning in his head, the risk weighing against the reward, the comfort of wealth versus the consequences of thievery. Ana realised she had to say something, otherwise there was a very real risk that Sigrad might do something foolish. If anything could turn him into a liability, it was the temptation of even more money than the Fialas were giving him.

"What do you want for yourself after you leave this manor, Sigrad?"

"I want to be a lord with subjects who have to do as I say."

"Well you'll never get that if you're caught with those shillings. You'll be dismissed from Lord Oswin's service in disgrace. Do as I say, and you'll earn far more than what's in that bag. When you have a household of your own, you can dig it back up and spend it on whatever you want. But for now, it stays hidden. Don't make anyone suspicious by suddenly becoming wealthy overnight."

Sigrad kept staring at the silver as if he hadn't heard her. In a flash of frustration, Ana seized his arm, digging her nails in hard. Sigrad gasped in pain.

"My mother and I can tell Lord Oswin about every dirty little scheme you've had your hands in, and it'll be our word against yours. Don't you dare think you can do better on your own."

In the guttering candlelight, she saw Sigrad's eyes widen with fear.

"Alright, alright! I'll bury the bag."

"Somewhere no one will look."

"I know."

"And don't be seen. Go now, while it's dark." She hurried Sigrad out into the great hall, taking care to make sure no one saw her behind him. When she returned to the solar, she found Vesna sitting up by the hearth.

"Well?" her mother said under her breath. Lord Oswin and the castle chaplain were conversing at the other end of the room, but they were far enough away that their voices didn't carry.

"It's done," Ana replied in a whisper. "If Calia wants that cellar excavated, she's going to have to pay for it herself."

CHAPTER 11

"I'm afraid I can't grant your request," Lord Oswin informed Calia and Huwel in the royal chambers the following morning, glancing up from his breakfast with a guarded look that suggested he wanted to get this over with quickly.

A fresh wave of disappointment dragged on Calia's waning spirits. She'd needed this. After losing Goldie, she wanted something to feel positive about again. For a few brief days, the mystery of the old castle had filled that void.

"Why not?" she blurted out.

Lord Oswin frowned at her. It wasn't appropriate to make such blunt demands of a lord, but they were in an informal setting, and a look of annoyance was the only reproach Calia received.

"It isn't a question of intent. I spoke with your mistress yesterday and she agreed that it would be a worthwhile investment. Unfortunately, the tapestry fund is unable to cover the expense at this time."

"That can't be," Calia said. "We haven't been buying much lately, and with Goldie gone that's one less weaver to pay."

As if sensing that the exchange was about to turn hostile, Huw attempted to lighten the mood with a smile and a chuckle.

"She's a merchant's daughter, milord. They have a special sense for these things."

Lord Oswin didn't look amused. "I wasn't aware of that."

Calia's stomach tightened. She knew Oswin's opinion of her had suffered when he found out she wasn't part of a weavers' guild, and Huw's innocent comment might have damaged it even further. The bailiff was a staunch royalist, and the merchant class were seldom liked by men like him. To wield power and wealth was a privilege of the nobility, god-given and entrenched in centuries of culture. The ever-rising prominence of the merchant class flew in the face of that maxim.

"Might we ask when the money will be available, my lord?" Calia asked.

"That isn't your concern, nor is it your place to inquire into the queen's finances."

Calia sensed she was on thin ice, but she wasn't ready to back down just yet. She didn't want timidity to relegate her to a life of disappointment and dissatisfaction. Perhaps if she'd stood up for Goldie, her friend would still be here.

"Then would you consider financing the project in some other way? I'm sure the queen would want it to go ahead."

"Is that so? Perhaps you would like to go over the treasury records and tell her exactly how she should be spending the rest of her silver, too."

Calia shrank back, cheeks warming as she stared down at the floor. She'd pushed it too far. There was no way out of this now besides deference and humility.

"No, milord."

Oswin gave a satisfied grunt as he popped a slice of fruit into his mouth. "I've made my decision. The money isn't available. Besides, we don't want to go tearing up a historical monument like Castle Ashmount, do we?"

"No, milord."

"Good. Then it's settled. I'm sorry for this inconvenience,

Huwel. You may go."

They backed out of the solar and retreated downstairs.

"We could've handled that better," Huw said as they passed the chapel.

"I could have, you mean."

"He's a proud man, Lord Oswin. If he thinks you're getting above yourself, he'll object to whatever you say on principle."

"I thought standing up for myself would help."

Huw patted her on the shoulder. "There's a time and a place, but it isn't during an audience with a man like him."

"I've ruined our chances, haven't I?" Calia hated to hear the despondence in her voice.

Huw sighed. "Well, no, not all the way. But I don't think we'll be getting that money from Oswin. He's probably decided he's against the whole thing now."

"I could help pay for some labourers, but it would cost a lot of my wages."

"No, no, you save that money. No use making yourself poor over something that might lead nowhere. Maybe the next time the queen visits you can put the idea to her. She won't blink at hiring a few workmen."

They went out into the great hall. Calia saw Rovena standing by the door talking to an apprentice from the weavers' guild who was delivering a roll of cloth. Watching the two of them, an idea occurred to her.

"Perhaps we won't have to wait that long. There's someone else I know who might want to get involved with the tapestry."

The next time the weavers' guild gathered for their monthly meeting, Calia and Rovena attended. Before today, Calia hadn't planned on showing her face at the guild hall during her time in Ashmount. Her admission was largely ceremonial. She didn't live here and was unlikely to stay after the tapestry was finished, so she had little investment in the local trade. Besides which, she didn't want to run afoul of Leander again. But ceremonial or not, she was a recognised guild member and thus entitled to make her voice heard at meetings.

The guild hall was shared by several prominent organisations in Ashmount. It stood in the centre of town adjacent to the marketplace, its smart stone walls and glazed windows a testament to the wealth of the tradesmen who'd built it. As Calia approached the door, she saw that a pair of scales had been carved into the lintel overhead. Like a church spire, it was an icon to those who conducted their business here. Wealth was the sacred precept of this house.

There were about twenty other people present at the meeting, most seated at circular tables around a central hearth. The place was clean and fragrant, the windows thrown open to let in fresh air that wafted through bunches of herbs hanging from the ceiling. Calia shuffled her feet through the carpet of straw around the doorway before stepping onto the rush mats. No sooner had she entered than a servant appeared with a broom to sweep up behind her.

"Nervous?" Rovena whispered in her ear.

"Terrified." Calia didn't like being the centre of attention. She'd worn her good dress and brushed her hair to appear presentable, but aside from Leander and a couple of others, no one was dressed as finely as her. They gawked with undisguised curiosity. Outsiders were always greeted with a mixture of wariness and fascination, even in trading towns like Ashmount. Most of these people had voted in favour of her admission to the guild the last time she was here, but they clearly hadn't expected to see her again so soon.

Calia and Rovena picked an empty table near the wall and sat down as the meeting got underway. Leander led the proceedings as alderman. He was an oddity in a trade dominated by women, though it was sadly commonplace for men to hold positions of authority even when they were the exception to the norm. Lords, aldermen, bailiffs, and bishops tended to be uncomfortable dealing with women in positions of power, so they exerted their influence to jostle men like Leander into leadership roles.

The local trade was discussed at length that evening; prices and fees, commissions and clients, apprentices and partnerships. Most of the weavers were there to protect their interests and ensure they got enough work. The guild was a collaborative institution where everyone had a voice. While Leander acted as the figurehead, he had little more power than anyone else to dictate decisions. Everything had to be agreed upon by popular vote.

It was here that Calia realised the alderman wasn't as prideful and pompous as she'd taken him for. He certainly had an ego, as his fine clothing and aloof manner attested, but a guild alderman did not survive without the support of his peers. Whether he'd been elevated to his position through nepotism or not, he'd held on to it through competence and conviction. He was a good mediator. Many guilds consisted of small groups of family and friends, which naturally led to factional divisions and cliques. Calia observed that the people who shared the same tables all seemed to know each other, often clashing with those who sat apart from them. Leander acted as a neutral arbiter in these disagreements. Perhaps being a man helped him in that regard, for it set him apart in a way that lent him a sense of impartiality. He treated each dispute like a judge sitting at court, hearing the arguments, weighing the precedents, and asking others to lend their voices before proposing a compromise. More often than not, the guild's majority voted in favour of his solutions.

Seeing the professional side of Leander, not the bitter agitator she'd met at the manor, gave Calia hope that he might be a man she could deal with. But she held off on presenting her idea to the group, not wanting to appear presumptuous by speaking up before the more senior weavers had their turn. She'd learned her lesson with Lord Oswin. When the meeting finally seemed to be winding down, she raised her hand and cleared her throat. Leander looked at her, a brief scowl pinching his expression.

"Our newest member, Calia Tailor, has a proposition for the guild."

Calia rose to her feet, her heart already pounding.

"Thank you, Alderman. I know I have little business being here compared to most of you, but I have a proposition that I think might be in the guild's interest."

"Go on."

"Huwel Ward–the castle watchman–and I have been investigating the history of the old keep in relation to the Farren Vale tapestry."

"Yes, we all know you're working for the queen," one of the weavers said, drawing a few dry chuckles from the others. Calia felt her ears burning.

"This doesn't concern the new tapestry, but rather the old. We believe there is a chance that some remnants of it, or perhaps other records and treasures, may still exist beneath the castle." She went on to explain in stumbling detail the dimensions of the keep hall and the discrepancies she'd found in Haelcar of the Vale's journals. She wished Huw was here to help. He was a respected and well-liked member of the community, far more likely to sway the weavers than her. She made sure to mention his name often, explaining how he had petitioned Lord Oswin for funds only to be rebuffed. She feared she was doing a poor job of making her case, but to her surprise, she saw that a few weavers were listening with interest. The mystery of the old keep intrigued them. Perhaps they shared her artistic curiosity about the Farren Vale.

"Sounds like a waste of time and money to me," one of the others said. "If there's something down there, why's no one dug it up before?"

Calia was glad she'd prepared herself this time, for she had an answer ready to go.

"Huw says people have tried, but the cellar is encased in a thick stone vault and the stairs are completely blocked with earth and rubble. It'll take heavy tools and skilled workmen to open it up."

"That sounds costly," Leander said. He seemed interested, but there was still a sardonic edge to his voice when he addressed Calia.

"It will be. Lord Oswin says the tapestry fund is too poor to finance the excavation, so I'm asking the guild for help."

A murmur of conversation ran around the room. The weavers seemed hesitant. Not all of them were as well-off as others, and there was nothing for them to gain from the project beyond the prestige of their involvement. According to Huw, any historical artefacts they uncovered would belong to the crown.

Calia suspected that at least one person in the room valued prestige over wealth, however.

"Exactly how much will this cost?" Leander asked.

Calia felt a flutter of excitement. She took out her wax tablet and read off the details she and Huw had worked out.

"Pete Builder says he can begin work within the week. He's quoted us twenty-eight silver shillings to get started with the men he needs, and a further twenty-four shillings each week thereafter."

"That's expensive for a bit of digging," one of the weavers said.

"It's skilled work. They don't want to damage the site too much, and working underground beneath old buildings can be dangerous."

"I'm assuming this hasn't been sanctioned by the queen," Leander said, "otherwise Oswin would've taken charge."

"That's right. We were hoping to present our discoveries to her the next time she visits."

"Are we within our legal rights to dig up Castle Ashmount?"

"Huw is, and he'll be in charge of the project."

Leander smiled. "Good. Then I'll speak with him first thing tomorrow."

Three of the other weavers banded together to put money into the fund, but it was Leander who covered the lion's share. Once they had assurances from Huw and Pete Builder that the project was legally and financially sound, they handed over the silver. Work began at the end of the week. A crowd gathered over the day as word spread about town that a team of workmen were excavating the castle. Calia was only able to visit after she finished work, and it looked like a small fair was taking place in the courtyard by the time she arrived. Someone had brought out a table from the gatehouse and was selling ale from a big barrel. The keep had been cordoned off with rope, but people clustered around the doors and climbed up to peer through the windows, excited to see what the workmen would find as they lifted flagstones and scraped away old mortar. It was like a treasure hunt.

Leander was in his element, standing with Huw at the centre of a small crowd as he explained in marvellously embellished detail how the journals of the old steward had revealed a secret buried beneath the ancient keep. Huw seemed to be enjoying himself as well, suddenly having all the company he could ever wish for.

Lucy had accompanied Calia up the hill, and she folded her arms with a frown when they saw Leander boasting to his audience.

"He's taking all the credit. You're the one who worked it out."

"I'm glad, truth be told. I wouldn't want all that attention. I didn't think so many people would be interested."

"Of course they're interested. It's a fine day, they've finished work, and something new's going on at the castle."

"I expect it'll quiet down once they realise there aren't any gold statues hiding under the flagstones. Pete said it might take weeks to find anything, especially if the cellar's packed with rubble."

"You're probably right. At least Leander's the one paying

for it."

Calia grinned. "He can't wait to rub it in Oswin and Ana's faces the next time the queen visits. He wants to prove to her that he should've been involved with the tapestry all along."

"If he's the one who finds what's left of the original, she'll have no choice but to acknowledge him. How did you think to play to his ego like that?"

"I don't know. I just saw Rovena talking to an apprentice from the guild the other day and thought of him."

"Well, you've got good intuition. That's what makes you good with thread. You see all those little patterns without having to stitch them out step by step."

Calia shook her head. She never felt worthy of such praise.

Lucy put an arm around her. "Stop that. It's only been a few months and you've already made all this happen." She gestured at the crowd. "Confidence, Calia!"

"I never planned on anything like this. I just wanted to do some weaving."

Lucy pressed her lips together, her expression forming a fond frown. "You remind me of Ana, you know, if she wasn't such a bitch."

"I can't see how."

"Maybe that's the difference between you and her. She thinks the world owes her something for her talent. You can't accept that you deserve anything at all."

Calia allowed herself a little glow of pride. She had done this, hadn't she? Just like Livy and Wolfram, she could be bold and successful if she set her mind to it.

"I'm glad to have a friend like you," she told Lucy. "I think you're exactly what I need."

Lucy snorted with amusement. "I like people to be their best. That's why I keep their clothes looking as fine as possible. Come on, let's rescue Huw from that crowd. He's starting to look a bit overwhelmed."

They made their way across the courtyard, but before they

could reach the crowd of visitors they were interrupted by the sound of hooves clattering through the gate. Lord Oswin, sharply dressed in a black cap and cloak, rode in on his sable steed. Three mounted men-at-arms followed him with swords at their belts. A nervous hush descended over the crowd as the bailiff and his men reined in their horses. When a lord showed up with armed men, he usually meant to throw his weight around. There was a stormy look on his face as his gaze swept over Calia, but his attention settled on Huw.

"Huwel Ward!" he barked, silencing what remained of the hubbub as his voice echoed off the crumbling walls.

Huw shuffled forward and made a bow. "Milord."

"What's the meaning of this? When you came to me about this project, I explicitly forbade it."

"I apologise, milord. If that was your intent, I must have misunderstood. I only thought you were withholding the funds."

The look on Oswin's face was one Calia had seen before. He knew he'd made a mistake, and now he was trying to overcompensate by putting his foot down. Had Ana and Vesna put him up to this? He'd said Ana supported the project, but Calia didn't believe that. The painter would see anything that took focus away from her tapestry as a threat.

"Indeed I was," Oswin said hotly. "I should have thought that made my feelings on the matter clear."

"My apologies again. I'm a simple man when it comes to such things."

Huw was anything but simple, Calia thought. He was playing dumb on purpose, refusing to give Lord Oswin any reason to rebuke him. The implication was that he wasn't the man in charge: that was Leander. Once again Calia felt a great sense of relief that the alderman had styled himself as the architect of this project.

Sure enough, when Huw continued to respond with deference and platitudes, Oswin turned his attention to Leander.

"I suppose you're the one behind all this?"

"I am the main investor, yes." There was anxiety in Leander's voice—no one wanted to get on the wrong side of their lord—but his pride wouldn't allow him to back down in front of an audience.

"And you didn't think to consult with me first?"

"I wasn't aware that was necessary. Huwel assured me that any work of this nature would fall under the purview of Castle Ashmount's custodian."

Huw raised his hand sheepishly. "That would be me, milord."

"This castle belongs to the king and queen, damn it, and I am the royal bailiff!"

"Though not the castle custodian," Leander pointed out. "Legally, Huwel is the man with the authority to approve or deny any building work here."

"That's a ceremonial position! He's here to scare off birds and tidy up rubble, not tear down half the keep!" Oswin was blustering, rapidly losing steam as he realised the letter of the law was against him. Huwel *was* the castle custodian, and he had every right to hire builders to repair or demolish parts of the old structure as he saw fit. Oswin had a reputation for adhering to tradition and legality in all things. If he kept this up, he would look like a hypocrite in front of half the town.

"You're right of course, milord," Huw said. "We should have consulted with the queen beforehand. It's only proper."

Oswin glared at the warden, but he recognised the lifeline he was being thrown. The only way he could back down while saving face was to appeal to a higher authority.

"Quite right. We'll see what she has to say about this. I will have a message dispatched to her immediately."

Huw bowed once more, but Oswin was already tugging at his reins, wheeling his horse around and kicking it out the gate. His men followed, looking disappointed that they hadn't gotten the chance to drag the builders off the site.

Calia breathed a sigh of relief and hurried over to Huw.

"You handled that so well."

He gave her a nervous smile. "That's how you speak to lords. Always make them think they're right, and always make them think they need to talk to someone else if they want answers."

"Let him send word to the queen," Leander scoffed. "I'm certain she'll give this project her full approval."

"As long as we find something," said Calia.

CHAPTER 12

The excavation of the great hall took several weeks. Pete Builder tried opening up the stone vault at first, rationalising that it would be easier than digging through yards of rubble in the old stairwell, but that idea proved unworkable. After finding one too many instances of cracked stone and powdered mortar, he concluded that the vault was too badly damaged. Attempting to remove any part of it ran the risk of collapsing the keep floor. They would have to go in through the stairwell, slowly and carefully, setting up frames to support the stonework as they went.

A small crowd gathered at the castle most evenings, though the initial flurry of interest quickly died down. Calia visited after work as often as she could, checking in with Huw, Pete, and Leander when she ran into them. Lucy and Karaline sometimes joined her. The digging didn't particularly interest young Karaline, but she was fascinated by the sewing Lucy sometimes brought with her. They would sit together watching the builders, eating their supper, embroidering cloth, and talking about their days.

"You could be a tailor's apprentice if you aren't going to be a painter," Lucy told Karaline one evening.

The girl shook her head. "Mother says she won't have me being a tailor."

"What does your sister say?" Calia asked.

"She lets me stitch her old clothes sometimes."

"At least she's letting someone work the way they want," Lucy said under her breath.

Calia ignored the comment and said to Karaline: "Tailoring's a very respectable profession. You might end up sewing clothes for the queen like Lucy."

"Mother doesn't want me learning a craft. She says I'll have to marry someone."

Calia wrinkled her nose in distaste. Karaline's situation was a sadly common one. In many families, both humble and noble, marriage was seen as a convenient way of pawning off unwanted children. If they couldn't make something of themselves, they could at least bind the family to someone more successful. Sometimes it was done out of necessity, like when a farmer couldn't make ends meet and needed a wealthy neighbour to help ease his burden. Other times, it was political, bridging a gap between rival families or securing bonds with powerful allies. Calia understood that it was just the nature of the world, but she still didn't like it. Having never had any interest in marriage herself, she would've been miserable if her parents insisted she marry someone instead of pursuing her apprenticeship. It seemed neglectfully selfish for Vesna to insist on such a fate for her youngest daughter. Karaline was not stupid or talentless. She was easily as good at sewing as Calia had been at her age, and she had the focus to sit still and listen while she learned. She could have found her calling in a dozen walks of life.

But Vesna did not want a tailor in the family, she wanted a master painter, and if Karaline was not as skilled as her sister, she would have to advance the family's social standing in some other way. She could piggyback on Ana's prestige to attract the affections of some lesser lord in another five or ten years, then she would be able to play her part in burnishing her mother's golden legacy. Thinking about Karaline's future made Calia's heart ache the same way it did when she thought of Goldie. On a whim, she opened the little bag she kept on her belt and took out her favourite bronze sewing needle. She offered it to Karaline.

"Here."

Kara held up the needle Lucy had lent her. "I've already got one."

"This one you can keep. Take it back to your room and put it somewhere safe. Whenever you're on your own, you can practise sewing."

"I'll lend you some spools of thread," Lucy said.

Karaline looked nervous. "Mother wouldn't like that."

"Then you'll have to keep it a secret from her," said Calia. She could tell Kara wanted to accept the gift. She spent so many of her days wandering the manor restlessly. A real hobby would do her wonders.

Karaline picked up Tappy. The doll was a simple thing, but very well made. Her wooden torso had little holes drilled in the bottom and sides where pegs held in pieces of cord connected to the arms and legs. Her wooden limbs were able to wiggle about as a result, making the doll far more expressive than most. Karaline took Calia's needle and slipped it into one of Tappy's leg holes, where it fit snugly alongside the cord with its end poking out. The doll's miniature cloth dress came down to cover up the hole and conceal it from view.

"That's a clever hiding place," Calia said.

Kara nodded. "Not many things fit in there."

"Well, I'll trust Tappy to keep my needle nice and safe."

Calia secretly hoped that Ana and Vesna would notice Karaline's new hobby someday. She hoped they would recognise how good it was for her and reconsider her future. It was a thin hope, but Calia was an optimist at heart. She wanted her needle to do some good.

Huw came over from the gatehouse with a cup in his

hand and sat down next to them. "Evening, miladies."

"What've you got to tell us, Huw?" Lucy asked. "I know that look."

The warden smiled. "I just had a chat with David Pedlar. Sold me this nice cup." He tapped the side of his drinking vessel. "He's been up west. Says the queen was hunting with Lord Lanter of Redland last week."

Lucy gasped. "I didn't know she was back in the area."

"She loves to travel, our queen."

"Is Redland nearby?" Calia asked.

"Aye, only about three days walk down the king's road. I expect we'll be seeing her again soon."

"I hope we have something to show her by then."

"We might, we might. Pete thinks he's almost through the worst of the rubble. If the queen decides to stay for a bit, she might get to see us open up that cellar in person."

Queen Meredith arrived a week later. Lord Oswin was on edge, personally overseeing every aspect of manor life to ensure nothing was out of place. He paced the rooms restlessly, snapping at servants and adjusting furniture until everyone felt like they were walking on eggshells. Calia couldn't help but share some of his apprehension. If the queen disapproved of the excavation at Castle Ashmount, all of their efforts would be for nothing. Huw might even get in trouble. Everyone seemed to have forgotten that Calia was the original mastermind behind the project, but she still worried for her friends. She tried in vain to listen to what was being said at the high table during meal times, desperate to garner any insight into the queen's mood.

It was two full days before the weavers assembled upstairs for a viewing of the tapestry. Calia had been working diligently on her second square, another segment in Ana's skyline, and it was coming along well. She'd been more subtle with her creative flourishes this time. Most of this square consisted of sunbeams and swirls of colourful cloud. There were no prominent details like the angels. She suspected that was intentional; Ana had assigned her a particularly simple piece so that she wouldn't have much to work with. But while there was only so much that could be done with the cartoon's brushstrokes, the colours were another matter. Once again Calia had neglected to use gold and silver thread for the sun rays reflecting off the clouds, opting instead for shades of orange and mauve that looked like a reflection of the light shining off a river in one of the lower squares. Ana had criticised the choice, of course, but Calia stuck to her convictions, and she was happy with the result. Once again her piece looked distinctive without breaking the harmony of the tapestry. There was a gentleness to her square of sky that evoked feelings of wistful romance rather than bombastic grandeur. Queen Meredith took note when she stopped to admire it.

"You see?" she said to Anastasia. "Once again Calia Tailor is breathing such character into your design."

"Indeed, Your Majesty," Ana replied with great restraint. "Unfortunately, we will run out of squares for her to work on soon. I believe you insisted that she only be allowed to work on the new ones."

"Did I? I can't recall."

Ana's clasped fingers visibly tightened behind her back. "The deviations in her style are unsuitable for recreating the original design."

"You know, I think I'm changing my mind. We're already deviating from the original, are we not? I'd like to see more changes. More uniqueness. A new Farren Vale for the modern era."

"Perhaps your next tapestry could be something more exotic, Your Majesty."

Meredith considered for a moment before letting out a sigh. "Yes, yes. I suppose it's too late to change things now." She turned to acknowledge Calia directly for the first time. "I hear you've been quite the little instigator in your time here."

Calia tensed up. "You have, Your Majesty?"

"Indeed. It was your idea to dig up the old castle, wasn't it?"

"Oh–not entirely. Huwel Ward and Leander–"

"I know the alderman is trying to take credit," Meredith interrupted. "But Anastasia and Oswin tell me it was you who first proposed the idea."

Of course, Calia thought. *When it goes wrong, they'll want to blame it all on me.*

"Well, yes. I noticed some inconsistencies in the old steward's journals that led me to believe the Farren Vale might have hung in the cellar rather than the main hall."

"Barking mad!" the queen exclaimed with obvious relish. "I'm fascinated to see where it all leads. I've informed the foreman that he's to send word the moment the cellar is opened. We three shall be the first people to see what's inside." She smiled at Calia and Anastasia in turn. "The architects of my tapestry and my antiquarian dig."

Ana gave Calia a smile that could have curdled milk.

It was another week before the builders broke through into the cellar. The queen was there for a leisurely stay, enjoying the summer months at her manor house while the king dealt with politics in the capital. Ashmount House was busier than ever. The queen liked to entertain when the weather was fine, and throughout the week there was no shortage of aldermen, abbots, prioresses, bailiffs, judges, constables, knights, barons, tax collectors, and minstrels present at the high table. The servants were busy from dawn till dusk stocking the cellars and emptying them again to the rhythm of the festivities. Calia was glad she could escape upstairs where things were a little quieter.

The news from the castle arrived just before midday. Sigrad interrupted Calia in the middle of work to tell her that Pete builder's apprentice was downstairs and her presence was demanded by the queen. She considered changing into her nice dress before joining the royal entourage, but decided against it. If they were going down into an ancient cellar, she didn't want to be wearing something that would suffer from dust and grime.

The Fialas were dressed resplendently, of course. Calia felt like a peasant when she stood alongside them. Vesna looked down her nose at her, but Karaline smiled and waved. Calia answered with a smile of her own, which had the added effect of provoking a look of confusion from Vesna. Despite not having a combative nature, it did amuse Calia how rudeness could so often be blunted by courtesy.

The royal party was mostly comprised of the queen's retainers and a few local figures who had taken an interest in the excavation. Leander was foremost among them, having finally charmed his way into Meredith's good graces. He walked alongside her as they strolled down the path into town, explaining in obsequious terms how important this excavation would be to the cultural history of Ashmount. He made little mention of the old tapestry, Calia noticed. He was being clever, covering his back in case the dig turned up nothing. The damage could only be limited so much, however. If the project ended in disappointment, Anastasia would leap at the opportunity to point out how wasteful and disruptive it had been.

Despite her trepidation, Calia was excited. This day had been weeks in the making, and the prospect of uncovering some new evidence of the Farren Vale filled her with wonder. The tapestry had become her life over the past months. Long after she finished her job here, it would stay in her memory as the most important thing she had ever worked on.

She heard her thoughts echoed from a surprising source as they made their way up the hill toward the castle gate.

"I wonder if it's really down there," Anastasia said.

Calia looked around to see if she'd been speaking to someone else, but Vesna and Karaline had fallen behind. She felt suddenly awkward. This might be the first time Anastasia had ever attempted something approaching casual conversation with her.

"I hope so."

Ana didn't make eye contact, keeping her gaze fixed ahead. She seemed to be talking to herself more than Calia, merely wanting an audience for her thoughts. "There aren't many tapestries that have survived for a hundred years without repair. Moths eat them and bright rooms make the colours fade. But there wouldn't be any moths in a sealed cellar. Certainly no light."

"It would be damp."

"Not necessarily. Some cellars are used explicitly for dry storage. If the damp problem the steward mentioned was resolved then it may have remained dry. Groundwater doesn't settle on top of hills unless you build something to hold it in."

"You're very knowledgeable," Calia said, wondering how Ana knew about the damp problem mentioned in Haelcar's journals. Had she poured over them herself in the preceding weeks, just as Calia had, searching for hidden clues?

Ana gave her a stiff look. "Some of us have been educated."

"I was educated."

Ana clicked her tongue and quickened her pace to join Leander and the queen, leaving Calia feeling slightly bemused. For a moment, it had seemed like Ana actually cared about something other than herself. Perhaps this was the side of her that Karaline saw. If only that passion for art and knowledge had been strong enough to displace her less savoury traits.

Huw and Pete Builder greeted them at the castle gates. Pete's face was dirty and he had what looked like stone dust in his hair, but he wore a smile as he bowed to the queen.

"Good news?" Meredith inquired.

"Yes, Your Majesty. We thought the end of the cellar was quite badly damaged, since we've been digging through rubble in there for a few days now. But most of it seems to have fallen in from outside. The interior isn't too bad. We've cleared a path and made it safe to go down, though I wouldn't recommend touching anything until we've given it a proper inspection."

"We will be the first ones to see what's inside, yes?"

"Of course, Your Majesty." Pete dipped his head respectfully, but Calia could see that he was still grinning. Obviously he and his team would have been inside already. Huw probably had, too, and by the looks on their faces, it was exciting news. Calia itched with anticipation.

"Show me," Meredith commanded. "Anastasia, Calia, to the front, please."

Leander took a reluctant step back as the two women joined the queen. She was in high spirits, striding forward with a jaunty gait as Huw and Pete led them across the courtyard. A great crowd had gathered, and several of Lord Oswin's men were present to ensure they remained on the sidelines. Even more people trailed up from the town in the royal party's wake. Everyone wanted to see what secrets the old castle held.

The interior of the keep had been transformed since Calia's first visit. The flagstones had been lifted and then replaced, tearing up moss and weeds in the process. The result was a strangely clean floor with gaps between the cracked stones. It looked both old and new at the same time. Buckets and barrows near the back wall surrounded a heap of debris comprised of broken stone, earth, and pieces of decomposing timber from the cellar passage. There was a lot more of it than Calia had expected. Pete picked up a fresh torch and dipped the end into a brazier on a stand, igniting the linen-wrapped tip before slipping the whole thing into a metal holder similar to a wall sconce. Torches were messy things, ill-suited to indoor use, as they had a habit of dripping burning fat or pitch. The fact that Pete had taken the precaution to bring a holder indicated that the cellar held something more flammable than bare old stone.

The builder led the way down the stairs, offering Meredith his hand as she followed, but the queen ignored it, hitching up her dress and hurrying down with gusto. The stairwell was broad and long, with thick steps sloping down at a gentle angle. This was no steep servant's staircase. It had been built for style and comfort. Dirty stains still clung to the walls and ceiling, illuminated by the licking flames of Pete's torch. Huw brought up the rear with a torch of his own. The passage narrowed halfway down as thick timber frames erected by the builders closed in on either side. Anastasia and the men had to watch their heads as they ducked under each crossbeam. When Calia looked up, she saw cracks in the stonework, and she wondered just how much weight the new beams were supporting. At the foot of the stairs, the passage turned left, opening into the cellar beneath the hall.

"Mind your feet," Pete called back. "There's a lot of loose rubble here. Follow me and I'll take you through the worst of it."

A veritable mountain of broken stone and mortar rose on Calia's right, with another, slightly smaller mound on the left, though it was still high enough to block her view of the chamber beyond. The cellar was a deep one, the torchlight picking out thick stone columns that splayed into the ribs of great arches overhead. Pete guided them forward to where the rubble ended. Anastasia muttered something that sounded like a curse as she stumbled over a loose stone, holding up her dress in a futile attempt to save the hem from the dusty wreckage littering the floor. The rubble was like a great snowdrift spilling out from the stairwell. The further they went, the lower it became until they were standing in the open close to the southern end of the room. The torchlight reached far enough to reveal more wreckage strewn about the floor, but the far end of the chamber was still shrouded in darkness.

"How thrilling," Meredith said, her voice echoing loudly

in the gloom. "To think, no one has set eyes upon these stones in almost a century."

Calia nodded in mute agreement, admiring the finely carved lines of the ceiling overhead. It was as opulent as a cathedral crypt, each arch wrought with patterns of leaves and flowers intertwining. Calia wondered what sort of person would commission a beautiful underground hall styled with images of nature. It was a fantastical refuge, unique from the halls of other lords and ladies. Excitement bubbled up in Calia's chest as her eyes followed the carved pillars. No mere storage cellar would have been so beautifully decorated. If the Farren Vale had hung anywhere, it would have been in a room like this.

Upturned tables and the frames of broken chairs rose like skeletons amidst the rubble. Some kind of desiccated fibre clung to the floor that might have once been a rug. At the edge of Pete's torchlight, more angular shapes jutted out between the columns, tables and benches that had survived the avalanche of rubble. Calia crept closer to one of them, entranced by the mystery. Huw stayed close by, holding up his torch to give her light.

"It looks like you were right, miss Calia."

She nodded absentmindedly. She felt like she was in another time and place, seeing things that only the dead remembered. Huw's light fell upon a table with discoloured stains on the surface. Calia looked up and saw similar discolourations on the stonework overhead. Huw leaned forward and touched the table, rubbing his fingertips together.

"It's damp. Must be a new leak from when we took up the stones. This wood would be in much worse condition if it was any older."

"Do you think this place stayed dry while it was sealed up?"

Huw nodded. "Aye, more or less. I think water used to run down the stairwell back there; we found plenty of stains and rotted wood. But after a while, someone either filled it in with earth or the mud blocked it up naturally. It turned into a big plug that kept the rain out."

Queen Meredith said: "Is any of this furniture in good enough condition to be moved?"

"Yes, Your Majesty," Pete replied. "It's well made. The pieces that haven't rotted could probably survive another hundred years down here."

"Not with the ceiling leaking. I want everything moved as soon as possible. We'll make room at the manor."

They crept deeper into the room, passing by a long table that was still set with a scattering of platters and drinking vessels. Instead of rubble, the floor was now strewn with more recognisable items: cups, stools, knives, more shreds of fibre that had either been mats or wall hangings, and even a soldier's longsword. Calia stared at the tarnished blade, remembering that this room had last seen use when the castle was sacked. Close to the sword was a pile of mail. She looked at it for a moment before taking a startled step back when she saw a knee bone poking out from the rusty links. Huw lifted his torch a little higher. The light fell upon a twisted mummy entombed in a husk of brown armour. Some of the flesh had rotted, exposing bones beneath flakes of ashen fabric, but much of the skin still clung to the body like a ghastly shroud. The figure was partially propped up against one of the pillars, the head and right arm lolling sideways as if they were about to fall off. It was one of the most ghastly things Calia had ever seen.

"Don't look here, miladies," Huw said softly. "There's dead folk."

Calia averted her eyes, but Meredith and Ana ignored Huw's advice. The queen in particular seemed morbidly fascinated by the spectacle.

"I suppose he must have been a soldier. Do you think he was one of the attackers or a defender?"

"No way of knowing," Huw said. "Any colours he wore

are long faded."

Calia deliberately moved forward, putting the grisly sight behind her as she approached the end of the room. She wanted to see the far wall where the Farren Vale would have hung. Pete followed with his torch so that she didn't blunder into the darkness. Inch by inch, the light crept across a set of steps leading up to the high table. Another human-sized shape lay across them. Calia averted her eyes and moved around it. The high table itself had been overturned like a barricade, though there were no signs of it having been damaged. Calia's pace quickened, her careless feet sending a cup clattering down the steps and she hurried around the fallen table.

She let out a gasp of unreserved joy as the light of Pete's torch hit the wall like a splash of fire.

It was there.

The fibres at the bottom had disintegrated like a ragged cloak with a bite torn out of it, leaving only a few brave warp threads clinging to the lowest hooks. Other pieces were stuck to the wall like matted fur, fused and unrecognisable, tangles of brown and grey fibre emaciated with age. Whether it had been damp, moths, or simple vandalism, the Farren Vale was a ruin of its former self. More than a third of the tapestry was gone beyond repair.

But only at the bottom. The top squares, those whose designs had been lost, were almost all intact. Calia stared up at them with a surge of giddiness. The torchlight could only reveal false shades of their faded colours, but the design was still there. The sunbathed valley stretched up to a skyline that did not contain heavenly angels or golden sunbeams, but leaves, birds, and flowers. The top of the tapestry matched the carvings on the arched ceiling.

Anastasia stepped up beside her, equally awestruck.

"I never thought it would really be here," Calia said under her breath. "Not in such good condition."

"Good condition?" the queen said. "There's barely any of

it left."

"But the parts we need are here," Anastasia said, pointing to the top row of squares.

"Indeed they are. Very strange. It looks like a garden growing in the sky."

Ana shook her head. "Not in the sky. It's hard to see without the lower parts here, but you'll recall that our design shows a view of the valley from the top of this hill. The landscape beyond is fantastical, but the spot it was painted from is very real. The artist must have sat beneath a tree when they made their first sketches. Those leaves are its boughs creeping in overhead."

Calia saw it immediately: a grounded border framing an ethereal panorama. Unlike Ana's design, it drew attention to the centre of the piece, conveying the feeling that you were gazing out from the mundane into the magnificent. It wasn't at all what she'd expected, but now that she saw it, it made perfect sense. She wanted to weave those birds and branches into the new design and study every weft from front to back. She wanted to understand how the original weavers had worked their looms and compare their techniques to her own.

Anastasia must have read her thoughts, for the look of wonder on her face slowly gave way to a worried frown. The reverence she felt for this piece of history was warring with a far more selfish desire.

This was a threat to her masterpiece.

CHAPTER 13

Much to the disappointment of the townsfolk, there was little hidden treasure to be found beneath Castle Ashmount. It made sense, Huw explained, for the place had likely been looted before it burned down. Besides a few nicely-carved chairs, some pieces of silver tableware, and the tapestry itself, nothing of particular value was found amongst the wreckage. It was possible some of the missing tapestry pieces had been stolen as well, but the looters would have quickly realised how heavy and cumbersome they were. The upper parts might only have survived due to the inconvenience of taking them down.

Over the next few days, Pete and his team emptied the hall of debris while a group of Leander's weavers disassembled the tapestry a piece at a time. Several segments were found to be damaged beyond repair, falling apart or losing threads when they were removed from their hooks. These fragments were preserved as best as possible, but they would never be anything more than a historical curiosity. The well-preserved pieces, those nearest the top, were laid in specially made wooden boxes that were flat and shallow, with hooks inside to secure each square as if it was still hanging from its fastenings. These boxes were carried reverently to the manor one at a time, to be stored in the weaving rooms alongside Anastasia's cartoons.

The queen's visit continued as the season wore on. According to Lucy, she often spent long stretches of her summers in Ashmount, only returning to the capital when the autumn rains were on the horizon. A fresh influx of guests arrived once news of the discovery spread. Nobles who wanted to toady to the queen used the discovery of the Farren Vale as an excuse to visit, and a few genuine scholars even joined them. Lord Oswin began to organise viewing parties with the surviving pieces of the old design hanging alongside the new.

It was during this period that Calia found her social standing quickly and unexpectedly advancing. She thought nothing of it at first; she was only called to the high table once or twice to answer questions about the tapestry for the queen's guests. But then it began happening more often. The queen started to insist that she stay, take a seat, and explain at length the artistic insight she held into the Farren Vale and its recreation. Her opinions were often contrasted with Anastasia's, much to the delight of the queen's more artistically-minded guests. They enjoyed the abutting viewpoints of weaver and painter. For many of them, it was novel seeing two female craftspeople in positions of such esteem. Some found it admirable, others silly, but in the presence of Queen Meredith they always kept their comments respectful.

These evenings daunted Calia at first. She spoke only when spoken to, avoiding eye contact as she focused on keeping her hands from shaking while she ate her food. She felt ill-equipped to deal with such company, especially with Anastasia's overbearing presence always on the periphery of her awareness. But to her surprise, the painter was uncharacteristically withdrawn. She too seemed quiet, though her overall mood was one of brooding rather than anxiety.

Calia kept expecting her to chime in with criticisms and dismissals whenever she was asked to explain something, but the usual rebukes rarely came.

Free from the put-downs that would have made her retreat further into her shell, Calia found her confidence growing. By the end of the month, she had her own seat reserved at the high table. Leander sometimes dined alongside her, all charm and smiles, fabricating stories about how he had identified her as a rising prodigy when she first came to Ashmount. It was at his insistence, of course, that she had been admitted to the guild, and thanks to her clever insights he had struck upon the idea to unearth the hidden tapestry with his team of workmen. Calia played along, finding that Leander was an amusing man to be around provided you were willing to stroke his ego.

Though many of the topics discussed at the high table went over Calia's head, she was educated and knowledgeable enough to hold her own when pressed for input. Despite being no social butterfly, she at least managed to avoid making a fool of herself, and that, in her estimation, was a victory. She told Lucy about it every evening before they went to bed, trusting that her friend would not repeat anything too gossipworthy to the servants. They both had experience as intimates of the queen's entourage now, and Calia was glad to have someone who understood her position. Lucy was a woman of comparatively humble birth, too, and she had been equally intimidated when she started taking the queen's measurements and tailoring her dresses.

"So, do you enjoy it?" Lucy asked her one evening as they sat up sewing felt slippers by candlelight.

Calia set her work down in her lap as she thought. "I like the food. They always serve the most wonderful dishes at the high table."

"You could stand to get a little plumper. I don't know how you survive the winter being that skinny."

"I can't eat much. Some of those sauces are so rich. And I

can taste the wine in them. I have to ask for water so it doesn't go to my head."

Lucy chuckled. "I've never heard of anyone getting drunk from a fancy sauce."

"Well, it's more Leander insisting my cup stays full every time he's here."

"He's getting fond of you, I'd say."

Calia frowned. "How do you mean?"

"Oh, you know. He must be close to forty and not married. Wedding an alderman, you could do worse for yourself."

"I don't think he's like that. I mean," Calia chuckled, "I think he might be more interested if I were a man."

"Well, yes, everyone with any sense knows that about him, but he probably still wants children someday. A wife of good standing, too. Someone like you or Ana would be perfect for him."

Calia smiled and shook her head, knowing that Lucy was mostly teasing. "No, I don't think so. I'm much happier here with you."

"Oh, it's like that, is it?" Lucy gave her a suggestive wiggle of her eyebrows.

"Stop it, you silly hen. You should talk to my sister. She'll fall in love with anyone who catches her eye, man or woman."

"Well, I wouldn't mention that in front of the queen. She's a pious woman, and the church doesn't approve of that kind of scandal."

"No, I suppose not." Calia picked out a misplaced stitch with the tip of her needle. "That's what makes me nervous about Queen Meredith. Her piety. You don't see it often, but the moment she catches a whiff of anything that goes against the church's teachings, she puffs up like a pigeon. I'm always worried she'll ask me something about the saints or the scriptures and I won't have an answer."

"Just be humble. That's what Huw says. You don't need to understand God's will to defer to His sacred precepts."

"I wonder if I should be more bold, though. My mother said I could learn a lot in my time here. Shouldn't I be trying to impress everyone? I can't do that if I'm acting like a serf who's never left her village."

"Do you *want* to impress everyone?"

Calia shrugged. "It isn't that I want to, it's just that when you're at the high table it feels like it's what you're supposed to do."

Lucy scoffed. "That's how people like Anastasia think. They have to put on an act every time there's an audience."

"Perhaps I'm getting a bit above my station."

"Oh, to hell with all of that. It's just nonsense made up by lords and ladies so they can look down their noses at people like us. If working here's taught me anything, it's that nobles fart and fornicate like everyone else. Do you want to be like them, or do you want to be like you?"

Calia smiled. She liked Lucy's blunt, no-nonsense way of thinking. It was like having an older sister who was always looking out for her.

"I suppose you're right. But you did say I have a lot in common with Ana. I'm not sure how I can become a respected master like her if I don't impress anyone."

"Proper respect invites itself. It's not a show you put on. The only attention that'll attract is from people whose respect isn't worth much in the first place. Huw, he's a respectable man. Pete, too. But Ana?" Lucy scoffed again. "I respect the sheep my wool comes from more than her."

"You're so wise about these things, Lucy." Calia put her sewing down and went over to give her a hug. "I'm going to bed. Would you brush my hair?"

"Only if you do mine first. I'm going to see a dressmaker from Tannersfield tomorrow. You'll have to wake me up early."

"I will."

Despite progress on the tapestry slowing down with the

recent excitement, Calia still finished her second square before the summer's end. Queen Meredith didn't check on their progress regularly, for she said that seeing the pieces half-finished was like eating an undercooked meal, but every time a new square was ready she ordered them hung downstairs in the great hall alongside Ana's cartoons.

"Beautiful, beautiful," the queen mused, gazing up at Calia's second piece. "When I next visit in the spring I want to see the whole thing finished."

A viewing party had been arranged that afternoon, though only a few prominent locals were in attendance. They milled about in the great hall conversing quietly as they admired the half-finished tapestry. Vesna was deep in conversation with the bishop of Farrenwold, who was here on another of his flying visits, while Leander recounted anecdotes to a bored-looking Lord Oswin.

"We may need more weavers if the tapestry is to be finished before the end of winter, Your Majesty," Ana said.

"I'll find some for you."

"If I could be allowed to hire them myself–"

"No," Meredith interrupted her. "I want to select them. You've been very dour lately, Anastasia, and I want weavers full of vigour."

Ana fell silent, but Calia saw the flash of resentment that crossed her face. Perhaps this was the moment to suggest an idea that had been on her mind since they discovered the old tapestry? She'd been reluctant to bring it up to the queen, for she was certain Ana would object, but if the painter was feeling humbled then this might be her chance.

Proper respect invites itself, she thought. If her ideas were good, they should stand on their own merits.

Calia cleared her throat. "Your Majesty, might I make a suggestion?"

The queen raised her eyebrows. "You may."

"Forgive me if it isn't my place, but I can't help thinking of the old design whenever I look at the tapestry these days;

the branches at the top, that wonderful natural framing. I know it's too late to change the whole thing, but we still have two squares from the top row that haven't been started. I was wondering if it might be possible to incorporate a hint of that of that old design into the new? A framing of tree branches at the top right corner, perhaps."

The queen looked at Ana. "Could that be done?"

The painter shook her head. "Out of the question. The design has already been finalised. Changing one part of it would throw the rest out of harmony. The colours have been selected and the thread purchased. One can't simply change a painting halfway through."

Calia disagreed with that. She didn't want to escalate things into an argument with Ana, but in her heart she longed to weave those gentle branches into the tapestry. She wanted to create a piece that was natural and calm, full of earthy colours like the ones she'd learned to weave with, not flashy silk and silver thread.

"We've made alterations before," Calia said. "And not all the thread has been purchased–nothing we can't repurpose for other parts of the tapestry, at least."

"You don't understand how these things are managed," Ana retorted. "And you certainly don't understand fine art."

"Don't behave like children," Meredith said, flashing both of them a glare. "This isn't the first time I've noticed the pair of you at odds. Do you know how tiresome I find it when people vie for my favour?"

An uncomfortable silence followed in which Calia became very aware of Vesna staring at her from across the room. She never knew where she stood with Meredith. The day Goldie had been dismissed, the queen seemed to have been revelling in her subjects' bickering. Today, she would have none of it.

"Forgive me, Your Majesty."

"I enjoy your work immensely, both of you, but I don't want any of this squabbling."

Leander sidled into view, apparently having been hovering

on the edge of the conversation.

"Your Majesty, if I may?"

Meredith still looked annoyed, but she motioned for him to continue.

"Calia and Anastasia are passionate women, both possessed of strong artistic convictions. It is only natural that they find themselves butting heads when forced to work together. I've seen it a dozen times. You can't have two chickens hatching the same egg. But I believe there might be an answer to Calia's suggestion that doesn't impinge on Anastasia's vision of the tapestry."

Calia listened with curiosity. She'd told Leander about her desire to weave the original design several times over supper. While he was far warmer to her these days than he'd used to be, it was unlike him to go out of his way to do her a favour. What was he up to?

"Are you going to suggest we weave two separate tapestries?" the queen asked drily.

"As a matter of fact, I am. Not another full-sized Farren Vale, of course, but perhaps a smaller piece, say, a couple of yards across. A miniature recreation of the original so that we might revive its spirit."

"That would mean taking Calia away from my project," Ana said.

"Precisely. She would no longer be getting under your feet. She would still be working on the Farren Vale, albeit in a different capacity."

"Well?" the queen said. "What do you think, Calia?"

She could hardly contain her excitement. "If it would please you, Your Majesty, then it would be my honour."

An amused smile twitched Meredith's lips. "I quite like the idea. I did say, didn't I, that I would like to see a full tapestry rendered in Calia's style? It could hang in my solar opposite the hearth. Yes, what an elegant solution! Calia will have her tapestry, and Anastasia will have hers."

Leander bowed. "I would be happy to organise the

commission through the guild."

So that was his plan. The queen had sidelined him by bringing in her own weavers the first time around, but if Calia was commissioned directly, the formal process would have to go through the Ashmount weavers' guild. They would take a fee, and, more importantly, they would share in the prestige.

Well, they could have their prestige and their fee. If it allowed Calia to work on her own, free from Ana's overbearing presence, then Leander could take all the credit he wanted. She was already envisioning picking out the colours she would use, studying the faded browns and greens of the original and working out how to translate them into a smaller design. Small tapestries had always been her speciality. She could experiment on her hand loom, testing out new patterns and combinations of colour before committing them to her final design.

"There is no cartoon for her to work from," Ana said.

"I can work from the existing cartoon and use the pieces of the old tapestry as references for the top parts."

"They're far too big."

"I can scale them down into something smaller. It won't be an exact copy, of course, but it'll have to be different to convey the same design on a smaller warp anyway."

"Well then," the queen said, "that's settled. With Calia gone, we shall have to find new weavers for Ana sooner than later, I think. Perhaps we can organise a craft fair of some sort. I want to be impressed by weavers I've never heard of."

Calia felt like a warm ray of sunlight was shining on her back. The cloud that had been following her since Goldie's dismissal had finally lifted.

CHAPTER 14

"I thought you'd be happy," Anastasia said as her mother paced the length of the room. She had a headache, and Vesna's irritable footsteps were only making it worse. She couldn't concentrate on her painting like this.

"Why should we be happy? Now you have a rival making her own tapestry, a direct copy of yours! What if people look at the two side by side and decide hers is better, hm? You'll be second to a half-trained tailor. Is that what you want?"

Ana pinched the bridge of her nose with a thumb and forefinger. "No one is going to make that comparison, Mother. Hers will be a fraction of the size. She's copying a weary old nature design. Mine is far more dynamic. She doesn't even like using silver and gold thread. Our styles are a world apart."

Vesna pinched her arm. Ana swatted her hand away in annoyance, then gasped as her mother slapped her across the face.

"You're slipping, Nastya. You couldn't get the queen to dismiss her. You couldn't stop them from digging up the old tapestry. Now you're not even going to fight back when the girl is poised to become the queen's new favourite! I'm ashamed of you."

"What am I supposed to do?" Ana said angrily. Her cheek stung from the slap, but the warmth spreading across her skin was nothing compared to the blaze of her mother's scorn.

"*Think*. Use Sigrad. Use Oswin. Find a way to put a stop to this and force Calia out of favour. If you can't do it, I will. I won't let my daughter disgrace her legacy."

"My legacy, or yours?"

"They're one and the same and you know it. I lifted us up to where we are now. It's your duty to keep us here."

Ana knew she was right. Vesna had brought them across the sea from a war-torn kingdom, worked tirelessly for their wealth, and ingratiated them with the royal court. Without her, Ana and Kara would have nothing. For as much as she hated her mother in that moment, she knew she could never disobey her.

"I'll think of something," she said miserably.

But she couldn't. As the days passed and she watched Calia setting up her new loom, she struggled to think of anything that might force the woman out of favour. She couldn't muster the passion for it, because, in truth, part of her was glad. She was tired of being at odds with Calia. Every time they butted heads, there was always an undercurrent of doubt. Ana wondered whether she deserved to be outdone. When she looked at Calia's work, she saw the unique talent that went into it, the eye for colour and contrast that, while different from her own, still held an equally powerful sense of character. The day they'd gone into the castle cellar, Ana had been enraptured by the old Farren Vale. It had brought her back to those days she'd spent staring up at ancient frescoes as a child, full of admiration for the wonders of the past. If she'd succeeded in thwarting the dig, she would've deprived herself of that moment.

The problem was, Calia had no obvious weaknesses to take advantage of—none that were relevant, anyway. She seemed to be of relatively humble birth, but the queen was one of those people who saw virtue in humility. Cloth weaved by the poor and books scribed by nuns held a special kind of charm to her. Calia's biggest weakness of character was that she was shy. At first, Ana had thought that would make her easy to bully, but she'd since learned otherwise. Calia's timid disposition wasn't born of cowardice or stupidity, but a painful lack of ego. Such people were always difficult to deal with, like pious monks who put their vows first and their personal interests second. That was probably why the queen liked her.

In the end, Ana reached the same conclusion she had before: if there was any way to push Calia out of favour, it would have to be via the people she associated with. First and foremost among those was Leander. He had styled himself as Calia's patron, and people who didn't know them often took her to be his apprentice. Ana and Vesna had spent a long time learning about Leander when they first came to Ashmount. He'd been their first major rival, constantly insisting that he, as the foremost weaver in town, should head up the project with a team of his choosing. Fortunately, the queen hadn't taken much convincing to cut him out of the picture. His persistence had been his undoing, and in the end he'd proven himself to be a man who was more talk than action.

Still, there were things they'd learned in those early days that might yet prove useful. Leander did not get on well with the local clergy. The root of this animosity, it seemed, was a short-lived stint as a novice monk the alderman had undertaken in his youth. Leander had left his monastery in unusual circumstances. There didn't seem to have been any formal expulsion, nor had any charges been brought against him, yet everyone said he'd been forced out against his will.

It hadn't taken long for Ana to come up with a theory as to why. There were rumours abound that Leander had an intimate preference for male company. At first she'd assumed the talk was just a by-product of his slightly effete manner, but his abrupt ejection from the church was too conspicuous to ignore. An illicit love affair was exactly the sort of thing the clergy would want to keep quiet. It was also the sort of thing that would brand a man with a lifelong resentment of the church. In Ana's experience, men with Leander's preferences were quietly overlooked most of the time. She suspected there were numerous affairs going on behind monastery walls that no one ever talked about, but the formal line of the church was that such relationships were sinful, and they ran the risk of prosecution in ecclesiastical court. Perhaps Leander had found love with a fellow monk and been forced out when he was exposed? Taking the matter to court would have been far messier, and no one would have come out of it looking good, least of all the monastery.

Ana sat in the shade of a tree outside the manor pondering her problem. The queen had insisted on a picnic in one of the meadows to take advantage of the last of the summer weather. She and her guests sat at a long line of tables while the servants stood around sweating in the sun. Vesna had complained about the heat and gone back inside, and Karaline had been scared of the wasps that kept landing on her goblet, so Ana took her into the shade where they could finish their meal in peace. Kara had a small square of leather in her lap that she was embroidering with a pattern resembling the queen's crown. The bronze needle she was using looked familiar to Ana, but she couldn't remember where she'd seen it before. She watched her sister for a moment, reflecting that the design was surprisingly good, before reluctantly returning to her plotting. Vesna had told her what she needed to do, and the more days that passed without any progress, the heavier the weight of her mother's disappointment became.

The queen took a low view of anyone who flouted the church's teachings. Fortunately for Leander, she seemed quite oblivious to the rumours people spun about him, but that could easily be changed. A rumour was not enough on its own, however. He would need official condemnation, something that brought him before the ecclesiastical court. Perhaps Calia could be drawn in as a witness to speak on his behalf. Surely she'd want to defend him, then if the ruling found him guilty...

Ana sighed and shut her eyes, leaning her head back against the tree trunk. It was all so insubstantial. Just hopeful ideas, none of them guaranteed to get her what she wanted. With enough time and plotting, those ideas might coalesce into a plan, but without the drive to see it through, it seemed a herculean task. This should have been a pleasant time, one of her few precious moments alone with Karaline, yet she was so preoccupied with appeasing her mother that she couldn't relax. Perhaps she should just give it all up; accept a future of mediocrity and Vesna's disappointment. But even contemplating that thought made her skin itch and her throat tighten with indignation. She wouldn't be a failure.

"Does this look like a crown?" Karaline asked, holding up her embroidered scrap of leather.

Ana took it from her and ran her thumb over the stitches. "I was just thinking that it reminded me of the one the queen wears."

"Is it good?"

"It is. Very nice thread, too. Where did you get it?"

"Lucy Tailor lent it to me."

Ana frowned. She wasn't especially fond of Lucy, being part of Calia's circle as she was, but she'd always respected the woman's work. "Do you see Lucy often?"

Karaline fell quiet, and when she responded it was not with an answer, but a question of her own: "Could I be a tailor?"

"I'm afraid not."

"Why?"

"Mother doesn't want it for you."

"What's wrong with being a tailor?"

"It's too humble a trade for a family like ours."

"But Lucy is the queen's tailor! That's not humble."

Ana wished she could indulge her sister's new passion, but it was better to nip this fantasy in the bud. "Very few tailors get to serve queens. Besides, you'll have a tailor of your own if you marry a nobleman. Wouldn't you like that more?"

Kara shrugged. "I don't know."

No, you wouldn't at your age, Ana thought.

She wondered sometimes whether she herself might have preferred a domestic life. It had never been a realistic option; she'd always been too busy with her painting. The closest she'd come to romance was batting her eyelashes at a handful of courtiers her mother wanted to impress. Vesna had insisted on more than flirting with a few of them, Lord Oswin in particular, but that was where Ana drew the line. She found the idea distasteful, fearing that the shame of it would be even worse than Vesna's wrath.

No man had ever captured her heart. She was a fine-looking woman when she dressed for it, though her tall stature and severe bearing made her what most people would call handsome rather than beautiful. There had been times as a teenager, before she'd fully come to terms with the responsibilities of her life, when she'd wondered whether some of her friends might become something more. It was always the ones who admired her paintings, studied trades of their own, and talked about art with a passion that made her believe there was more to it than wealth and prestige. Such people enchanted her. More than once she'd pictured a future in which she lived in a bright house designing frescoes for cathedrals and panel paintings for wealthy merchants alongside a partner who viewed her work not with judgement, but admiration.

That wasn't the life for her. A woman of her talents couldn't be shackled to a husband beneath her station. Vesna often spoke of the burdens Ana's father had heaped upon them when he was still alive, and she had no intention of hobbling her eldest daughter with the same fate. Karaline, on the other hand, faced the opposite problem.

Ana wished she had some advice to give her sister. After she got married, they probably wouldn't see each other very often, and as the years went by they would only grow further apart.

"You don't look very happy today," Kara said.

"I'm really not." Ana surprised herself with her honesty, but if there was one person who could wring the truth from her, it was Karaline.

"Why?"

"Being an adult is very complicated, and sometimes I wish it weren't."

"Oh."

If only Karaline was a few years older, old enough to empathise with her troubles and lend a sympathetic ear. Maybe she could even have offered some advice of her own. The only person Ana could talk to about such things was Vesna. She'd never really had close friends, only those fleeting companions scattered across her teenage years. They'd moved around so much that she'd never stayed in contact with any of them for long. One day, when the Farren Vale was complete and she was the foremost artisan in the kingdom, perhaps she would have time for friends again.

By the time the queen departed that autumn, Calia's tapestry was coming along well. Each thread added to it felt like another moment slipping through Ana's fingers. She stared at it every evening after the weavers left the workroom, marvelling at how carefully considered the choices of thread were, how Calia could pattern thin pieces of wool between thick ones so that only playful hints showed through, creating an effect of colour and texture that was wholly unique to her style. There were dozens of tiny tricks like that in her work. Small, practical things she must have learned from a skilled master. Comparing Calia's work to the other weavers', Ana suspected she'd learned from someone who was self-taught, or else confident and experienced enough to have moved away from the traditional techniques. Most of the weavers in Ashmount had a formal rigour to their style that made their work tight and consistent. "Professional weaving," as Ana would have called it. That was why she'd disliked Calia's style at first. It wasn't that it was bad, simply that it was different, and because it did not fit the conventional style, she'd assumed it to be the work of an amateur.

Calia didn't copy her cartoons exactly, she improvised around them, getting rid of the characteristics that only worked in paint and replacing them with ones better suited to thread. This style of hers was even more apparent now that she was working on a full tapestry rather than a segment of something larger. Her new loom would hold the entire thing. It was two yards wide by a yard and a half tall. She was still using the mirror setup to copy from a piece of Ana's cartoon behind her, but rather than creating an exact imitation, she was only using it as a reference for part of her smaller version. Right now, she was working on the lower-right section of the tapestry that depicted a king riding with his knights. It was impossible to portray so many figures on such a small warp, so Calia had improvised. The knights were now a scattering of brown and grey threads, abstract up close, but resembling a host of horsemen when viewed from afar. The king had been moved further up the hill, closer to the perspective of the viewer, so that his outline could be depicted clearly with a sable horse and a crown of yellow thread. It was the same colour Karaline had been embroidering with.

Ana was dragged from her reverie by the sound of Vesna's footsteps entering the room behind her. They were slow and deliberate, holding a cat's predatory poise, coming to a halt with a slight shuffle that reminded Ana of a person clearing their throat. She'd listened to those feet pace her workroom for years.

"Are you joining us for supper?" Vesna asked.

Ana shook her head without turning. "Not yet."

"Lost in thought, are you?"

"No, Mother."

"Well, you should be. The queen's gone now. We don't have to walk on eggshells."

Ana sighed. "I don't know what to do. Her work is excellent. The queen likes her. She isn't up to anything suspicious or unsavoury." It pained her to admit that she'd come to a dead end, but the sooner she confessed, the sooner she could get it over with.

"Then we'll have to find something we can *make* suspicious and unsavoury."

"All I can think of is Leander. You remember his history with the church?" Ana went on to explain the thoughts she'd been mulling during the summer. Vesna nodded along, coming to the same conclusion.

"It isn't enough to accuse Leander on his own. Calia could easily distance herself from him."

"So there's nothing to be done."

"There is always something to be done, Nastya. Look at you, giving up the moment things become difficult. I forget that you're still a child."

"I'm twenty-five."

"And you still need your mother to look after you," Vesna said sharply, then her voice softened. "Perhaps I've burdened you with too much. I'm asking you to fly when you're still learning to run."

Ana had been preparing herself for a fight, steeling her nerve so that she could endure whatever her mother threw at her, but sympathy was not what she'd expected. It made her feel like the child Vesna saw her as, still in need of guidance and protection. The anger that had been building in her chest flooded out of her, leaving behind a shrivelled nugget of guilt.

"What do we do?" she asked meekly.

"We get our hands dirty. If there isn't an elegant way to

deal with Calia, we'll have to be inelegant."

"What do you mean?"

"It's better if you don't know. Let your mother shoulder the burden for you."

The underlying judgement in her voice made Ana look away uncomfortably. She'd failed, and now her mother had to take over. Vesna knew best, of course. If only Ana could have been cleverer. More ruthless. More like her.

CHAPTER 15

Working on her own tapestry free from Anastasia's interference was a dream come true for Calia. The cooling weather had taken the edge off those long, hot summer days, and the queen's departure meant she could stop worrying about how she conducted herself at the high table. She was back to having supper with Lucy and the others at the end of the hall where the atmosphere was light and companionable. Karaline even joined them on occasion when her mother and sister weren't around.

There was no place for a young girl at the table that evening, however. They were entertaining a tinker named Jacob who came by to mend kitchen utensils every few months. Calia had quickly come to realise that he enjoyed sharing his supper with the young women of the household more than mending their tools. He was devilishly handsome in the way of a man who was used to getting his hands dirty, sporting an easy smile, sparkling eyes, and stubble that was always a couple of days overgrown. He never had any difficulty winning himself the affections of the manor servants. He was sitting between Calia and Lucy, enthralling the group with a bawdy story about Lord Lanter of Redland, who apparently had an obscenely plump mistress and a wife as thin as a rake. Rovena and a few others were hanging on his every word, but it was Lucy who'd managed to monopolise the charming tinker's attention that evening. Every now and again, Calia caught a glimpse of her friend's hand on his thigh beneath the table. She leant in close against him every time he made her laugh, and sometimes he put his arm around her waist in response. Calia didn't know how to flirt. She felt uncomfortable sitting there, feeling like she should move aside for someone else to take her place, but Jacob was polite and respectful to her, perhaps sensing that she wasn't the sort of woman he could woo.

"I might go upstairs," she told Lucy when Jacob got up to visit the latrine.

"No, stay! You're keeping anyone else from sitting next to him," Lucy whispered.

"I don't know. You seem to be doing well enough by yourself."

"Please. You'd be the best friend in the world."

Calia sighed, but Jacob came back before she could offer another protest.

"What're you two arguing about?" he said in a jovial tone, clapping them both on the shoulders as he clambered over the bench.

"You, obviously," Lucy said.

"As if a pair of angels could be so vain. Can you pour me some more ale, Calia?"

She flushed bright red as Jacob's loud comments drew the attention of the other diners. Lord Oswin frowned at them from the high table.

"You'd better keep your voice down," she said under her breath. "Or Lord Oswin will have you thrown out."

Jacob pressed a finger to his lips and winked at her. She focused her attention on pouring the ale to avoid any further embarrassment. She wouldn't have minded this in a private context, but not in front of the whole household. Her discomfort must have been plain to everyone, and that made it worse. After sharing the queen's table, she felt like she should be conducting herself with poise and refinement like Anastasia, but at the end of the day she was still an awkward twenty-year-old with little worldly experience. Sitting at a loom all day did not prepare one for situations like this.

Nevertheless, she wanted to be a good friend, so she endured her discomfort and drank her ale until Jacob's jokes started making her laugh again. As the evening wore on and people got up to leave, it seemed like Lucy had succeeded in getting her man to herself. The other weavers, realising they'd been sidelined, drifted away until it was just the three of them left.

"So, where do you two keep your beds?" Jacob asked with a casual sip from his cup.

"Why do you want to know?" Lucy replied.

"Oh, I just hope it's somewhere safe. The kitcheners leave their door wide open in the evenings. It's to let the room cool, they say, but I don't know... any ruffian could walk in and slip his way into someone's cot."

"I never have any ruffians in my workshop. It's all the way upstairs from the servants' hall–to the right at the far end of the landing."

"Ah, I thought that might be the one."

"Luckily the boards creak, so no one ever surprises me. They'd have to walk very carefully–right along the edge of the left wall. If they did that, they'd be able to sneak in without anyone noticing."

Calia saw Lucy walking her fingers up Jacob's thigh as she spoke. The pair of them were completely absorbed in each other, ignoring her as if she wasn't there. Jacob leaned back and put his arm around Lucy, nudging Calia's foot beneath the table as he shifted position. The touch made her jump, sending her cup clattering to the floor as she banged the table with her knee. Everyone looked at her again. She stammered an excuse and hurried out to the latrine, though she didn't need to go. When she came back, Lucy was waiting for her by the door.

"I'll sleep down here tonight," Calia told her.

"You don't have to."

"I wouldn't be able to get any rest if... you know. You have visitors."

Lucy chuckled. "I'm crossing my fingers. Thank you. You really are the best friend." She squeezed Calia's hand and gave her a peck on the cheek before heading upstairs. Calia collected her fallen cup and went to ask Rovena if she could share her mattress by the hearth.

* * *

"Go over to the weavers," Vesna murmured into Sigrad's ear, "and ask them what Calia and Lucy were fighting about. Do it loudly enough that people hear you."

"Are you sure they were fighting?"

"It doesn't matter if they were or not. I want people to think they had a disagreement."

Sigrad nodded. He knew he wasn't as clever as Ana or Vesna, so he didn't bother trying to second-guess their plans. They knew what they were doing, and following their instructions had made him rich. He'd always been willing to put about rumours and listen at doors for them. That had earned him a few shillings of precious spending money, but it was the incident outside the treasury that had confirmed to him without a shadow of a doubt that his fortune lay in steadfast loyalty to these cunning women. He was afraid of what they could do to him, but his hunger for wealth and power eclipsed that fear. After Ana had given him the bag of silver from the treasury, he'd buried it in the woods just as she asked. He'd tried to forget about it, but the temptation kept returning. He thought about those glittering coins every night. It was enough money to buy a good horse, a strong sword, and a smart surcoat. He could ride off and sell his services as a man-at-arms anytime he wanted. But by staying here, he stood to earn far more. He had to be patient. Become a squire. Become a knight. Then he would be rich and powerful.

In the end, he'd compromised with himself. He wanted to feel rich even if he couldn't show it off, so he'd taken some silver from the bag and used it to buy a knife from one of the jewellers in town. The blade was mirror-polished steel fixed into a glossy bone handle inlaid with silver that swirled down the grip in elaborate patterns that culminated in a cloudy purple gemstone at the pommel. It was the most beautiful possession he'd ever owned. He kept it in a leather sheath that hung from a thong around his neck so that it was always close to his heart. Feeling its weight there brought a confident smile to his lips everywhere he walked. It was like a secret power. Even though he was just a page, having his knife made him feel like a lord.

Following Vesna's instructions, he went to the other end of the hall where some of the weavers were still talking. Lucy had gone upstairs and Calia was bedding down for the night with her friend Rovena. Keeping his voice low enough that Calia wouldn't hear, but still loud enough to carry to the nearby tables, he asked: "What were Calia and Lucy fighting about?"

Elaine and Bess, two of Anastasia's staunch loyalists, snorted in unison.

"That tinker, I expect."

Sigrad nodded, looking intrigued. He'd always been fascinated by other people's dirty secrets, and it wasn't hard for him to pretend he'd come gossip-hunting. "Calia threw her cup and stormed off, didn't she?"

"That's not like her," Elaine said.

"A cock causing trouble in the hen coop," said Bess. "Quiet girls like that often get riled up when they have eyes for a man. Don't know how to handle them, especially when their friends are involved."

Sigrad didn't need to stir the pot much more after that. Once the women latched on to the narrative that Lucy and Calia had been fighting over the tinker, their imaginations and prejudices filled in the rest. He nodded along, only adding occasional comments to stoke the gossip. After a while, he saw Vesna staring at him and slipped away to rejoin her.

"Did you do it?" she asked.

"Yes. Everyone thinks they had a fight."

"Good. Now listen to me. This needs to be done tonight while that rumour's still fresh in their minds. If you get caught, you'll be dismissed from the household, but if you do as I say, I'll have Oswin make you a squire before the year's end."

Sigrad's heart leapt. "I don't want to be dismissed."

"Then don't get caught."

"What do I have to do?"

Vesna nodded in the direction of Lucy and Calia's bench. "Lucy left her cloak there. Do you see it? The one with the red pattern on the back."

"I see."

"Go and take it. Make sure no one notices. Put your own cloak on top and pretend you're clearing the table or something, then pick it up when you leave. Go outside and wait till everyone's gone to bed. Then put on Lucy's cloak and come back in here. You're about the same build as her. Let people notice you, but make sure they can't see your face. Then go upstairs to the weaving rooms. There's a stack of special boxes holding the pieces of the old Farren Vale in there. I want you to destroy them."

Sigrad blinked. "Why?"

"Because Calia's copying her tapestry from those pieces. She can't make a copy if she doesn't have a reference. Try and find the ones from the top row. Make sure they go first. It doesn't matter about the rest."

"Alright. I'll cut them up and pull the threads out." Sigrad knew he would be in dire trouble if he got caught, but he was good at sneaking around. He'd crept about the manor's upper floor many times when he couldn't sleep, exploring all the places that were normally forbidden to him. He knew which doors were locked and which weren't, which boards creaked and which were silent. He even knew which rooms people slept in.

"If you're caught, Sigrad, then bringing up my name would go very poorly for you."

"I won't."

Vesna closed her fingers around his wrist, gently at first, then with painful pressure. "They might put you on trial. You'll be dismissed from this household in disgrace. Perhaps you'll be flogged, but you'll live." Her nails dug into him. "If you mention my name, I'll deny everything and see to it that you hang."

Sigrad's mouth went dry. He nodded mutely. Seeing that he understood her, Vesna let go and her thin lips spread into a smile.

"But you won't get caught, will you? You'll do well, become a squire, and in five years you'll be a knight. My Karaline will be old enough to marry by then. She might be a good match for an up-and-coming nobleman like you."

"Oh, yes." Sigrad was bemused by the offer. He struggled to think of Vesna's young daughter as a woman he might one day marry, but when he thought about it, it made sense. He would be powerful, and her family would be rich. Maybe he could be a baron someday with that kind of money behind him. He saw a future where the Fialas backed him with their money while he threw his weight around in the courts. He liked that idea. They could be the brains and he'd be the brawn. He just had to do well tonight.

Vesna retired to the royal solar shortly thereafter, leaving Sigrad to his task. He drank some ale to steel his nerve, his foot drumming restlessly beneath the table. Once people began settling down for the night, he started gathering leftover cups. He moved quietly, barely making a noise as he went about his made-up task. People were used to him being in the background, and no one looked his way when he dropped his cloak over Lucy's, collected a pair of empty jugs from the table, and took the whole bundle out with him to the servants' hall.

After that, he waited. It would be best if no one saw him walking around, so he went outside and stood behind the stables, hopping from foot to foot to keep himself warm. The evenings were getting chilly again. After what he judged to be about an hour, he donned Lucy's cloak over his own. Vesna had been right; they were of a similar build. Sigrad wasn't yet a full-grown man, and Lucy was a broad-shouldered woman. He put up the hood and drew it forward to conceal his face.

By now, he'd figured out Vesna's plan. She wanted people to think Lucy had destroyed the tapestry in a fit of jealousy after getting into a fight with Calia. It was very cunning. The old woman must've been waiting a long time for an opportunity like this. Or perhaps she'd seized the moment and come up with the idea on the spot. He didn't know how people like her thought.

Creeping out from behind the stable, he went back into the manor and crossed the great hall. He didn't dare raise his head in case anyone saw his face, but he did walk loudly, letting his footfalls draw the attention of anyone who was still awake. The manor was warm and quiet, filled with sleepy snores and the crackle of low fires. He knew the rooms well enough to navigate by the light of the hearths and feel his way past the slumbering servants. Once he was in the servants' hall, he followed the wall with his palm until he reached the stairs, once again making no effort to silence his footfalls. Only when he reached the top of the stairs did he slip his boots off and tuck them under one arm. He waited patiently on the landing, listening to see if anyone was moving around. The only sounds he heard came from downstairs.

Treading carefully, he moved across the landing until he found the door leading to the weaving rooms. It was usually left open during the day, covered by a light curtain, but now it was shut and locked. That was no obstacle to Sigrad. There were only two types of warded lock in the manor, and he'd worked out that a simple crooked iron rod could unlock most of them. The ones in the treasury were of a more elaborate design, but for doors like this, he had a homemade tool that worked just as well as any key. He slipped it out of his bag and groped for the keyhole in the darkness. Working by touch and feel, he pushed the rod in and turned it until the lock clicked.

The room beyond was pitch black. He would need a light to find the tapestry pieces. All the large rooms in the manor had alcoves where fires could be lit. Not all were full hearths, but they did hold candles, rushlights, and fire strikers. Sigrad shut the door behind him and felt his way along the wall until his foot hit the stone lip that marked the edge of the hearth. His fingers found a fire striker hanging from a peg and a chunk of flint below it. A cup of rushlights sat nearby. He could even feel a handful of tinder in the back of the alcove, dry grass from the meadows and wood shavings from the carpenter's workshop. Striking the flint against the curved chunk of steel, Sigrad was rewarded with a shower of sparks. He used the brief flash of light to aim them towards the tinder, then struck again. A few small embers sprang to life in the nest of dry grass. Blowing them into a flame, he pressed one of the rushlights against the ball of tinder until it ignited. His nose wrinkled as pungent smoke wafted into his face. The stalk of fat-soaked pith burned brightly, but tallow lights always smelled terrible compared to the expensive wax candles they used downstairs.

With the rushlight in hand, Sigrad lowered the hood of Lucy's cloak and crept across the room. Anastasia's cartoon panels hung on the wall to his left. The last time he'd been in here, the tapestry boxes had been stacked on a table by the opposite wall. An intrusive creak of the floorboards made him draw a sharp breath. It rushed out a moment later in a sigh of relief when he saw the boxes still piled on the same table. Holding the rushlight in his mouth, he lifted the topmost box down to the floor. It was much heavier than he'd expected, and there was a metallic knocking sound when he propped it up against the table leg. The source of the noise was a shackle lock affixed to the lid. That hadn't been there last time. Sigrad gave the lock a rattle. It felt light and loose, but the keyway was too small for his skeleton key. If he could find the right angle, he might be able to force the lock and break it, but that would be noisy. He clicked his tongue in frustration. All the other boxes had the same locks on them. How was he going to find the right pieces? It would take all night to break into each one in turn. The longer he dallied, the more likely it was that someone would catch him.

He unlooped the thong from around his neck and pulled out his knife. Along with looking pretty, it was both strong and sharp. Working the blade beneath one of the box's metal hinges, he began to wiggle and pry. There was a small amount of give as the nails loosened. He tried the second hinge, but this one proved to be more difficult. It had been hammered tightly into the wood, and no matter how hard he tried, he couldn't fit the tip of his knife underneath it.

Sigrad sat back and wiped his brow. Warm sweat clung to his clothing. He'd never get the tapestries out at this rate. If only he didn't need to be quiet, then he could fetch an axe and smash the boxes apart. How was he going to do it? He was afraid of failing Vesna. Maybe they could try again another night, but she wanted it done now. They might never get another opportunity with Lucy and Calia like this. Perhaps he could drag the boxes into the next room and toss them out the window... no, that was stupid. With better tools, he might be able to remove the locks and hinges, but he couldn't go searching through the workshops in the middle of the night.

Sensing that he was wasting precious time, he leaned forward again and began whittling at the box with his knife, trying to pick away the edge of the lid until he had room to slide his blade under the second hinge. It took a lot longer than he'd hoped, and a small pile of wood shavings had collected on his knees by the time he finished. Easing the hinges up one at a time, the lid came off. He cursed at what he found inside. It was one of the half-ruined pieces, not the ones Vesna wanted him to destroy. He heaved the box aside and pulled down another, then began the process again.

An hour later, his brow damp and his fingers aching, Sigrad realised he wasn't going to finish in time. He'd only opened five boxes, and there were dozens more to go. It was hopeless. He'd burned through two more rushlights as he worked, and every time he looked down their flames revealed the horrible mess of splinters and wood shavings he'd left on the floor.

As he pondered giving up, a terrible realisation struck Sigrad. There was no way to repair the damage he'd done. Even if he could force the nails back into the holes and reattach the hinges, the mangled wood would make it obvious that someone had forced the boxes open. He looked around in a panic. If he failed now, Lord Oswin would order the boxes kept under lock and key, probably downstairs in the treasury. There would be no hope of trying this again. Vesna would be furious with him.

He stared at the wood shavings. Some of them were as fine as the tinder in the hearth. What if he lit a fire? He could set the boxes alight. That would all but ensure the destruction of the right pieces.

Arson was a far more serious crime than destruction of property. People were hanged for it. And yet, the thought excited him. He didn't have to slink back to Vesna with his tail between his legs. He could still finish what he'd started. Just like the sensation of having his beautiful knife close to his heart, the thought of starting a fire in the queen's manor made Sigrad feel powerful. No one knew he was up here. Little Sigrad the page boy held the fate of this ancient tapestry in his hands.

He'd do it. He'd start the fire and slip out before anyone smelled smoke. By the time they realised what was happening, it would be too late. He didn't need to worry about the manor burning down; there were water cisterns in the house and buckets of earth for smothering flames. There had been two fires in the night during his time here, and both had resulted in little more than a few scorched timbers and blackened walls. Someone would extinguish the blaze before it got out of hand.

Taking his rushlight back to the stone alcove, he scooped up the leftover tinder and brought it to the table. He'd made dozens of fires in the woods as a child. It had always enthralled him, the process of gathering tinder, splitting wood into kindling, and arranging it in a pile until an ember in a handful of smouldering grass became a conflagration that could ignite a whole tree. It was a beautiful kind of destruction.

At first he thought to stack the boxes in the middle of the room, leaning them up against one another the way he would've arranged logs for a bonfire, but if he set the fire directly on the floorboards, it might burn through into the great hall below. The hearth was far too small. He would just have to light it on top of the thick oak table instead. He heaped up the kindling and wood shavings, then adjusted the stacked boxes so they leaned over it in a small arch. He added the cup of rushlights to the kindling, cracked a few large splinters off the edges of the boxes, and arranged them over the top in a conical shape. It was a good fire. The boxes would catch.

Taking one of his still-burning rushlights, Sigrad pushed the tip into the pile of kindling until the flame spread. A bead of fresh sweat rolled down his temple as a flare of light illuminated his face. He should go now, before anyone smelled smoke. But there were always phantom smoky smells in a house like this. He could afford to stay and watch a while longer. The flames transfixed him as they ate away at the rushlights, spread to the big splinters, and finally started to lick at the box frames. Shadows danced about the room as Sigrad fiddled with his knife, stroking the silver patterns and fingering the keen edge. He loved to feel the heat of a fire pressing up against his face like a warm hand, raising the temperature of his skin until it began to tingle. Little embers rose from the kindling as the updraft caught them. The boxes were burning on their own now. He knew he should go, but he kept on staring.

Only when the warm tingle on his cheek suddenly grew sharp did he step back. He swatted at the flash of pain, thinking that an ember must have fallen on him. A second spark fell on his shoulder, and he looked up with a start.

It was worse than that. Some of the embers had drifted all the way to the ceiling and ignited whatever flammable detritus had accumulated atop the roof beams. Another burning fragment fell on his face, this one bouncing off his cheek and landing inside his hood. He let go of his knife and tore off Lucy's cloak in a panic, feeling the ember stinging his neck the whole time. The realisation that he'd waited too long struck him like a blow, the mesmerising warmth of the fire immediately dispelled. He threw off the cloak and ran to the door, suddenly afraid that he would find it stuck and be trapped in here with the flames. But it was only a momentary fear. The door swung open, and he found the landing empty. No one had been woken by the smoke yet. He forced himself to close the door carefully and crept to the top of the stairs.

His feet locked in place when he saw two shadowy figures coming up from the servants' hall towards him. Praying that he hadn't been seen, he scuttled back into the darkness and cast about for another escape route. There was nowhere for him to go except into one of the rooms, and most of those had people sleeping inside them. He retraced his steps and slipped back into the weaving room. The heat of the blaze seemed to have grown in the few moments he'd been outside. A second door led out of this chamber into one of the weaving rooms. He went through it, emerging into Calia and Rovena's work area. There wasn't much of a moon that evening, but Sigrad could see just enough light shining through one of the windows to navigate his way past the shadowy looms towards it. It was glazed with diamonds of translucent glass set into metal latticework. Windows like this couldn't be opened. But he knew there were shuttered windows in this room as well, so he felt his way along the wall until he found one. To his relief, the shutters were only held closed by a simple latch. Throwing them open, Sigrad clambered out into the cold night air and lowered himself over the windowsill.

It was a daunting drop to the courtyard below. If he jumped from here, he might break his legs. Clinging on with his fingertips, he lowered himself as far as he could, his bare toes scraping the plastered stone in search of a foothold. He hesitated, realising that he'd left his boots inside. And where was his knife? He couldn't feel its reassuring weight against his chest anymore. A gasp of anguish left his throat. He must've dropped it when he tore off Lucy's cloak! He tried to pull himself back up, but it was too late. His fingers slipped off the windowsill, one hand and then the other. The ground rose to meet him with a jarring slam. His legs folded beneath him and he rolled over with a grunt of pain. He lay there for a second, staring up at the sky, thinking that he might still be able to hurry upstairs and fetch his knife back, but it was too late. Even as he picked himself up, the cries of "Fire! Fire!" began sounding from inside.

Sigrad swallowed his distress and crept into the shadows behind the stable. He could always buy a new knife. He'd done what Vesna asked of him. The old tapestry had been destroyed, and he would be rewarded for it.

CHAPTER 16

The cry of "Fire!" was a terrible one to wake up to. Every child was taught to fear it. When Calia was a baby, her parents' house had burned to the ground. She couldn't remember anything about that night, but there was something about the flash of heat and the cloying taste of smoke that always sparked terror in her, as if her unconscious mind still recalled the danger she'd faced as an infant.

She shot upright, clutching Rovena's arm as her friend rose beside her. Everyone else in the great hall was in a similar state of groggy confusion. The cries came again from the servants' hall.

"Fire! Upstairs! In the weaving rooms!"

Calia scrambled to her feet, still clothed in the work dress she'd worn to bed. It couldn't be, not the weaving rooms! No fires were ever lit up there unless it was exceptionally cold, and those were always extinguished well before bedtime. There hadn't been so much as a candle burning when she came downstairs earlier. The cry from the servants' hall came again, then the door burst open and one of the laundresses bellowed her warning into the great hall. Calia was the first person to reach her, her feet made quick with fear. All the tapestries were up there. Lucy's room was far away at the other end of the landing, but Calia was afraid for her friend as well.

She ran to the foot of the stairs where a group of people were already hauling heavy fire buckets out of the storeroom. Toby the cook pushed one into her hands, and before she knew it she was hurrying upstairs, sandy earth spilling over the bucket's rim with each frantic step. Ahead of her, a flickering light silhouetted the other firefighters. About a dozen people had gathered on the landing, Lucy among them. Some were pushing their way into the weaving room with buckets while others looked on in horror. Calia felt a terrible pinch of anguish as she glimpsed flames raging like hellfire through the open door. The tapestries and Ana's cartoons were all in there. The thought of so much precious art going up in flames hurt her like a physical wound. Lucy grabbed her arm, urging her to stay back and give her bucket to one of the men, but Calia threw her off and went in.

The weaving room was like a furnace, the table in the far corner completely engulfed in flames. They clawed at the walls, reaching up for the ceiling where one of the beams was already charring in a blaze. Calia remembered the hollow shell of Castle Ashmount, those empty gaps that had once held roof beams, and had a vision of the manor being reduced to a similar blackened ruin. Once a roof caught fire, it was almost impossible to put out.

A pair of Lord Oswin's burly men-at-arms were fighting back the blaze. They'd dragged over one of the step ladders used for hanging the cartoon panels and repurposed it to reach the beams. The first man perched on the topmost step swinging a wet wool blanket at the flames licking the roof. His partner was soaking a second blanket in a bucket of water getting ready to pass it up to him. The fire in the corner was being ignored, though Calia could see puddles of water and scattered earth where people had emptied fire buckets in its direction. Anastasia's cartoons were still untouched, but the stack of boxes that held the original Farren Vale blazed like a pyre, sending another spike of agony through Calia's heart. Running forward, she got as close as she dared and upended her bucket over the boxes. A gust of hot air hit her face. For a second, it looked like the flames had died down, but it wasn't enough. Most of the earth she'd thrown scattered to the floor, and the fire sprang back to life.

She took a step back and almost tripped over a pair of discarded boots. She kicked them aside and turned to take another bucket from the person coming in behind her. The beginnings of a bucket chain began to form with Calia at the front. She hurled water and earth over the pile of boxes, her thin arms straining with the effort. Her face stung from the heat, and she could smell something horrible like burning hair. Each breath made her cough and retch, her vision blurring as the smoke brought tears to her eyes. One of the men-at-arms pushed her aside and took her place, seizing the next bucket with greater strength than she'd been able to muster.

"Save the boxes!" she cried in a raspy voice.

The man shook his head, hurling water up at the roof beams instead. "We have to stop it reaching the roof!"

Calia knew he was right, but it didn't make the pain of watching the boxes disintegrate beneath the flames any easier. For a hundred years, the Farren Vale had hung in that cellar beneath Castle Ashmount. Now it was dying before her eyes. Dashing forward, she reached up and grabbed the edge of a box at the top of the stack. The wood was warm and covered with wet mud, but only the far corner was on fire. Calia heaved with all her strength, her sore muscles protesting as the heavy box slid down and toppled to the floor. She dragged it away from the flames, then went back to get another. Some of the people behind her saw what she was doing and hurried forward to help. They beat at the still-burning edges of the rescued boxes with their clothes, smothering the flames until they were extinguished.

When Calia pulled down a third box, a flame scorched the back of her hand, forcing her to let go with a cry of pain. The box toppled, fell, and struck the top of the table with an almighty crash. It was a miracle the table had remained standing as long as it had. The impact strained the burning timbers beyond their limit, and the far end collapsed in an eruption of smoke and sparks. Calia threw herself back as the stack of boxes toppled towards her. She felt arms around her waist yanking her away. The avalanche of blazing wood barely missed her, and she fell to the floor in a tumble. The boards shook with the impact of the boxes. One after another, their heavy wooden frames cracked into the timbers, some of them splitting apart, others bouncing and sliding as they toppled crazily end-over-end. Calia pushed herself away in a panic, but not fast enough. One of the boxes landed on its edge and seemed to hover there for a split second, a border of fire guttering around its frame, before it crashed down on Calia's right hand. She screamed as she felt bone breaking. The sting of the fire was nothing compared to the sudden numbing pain that shot up her arm. The person who'd grabbed her pulled her away, dragging her into a corner. Calia cradled her hand to her chest, afraid to move anything. Every twitch of her muscles sent a shock of pain up her wrist.

"Oh, Calia, I told you not to go!" Lucy's voice cut through the chaos. She put her arm beneath Calia's shoulders and helped her to her feet. The door had been blocked by the bucket chain behind them. Knowing there was nothing more she could do, Calia allowed her friend to lead her away into the adjoining workroom. She managed a final glance over her shoulder as they left. The blaze was finally dying down thanks to the stubborn efforts of the firefighters, but the sight of the shrivelled and smouldering tapestry fragments littering the floor dragged a sob of anguish from her throat. They were scattered like fallen soldiers amidst the wreckage of the burning boxes, their ancient threads torn and twisted into unrecognisable lumps. They looked so sorry and helpless, those precious squares. Calia couldn't help but bring each picture to life in her mind, imagining the king's entourage burning, the golden sunset turning black, those beautiful tree branches turning to ash.

That tapestry had been an inspiration to her. For a few joyful weeks, it had come back from the dead. Now it was gone forever. She wept as much for its loss as she did from the pain in her hand, leaning heavily against Lucy as they crossed the workroom.

Lord Oswin and a few others waited anxiously by the far door with candles. They must have come through from the royal solar. Anastasia and Vesna were with them. Through her tears, Calia shot the painter a vicious glare, as if to say, "Well? Are you happy now?" but Ana wasn't looking at her. Her face was pale and drawn, her eyes fixed on her mother.

"Calia's hurt her hand," Lucy said.

Lord Oswin, still dressed in a nightshirt, blinked as if suddenly remembering he was in charge. "Send for a physician," he told one of the servants. "Other people may be injured as well. Lucy, take her to the chapel and find Alan. He can tend her in the meantime."

"He's probably still in there," Anastasia said distractedly. "He was lighting candles for the eve of Saint Goldin's Day."

They went through the solar and downstairs to the chapel. Alan Treasurer was there praying beneath the candles on the altar. He had some basic medical training from his cloistered days and quickly diagnosed Calia with two broken bones in her hand. She grit her teeth through his poking and prodding, almost screaming in pain when he pressed down to make sure the break didn't need setting. She felt lightheaded and breathless, the taste of smoke sticking like tar in the back of her throat. Lucy sat with her arms around her, letting her rest her head on her shoulder as a few other people came in with minor burns. They told them that the fire had been put out. Not long after, a physician arrived from town. He applied ointments and dressings to the burns and bound up Calia's hand in a splint. Tomorrow, he would come back and put on a cast. When she told him she was a weaver, he said she wouldn't be able to work for at least a month.

That made her start crying all over again.

Calia didn't think to question how the fire had started until Lucy told her Lord Oswin was gathering the household in the great hall the next morning. They'd slept on blankets in the chapel, for the other end of the manor was still noisy with people cleaning up the damage. The pain in Calia's hand kept her up most of the night, only allowing her a few fitful hours of rest before dawn. Rovena offered her a potion of hot wine mixed with herbs that she said always helped her great-aunt with rheumatism. It had the desired effect of blunting the throbbing ache in Calia's palm, but whatever the herbs were, they were potent, and her head became foggy within minutes of quaffing the drink.

"Why does he want us in the hall?" she asked Lucy when she delivered the news.

"He says it's an inquest. He wants to know who's responsible for the fire."

"Is he holding court?" As lord of the manor, it was Lord Oswin's duty to preside over the local judiciary. His purview was typically minor disputes and offences, with serious crimes being handled by the king's judges and religious matters by the ecclesiastical courts.

"I'm not sure," Lucy replied. "Not formally, I don't think. But whatever he finds out, I'm sure it'll be important if someone ends up on trial."

"Who would set a fire on purpose? It's so spiteful!" Calia swallowed as she felt her anguish bubbling up again.

"It must have been an accident. Not even Ana would do something like that. It's a miracle her cartoons weren't damaged."

Calia agreed. She knew the Fialas weren't happy about her

new tapestry, but she'd seen the way Anastasia reacted to the discovery of the Farren Vale. She'd been just as enthralled by it as her. For an artist to destroy such an artefact would be a cardinal sin. But she also remembered the look Ana had given her mother last night. What had it meant? Calia frowned as she tried to clear her head, pain and grogginess slowing her thoughts. Had it been a look of guilt? Disbelief? Fear? If that look had concealed some dark secret, it wasn't one she could decipher right now.

She wished she could stay in the quiet chapel and rest, but if Lord Oswin had summoned everyone then she was obliged to make an appearance, even if her hand was hurting and her heart heavy with grief. She didn't want anyone thinking she'd had something to do with the fire.

The great hall was unusually quiet. Without the queen and her entourage present, there were only a few dozen people living at the manor permanently, most of whom were now clustered around the high table. Lord Oswin sat in the large chair he used when holding court, and the town constable was with him. Whether this was a formal proceeding or not, the royal bailiff was clearly serious about unearthing the truth. The constable and his menacing deputies would be ready to escort any suspects to the town jail where they would await trial.

Calia felt too woozy to stand, so she and Lucy found seats with Rovena off to the side. From where they were sitting, they could see Anastasia and Vesna standing close behind Lord Oswin's chair. Calia studied Ana's face, trying to unearth some hint of the expression she'd glimpsed last night, but all she found was a wall of stony composure.

"I have gathered you all here to determine exactly what happened last night," Lord Oswin began once everyone was present. "As you know, there was a fire in the weaving rooms. The reclaimed pieces of the Farren Vale were irreparably damaged, as was a substantial amount of the queen's property. Had the fire burned much longer, the roof would have caught alight." He swept his gaze over the crowd, his thunderous expression underlining the severity of the situation. He was out for blood. "Most fires are accidental. Some are not. Arson is a serious offence, one that bears the full weight of the king's law. I want to begin by establishing everything that happened in that room last night. Would all of our weavers step forward."

Calia reluctantly rose and joined the others. They stood before the high table in a line like petitioners awaiting their lord's judgement. One by one, they were asked to recount what had happened before they finished work. Everyone's testimony was consistent; no fires had been lit in the weaving rooms that day, not even candles. Everyone had left before the light faded, and Anastasia herself had locked the doors.

The servants were interrogated next. Several of them had keys that could have opened the weaving room. Had they gone in at any point after the weavers finished work? Had anyone carried a candle with them? Once again the responses were consistent and unanimous. No one had entered the weaving room yesterday evening. Someone might have been lying, but as the interrogation went on it seemed like everyone had an alibi with witnesses to corroborate it.

"The question, then," Lord Oswin continued, "is whether anyone entered the weaving rooms after the household was abed. A thief, perhaps, hoping to steal something valuable."

"Jacob Tinker was here last night," one of the cooks said. "That man's a rogue."

"He's no thief," Rovena countered.

"And he always does good work for us," said another cook.

Lord Oswin frowned and steepled his fingers. "Did he stay in the hall last night?"

"Lucy was with him last. She'd know."

Calia felt Lucy shift uncomfortably as all eyes turned in their direction. If Jacob had been in her bed, she could give him an alibi, but doing so would damn her. Not everyone cared about unmarried couples sleeping together; they might tut and gossip, but it was a normal part of everyday life, even if the church did frown on extramarital relations. Unfortunately for Lucy, the church held great sway in this household. Queen Meredith did not stand for fornication under her roof, and Lord Oswin enforced her will aggressively. Lucy would probably be dismissed on the spot if the truth came out. To Calia's dismay, she saw the guilt written all over her friend's face.

"He was leaving just as I went to bed," Lucy began. "He didn't plan on staying the night."

"Did anyone see Jacob Tinker go upstairs?"

Silence answered Lord Oswin. He looked disappointed, as if he'd been expecting a swift and decisive conclusion. Instead of pressing Lucy further, he picked up a shiny object from the table and held it out so that everyone could see. It was a knife with a gemstone pommel and a handle inlaid with silver filigree.

"Was he using this knife at supper? It was found on the weaving room floor."

"No," Calia answered. "He had a plain one."

The other weavers murmured their agreement. Such an eye-catching knife wouldn't have gone unnoticed.

"This is a fine piece," Lord Oswin said. "Expensive, certainly. Not the sort of thing just anyone would carry around. I expect the owner is either wealthy or light-fingered." He let that hang in the air for a moment, letting everyone draw their own conclusions. If the knife belonged to a member of the royal household, that narrowed the list of suspects considerably. Only the senior servants and artisans would be able to afford such a treasure. Calia felt queasy, her anxiety mingling with the pain of her broken hand and the fog of Rovena's potion.

"There was that other article as well, my lord," Vesna Fiala said.

"Yes. Do you have it?"

Vesna turned around and picked something up off the floor. It was damp and dirty: a damaged cloak that had been singed in several places. When she turned it around, Calia's heart dropped to the pit of her stomach. The red pattern on the back was unmistakable. It was Lucy's.

For a dreadful moment, nobody spoke.

"That's Lucy's cloak," Elaine Weaver said.

"Yes," Lucy confirmed in a small voice. "It's mine."

Lord Oswin's expression darkened. "Anastasia and Vesna went over the room this morning and confirmed that the knife and this cloak were the only items out of place. Can you explain how they got there?"

A sudden thought occurred to Calia, something she'd all but forgotten in the chaos of the fire. "There were some boots, too! Right in the middle of the room. I remember because I tripped over them. No one ever leaves their boots in there. Perhaps if they match someone's feet–"

"They must have belonged to one of the firefighters," Vesna interrupted her. "There were no boots there this morning."

"Well?" Lord Oswin said, still glaring at Lucy. "Did you drop your cloak by accident?"

She shook her head, her words a frightened mumble. "No. No, I don't know how it got there. I was wearing it last night, but not when the fire started. I went straight to bed after supper."

"No you didn't," Bess Weaver said. "I saw you sneaking around down here later on. I thought you'd slipped out to go and see your tinker. Then you went upstairs. That wasn't too long before the fire started, as I recall."

"That's true," said Toby Cook. "I saw her wearing that cloak as well. Couldn't have been more than an hour later when I went up and found the fire."

Lucy had gone pale. She shook her head, but when her lips moved no sound came out. She was trapped in an impossible limbo. The evidence was mounting against her, and her only alibi was to admit that she'd been with Jacob. Calia felt sick. This was just like what had happened with Goldie. The interrogation. The judgement. The accusations coming from all sides. Was this Anastasia's doing again? The painter's face was set like a statue. She stared at the far wall, stoically detached from the proceedings. Only Vesna seemed engaged. She was watching Lucy intently. Calia couldn't be sure, but she thought the woman looked almost excited.

Guilty memories yanked at Calia, reminding her that Goldie might still be here if she'd argued harder in her defence. She had to make her voice heard. Gripping Rovena's arm, she rose to her feet.

"It sounds like you're all accusing Lucy of this! Well, it wasn't her. She'd never do such a thing."

"Then what was she doing last night, and how did her cloak end up in that room?" Vesna's voice snapped like a leather whip.

"There could be a hundred reasons! Perhaps she left it there and forgot. Perhaps she dropped it in the commotion and someone used it to smother the fire. Perhaps–" Calia tried to finish with a convincing third point, but she suddenly felt dizzy and had to clutch Rovena's arm for support.

"You're only making guesses," Vesna said. "That cloak is firm evidence, as is the knife. It couldn't belong to any of the servants. Lucy is one of the few people in this household who could afford it."

Calia struggled to come up with a rebuttal. Her hand throbbed like a hot bruise. Her eyes itched from lack of sleep. Vesna had already begun speaking again before she cut her off with the only desperate plea she could think of: "Why?! Why would she do something like this? It's absurd! Burning the house she works in, putting everything at risk, ruining my tapestry!" Calia realised there were tears in her eyes. She wasn't sure which tapestry she was talking about, the Farren Vale, or her smaller copy. The art she loved had been taken from her. She couldn't lose her best friend as well.

"Temper your emotions, Calia," Lord Oswin said impatiently.

"But just think! We all know Lucy. She's no troublemaker."

It looked like Vesna was desperate to say something. Her eyes flashed about the room, her lips parted, some comment on the tip of her tongue. But she held off, and her patience was rewarded.

"Then what were you two fighting about last night?" Bess asked.

"Mhm," Elaine chimed in on cue. "You got so upset that you threw your cup and stormed out."

"No I didn't!"

"Oh, come on. It's obvious. Lucy looked guilty as sin the moment Jacob Tinker's name came up. You two were fighting over him, weren't you?"

"Several of our weavers were, as I recall," Vesna said. "He was charming everyone at their table last night."

Calia shook her head as she felt control of the situation slipping away from her. "That isn't true!"

"Calia isn't that kind of woman," Rovena said.

"Isn't she?" Vesna retorted. "She's managed to make Alderman Leander very fond of her." She turned to Lord Oswin. "I think we're starting to paint a picture of what happened, wouldn't you agree, my lord?"

The bailiff nodded, though he still looked uncertain.

Vesna went on: "If what everyone says is true, Lucy and Calia fought over the handsome tinker last night, and Lucy was later seen up and about after the household had gone to bed. Perhaps she made a reckless blunder. We all know how temperamental young women can be." She looked at Oswin again, who offered another nod. He was always ready to believe that women's tempers were the bane of sensible men like himself. "One too many cups of wine and a broken heart spurred her to rashness. She has a key to the upstairs rooms, doesn't she? I think she set that fire on purpose as a means of getting back at her friend, and before she knew it, it was out of control."

"No!" Calia cried. The throb in her hand had spread to her skull, pressing behind her eyes and pulsing in her ears.

"Lucy Tailor's service has never come into question before," Lord Oswin said. "I'd be disinclined to believe this were it not for the cloak and the knife. And we do know Lucy is a woman fond of her wine. Do you have anything to say for yourself?"

"I didn't do it," Lucy answered meekly. "Calia and I never fought."

"They've made up now, I'm sure," Vesna said. "Full of tears and regret. But that doesn't change the fact that her selfishness destroyed priceless property and endangered the lives of everyone in this house."

Calia looked around in desperation, searching for a friendly face that might speak up in their defence. Lucy was stunned. Rovena looked like she was still trying to process what was happening. They were all tired and hurting from last night's tragedy. Some of the servants wore sympathetic looks, but just as many seemed willing to believe the narrative Vesna was spinning. Even the other young weavers appeared all too ready to let their lingering jealousy over Jacob guide their feelings that morning. Lucy was drowning in a sea of accusations, and Calia felt too faint to rally her thoughts into an effective defence.

They would have to admit the truth about Jacob. It was the only way. If he could come forward and testify that he'd been with Lucy in her room last night, at least she would be spared the punishment of a criminal trial. But she would lose her job, and Calia would lose her closest friend. The tears that had been brimming in her eyes rolled down her cheeks. Damn Vesna. Damn that old witch and her daughter to hell. Calia had never been prone to hatred, and the realisation that someone had managed to drag that ugly emotion out of her made her tears fall all the heavier.

Then Anastasia spoke.
"Where was Sigrad last night?"

CHAPTER 17

"Why? Do you think he had something to do with it?" Lord Oswin said. "Sigrad! Where are you? Step forward."

There was the sound of a bench scraping and a shuffling of feet as the page approached the high table. It was the first time Calia had seen him all morning. He must have been hiding behind the cooks. What was Ana up to now? Did Sigrad have some fresh lie to spill that would further incriminate Lucy? But whatever this was, it didn't seem to be part of Vesna's plan. She grabbed her daughter's arm and whispered something urgent in her ear, but Ana paid no attention.

Sigrad stood before the high table with his hands clasped behind his back, eyes downcast.

"Where were you?" Anastasia repeated.

He didn't answer immediately. His eyes flicked up, going from Ana to Vesna like an ill-prepared minstrel suddenly called upon to perform before a crowd.

"I was with you, milady."

"No you weren't. I didn't see you all evening."

There was a rumble of dissent from the onlookers. The stone-faced composure Anastasia had worn all morning cracked as she stared at Sigrad with fire in her eyes. She looked angrier than Calia had ever seen her. When she spoke, there was a tremor in her voice that held the same pain Calia had felt when she saw the Farren Vale go up in flames.

"Explain yourself!"

Sigrad shifted from foot to foot, his fingers clenching and unclenching behind his back. "Well, I mean to say, I was in the royal solar."

"What were you doing there?" Lord Oswin demanded.

"I called for him," said Vesna. "You know how I like a bowl of warm water for my feet, especially when it's cold."

"It wasn't very cold last night, Mother," Ana replied acidly. The entire room had fallen silent, enthralled by this unexpected twist to the drama.

"You're always busy with your work. Of course you wouldn't have noticed. You were sketching by candlelight long after I put your sister to bed."

"What are you driving at with this, Anastasia?" Lord Oswin asked. "Do you think young Sigrad was involved in the fire as well?"

"I do, my lord. In fact, I think he was the only one involved. Calia is completely right; it's absurd to think that Lucy Tailor set fire to the manor. She isn't the type to act so rashly."

"Then how do you explain the knife and cloak?"

"I'm not sure. But before we jump to hasty conclusions, I'd like to know where Sigrad was when the fire started. I think we'd all agree that it's far more in his character to do something like this than it is Lucy's."

Oswin frowned. "Sigrad has performed his duties well during his time here."

"We all know him," Ana almost snapped at the bailiff. Vesna tugged at her arm again, and this time the two women exchanged a look that seemed to take some of the wind out of Ana's sails.

"I didn't do anything," Sigrad protested. "I was minding

my business in the solar making sure the lady Vesna had warm water, as she said."

"Is that true, Vesna?" Lord Oswin asked.

"Well," she replied hesitantly, as if realising that her answer might make her a target of suspicion, "I can't say that he was there all night. I dozed off on my cushions by the hearth."

"He wasn't there when the fire woke us," Ana said.

Sigrad's eyes were wide as he stared across the high table. Calia could see sweat beading on his brow. Had he really been involved? Her gut told her that Vesna was behind this, and it would make sense for her to send someone like Sigrad to do her dirty work. Surely Ana would be in on the plot as well, but the passion in her voice was that of a woman who felt deeply wronged. As ruthless as she was, perhaps even she had her limits. Vesna might have gone behind her back. There was a thread of shared purpose connecting them now, and Calia knew she had to seize it before it was too late.

"Who else would have seen Sigrad upstairs?" she asked.

"Myself and the Fialas were the only people sleeping in the royal solar," Lord Oswin said. "I went to bed early last night. I assume young Karaline was asleep as well."

"She was," Ana said with a frown.

"What about downstairs?" Calia asked. "There's only one set of stairs leading to the solar."

Ana's expression lit up again. "Alan Treasurer. He was keeping his vigil in the chapel all night. Anyone who went upstairs would have had to walk past him."

"Yes! He was still there when we came down after the fire."

"Alan?" Lord Oswin called. "Did you notice anyone using the stairs last night?"

The monk stepped forward. He was known for his keen eye and meticulous nature. Whatever he said here would carry weight.

"You went upstairs first, my lord, with two servants as I

recall. I recognised the sound of your walk, but not theirs, alas. They came back down less than half an hour later. Mistresses Anastasia and Karaline went up next, then Mistress Vesna after another hour. No one else."

"Perhaps I called for Sigrad earlier, then," Vesna said. "I forget sometimes." She reached up to brush her hair away from her face. It was a subtle motion, but it called attention to the persistent tremor in her hand. She was playing the part of the doddering old woman, though Calia was certain she couldn't have been much older than fifty. It seemed to work on Lord Oswin, for he accepted her explanation with an exasperated huff.

"So, Sigrad was not in the solar."

"I was!" the page protested. "I just didn't use those stairs. I came in through the upstairs door."

"The one that's kept locked?" Ana said. "The one that only the senior servants hold keys to?"

"Alright, maybe I wasn't up there. I slipped out to visit an alehouse in town. I didn't have anything to do with the fire! It was Lucy's cloak you found up there, wasn't it?"

"Lucy, are you sure you didn't leave your cloak somewhere else?" Calia said. She felt like they were teetering on the brink. If the cloak could be explained, Lucy might be saved.

"I was wearing it during supper. And I went upstairs. I didn't go to bed with it, though. I remember I had to get another blanket."

"So you could've left it down here?"

"Yes. Yes, I suppose I could've."

Ana held up the cloak for everyone to see. "Did anyone see this cloak lying around the hall?"

"You know, I think I did," Bess Weaver said. She'd changed her tune now that her mistress was on Lucy's side. For better or worse, she and Elaine could always be counted on to fight Anastasia's battles. "I saw it on the bench after everyone left."

"So anyone could've picked it up and worn it upstairs."

Lord Oswin gave another grunt of impatience. "Now we're even less certain of the culprit. I agree, I find it unlikely that Lucy would do something like this, but I'm not convinced Sigrad was involved either. He comes from a respectable family."

Calia sat back down, squeezing Lucy's arm with relief. Her friend wasn't out of the woods yet, but at least she was no longer the prime suspect. How could they prove that Sigrad and Vesna were in this together? They could ask Sigrad which alehouse he'd supposedly been to, but he could always lie again, and even if he had no alibi, that didn't prove he'd been the one to set the fire. The only thing she could think of was the knife.

"Are we sure no one's seen that knife before?" she asked. "It's so distinctive."

Everyone in the room shook their heads. Anastasia lifted the knife from the table, her eyes narrowing as she turned it over in her hands.

"Calia is right. It is very distinctive. So distinctive that I expect the maker recalls it very well–and who they sold it to."

"Indeed." Lord Oswin nodded as if he'd been thinking the same thing all along. "It bears the quality of a piece made in Ashmount. We'll show it to every jeweller in town until we get an answer."

The focus of the assembly had shifted away from Sigrad long enough that no one noticed him taking a step backwards. He looked pale and unsteady, but the second he acted it was with the alacrity of a bolting animal. He shoved Bess Weaver aside and vaulted the table behind her, putting it between himself and the others. The town constable shot to his feet, bellowing for his men to stop the page. But Sigrad was already one step ahead, weaving past the benches and kicking over a stool to trip anyone who followed him. A flurry of commotion forced the crowd apart as the constable's deputies and Lord Oswin's men-at-arms hurried to intercept the fleeing boy, but he made it to the door ahead of them. One of the men cursed loudly as he banged his foot on the fallen stool. The others squeezed past him, charging out into the courtyard where the noise of the chase receded.

Calia stood with her friends at the back of the group, unable to feel anything but intense relief. Sigrad had all but confessed his guilt by running. Lucy was safe. Lord Oswin and a few others moved to join the pursuit, but one of the deputies came back in before they reached the door.

"He went over the wall. We're getting some horses to go after him."

"I always knew he was a bad one," Bess said, making a show of nursing her elbow. "No compassion. A black soul."

That didn't stop you from gossiping with him every other evening, Calia thought, but she wasn't interested in getting into another argument. She was too exhausted. When she looked back at the high table, Vesna had disappeared. That was cunning of her. She didn't want anyone thinking too hard about her attempt to defend Sigrad. If she stayed out of the way, everyone would be talking about him instead of her.

"I think I need to lie down," she told Lucy.

"You and me both. I feel like I almost got run over by a cart."

"I was so afraid for you. It sounded like Lord Oswin was ready to throw you in jail."

"Let's go to my room. It'll be quiet there now."

"I don't suppose any of us will be working today," Rovena said.

The three of them crossed the room behind the high table to avoid the chattering crowd. Calia stopped next to Ana as they passed by.

"Thank you," she said haltingly, "for speaking up on Lucy's behalf."

Anastasia folded her arms with a look of irritation. "Inquests are supposed to unearth the truth. It was obvious she had nothing to do with it. I want that little runt to pay for what he did."

"Why do you suppose he did it?" Calia sensed she was treading dangerous ground, but she was desperate to understand what was going through the painter's head.

Ana looked away. "I don't know. He doesn't have any scruples."

She was lying. Even Calia could tell that much. Was there some deep hurt in her? A twisted guilt that had been edged out by righteous indignation? It angered Calia to think that she was covering for her mother, but it was different from the anger she'd felt before. She didn't think Ana was evil. Like all people, she was complex. Alongside her bitterness, her pride, and her arrogance, Calia had seen a woman who shared her passion for art the day they found the Farren Vale. That was the woman Karaline loved; a woman decent enough to do the right thing when it truly mattered.

Calia longed to say more, but her hand was throbbing and she felt lightheaded. She was still wrestling with her tumultuous feelings when they left the hall. Ana hadn't done the right thing with Goldie, that was for sure. Perhaps this flash of decency was a one-off. But it had been enough to rekindle a glimmer of Calia's respect for the woman.

* * *

Lord Oswin returned to the manor half an hour later. He'd gone out with his horse to join the pursuit while Ana waited anxiously in the courtyard. Part of her was worried about what Sigrad might say. Another part was desperate to see him punished. The rest was afraid to go inside and confront her mother.

"Damned fool boy went straight down the hillside into the valley," the bailiff said as he climbed off his charger. "He'll fall and break his neck more likely than not."

"You didn't catch him?"

"We couldn't take our horses down those rocks, and I wasn't about to risk a man's life sending them after him. The constable's riding down to try and catch him in the valley if he makes it that far. The problem is, he could hide on the hillside all night and force us to climb down to get him. Or he'll wait till dark, climb up again, and sneak off into the woods. We'll round up some hounds tomorrow and try to catch him if he makes it off the hill."

"A pity." Ana didn't know whether to feel relieved that Sigrad couldn't spill the truth or outraged that he might get away with what he'd done. Vesna was the true culprit, of course. Ana had suspected as much all night, yet she'd dared not ask. It wasn't until Vesna started accusing Lucy that her suspicions had been confirmed. The best way to get away with a crime was to put it on someone else.

Ana wondered whether this was her fault. Her mother had said something ugly would have to happen if she couldn't handle things herself. But it was easier to blame Sigrad. He was the one who'd set the flame. If she directed her anger at him, she didn't have to think about the part she or her mother had played in it. She took a deep breath to steady herself. Perhaps this was for the best. Calia couldn't finish her tapestry with the reference material destroyed. That was good. It was what they'd wanted.

Ana told herself that over and over as she paced the courtyard, but she couldn't believe it. The price was too high. She wanted to scream and weep when she thought about that priceless tapestry shrivelling up in flames. Being ruthless was one thing–putting others down to lift yourself up was only necessary if you wanted to get ahead–but how much was too much? Once you started destroying the very things you professed to love, was any reward truly worth that price?

An idea for a painting crept into Ana's mind as she paced. A victorious soldier, his armour bloodstained and torn, holding a banner aloft as he stood on a mound of ashes that had once been a great manor. He was at the top, alright. The top of a ruin. Something beautiful reduced to ash in the pursuit of his victory; an end rendered pyrrhic by its means.

Had last night's alarm sounded just a few moments later, would she have been standing on her own mound of ashes that morning?

She was thinking like an artist, she told herself, losing her good sense to whimsy and emotion. That wasn't how Vesna had taught her to be. She should be focused on Sigrad, what to do if he was caught, how she might defend her mother if he revealed the truth.

But just like her efforts to undermine Calia, she couldn't muster the enthusiasm for it. She was tired. For years she'd been rising to the challenges her mother placed before her, climbing step after heightening step and stamping down anyone who tried to come after her. Was this to be her whole life? An endless struggle to stay on top? When would there not be some bright new artist rivalling her for the queen's favour? She couldn't fight them all.

She didn't realise how long she'd been pacing the courtyard until the bell rang for the midday meal. Her stomach twisted at the thought of seeing Vesna. How was she going to explain what she'd done? She'd betrayed her, weakened their standing, and incriminated the most useful ally they had in Ashmount House. In one fell swoop, she'd undone months of work. The guilt shivered up her spine, scratching at her body like a cloak of briars.

In her heart, she felt like she'd done the right thing, but her mind told her otherwise. Perhaps she'd done the right thing for Lucy and Calia, but not Vesna or herself. Who did she owe more to, a pair of women she barely even knew, or the mentor who'd made her everything she was?

With faltering steps, she went inside to face her mother's wrath.

Vesna wasn't in the great hall with everyone else. Hardly anyone was eating; the house still bubbled with gossip about the dramatic events of that morning. Ana went upstairs to the solar and found her mother in their room. Karaline sat in the corner clutching Tappy to her chest. It looked like she'd been crying. Feeling a surge of compassion for her sister, Ana went to her.

Vesna grabbed her arm before she could make it across the room and hit her in the face. It wasn't a chiding slap, but a full blow. Despite the act she'd put on earlier, she was no doddering invalid. Ana's vision flashed red as her mother's knuckles cracked into her temple. She stumbled and fell, her knees bursting with pain as they hit the floor hard. Karaline screamed.

"Shut up!" Vesna yelled at her. "Why are you such children, both of you?! Do you realise what you've done, Nastya?"

The guilt writhing in Ana's stomach made her want to vomit. She nursed her aching cheekbone, torn between shame and anger.

"He almost burned the manor down! My paintings, my tapestry, everything!"

"So you thought you'd make things even worse? The boy was a fool. I told him to tear up the old tapestry, not set a fire. They were all ready to believe Lucy Tailor was the one responsible until you opened your stupid mouth."

"That tapestry was priceless."

"And who was it helping? Us? No, it was Calia's pet project. Now that it's gone, everyone can focus on the one that matters again, no thanks to you."

Ana shut her mouth and looked away, bottling up her rage until tears filled her eyes. What could she say? That she cared more about the old Farren Vale than her new copy? That she'd rather see Sigrad punished than keep him around as a lackey? Those were stupid, self-defeating thoughts that would only make Vesna angrier. She stayed there on the floor, wretched with shame.

"I'm glad Lucy didn't get in trouble," Karaline said quietly.

Vesna stared at Ana for a moment longer before turning to her younger daughter. She bent down so that they were at eye level. Kara shrank back in her seat, holding Tappy up as if the doll would protect her.

"Put that thing down, Karaline."

She shook her head fearfully. Vesna stared at her in silence, waiting patiently, then with a sudden burst of anger she grabbed Tappy and ripped her from Karaline's grasp. The girl wailed in anguish, trying to grab the doll back, but Vesna shoved her into her seat.

"You're not a child. Neither of you are!" Vesna threw Tappy to the floor with such force that the cord holding the two legs broke. They rolled away as Vesna brought her boot down on the torso, shattering the finely made toy into splinters. Karaline choked a scream through her sobs.

Ana felt numb. She was just as much a child as her sister in that moment, a thousand leagues away from the woman who'd confidently addressed the inquest that morning.

Her throat felt tight and swollen as she stared at the shattered splinters of Tappy's body, the doll's painted face split in two, the cloth dress crumpled with the imprint of Vesna's boot.

"I hate you," she whispered. The words were so quiet she barely heard them. Pathetically quiet. Her hands began to shake as she listened to the sound of her sister sobbing. The shame inside her flared up like wildfire, angry and delirious and desperate. "I hate you!"

Vesna took a step toward her. Fear shot through Ana as her arm tingled, imagining Vesna's sharp fingernails digging into her, the slash of her palm, the crack of her knuckles. She flew to her feet and shoved her mother in the chest as hard as she could. Vesna's eyes widened as she stumbled back, tripping over the painting stand and dragging it down as she fell to the floor with a crash. She stared up at her daughter, incredulous with rage.

"You ungrateful sow!"

"Get out!" Ana shrieked. "Get out of my room!"

"This is *our* room!"

"The queen hired me, not you! Get out!"

Vesna regained her footing in an undignified scramble. Her expression was drawn with anger, but there was uncertainty there now. Ana wasn't a little girl she could bully anymore. The balance of power between them had shifted. A mutual understanding had just been strained to breaking point, and something had snapped.

"When you realise how stupid you've been," Vesna said through gritted teeth, "I'll be waiting for your apology." She turned and marched out of the room, slamming the door behind her.

Ana hurried to her sister's side. She swept Karaline into her arms, hugging the weeping girl as tight as she could.

"Tappy," Kara sobbed.

Ana sat on her bed and slumped against the wall. She held Karaline close, her throat so tight she couldn't speak. Eventually, her sister's sobs softened into sniffles. Ana stroked her hair, soothing her into the miserable doze that followed a child's anguish. She couldn't bear to think about what she'd just done, nor what it meant for her relationship with her mother going forward. Just like the Farren Vale disintegrating in that fire, something that had been meticulously woven over the course of years had just been rent asunder.

But as long as she was holding Karaline, she didn't have to think about it. Comforting her little sister was more important. Miserable though she was, the warmth between their bodies brought a kind of peace to her soul.

A while later, when Karaline had grown quiet, Ana bent down to pick up one of Tappy's legs. Her sister whimpered fitfully. With a soothing "shh," Ana returned to her sitting position, and Kara quietened once more. She turned the doll's leg over in her hands, wondering whether it might be repaired. It seemed unlikely. The body was the most delicate part, and Vesna's boot heel had split it into pieces.

There was a length of metal protruding from the leg that Ana didn't recognise. It had been tucked into a hole alongside the piece of cord that attached the leg to the body. She drew the metal piece out, revealing it to be a sturdy bronze sewing needle. It looked familiar. She'd seen Karaline sewing with it before, hadn't she? But no, there was something else. She thought about it for a moment, then it came to her. This was the needle Calia had used when she first came to Ashmount House. She recalled thinking of it as a tailor's quirk, a little tool she was fond of using when she worked with thread.

"Was this a present for you?" Ana murmured, but either her voice was too quiet or Kara was in too much of a doze to hear her. A swell of jealousy rose in her chest as she pictured her sister playing at sewing with Calia and Lucy, stealing away the time she should've had with her. For an instant, she wanted to press her thumb into the middle of the needle and snap it. Then she thought of Vesna stamping the doll to pieces, and her resentment turned inward.

She tucked the needle safely back into Tappy's leg and pressed it into Karaline's hand.

CHAPTER 18

The day after Sigrad went missing, Anastasia moved out of Ashmount House. The news came as a surprise to everyone. She told Lord Oswin she needed peace and privacy for her painting after the recent commotion, but she would still visit every day to make sure work on the tapestry continued as planned. Rovena and the other weavers suspected there was more to it than that. People had heard banging and raised voices coming from the Fialas' room on the day of the inquest. When Ana moved out, she took Karaline with her, but Vesna remained behind. There had obviously been some sort of row.

For Calia's part, she was happy. Seeing less of Anastasia could only be a good thing, and Karaline would surely get on better without her vile mother around. It helped take the edge off the malaise she threatened to fall into in the aftermath of the fire. With her hand sealed in a wax cast and her arm in a sling, she could do no more than the most basic work, and even that was at a snail's pace. Every time she sat down in front of her loom, her fingers itched to tie knots and tug at the heddle, but the physician had impressed upon her the importance of keeping her hand still if she didn't want the damage to become permanent.

She didn't know what would become of her tapestry now. Without the original to copy from, she doubted she could recreate the beautiful border of hanging branches accurately. Perhaps the queen would call off the project and Calia would go back to weaving squares for Ana again.

Lord Oswin's men failed to track down Sigrad. For several days they roamed the valley and woods with hunting dogs to no avail. Either the boy had fallen to his death on the hillside, or he'd escaped and become an outlaw. One way or another, they probably wouldn't see him again. Calia didn't know much about outlawry, but it seemed almost as dire a fate as going to the noose. Wanted outlaws couldn't return to civilised society. They would be arrested if they did. They had to live in the woods and survive on their own, or else go far, far away where no one knew them and try to start over. The thought of abandoning friends and family seemed horrible to Calia, but perhaps Sigrad didn't have anyone he cared about. Did people like that mind being outlaws?

She tried not to dwell on such things, but it was difficult when she didn't have work to distract her. After a few days of glacial progress on her tapestry, she told Lord Oswin she wouldn't be able to continue until her hand was better. To his credit, he was sympathetic. He seemed to harbour some lingering guilt over his willingness to believe that Lucy had started the fire. He told Calia she was welcome to stay at the manor while her hand healed, but he would have to pause her wages. That was alright with her. Besides the occasional article of clothing, she barely spent money on anything. Most of it went home to her parents, and the rest was more than enough to see her through a month without work. She would just have to find one-handed jobs to keep herself busy. At Lucy's insistence, she put the word about that she was looking for some temporary light work, but no one at the manor had anything for her. It was a quiet time of year for them, and no employers in town were looking for a one-handed assistant either.

A week and a half into her recovery, Calia was surprised by a knock at Lucy's door. She'd been helping her friend organise her workshop, folding and cutting fabric while Lucy was at market. When she opened the door, she found Anastasia staring down at her.

"I hear you're looking for work."

Calia blinked in bemusement. "Yes. Something simple while my hand mends."

"I need someone to mind Karaline. I don't like leaving her on her own while I'm here at the manor. People say you're good with children." Ana paused, then with some reluctance she added: "She's been asking after you and Lucy since we moved out."

"Can she not come here with you?"

"No." The warning look on Ana's face told Calia to drop this line of inquiry immediately. Apparently visiting the manor and entrusting Karaline to Vesna were off the table.

"Very well. I can go right away if you'd like. I've missed her too. Where are you staying?"

"We're renting a room in Ferald and Sara Goldsmith's house. They'll be there during the day, but they don't want Karaline bothering them in the workshop. Don't you want to know your wages?"

"Oh, I don't really mind. I'm not wanting for money. I just need something to keep me busy."

Ana frowned. "Well, I'll pay you a silver shilling a week."

"That's very generous of you."

"I expect you to earn it. Karaline's interested in sewing. Why don't you teach her something useful?"

"Gladly." Calia decided not to ask about what had happened to the plans for Kara to marry a nobleman instead of becoming a tailor. Ana was easier to deal with when she was being tight-lipped and professional. As long as they avoided the topic of Vesna, perhaps their relationship going forward could be a cordial one.

"Come along then. Fetch whatever you need and I'll show you to the house."

Calia finished tidying Lucy's work table and went to collect her sewing box. She'd left it by her work area in the weaving room. Ana followed her in silence. Rovena looked up from her loom with a raised brow when they came in. She was making good progress on one of the central segments of Ana's tapestry, her weft shining with silk and silver sunbeams lancing across the sky.

As Calia packed up her sewing box, Ana came to stand in front of her loom.

"Will you finish it?"

Calia's spirits fell when she stared at the half-finished tapestry. She didn't want to have this conversation with Anastasia. They always disagreed when it came to weaving, and she had no desire to rub salt in the wound of her faltering project.

"I don't know."

"Why not?"

Calia sighed. "Because the original is gone. I can't copy something that doesn't exist."

"You never copied my cartoons accurately."

Calia almost voiced a sharp retort before realising that Ana hadn't meant it as a criticism.

"Well, no. But I still needed them as a reference."

"You have a reference for most of the tapestry. I don't see why you can't complete it and improvise the missing details once you get to the top."

"It wouldn't be the same. The queen commissioned me to recreate the original, not make up something new."

Ana scoffed. "How is she going to know? The original is gone. As long as you weave something that captures the same effect, I doubt she'll remember the difference. You'll be praised for preserving it in your memory."

"That sounds dishonest."

"What does it matter? It'll please the queen, won't it?"

"I suppose it might," Calia conceded.

"I thought you'd leap at the chance to do things your way."

There was something odd about Ana's behaviour. She was still her sharp, hard-edged self, but she wasn't berating and criticising. She sounded more like an impatient mentor trying to instruct a troublesome student.

"You're right," Calia said. "I would like that. I've always been told I work best when I have a little freedom."

"It's not the way weaving's usually done."

"No. People want weavers who do exactly as they're told."

Ana frowned, but she held her tongue. "Have you got your things?"

"Yes."

"Come on then."

They left the manor and headed into town. Calia had heard of Ferald and Sara Goldsmith, but she didn't know where they lived. They were among the respected jewellers of Ashmount, with a reputation for high-quality work that took a long time to finish. They didn't live close to the marketplace like many of the more commercial jewellers, but at the end of a street on the south side of town near the castle. Their house was a sumptuous and expensive one, nowhere near the size of Ashmount Manor, but built in a similar style with a stone storey housing their workshop beneath upstairs living chambers built from timber. The middle-aged couple were working when Calia came in, Sara delicately bending wire around a ring with a set of pliers while Ferald tended a hot crucible in a wall-built forge. They seemed quiet and gentle people, welcoming her politely when Ana made the introductions. They said their son and daughter had both moved out to start families within the past year, so they had ample space for guests.

Karaline was sitting by herself in a parlour upstairs, poking at a torn stocking with Calia's needle and a too-short length of thread. Her expression lit up when they came in.

She hopped to her feet and threw her arms around Calia's waist.

"You brought her!"

Calia couldn't help but smile. It had only been a couple of weeks since they last saw each other, but that could be a long time for a child. She wondered whether Ana approved of their friendship. She'd always been careful to hide her affection for Karaline in public lest it caused any upset.

Ana seemed momentarily pained, resentful of her sister's affection for this other woman, but any ill feelings she might have harboured melted away when she saw the look on the girl's face. She actually smiled. Calia couldn't be sure, but it might have been the first time she'd seen Ana looking happy. It was an odd emotion for the painter to wear, pleasant, yet sad somehow, as though she knew it didn't really belong.

"Calia will be minding you while I'm out. Make sure you behave for her, and I'm sure she'll teach you how to use that needle properly."

"Can Lucy come too?"

Ana pressed her lips into a tight line.

"She's very busy," Calia interceded. "But perhaps we could all go for supper at Huw's together like we used to?"

Ana nodded. "Yes. That would be best. The Goldsmiths like their peace. They wouldn't take kindly to me filling their house with strangers."

Calia suspected Ana just didn't want to see Lucy after what had happened at the inquest, but she kept that to herself. Professional and cordial.

"I'd like that," Kara said. "I want to show her all my sewing."

"Have you been doing lots?" Calia asked.

"Yes. There's nothing else to do here. I'm making mittens for winter."

"Why don't you show me?"

Karaline took her into a bedroom and Calia heard the sound of the parlour door shutting behind them. When she looked back, Ana had gone.

Anastasia remained distant in the following weeks. Sometimes she was gone all day, leaving the Goldsmiths' house before Calia arrived and only returning after she left. It was almost as if Karaline was being neglected again, but at least this time Ana left her with company. Calia did her best to keep the girl occupied. They sewed together in the mornings, visited the market to get their meals at midday, and went out walking in the afternoons. Their treks took them around the town, up to the castle, and a short ways into the valley, but neither of them were enthusiastic hikers. They preferred to meander along as they absorbed the world around them, watching ants march their trails and rabbits nibble at dandelion stems. Two nights a week, they met up with Lucy for supper at Huw's house. It was during those evenings that Karaline seemed happiest of all. Calia wished she could have said the same for the other days. Whatever had happened between the Fialas, it was serious. Calia tried her best not to pry, for she was worried that Ana would stop her from visiting if she poked her nose where it didn't belong, but in the end she couldn't help herself.

"I haven't seen Tappy recently," she said to Kara one rainy day when they were sewing at the parlour table. Calia couldn't do much one-handed, so she watched and gave instructions instead.

Karaline seemed to shrink into herself, clutching at the mitten she was making the same way she'd used to clutch her doll. A tearful edge entered her voice as she said: "Mother broke her."

Calia's heart went out to Karaline. She knew that losing a treasured toy held a special kind of pain for a child.

"I don't know why," Kara continued. "She just took her and stamped on her, and she hit Ana and pushed her on the floor. But Ana pushed her back and made her leave. We hate her."

"I don't think she's a very nice woman."

"She's horrible. I wish it was just me and Ana."

"Does Ana want that too?"

Karaline shrugged. "I miss Tappy."

Fearing the poor girl might be about to cry, Calia said: "Why don't we make you a new doll? You could make it yourself. I'll help you measure out some cloth and cut the pieces, then you can sew them all together. We'll stuff it with straw so that it's nice and soft when you hug it."

Kara's expression brightened. "Can I really make something like that?"

"You can make anything out of cloth and thread. Anything you like. I'll show you how."

"Could we make a tent?"

Calia smiled. "Best we stick to small things first. What sort of doll do you think you'd like?"

They spent the rest of the morning drawing ideas for dolls on birch bark using Ana's sketching charcoal. Once Karaline had settled on a design, Calia showed her how to measure out the pieces and trace their shapes on a sheet of vellum. Using a sharp knife, they cut them out to use as guides once they had the right cloth. That way, Calia explained, Karaline could always make more dolls as long as she kept the guides.

"I could be a doll maker! I could sew them every day and sell them at market."

"You could! I expect there are lots of rich families who'd like to buy dolls in Ashmount."

"Then that's what I'll do. Ana can paint and I'll make dolls, and we can work together every day."

Karaline's spirits visibly improved after that. She was enthusiastic to go to market the next day and pick out cloth for her doll. Calia paid for it using her own money, letting the girl choose whatever she wanted. By the evening, Karaline had made an oddly-shaped torso out of blue felted cloth. A floppy head clung to the top waiting to be stuffed with straw and stitched on properly. After that, they would add arms, legs, and embroider a face. They could even make tiny clothes if Karaline wanted.

Calia stayed longer than usual that day, for her charge was impossible to pry away from her sewing. The Goldsmiths invited her to eat with them when supper was ready. Despite what Ana had said about guests, the couple seemed happy to have her. With their children gone, they enjoyed having young folk at the table.

Ferald went out to visit a friend after supper while Sara cleaned the cooking utensils with Karaline. She was a hard-working woman who abhorred the idea of hiring a housekeeper, and it was an attitude she was keen to impress upon Karaline. Calia expected she would have been roped into cleaning duty as well if it hadn't been for her hand.

The light was fading earlier than usual these days, so Calia said her goodbyes, kissing Karaline on the cheek before going upstairs to fetch her cloak. A strange sound reached her ears as she approached the parlour. Her felt boots were silent on the steps, and she hesitated outside the door, realising that whoever was inside wouldn't have heard her. Someone was sobbing, deeply and breathlessly. For a moment, Calia wondered who it was, for she had never heard that voice wrought with such pain and vulnerability before. But there was only one other person staying at the house. Ana must have slipped in while they were having supper.

Calia's first instinct was to back away and pretend she hadn't heard anything. She didn't have any business eavesdropping. Whatever was going on between Ana and Vesna, it was for the two of them to sort out.

But for some reason, she stayed where she was. Ana sounded uncomfortably like Karaline when she cried. A lonely girl, bereft of affection.

Calia eased the door open and peered through the crack. Anastasia was sitting at the parlour table with her forehead on the heel of her palm. It must have rained again that evening, for her long, copper-coloured hair hung in damp strands either side of her face. She was clutching Karaline's half-finished doll in her hand.

A lonely girl, bereft of affection, a doll the only vessel for her love.

Calia opened her mouth to speak, but she didn't know what to say. If she mentioned her cloak, it would sound like she'd come in by accident. That didn't feel like the right approach. She'd opened the door for another reason.

"Ana?"

A sharp intake of breath interrupted Anastasia's sobs. She coiled up like a flinching spider, rounding on Calia. She was ready to lash out, throw her misery in Calia's face, push her away with a burst of outrage.

Calia backed away in fear. When Ana saw the way she recoiled, her shoulders slumped, the angry cry that had been building in her throat diminishing into another sob.

"Leave me alone."

For a long moment, Calia stood there in silence, afraid that she would only make things worse by staying. But she'd opened the door for a reason. She went to the table and sat down opposite Anastasia.

She'd comforted many people before, friends, siblings, tearful children, but never an enemy. Never someone she held such mixed feelings for. She had a terrible fear that whatever she said would backfire and Karaline would pay the price for it. Yet Karaline was the reason she was here. Calia cared for the girl deeply. She'd grown fonder and fonder of her with each passing day, but she couldn't be her mother. Ana was the one who had to fill that role now. Whether she was comfortable with it or not, Calia needed to care about both of them, for Karaline's sake.

Ana refused to meet her gaze. She was still clutching the doll, staring stubbornly at the far edge of the table with red-rimmed eyes.

"Is it Vesna?" Calia asked.

Ana looked at the wall and scrunched up her face as if she wanted to scoff, but again she said nothing. The silence stretched out until her tears began to dry and her eyes narrowed back into something resembling her usual expression. Her heel began to drum the floorboards in tandem with a finger tapping the tabletop.

"Do you have a mother?" Ana's tone was still combative, but the question seemed honest enough.

"Of course."

"And what sort of woman is she?"

"She's quite blunt. A bit too blunt, most people would say. But she works very hard. She was away from home quite often when I was growing up. She's a merchant, you see. So my brother and sister and I took care of each other, like you do with Karaline."

"Did she send you here to make tapestries?"

"No. But she did encourage me. I wasn't sure at first. She said it would be a good experience, and I think she was right."

Ana sniffed. "Really?"

"Yes."

"You don't regret what's happened?"

Calia looked down at her injured hand. It didn't hurt anymore, and while the loss of the old Farren Vale still weighed heavily on her, she no longer felt bleak about it.

"My mother always told me that the bad things in life make the good shine all the brighter. I'd still like to finish my tapestry the way you suggested. I'll improvise what I remember from the old design."

A sardonic smile twitched the corner of Ana's mouth. "Your mother sounds nothing like mine. If I could choose another, I'd do it in a heartbeat. But I can't."

"Can't you?"

"What do you mean?"

"Well, my mother, the woman who raised me, she's actually my aunt by blood. Her brother was my father, and

I've never known the woman who bore me. If you want to look at it that way, my siblings are my cousins, and I'm not related to my papa at all."

"How miserable for you."

Ana's answer was so bemusing to Calia that she laughed. "Not at all. I can't think of anything that matters less. They raised me. My parents are my parents and my siblings are my siblings because that's what we've decided we mean to each other."

"Don't you want to know who your real mother is?"

"I do know who my real mother is. I suppose that's why I've never asked after the woman who bore me. It doesn't seem important. My parents would probably tell me if I asked, but I've never felt the need to."

Ana frowned. "I can't understand that."

"I just think family is who you love. I didn't have many blood relatives growing up, but I was always surrounded by family. My nana was an old friend of my mother's. My uncle and auntie were the stabler and his wife. We had dogs and horses and lots of visitors. It was as good a family as anyone could ask for."

"I don't believe in that at all. I don't love Vesna, but she's still my mother. I owe her everything I am."

Calia's heart sank. She thought she knew why Ana had been crying now.

"You don't have to go back to her if you don't want."

"Of course I do! How else am I supposed to keep going? She's the one who knows half the royal court. She fought for everything we have so that Kara and I could live comfortable lives. She taught me how to paint, and it's my duty to repay her."

"Even if she's making your life miserable?"

"I'm not a soft-hearted child."

"But Karaline is," Calia said, raising her voice for the first time. "And anyone can tell that she's far better off without Vesna around."

"You don't know anything!"

Calia felt her lip trembling as she met Ana's gaze. "I know you're a better person than your mother. She told Sigrad to start that fire, didn't she? You could've stayed quiet and let Lucy take the blame, but you did the right thing instead."

Ana's face paled and she looked away. "I didn't know she'd take it that far."

"Well, she did. She destroyed our tapestry and tried to blame Lucy. They could've hanged her."

"I won't let anything like that happen again."

"How can you be sure?"

"Because it was my fault!" Ana dropped the doll and banged her palm on the table. "I couldn't do what she asked of me, so she went and did it herself! If I'd only thought of a better plan, none of this would have happened!"

"She asked you to destroy the tapestry?"

Ana shook her head. "I wouldn't have done that. I was supposed to stop you from outdoing me. It's obvious the queen likes you more, inviting you to her table every night, letting you start your rival project." She sounded bitter, but Calia didn't think she truly believed the things she was saying. They sounded like someone else's words.

"It isn't a competition, Ana," she said softly. "I don't like sitting at the queen's table. I'd rather be in the corner with my friends. And as glad as I am to be weaving my little tapestry, it's nothing compared to yours."

"What about in five years' time? What about ten? You're the youngest weaver here, and you're already as good as some of the masters. You'll be at the royal court taking commissions from dukes and cardinals soon."

"I don't think so. And even if I am, why does it matter? Just as many of those people will be commissioning you to paint for them."

"That's not how success works."

"Then how does it work?"

Ana glared at her. "You have to stand out. You can't be

like all the others. That's why the queen likes you. You're a curiosity to her, and your weaving is just as curious. I used to be her favourite."

So many of the things Ana said puzzled Calia. She seemed to live in a different world, one where everything was a battle and everyone an enemy. How could she get through to a person like that?

"Lucy says you and I have a lot in common. Couldn't we do more if we worked together? If being the best is all you care about, wouldn't you rather we be friends than enemies?"

"I don't have friends." That statement coming from Ana might have sounded prideful on any other day, a badge of honour she wore to distinguish herself from others. Now it just sounded sad.

"Was that something Vesna insisted on?"

Ana averted her eyes.

"Stay here with the Goldsmiths. Don't go back to her. Things could be so much better for you and Karaline."

"You don't understand. I haven't been myself lately. I have to take charge and put my foot down. I'll make sure Vesna doesn't do anything reckless again. Things will be different when we go back."

To Calia's dismay, it wasn't confidence she heard in Ana's words, nor even arrogant self-assurance. It was desperation. She was afraid of letting go. Some deep bond still tethered her to Vesna. It wasn't love, but a similar, far more insidious dependency. Calia had seen it before in some of the children she'd minded at her mother's inn. The ones who were very quiet, very obedient, and who always hid their bruises beneath their clothing. The only thing those children feared more than their parents was the thought of being without them, for they were the only lens through which the world made sense.

Calia's resentment towards Anastasia began to wash away as she wove the connecting threads together. She understood now why Karaline cared for her. She wasn't a bad person, not at heart. She just didn't know any other way of being. All her talent had been twisted into something bitter and miserable by her ruthless mother. She was one of the most gifted women in the kingdom, yet she felt insecure and inadequate, because in the world she'd been taught to see, everyone was an enemy. Her hostile attitude was a suit of armour she'd built to protect herself from the fears Vesna had cultivated.

Calia wasn't sure how to put her realisation into words. It might not have done any good even if she had. Ana probably knew the same thing herself, deep down. Hers wasn't a problem that could be solved through a simple conversation. It was ingrained deep into her soul.

Calia reached across the table and took her hand.

"I'll be here every evening if you want to talk."

"What good will that do?"

"I don't know. But I'll be here all the same."

Ana held on longer than she needed to before pulling away.

CHAPTER 19

A week later, Anastasia asked Calia to help her sort through a box containing some of her drawings. She'd packed it hastily when she left, and the contents were all jumbled up. Karaline had been enlisted to help Sara in the kitchen, so the two of them had the upstairs parlour to themselves. It was the first time Calia had seen any of Anastasia's work besides the Farren Vale.

"Are all of these in charcoal and ink?" she asked as she looked through a stack of manuscript pages illuminated with beautiful illustrations.

"What else would they be in? You can't paint on parchment."

"I suppose not. It would flake off, wouldn't it?"

"Exactly."

"You're very good at drawing."

"I should hope so. I wouldn't be much of a painter if couldn't sketch out my designs first."

"Is that what you do?" Calia asked, genuinely curious. "Draw a sketch and then paint over it?"

"Yes. A builder needs a drawing floor and an artist needs a sketch, otherwise you don't know what you're doing."

"I thought you just picked up a brush and went straight at it."

"Some painters do," Ana said with a derisive curl of her lip. "I don't know how they get away with it. Half of what they paint ends up a mess; people with short arms and long heads, distant castles that are supposed to be close, designs that are too cramped or too empty. I use a measuring stick to space out everything properly, and I only start painting once I'm happy with the design."

"Like how weavers work from cartoons."

"Exactly."

"I think I'm one of those messy artists," Calia said. "I only make basic sketches for most of my weaving, and I barely end up following them."

"No, you see it all in your mind, don't you? That's why your work turns out the way it does."

"I've never really thought about it. It's just a sort of intuition. I have an idea of what the finished tapestry might look like, but it doesn't usually turn out that way. It changes as I go along once I see how the threads look on my loom."

"Is that why you changed my design? Because you thought yours would look better as you went along?"

"It isn't that I disliked yours. It's just that paint and thread are different. What looks good on a panel might not come across on a loom."

"Elaine and Bess always manage to make it work. Rovena, too."

Calia smiled sheepishly. "Well, I think they're better weavers than me."

Ana sighed. "Yes, they are. Better traditional weavers. Your style is more like–" She cast about in search of a comparison. "A twisted old tree that's grown through a wall, wrapping around the stones until they're moulded together. Compare that to a proper tree, a well-kept one in a lord's courtyard; straight and tidy, every branch trimmed, every leaf in its proper place. That would be a *better* tree, wouldn't you say? But put them side by side, and that odd twisted tree is the one that would draw everyone's eye. It's unique. It's interesting. And it has its own kind of natural beauty. That's what your weaving is like."

Calia laughed, though Ana's expression didn't suggest she'd been trying to make a joke.

"So I weave tapestries like twisted old trees?"

"More or less."

"And you paint things that are straight and perfect?"

"Exactly."

Calia set the manuscript pages aside in their own pile and moved on to a stack of larger sheets covered in charcoal sketches. Ana was right, her style was perfect. Every line looked like it had been sculpted by a mason. The shape of everything looked just right. Even the proportions, as she'd pointed out, held a kind of pleasant regularity that was simultaneously striking and unobtrusive.

When she'd first seen the cartoons of the Farren Vale, Calia remembered thinking that Ana's art was ostentatious. That was certainly true, and while it was not Calia's preferred style, the more she looked at the drawings, the more she came to appreciate the craft that had gone into them. Ana's art had a way of downplaying the mundane and drawing attention to the fantastical. The sheet in front of her bore a sketch of a woman casting a ribbon from her bedroom window into the hand of a knight riding off to battle. The moment was exquisitely captured. Calia's eyes were not drawn to the knight's horse, his armour, or the scene around them that subtly hinted at an entourage of men preparing for war. It was the ribbon that dominated the sketch. It coiled in impossible loops, swirling close to the viewer and then far away, delicately shaded with dark and light so that it looked like it was flashing in the sun. The hands of the man and woman clutching it at either end were rendered in fine lines that expressed a desperate, grasping need. Every part of the sketch portrayed what it needed to without distracting from the coils of ribbon that drew the viewer's eye inward to the centre. It was masterful. Calia felt like a novice when she thought about the painstaking consideration that must have gone into Ana's craft.

"I can see why the queen picked you for the Farren Vale. This is breathtaking."

"It's just a sketch," Ana said dismissively, taking the sheet from her and tossing it onto a pile of similar drawings.

"But it's wonderful."

"You don't improve by being self-congratulatory."

"You deserve to feel proud of what you've accomplished."

Ana's fingers hovered over the next sheet, hesitating before she picked it up. "Is that what your mentor taught you?"

"Old Milly, yes. Whenever I sewed something good enough for her to sell, she'd give me a silver penny at the end of the week. It always made me want to sew something even better next time."

"Vesna threw my sketches on the fire if they weren't good enough."

Calia shifted uncomfortably in her seat and tried to think of a way to change the subject. She'd been trying her best to avoid mentioning Vesna this past week. Ana became defensive when the topic came up, attempting to excuse or justify her mother's actions when Calia criticised them. The problem of Vesna couldn't be solved by attacking it head-on.

"I don't suppose you'd consider doing a sketch for me?"

Ana raised her eyebrows. "Of what?"

"The old Farren Vale. Or what you remember of it, at least. It would be easier to have a smaller cartoon to work from when I get back to my tapestry so we don't have to keep getting the big panels down. I haven't been able to look at the ones the other weavers are working from at all."

"I thought you didn't like working from cartoons. You didn't follow mine properly."

"I did," Calia protested, "I just changed some of the details. Remember those angels?"

"You turned them into something completely different."

"But the queen liked them, didn't she? They were still your idea. I just changed them into something I thought looked better in thread."

Ana dragged over a stack of parchment and leafed through it until she drew out a large sheet almost a yard wide.

Calia's eyes widened. It was the old Farren Vale. Not precisely—the charcoal was smudged and the lines were rough, obviously a quick sketch—but it had captured all the relevant details including an approximation of the branch border along the top edge.

"I drew it after we discovered the old tapestry," Ana said. "I planned on starting a proper painting when I had time."

"This is perfect!"

"It's a mess. I'll have it cleaned up on a fresh sheet of parchment by the time your hand's better." Hastily, she added: "Consider it your payment for helping me go through these."

"That's very kind of you. It'll make finishing my tapestry so much easier."

Ana frowned, perhaps wondering what her mother would say when she learned she was helping her greatest rival.

Calia said: "Now when the queen visits, we can tell her that both of her Farren Vales have your touch on them."

That seemed to placate Ana. She gave Calia a thin smile and went back to sorting.

"I don't know what you're hoping to achieve with her," Lucy told Calia a few days later. They were sitting up in bed together, Lucy embroidering a cap for Lord Oswin by candlelight while Calia nursed a cup of warm wine in her good hand. She'd slept on the floor when she first arrived, but now that the chill of autumn was pressing in she was happy to share the warmth of her friend's blankets.

"She's not a monster. I'm sure it's all Vesna's doing, the way she behaves."

"Vesna might be a wicked old bitch, but Ana makes her own decisions. She's not worth your time."

"Well, even if she isn't, Karaline is. I want her to have a chance to find some happiness in life. God knows Vesna isn't going to give it to her, but I think Ana will."

"I'm telling you, it's a lost cause. I tried being nice to that woman when she arrived and it didn't get me anywhere. The harder you try and change her mind about something, the more she digs in her heels."

Calia wriggled down beneath the blanket, resting the warm mug on her belly. "I know. I've given up trying to argue with her about Vesna."

"Then what's your plan?"

"What changes your mind about things, Lucy? I mean, what *really* changes it? Not when someone browbeats you, but when you get there on your own?"

Lucy shrugged. "I suppose if an idea makes sense, and if I respect whoever put it to me, then I'm willing to reconsider things."

"That's what I think, too. And the people I respect are the people I like. All the folk I've learned the most from are the ones I admire."

"So that's your plan, is it? Trick Ana into liking you so she does the right thing?"

"Don't tease. You were right about the two of us. We do have a lot in common. We spent all evening talking about her drawings the other day. Our styles are so different, but I think that's what makes it so interesting. We don't agree, but we can each see where the other is coming from. I like her art, and I think she likes mine, too." She let out a sleepy sigh. "Maybe if she starts to think of me as a friend, she'll see that things don't always have to be the way Vesna taught her."

"You're a nobler soul than I."

"Am I? You don't think I'm being foolish?"

Lucy smiled and shook her head. "You're being you."

"Is that good?"

"Well, it's good enough for me."

As the days grew shorter and the weather colder, Calia's opportunities to go walking with Karaline grew fewer and farther between. When the clouds finally parted after a long week of rain, the girl pleaded with her to go out on a trek.

"It's too late," Calia said. "I have to get back to the manor soon, and you need to have your supper."

"Please? Who knows when the sun will come out again."

Anastasia's voice drifted into the parlour from the adjacent bedroom: "We could have supper outside. Take a picnic up to the castle. It might be our last chance to watch a good sunset this year."

"Yes please!"

"Alright," Calia conceded. "I'll ask Sara for a basket."

Ana came through to the parlour. She'd been spending more time at the Goldsmiths' lately, using the bedroom as her studio when she wasn't at Ashmount House.

"Will you be coming with us?" she asked Calia.

"If you'll have me, I'd be happy to."

Ana gave her a brisk nod. "I'll take care of that basket. You get your things and make sure Kara's ready."

They set out for the top of the hill half an hour later. The ground was still damp, but the gritty path gave them firm footing, and the sinking sun had painted a beautiful rainbow through the distant clouds.

"What are rainbows?" Karaline asked.

Calia shielded her eyes to gaze across the valley. "My nana always told me they were forest faeries waking up when the sun came out."

"That's nonsense," Ana said chidingly. "It's the sun shining through distant rain."

"How does that work?"

"I saw a monk give a scientific demonstration at the

capital once. He used mirrors to focus a beam of sunlight through a crystal chalice filled with water. When he rotated the chalice, it created different patterns on the table. Some of them were the same colour as a rainbow. Then he filled a bladder with water and sprayed it through the beam in fine droplets, and I saw a rainbow appear right there in the room."

It sounded to Calia like the miracles priests described in sermons.

"Can only monks do that?"

"No. It's not a blessing from God. Water has a way of putting colour into light when it shines through it."

"Maybe sunlight is supposed to be rainbow-coloured," Karaline said. "But it's all dried out and yellow, like grass after a long summer. So when it gets watered, it goes back to being colourful again."

Ana scoffed in amusement.

"Maybe so," said Calia. "That's a very clever idea."

Karaline beamed and squeezed her new felt doll, appropriately named Blue after its colouring. She was a creatively-minded girl. It was a talent she shared with her sister, even if she wasn't as gifted of an artist. She would make a good tailor. Sewing charming dolls and unique dresses would come easily to her. The more Karaline felt able to express herself, the more she came out of her shell.

They walked through the old castle gates and Kara hurried off to find them a place to sit. Calia knocked on the gatehouse door to check on Huw, but he seemed to be out that evening. They crossed the courtyard and went through a gap in the crumbling south wall. A broad, flat piece of masonry had fallen there, its surface dry and warm from the fading sunlight. After setting down a blanket, the three of them perched on the edge to have their supper. The rainbow stretched over the vale in the distance, fading into the misty clouds as the sun went down.

"I'll never get tired of this view," Calia said as Ana poured them cups of sage water.

"Me neither. I could paint it a hundred different ways."

"Do you think you might stay in Ashmount after the tapestry's done?"

Ana shook her head. "We have to return to the capital."

"We've got a house there," Kara said gloomily.

"If you like nice views, perhaps you could come and visit my family one day. My mother has an inn in Tannersfield."

"I thought Tannersfield was flat and covered in forests?" Ana said.

"The part where most people live is, but there are lots of old hills in the north. They go up for miles and miles. Just about anywhere you stand, you can look down and see half the county spread out before you."

"Hm." Ana handed everyone a small loaf of bread and took out her knife to cut some thick slices of ham and cheese. Karaline showed Calia how to tear the end off her loaf and hollow out the doughy inside so she had a crusty pocket for her food. They watched the rainbow fade as they ate, Calia and Karaline doing most of the talking. Ana wasn't a very chatty woman. When she spoke, it was usually about serious, practical, or intellectual matters. She didn't seem to be one for idle gossip. Yet quiet though she was, she looked as content as Calia had ever seen her that evening, her copper hair drifting about her face as she stared into the middle distance sipping at her sage water. Did she have the soul of a romantic buried in there somewhere? The kind of soul that longed to wander ethereal moors, share quiet summer picnics with her friends, and muse on the scent of the wind and the sound of the rain?

Calia was that sort of person. She shied away from places like the capital where everything would be busy like a marketplace, the streets cramped and smelly, all the green of the world smothered out by shingled roofs and plastered walls. She didn't want Ana and Kara to go back there. It was obvious neither of them were looking forward to it.

They finished their meal with some fresh grapes.

Anastasia always made sure to keep a bowlful on the parlour table when they were in season. The farmers in Ashmount cultivated a plump, sweet variety that Calia had never tasted before, quite different from the strong-tasting grapes she'd once pilfered from the nuns' vineyard when she was little. She and Karaline tried to see who could spit their seeds the furthest, the pair of them giggling at the chance to do something so unladylike in private. Ana ate all of her seeds, crunching them down along with the grapes.

A few other people were wandering the castle ruins that evening, but they had all been on the other side of the wall when they arrived. Now, as they finished up their meal, a group of teenagers came around the wall and approached them. Most were boys, but there were a couple of girls with them, one of whom glared at Calia when she saw her. She whispered something to a lad beside her, and he grinned and nodded. He swaggered forward with his hand resting on the head of a hammer that he wore like a sword at his belt.

"We always have this spot."

Calia offered him a companionable smile. "We're just finishing our supper. We shan't be long."

"Then you can be off right away."

Ana rose to her feet. She was taller than the boy, and the look on her face said she was ready for a fight.

"Ana," Calia whispered, tugging at her sleeve.

"I know your master," Ana said. "You're Pete Builder's apprentice, aren't you?"

"That's right."

"Find your own spot."

The lad looked back at his friends uncertainly, but the girl who'd whispered to him called out: "She's that mad woman who pulled a knife on Jack. Don't let her bully you!"

Anastasia bridled at the comment, pushing the young man out of her way and striding towards the girl. Calia leapt to her feet and ran after her. This time she grabbed Ana's wrist and pulled hard.

"Leave them be. Let's just pack up our things and eat the rest of our grapes on the way home."

"I'm not letting these little thugs intimidate me."

"They're just stupid teenagers. Come on, it isn't worth making a scene."

"Don't be such a pushover."

"You're upsetting Karaline."

The mention of her sister made Ana pause. She looked back and saw Kara clutching her blue doll tight, her eyes wide and fearful. The look of anger on Ana's face dimmed, and she let Calia pull her away. The group of youths watched from a distance, muttering inaudible comments that drew a few giggles from the girls. Ana looked back at them every time they laughed, but Calia made sure to keep one hand on her arm. They bundled their blanket into the basket and took their leave.

"Why don't we circle around the bottom of the hill?" Calia suggested. "We can have a little walk and enjoy what's left of the sunlight before we go home."

"Yes, let's," Karaline said. She was already perking back up. By the time they were out of sight of the teenagers, she looked like she'd already forgotten about the uncomfortable scene. Ana still brooded a few paces behind with her brow furrowed. Calia waited so that she could catch up.

"Have you ever come this way before?" she asked.

"No."

"It's a nice little walk. You get to see the woods behind the manor, and there's a stream running around the hill into the valley."

"And no teenagers," Kara said.

Calia laughed. "No, none of them. Did you see the look on that girl's face when Ana got up? I don't think she's used to people pushing her boyfriend around."

"I should have words with Pete Builder about him," Ana said.

"Oh, I think you scared him enough. Come on, this way."

Calia led them down the west side of the hill behind the castle. A gentle path circled behind the manor before curving back to rejoin the road leading into Ashmount. With the lingering awkwardness of the confrontation dispelled, Ana began to brighten up again. She smiled when Calia and Karaline showed her a spot down by the stream where at least a dozen frogs could always be found lurking beneath a bed of wildflowers. Karaline rustled the plants with her hand and ran away giggling as an eruption of tiny brown frogs hopped out in all directions.

"I'd like to sew a frog doll," she told them as they walked on. "Could I do that?"

"I've never heard of a frog doll before," Calia said. "But we could definitely try."

"There's a carpenter's wife in town who makes wooden animal figurines," said Ana. "I've seen some frogs at her market stall. I'll buy you one to use as a reference."

"Your sister likes to plan everything out, doesn't she?" Calia said to Karaline.

Ana folded her arms. "I won't have my sister making shoddy frogs."

The tone of her voice was so sincere that Calia burst out laughing. Karaline joined her. Ana looked irritated, then bemused. Eventually, the smallest chuckle left her lips.

Their meandering walk around the hill took so long that it was dark by the time they returned to the Goldsmiths' house. Calia said goodnight to Karaline and sent her inside with the picnic basket.

"Stay here tonight," Ana said. "You don't want to walk back to the manor alone in the dark."

"I'll be alright. Besides, Lucy will worry about me if I don't come home."

"Let me get you a lantern, then."

Calia waited outside while Ana fetched the lantern. It was an expensive one, made from metal with holes in the sides to shield the flame from the wind.

"Don't lose it," Ana told her. "Or Ferald will be very unhappy."

"Thank you. I'll bring it back with me tomorrow morning."

A moment of silence passed, neither of them knowing quite how to say goodbye, until Ana cleared her throat and said: "I'm glad to have you at the house, Calia."

"I'm happy to be here."

"Earlier," Ana continued, her tone faltering stiffly, "with those youths at the castle. I think you were right. I would have upset Karaline."

"Well, you didn't. And we had a lovely evening, didn't we?"

"I felt like I should have done something."

Calia shook her head with a smile. "It isn't always worth it. Better to be happy and get on with your day. That's what my papa always says."

"That's not what I was taught."

"You're a much lovelier person when you're not listening to what Vesna taught you."

Ana fell silent, drawing her arms about her body as the wind gusted. "Am I?"

"Yes. You're clever and creative and interesting, and I'm glad we've become friends." When Ana didn't respond, she repeated: "We've become friends."

Ana nodded, turning away and reaching for the door handle. "Thank you."

She went inside without another word.

CHAPTER 20

For as much as Vesna Fiala cursed her daughter's foolishness at being taken in by Calia Tailor, she cursed herself even more for having underestimated the girl. Anastasia's unexpected outburst at the inquest had taken her completely by surprise. Her daughter had never disobeyed her so openly before. There had been small acts of defiance, of course, as was to be expected as Ana grew older and more wilful, but those always happened in private, and usually only when Karaline was involved. Ana's soft spot for her little sister had always been her greatest weakness. They should have left the girl in the capital so they could focus on the tapestry without distractions.

But this latest incident hadn't been Karaline's doing. No, when Ana opened her mouth at that inquest, she'd taken everything they'd planned and burned it to cinders along with the old tapestry. The boy Sigrad was to blame as well. If he'd only done what he was supposed to without setting a fire, perhaps Ana wouldn't have felt the need to speak out. Now Lord Oswin thought Vesna was a fool for the way she'd mistakenly accused Lucy, and Calia's reputation hadn't suffered a dent. If anything, people thought even more highly of her than before, sympathetic to the injury she'd suffered while bravely trying to rescue the old tapestry pieces.

Vesna brooded over these thoughts for weeks, searching for a solution that would restore her standing and bring Anastasia back to her. She was infuriatingly helpless on her own. Without her daughter to command Lord Oswin's respect and Sigrad to serve as her lackey, she felt feeble and overlooked. She was a source of gossip now, living alone in the royal solar, abandoned by both of her daughters, no one sure exactly why she was there or what purpose she served. The thought of it made her so angry she wanted to scream.

Ana was her protégé. She'd realised the day she felt the first tremor in her hand that her daughter would have to be the one who carried on their legacy. She just hadn't had enough time. First it had been her husband saddling her with a child when she should have been wooing the royal court, then the war in their homeland, and finally the burden of raising Karaline as she tried to ingratiate herself with the nobility of this foreign kingdom. She'd been stretched all her life, constantly pulled away from the art that should have won her wealth and fame.

So she'd made sure Ana had no such distractions. Every waking moment since they set foot on these shores, she'd kept her daughter on the right path, instilling in her the drive that was necessary to succeed.

And now Ana was trying to throw it all away. This was exactly why Vesna had kept her apart from ill-advised romances and unnecessary friends. Calia was poised to become the queen's new favourite, and Ana couldn't even see it.

Vesna tried to find another servant like Sigrad whose loyalty could be bought with silver, but everyone in the manor was either too upstanding, too clever, or too incompetent to suit her needs. She needed Ana back. They'd barely spoken since their falling out. Ana never came to the royal solar anymore unless she had business with Lord

Oswin. She spent all her time in the workrooms where she could easily find excuses to ignore her mother, and since she was always surrounded by her weavers, Vesna couldn't bully her the way she might have in private.

The girl would come back eventually. Vesna knew her too well to think otherwise. Every time they met, she saw the fear in her daughter, the growing desperation, the need for guidance and affirmation. It was a fantasy, this newfound burst of independence.

But the longer she stayed away, the more damage was being done. Time was wasting. They should have been taking advantage of Calia's recovery period to try and get her project cancelled, to re-establish their position as the most important artisans in Ashmount, and to make sure everyone forgot about the old tapestry that had almost stolen their thunder. Instead, all those weeks went to waste. Calia recovered from her injury and returned to work, tending her loom with newfound passion using a sketched cartoon of Ana's own design. The one saving grace was that she no longer spent all day at the Goldsmiths' house with Karaline, but she still dined there every other evening. Once or twice, Lucy Tailor even went with her. Calia's influence over Ana was growing. How much would it end up changing her by the time she came to her senses?

One drizzly morning, Vesna rose at the crack of dawn to wait outside the manor for her daughter. Her fingers ached from the cold and the patter of rain on her cloak made her shiver, but she waited all the same, standing in the same spot by the gates for almost an hour before Ana came striding up the path. She had never looked finer, carrying herself with a poise so vibrant that Vesna's chest swelled with pride. The folds of her orange dress rippled beneath a dark green cloak that hovered a confident inch above the wet path. Her head was high, her shoulders back, and she wore a headband of polished wood and bronze filigree.

She acknowledged her mother with a cold stare and made to keep walking, but Vesna blocked her path and gripped her by the arms.

"Nastya, speak with me."

"I've nothing to say."

"It's been more than a month! Haven't you punished your old mother enough?"

Ana's eyes fell to the ground, some of the confidence seeping out of her. "What do you want?"

"I want you to come home where you belong. It's time we started focusing on the things that matter again."

"And what are those?"

"Your future. Your legacy. Your standing in the eyes of the queen."

"Oh, yes," Ana said dejectedly.

"Where's that fire, Nastya? You've never been soft. We've had our troubles, but it's nothing we can't recover from. I want to see the work you've been doing. I can tell you where you've been going wrong, hm? We can start with that sketch you did for the tailor girl."

"You know her name."

Vesna scowled. "It's not worth repeating. You've had enough time playing with her. Now you need to get back to work."

"I have been working. It's some of the happiest work I've done in years."

"Minstrels do happy work. Do you want to be like them? Farting and juggling for stupid noblemen? Or do you want to be the greatest painter this kingdom has ever known?" To Vesna's shock, it looked like Ana was genuinely considering the absurd question. "It's the tailor girl. She's got you thinking like a bumpkin. You know you can't keep seeing her forever, don't you?"

"I know."

"Good. Then come up to the solar with me. Bring your things with you. We can start putting all this behind us."

"You haven't asked after Karaline."

Vesna waved her hand dismissively. "She's well, isn't she?"

"No thanks to you."

"Then what's the matter?"

Ana gave her a long, hard look. "If I come back, I want a promise. I've always been your student, and I know how much you've done for me. But you've never shown any interest in Karaline. Let her live her own life. Don't make her marry someone just to get her out of the way."

Vesna pursed her lips. "If she ever wants to amount to anything–"

"I don't care," Ana spoke over her. "Leave her be. I mean it. If you hurt her again, I swear I'll walk out, and this time I won't come back."

She was almost convincing. Anyone else would have heard steely determination in her words, but Vesna knew her daughter too well. It was all an act. An act she'd taught her. It was the way she knew she had to behave to get what she wanted. Yet there was the faintest glimmer of truth in it this time, a kind of fervent desperation that Vesna feared might sprout into genuine defiance if she agitated it. Ana was like a fish on a hook sometimes. Tug too hard, and she'd tear her own lip trying to get away. Now was a time to ease her in gently. Later, once she was back to her old self, then they could revisit this topic. There was no hope for Karaline if she didn't marry well. Allowing her to waste her life on anything else was out of the question.

"Alright," Vesna said, offering her daughter a rare smile. "If that's what you want."

That was all it took. Ana's composure fractured like a puppy being thrown a treat.

"Thank you," she said. "I told Calia you'd see sense."

"So, you're coming back?"

Ana hesitated. "Soon. When Karaline's ready."

Anger flared within Vesna, but she didn't let it show. She'd done all she could for now. With a forced nod, she stepped aside and followed Ana through the gates. She fell behind as they crossed the courtyard, mulling over her next course of action. Calia Tailor still had her claws in deep. She'd been trying her hardest to turn Ana against her, and most likely Karaline, too. Vesna felt a bitter hatred towards the woman. For twenty-five years she'd moulded Ana into the perfect student, and in just a few months some scrap of a girl had come along and threatened to undo it all. Who did she think she was, changing Ana's designs, digging up the old tapestry, working on her own competing version?

Vesna would have happily seen the woman dead. Such things could be done. Many years ago, in the chaotic days of the war, she'd leveraged her money and influence to ensure that her brother-in-law didn't contest the family inheritance when her husband died. She hadn't cared to hear the details of what happened, but her brother-in-law and his family had been found dead on the road a few weeks later, apparently robbed by vagrant mercenaries. With the money from her husband's side of the family secure, she'd been able to make her flight overseas and establish herself once again. That was the first and only time she'd employed murder as a tool. It wasn't one she planned on using again, but the temptation was always there. She'd done it once before.

But the risk was too great. She was no longer living in a war-torn kingdom where random acts of violence were frequently seen and swiftly forgotten, nor did she have the luxury of sailing away before it had the chance to catch up to her. She was going to need a better plan.

To the west of Ashmount across the stream that ran around the hill, a small cottage stood near the edge of the woods. Vesna recalled that the woman who lived there was Rovena Weaver's great-aunt. She was old and mad, but in her younger years people said she'd been a wise woman who knew how to cure aches and pains with her potions. Not wanting anyone in town to know about her infirmities, Vesna had gone to see her when the cold weather started making her hands ache. She'd been visiting once a fortnight ever since, hoping she caught the old woman in one of her lucid moods where she could still heat up a jug of wine and mix in the right ingredients. She never remembered who Vesna was from one visit to the next.

It was during one of these visits that a stray comment caught her ear. The old woman, whose name Vesna had never bothered to ask, frequently rambled as she shuffled about the room. She spoke of people who were long dead, events that had happened far in the past, and disconnected anecdotes that seemed to hop from one topic to the next at random. Most of it was nonsense. On the rare occasions when Vesna was addressed directly, she offered short, simple responses, not wanting to distract the woman from her work. But this comment was different.

"Would you put out the bread for him?"

"What bread?"

The old woman gestured to a loaf sitting on a stool by the door. "Outside. Put the wine, too. Don't forget."

"Why are you putting bread and wine outside?"

"For the boy."

Vesna glanced out the door, worried about being seen at the cottage if someone was coming.

"Is he there?" the old woman asked.

"There's no one on the path."

"He comes from the woods with squirrels and rabbits for me."

"You give him bread and wine in exchange?"

"Other things, too."

"He must come often, for you to remember him."

"Oh yes. Every couple of days. More than my Rovena. He's a good boy."

"What's his name?"

The old woman paused, her attention seeming to drift, then she began telling a story that Vesna soon realised was about a completely different young man.

She wondered if it could be Sigrad. There weren't any foresters this side of Ashmount, nor were there reports of outlaws in the area. Sigrad knew how to hunt and fend for himself. If he was living in the woods, it would make sense for him to come here for supplies. The old woman was the one person in town who wouldn't care who he was and wouldn't be believed if she told anyone.

Vesna let the thought percolate as she waited for her potion. Could Sigrad still be useful to her, even as an outlaw? He might resent her for what had happened at the inquest. But if he'd wanted revenge, he could have incriminated her then and there. Instead, he'd stayed true to his word and kept quiet. Perhaps he thought she was still on his side.

Vesna lingered at the cottage all afternoon. It was no great task to impose on the old woman's hospitality. She was happy to ramble away until she fell asleep on a cushioned chair near the fire. If the boy she'd spoken of really was Sigrad, he would probably come at night. He couldn't afford to be seen so close to the town during the day. No one at the manor was going to miss Vesna for one evening, not now that her daughters were gone. Thoughts of her estranged family fired her resolve, and she slipped another log into the hearth.

About an hour after dark, she heard a noise outside. There came a hollow scraping sound like someone setting down an empty jug. She rose to her feet and crossed the room. At the door, she hesitated, wondering how the visitor would react if they weren't Sigrad. But the noise had already stopped. If she didn't look now, she might miss her chance. Pushing the door open, she saw a cloaked figure hurrying away into the gloom.

"Sigrad!" she hissed.

He stopped and turned back. The hair under his hood was tangled, his wispy teenage stubble unkempt, but it was him. He looked surprisingly healthy for a man who'd been living rough for over a month.

"Who's that?" he called back. He sounded cautious, but

not afraid.

"Vesna. Come here." She shut the door behind her and stepped out to meet him. Without the light coming from the cottage, she could no longer make out his face, but she saw his shadow edge closer.

"What do you want?"

"I want to help you. How have you been getting by on your own?"

"I manage. It's easy to set snares in the woods. But I don't have any bread or wine, so I come here to the mad lady. I didn't think she'd tell anyone about me."

"You'd better not come back again. She mentioned a boy earlier, and I guessed it was you."

Sigrad cursed. "Will you bring me bread instead?"

"I'll do more than that. I'll get you pardoned so you can stop hiding in the woods. But you're going to have to do exactly as I say."

"Alright."

Vesna was glad the darkness hid her smile. This would be easier than she'd thought. He was as gullible as ever, perhaps more so now that he was desperate.

"Where can we meet in daylight?"

Sigrad thought for a moment. "If you follow the hunting trail at the north end of the woods, there's a clearing a little ways in with a big fallen oak leaning up against a standing one. If you wait there, I'll see you."

"Look for me there the day after tomorrow. I'll come early in the morning."

"Will you bring bread?"

"I'll bring a whole basket."

"What do I have to do?"

"You let me worry about that. Just make sure you're ready when I need you."

"Alright."

Vesna let him go and took a lantern from the cottage to light her way home. She stumbled in the stream and got her feet wet, but she was too focused on her plan to feel annoyed. She had something to work with now.

Sigrad would do anything she wanted, and Calia Tailor was going to pay for poisoning her daughters against her.

* * *

Bishop Matthew of Farrenwold was never fond of tangling himself up in politics. It was an inevitable part of the job, of course, but for the majority of his twelve-year tenure as bishop, he'd managed to stay mercifully beneath the notice of the nobility. He offered favours, but he did not accept bribes. He was obedient to his superiors, but he didn't toady to them. To the best of his ability, he avoided audiences with noblemen, travelling often so that they could never catch him at home. He had cultivated a reputation as a slow-acting conservative who was difficult to strike bargains with; a robust and innocuous wheel in the machinery of the church. That wasn't the whole truth, but it was a reputation he was happy to indulge. It made his life quiet, leaving him with more time for the things he was truly passionate about.

God loved beauty, and so did Bishop Matthew. He wanted nothing more than to decorate Redland Cathedral, the seat of his diocese, with gilded ornaments, silken drapery, cushioned benches, and vivid carvings. He dreamt of an interior glowing with light and colour, so resplendent that it mirrored a hall of heaven itself. The embellishment of the cathedral was his pet project, and it was why he visited the town of Ashmount so often. The goldsmiths here had made dozens of the gilded icons and jewel-encrusted chalices he liked to display upon his altar during service. But more importantly, the painter Anastasia Fiala was working at the queen's manor, and he harboured a fantasy of commissioning her to create a great fresco behind his altar. He didn't know where he was going to find the money yet, nor whether the queen would let Anastasia go, but he was making progress. He'd dined with

Anastasia and her mother several times during his visits. The mother seemed the type who liked to ingratiate herself with men like him. With a little luck and a few more dinners, he expected he stood a good chance of currying their favour.

It was raining when he arrived in Ashmount, as it seemed to have been for the better part of a month now. Rain was pleasant when it arrived at the end of summer, but the novelty quickly wore off. Now it was icy with winter cold. The bishop wore two cloaks, one thick and warm, the other oiled to keep off the rain, but somehow he still ended up soaked to the bone. It was a relief to finally sit down by a fire and watch the steam rise from his drying clothing. Ashmount had no priory, so he always lodged with a priest who lived in a comfortable clergy house near the church.

Before nightfall, he received a visitor. He was annoyed at first when the housekeeper told him there was someone at the door. He'd arrived quietly and had been hoping to spend the evening resting before he announced himself tomorrow. Upon learning that his visitor was Vesna Fiala, however, his annoyance vanished. He had the housekeeper prepare two platters of leftovers from supper and set the parlour table for them. Despite having already eaten, he could always find room for more, as the subtle filling out of his frame made more apparent year by year.

He greeted Vesna with wide arms and a smile when she stepped into the parlour.

"The mother of the queen's painter. I couldn't ask for a more delightful welcome."

"You are too kind, my lord bishop."

"I wasn't aware anyone knew I was coming."

"A man of your distinction rarely arrives unnoticed."

They sat and ate, exchanging the platitudes that were routine for such dinners. Far from finding the exercise tiresome, it was one of Matthew's favourite parts of his job. He preferred it when people spoke of mild and pleasant things. Life should be mild and pleasant. It was much nicer than the cloak-and-dagger dealings some bishops handled over dinner. But, as he had expected, the true reason for Vesna's visit eventually reared its head through the warm, wine-muffled fuzz of conversation.

"Sadly, not everyone my daughter works with embodies the virtuous precepts as you do, Bishop. It troubles me to think that it goes on right under the queen's nose."

Matthew felt himself sigh internally. Here it was. Some personal squabble she wanted help with. He would have to find a way of saying no without undoing the goodwill he'd built up with her. The last thing he wanted was to invite the ire of the queen and her stuffy bailiff by meddling in the affairs of Ashmount House.

Vesna continued: "One woman in particular, Calia Tailor, has a reputation for unseemly behaviour. Do you know her?"

"I can't say I do."

"She was employed as a weaver under strange circumstances. No formal training. A tailor by trade, yet somehow she convinced the queen to hire her for the tapestry. Her work has a deceitful quality to it. She has been known to alter the design of angels in a mocking fashion, and she shares her bed nightly with another woman."

"If sharing beds were a sin, every commoner in the land would be guilty."

"Even if there is fornication involved?"

"That is an easy accusation to make and a difficult one to prove, especially when it concerns two women. The lack of any children tends to make evidence of such deeds rather hard to come by." Matthew chuckled in an attempt to lighten the mood.

Vesna didn't laugh, instead nodding as though this were a philosophical debate between monks in chapter. "Nevertheless, it would be a sin and a crime."

"Church doctrine is somewhat vague in that area. Fornication between women is not explicitly defined in the scriptures."

"Yet it is frowned upon."

Bishop Matthew inclined his head, conceding the point. "It's all academic. Problematic though it may be, it's impractical and ill-advised to try and bring such things to court. The few instances I recall presiding over led to nothing more than a fine and some light penance for the accused." He was hoping to dissuade Vesna from whatever vendetta she had against this Calia Tailor, but to his exasperation, the woman kept stubbornly on.

"Regardless of the penalty, it is only right that these things be exposed, wouldn't you agree? The queen would certainly want to know if it was going on beneath her roof."

"Ah, of course." Matthew saw where this was going now. "She is a principled woman, our queen."

"And she would dismiss Calia immediately if she knew the truth."

"If, indeed, it is the truth."

"That is why I would encourage you to hold a trial–so that the truth can be ascertained."

"Lady Vesna," Matthew said patiently, "ecclesiastical court is not a weapon to be wielded against one's enemies. It harms the church's reputation when we are seen to persecute frivolous dalliances that are not strictly defined in the scriptures."

"I should have expected this attitude."

Matthew straightened in his chair, his defences immediately rising. He'd heard that tone before, and he didn't like it. People didn't speak flippantly to men like him unless they had something to back it up.

"And why is that?"

"Do you know who's taken Calia Tailor under his wing? Leander Weaver."

Matthew kept his face impassive, but internally his thoughts began racing. "He's the alderman of the weavers' guild, is he not?"

"I think you might be more familiar with him as a young

monk. One who was involved in a similar 'frivolous dalliance,' as you call it."

Matthew's heart sank. Of course he remembered the incident. It had been a long time ago, back when he was still an archdeacon, but he vividly recalled the scandal that had almost fractured the reputation of Redland Abbey, the wealthiest monastic institution in Farrenwold. Leander, a novice at the time, had been caught in the prior's bed. It should have been dealt with behind closed doors, as such affairs usually were, but somehow word of it had leaked out to the town. Matthew and several other senior clergymen had met with the abbot to discuss how to resolve the matter. Some of the brothers at the abbey called for a trial, but Matthew and his then-bishop feared that such a spectacle would turn the abbey into a laughing stock. They couldn't afford that kind of escalation. The solution they'd agreed upon was for Leander to quietly give up his novitiate and return home to Ashmount. The monks were forbidden from speaking about the matter again, and most had begrudgingly complied. It was messy, but far less messy than it could have been if the rumours were confirmed in court.

"So," Matthew said carefully, deciding to probe for more information before he settled on a response, "you have concerns about this woman's association with Leander?"

"It's a black mark against her, surely. One that I'm sure the church would rather address in court rather than letting it spread about town unchecked."

"I see. So you're saying that if Calia Tailor were not brought to trial, you expect these rumours about her association with Leander—and the things he may or may not have done in the past—might resurface once again?"

"Exactly."

Matthew gave her a thin smile. On some level, he appreciated how cordially she was blackmailing him. He wondered how she'd found out about Leander. She was obviously a more resourceful woman than he'd taken her for.

But then again, did he really expect anyone who dwelt in royal company not to have a few daggers up their sleeve?

"Of course, I would prefer to avoid that. Perhaps we can come to an arrangement."

Vesna reached beneath her cloak and put a heavy purse on the table.

Matthew frowned and shook his head. "No, please. Let's not make this unsavoury. You're a concerned citizen acting in the interests of the church."

"Indeed I am."

"And, in the interests of the church, perhaps your talented daughter might see fit to visit me in Redland one day. I'd like to talk to her about painting my cathedral."

"Perhaps she could."

"I don't like obligations," he said, pushing the purse back towards Vesna.

"Good. Then I don't think we'll need to bring this up again—as long as Calia Tailor is called to trial before the end of the month."

Bishop Matthew picked over the remnants of his meal, his appetite for both food and conversation having deserted him. This was going to be a headache. He would have to keep it as quiet as he could. The Leander scandal couldn't be allowed to creep back into the limelight. One of his archdeacons would have to bring Calia Tailor to trial, for it would be strange for the bishop to summon her all the way to Redland on such thin charges. The whole thing was distasteful to him, but at least it seemed to stem from a personal squabble of Vesna's rather than some insidious scheme that might cause greater unrest in the diocese. Best to get it over and done with as quickly as possible, and hope he at least got his cathedral painted afterwards.

Anything for a quiet life.

CHAPTER 21

"On what charge?!" Lucy exclaimed when the quiet young monk delivered Calia's summons. He had wisely taken them outside and away from the manor before telling them that she was due in court next Tuesday.

He looked around the courtyard nervously before whispering: "Fornication."

"That's absurd. Calia doesn't fornicate with anyone."

"An accusation has been made."

Calia was utterly bewildered. Of all the things she thought she might one day get in trouble for, fornication was the least among them.

"What will happen?" she asked the monk.

"There will be a hearing. You will be presented with the accusation and have a chance to defend yourself, as will any witnesses you bring."

"Well, I'm going," Lucy said. "We'll bring Huwel Ward, too. And Leander Weaver. Let's see the archdeacon argue with him!"

The monk fidgeted with the sleeve of his robe. "I'd advise against bringing the alderman into this. Calia's association with him is part of the problem."

"What do you mean by that?"

The monk shook his head and backed away. "I'm afraid I shouldn't say any more. The trial will be held at the clergy house this Tuesday at noon. Please be on time. The archdeacon has been known to find people guilty in absentia before."

"Church courts," Lucy muttered as the monk left. "Who ever heard of a trial for fornication? I don't know what's more of a joke, this accusation or the archdeacon agreeing to try it in the first place."

"It does seem very odd. I wonder if there's been some mistake."

"More like Ana and Vesna's doing."

Calia frowned. Ana had moved back into the manor a few days ago. Their relationship remained friendly, but there was a definite weight to it now. It was obvious that Ana wasn't happy, yet for women like her, happiness wasn't always the driving force in life. The sense of duty she felt to her mother, and the unhealthy dependency it had produced, had won out in the end. Even so, she couldn't have fallen back into her old ways so quickly, could she?

"I don't believe Ana would do something like that, but you might be right about Vesna. She still looks at me like I'm cow dung."

In the past, Calia might have left her suspicions alone, but she wasn't the timid girl she'd been six months ago. She didn't want a repeat of what had happened at the inquest. No one would catch her out with accusations she wasn't ready for again. She went upstairs and found Ana with the other weavers. At Calia's insistence, they went into the room housing the cartoon panels where they could speak in private. The damage from the fire had mostly been repaired by now, leaving only a few scorched roof beams as evidence of the arson.

Ana looked perplexed when Calia told her about the summons.

"That doesn't sound like something my mother would do."

Calia gave her an incredulous look. "Really?"

"What I mean is, it isn't a very good plan." A flush of guilt coloured Ana's cheeks. "I considered something similar once, but the charge is too thin. You're a respectable woman— a member of a guild and a servant of the queen. The archdeacon will be looking for any excuse to find you innocent so he can move on and avoid the headache. Unless there are witnesses who can accuse you directly, there's no case to be made. Besides, if it's a charge of fornication then why are you the only one being accused? Fornicators usually come in pairs."

"Could Vesna have paid someone to lie?"

"I'm keeping an eye on her."

"Be honest with me."

"Fine. No, I doubt she'd pay a witness to lie, not unless she had some other means of pressuring them into it. That's the best way to get people to do what you want, especially when it's something as serious as lying in court. They have to be more afraid of the alternative."

"That's horrible."

"It's how you get ahead."

"You don't still believe that, do you?"

Ana scowled. "It's the truth, no matter how unpalatable you find it. I don't want to talk about this anymore. It isn't my mother's doing. You can't get someone convicted on hearsay, and I doubt she has the pressure to present false witnesses. You'll be fine."

Calia wasn't so sure, but she could see Ana retreating inside her armour. There was no point trying to argue with her when she was like this.

Calia struggled to concentrate on her weaving for the rest of the day. Even her near-finished tapestry couldn't absorb her the way it usually did. After a month with her hand in a cast, she'd been itching to get back to work and had attacked her loom with newfound enthusiasm. Progress was swift with Ana's sketch to help her. It held just enough detail to guide her without making her feel like she was deviating when she chose an unusual colour or altered some visual element. Karaline came in to watch sometimes, and Calia would explain what she was doing as she guided her bobbin through the warp. Thread by thread, her tapestry had grown like a thickening spider web until the glowing sun took shape and the first border branches began creeping in. It was a soft, rustic rendition of Ana's flashy masterpiece. She'd used no silk, instead focusing on earthy colours with deep orange and purple contrasts for the sunset sky. It was unquestionably the Farren Vale, yet no one could have mistaken her tapestry for Ana's. When she walked around to admire the front of her loom at the end of the day, she was continually amazed at how two artists could create such differing visions of the same scene.

Yet Calia's work was slow that day as she fretted over the impending trial. Her suspicions were all but confirmed when she caught Vesna giving her a self-satisfied look over dinner. She tried not to worry, trusting in Lucy and Ana's judgement that the accusation would come to nothing, but she didn't want to sit idle and let disaster creep up on her. Vesna didn't seem like the type of woman to engage in half-baked plans.

It was difficult to inquire into who had made the accusation without letting it become public knowledge. She didn't want gossip spreading about town. For now, it seemed like only Calia, her close friends, and the clergy knew about the trial. A few rumours would probably stir themselves up once she was seen attending court, but those would run their course if she was found innocent. If everyone heard about it beforehand, however, then the locals might settle on their own narrative before the archdeacon had the chance to pass his verdict.

With Ana being uncooperative, Calia went to see Leander instead. The alderman always kept one ear to the ground, and he had a vested interest in upholding Calia's reputation.

"It doesn't particularly surprise me," he said with a contemptuous snort when Calia explained the situation. "The church and I haven't gotten along for a while now. They become particularly aggravated whenever I remind them of that fact. The monk was right, though. You wouldn't want me testifying on your behalf. I think the archdeacon would see it as some sort of threat. You be careful. If the queen catches wind of this, she won't be happy. I'm half-sure the reason she refused to involve me with the tapestry in the first place is because of the things people say about me. Not that the church would ever dare make a formal accusation." There was great bitterness in his voice when he said that, some old hurt that had never fully healed.

"Would you keep an ear open for me?" Calia asked. "I'd like to know if there are going to be any other witnesses present. Ana and Lucy say I shouldn't worry, but I don't want to be caught off guard."

"Of course. I can't have my favourite weaver getting into trouble. I'll let you know."

Calia heard nothing from Leander in the following days. Huw came up empty as well, and Ana remained difficult to talk to. No one seemed to have any idea where the accusation had come from or where it might lead. Perhaps this was just a desperate, last-ditch effort of Vesna's to try and get back at her; a petty swipe with little substance to back it up.

On the eve of the trial, Calia felt as prepared as she could be. Lucy and Huw had both agreed to stand witness for her. As three highly respected local figures, it would take an almighty amount of opposition to paint Calia as the guilty party. She hoped that by this time tomorrow, it would all be behind them. Lucy advised her to settle her nerves and rest well that night, so she decided to try and take her mind off things for a few hours. She always went to Huw's for supper on Monday evenings, and the old warden's sensible outlook tended to reassure her when she was fretting.

Lucy thought she might be catching a cold and decided not to brave the drizzle that evening, but Karaline was eager to come along. One of these days, Calia would get Ana to join them. She wanted Ana to see that kinship could be so much more than the twisted bond she shared with her mother.

Donning their cloaks, Calia and Karaline hurried into town. It would have to be a quick supper, for it was getting dark very early these days, and thick grey clouds were already smothering out the daylight. They splashed through shallow puddles as they made their way up the gritted path to the castle. A very different picture of the Farren Vale could be painted, Calia reflected, if one were to stop and take in the view on a gloomy day like this. Castle Ashmount was a craggy ruin, its turrets dark bones against clouds the colour of charcoal smudged over linen. She heard a rumble of thunder in the distance and hurried Karaline along to the gatehouse.

"You ladies needn't have come in this weather," Huw said as he held the door open for them. "It's going to be a bad one tonight. I'll need the buckets out tomorrow. Now that it's all opened up, the rain's been filling the castle cellar like a pond. Saw a family of frogs in there last I went down."

Karaline gasped with delight. "Can we see?"

Huw chuckled. "Not tonight, milady. Maybe when it's dry we can get a lantern down there. Let's have some supper."

Calia was glad she'd come, for Huw's presence had the soothing effect she'd hoped for. They ate crusty bread with stew, listening to the patter of rain on the shingles while the crackling hearth kept them warm.

"Don't you worry about tomorrow, Miss Calia," Huw said when they began tidying up. "Everything has a way of feeling like it's the end of the world at your age. But the world keeps on going, and so do you, even when the worst happens. It'll be alright, and if it isn't, well, you'll still have us, won't you?"

Calia's cheeks warmed with a smile. "Yes, I suppose I will.

Thank you, Huw. I feel better about it already."

"Now hurry home before those puddles get deep enough to start swallowing young ladies." He went to the door and held it open for them. The sound of beating rain roared into the house. It had gotten even worse while they ate. Calia made to leave, but Huw held up a hand to stop her and took a half-step outside. "Who's that, then?"

The sound of a voice came through the crashing rain, its words muffled and indistinct.

"She is, yes," Huw replied when the stranger finished speaking. A hand shot through the doorway and grabbed him by the collar. He let out a cry of alarm as the stranger dragged him outside and hurled him bodily to the ground.

Calia stepped in front of Karaline, a spike of fear shooting through her gut as she saw a cloaked figure standing over Huw. They had a long club in one hand, and as the warden struggled to his feet, they swung it at him. The breath left Huw's lungs in an awful groan. For a moment, Calia was frozen, unsure of what to do. She'd never had to confront violence face to face like this before, not without someone else to protect her.

"Stop it!" she cried. "What are you doing?"

The cloaked figure looked up. Sigrad's face, wet and wild-eyed, stared out from beneath the hood. Calia backed away, almost tripping over Karaline as she looked for something to defend herself with. Sigrad advanced into the house. Karaline thrust a fire iron into Calia's hands and she raised it like a sword in front of her.

Sigrad hesitated and held up a palm. "Come with me, and I won't hurt you."

"What do you want?!"

"Just come with me." He lowered the club and held out his hand.

Calia's first instinct was to take it. She was afraid, and wherever Sigrad wanted to take her was probably a better alternative than trying to fight him. But when she heard

Huw's pained gasps coming from outside, a sudden anger flared in her breast. She swung the iron at Sigrad's arm. He moved back and raised his club with the quick reflexes of a swordsman. The iron banged against it, bending slightly from the impact. Calia swung again, thrashing clumsily at Sigrad's side to try and force him away from the door. Karaline screamed behind her. Sigrad blocked each blow with his club, but he was driven sideways and back, pushing him into the corner of the room. As soon as she had an opening, Karaline darted outside. Calia followed her, stooping to pick up Huw as she ran into the pouring rain. The old man was wheezing, but he managed to find his feet.

Their head start only lasted a second before Sigrad was on them again. Calia didn't hear him coming over the crash of the rain. It was beating down on top of her head, running into her eyes and soaking the neck of her dress. The back of her shoulder burst with pain as Sigrad's club thudded into her. She staggered away, dropping the fire iron to the ground. Her eyes scanned the courtyard frantically for anyone who might help, but the castle was deserted. No one would be up here in this weather.

"Run, Kara! Get help!"

The frightened girl bolted for the gates. Sigrad went after her. Calia groaned as she realised she wouldn't be able to outrun him. Huw staggered after them, but he was too slow. Sigrad lashed out with his club and cracked the side of Karaline's shin, sweeping her legs out from under her. She fell hard, her scream of pain lost amidst the thunderous deluge.

With a ferocity Calia had never before seen in the gentle man, Huw threw himself at Sigrad. He was bigger than the adolescent page, but Sigrad had the nimbleness of youth on his side. He managed to dart back before Huw could grab him and raised his club again. There was a terrible look on his face, not of anger or malice, but a kind of breathless excitement.

The next time Huw lunged, Sigrad brought his club up and swung hard, aiming for the head. The old warden didn't react in time. The blow slammed into his skull with a sickly cracking sound, and he crumpled like a bag of broken twigs. Calia screamed his name in anguish. He lay still on the ground, blood seeping into a muddy puddle beneath his face.

Sigrad looked back toward Calia. She picked up the fire iron, but he wasn't afraid of it this time. Some dark fervour had taken hold of him. He didn't even blink as he stepped forward, seized the rod, and twisted it out of Calia's grasp. In her terror, she knew she had to run, but Sigrad was so fast. She didn't get two paces before the club hit her in the stomach. A burst of nauseating pain made her double over, then Sigrad's fist hit her in the face, and the next thing she knew she was on the ground, her head spinning as cold water soaked through the back of her cloak.

She felt herself being dragged then, her cloak tie digging painfully into her chest as Sigrad hauled her like a sack of grain. She flopped about helplessly, still too stunned to get a grip on herself. Karaline cried out somewhere behind them, and Calia writhed in sudden panic until Sigrad hit her again. Cold stone ridges dug into her back as he pushed her down a flight of stairs. She tumbled head over heels, her muddy cloak the only thing sparing her from cracking her skull open as the steps jabbed at her like a mouthful of worn teeth. The light vanished, plunging her into darkness as she splashed into a pool of freezing water. The shock cut through her aches and pains. Fearing that she might be about to drown, she thrashed about until she found the steps and dragged herself out.

Sigrad must have thrown her into the castle cellar. She crouched there, hunched and shaking, afraid to look up. A few moments later, just as she dared to start moving again, she heard the sound of Karaline's voice. It echoed from the top of the stairs, shrill and terrified. In the square of dim light above her, Calia saw the girl struggling in Sigrad's arms. He pried her away and gave her a shove. Calia threw herself forward, managing to catch Karaline before she hit the steps. The pair of them tumbled and splashed into the pool of freezing water again. It was only a couple of feet deep, but the darkness made it seem black and endless. Karaline thrashed about desperately. By the time Calia managed to haul her back to the stairs, they were both soaked through. Fearing that Huw might be next, Calia clambered upwards on all fours, her sodden cloak dragging against the steps behind her. Huw's body didn't come tumbling down, but a thick sheet of wood slid across the top of the stairwell instead, laid flat against the floor so that it met the sloping ceiling and sealed the passage like a trap door. Only a tiny chink of light shone in around the edge. Calia grabbed the end of the wooden sheet where it touched the ceiling and tried to yank it down, but it didn't budge. Sigrad must have put something heavy on the other end.

"I told you to come with me," Sigrad's voice panted from the other side. "Now you can stay down there. I'll be back tomorrow night."

"What about Huw?!" Calia screamed, but she received no answer. Rain trickled in around the edges of the board, dribbling over her fingers and running down her back. The only warmth she could feel came from the tears in her eyes.

CHAPTER 22

During their time at the Goldsmiths' house, Calia had coaxed Anastasia into appreciating the soothing quality of rain drumming against a shuttered window.

It wasn't soothing her that evening.

As the clouds darkened, Ana kept thinking about treacherous puddles and slippery mud on the path to the castle. Karaline would be soaked through. Why did she insist on trotting off for walks in weather like this? Part of her itched to go out and find her, but she forced herself to relax and trust that Calia had everything in hand. Trust was a difficult thing for Ana to place in others. The only people she truly trusted were Karaline and Vesna. With her mother, it was a fearful dependency, a kind of blind faith that kept her doubts at bay. She'd never questioned it before, but she knew now that there was something wrong with that way of thinking. It had been on her mind ever since the night of the fire, but try as she might, she didn't know what to do about it.

Living apart from her mother had been frightening. Liberating, but frightening. Coming back to the manor was like slipping on a rough yet familiar dress. She knew what to expect here, even if it itched.

Finishing her daily tour of the weaving rooms, she snuffed the candles and went back to the royal solar, locking the door behind her. She found Vesna perched on the edge of her favourite chair.

"What are you anxious about?" Ana asked.

Vesna flinched as if she'd been bitten by something. "Nothing you need worry over."

"Karaline isn't back from the castle yet, is she?"

"No. I didn't realise she'd gone with that woman."

"They always go on Mondays."

Vesna glared at her. "I wish you'd told me."

"If you paid her more attention, you might notice these things." Ana turned away before her mother could retort with something argumentative. She was obviously in a prickly mood. "If she isn't back soon, I'll ride up and fetch her."

"There's no need."

"Do you want her dripping mud all over the solar floor? Lord Oswin won't be happy about that. You know what she's like. Leave her on her own and she'll jump in every puddle she can find."

"Nastya, listen to me. I don't want you going up to the castle tonight."

The knot of tension that had been sitting in Ana's belly all evening suddenly tightened. "What do you mean?"

"I mean you leave that woman be."

"Her name is Calia. What are you up to?" When Vesna didn't answer, Ana felt herself flush with indignation. "This is about her trial, isn't it? I told her you wouldn't be behind something so foolish!"

"I don't see why you're upset. It was your idea in the first place. I just thought of a way to make it work."

"What have you done?"

"Calm down. She'll be back soon enough–once she's missed her trial and the archdeacon's passed a suitable verdict. I'm told he's got little patience for people who miss their court dates."

"You stupid woman."

"Don't talk back to me, girl."

Ana felt like a fool. She went to her room, threw on a cloak, and hurried downstairs, ignoring the protests Vesna called after her. She quashed the anger rising in her belly, knowing it would do little good to waste time arguing with her mother.

She shouldn't have brushed off Calia's suspicions. She should have trusted her. Now she might suffer a damning judgement in church court, or at the very least an uncomfortable and prolonged fight to clear her name. Either way, she would become a public spectacle. What had Vesna done? Hired someone to kidnap her? Ana might have pressed the truth out of her mother eventually, but right now she was more concerned with getting to Calia before it was too late. She would never forgive herself if Karaline got tangled up in this.

Her pace quickened as she crossed the great hall and went out into the rain. It was worse than she'd thought, hitting her like a sheet of ice the moment she opened the door. Her boots sloshed through a muddy lake of water on the way to the stables. A groom saddled her horse for her, expressing concern for riding in this weather, but she snapped at him until he shut up and finished his job.

With the rain blowing in beneath her hood, she rode up the path through town, urging her disgruntled horse on as fast as she dared through the deluge. The streets of Ashmount were deserted, as was the path to the castle. She couldn't tell whether it was approaching dusk, or if the thick rainclouds were just making it look that way. The broken castle walls rose before her, eerily desolate in the gloaming. She rode her horse through the gates and turned toward Huwel's house. The door was unlatched, creaking back and forth on its hinges as the rain tried to push its way in. The gate to the warden's little stable was open, too, and his horse was missing. Had he left in a hurry?

Ana dismounted and looped her horse's tether around a hitching post. She pushed the gatehouse door open without knocking. A puddle of rainwater had collected inside. The hearth crackled next to a half-cleared table, its flames slowly dying. A scattering of muddy bootprints stained the floor beside an overturned chair.

"Karaline? Calia?" Ana called, but no one answered. Her anxiety growing by the moment, she went outside and scanned the courtyard, calling Karaline's name again.

She was too late. Whatever Vesna's plan was, it had already happened. Ana's eyes fell upon a long piece of metal lying in one of the puddles. She stooped to pick it up. It was a fire iron, bent in the middle as if someone had tried to snap it over their knee. A sickly feeling crept into her stomach as she saw a thin red rime edging the corners of a nearby puddle. Crimson wisps danced in the muddy water. Was it her sister's blood?

"Karaline?!" she yelled again. The shrillness of her voice strained her throat. Dropping the fire iron, she hitched up her dress and ran across the courtyard, screaming her sister's name futilely into the downpour. She went into the keep, but the place was empty, and it looked like the cellar had been boarded up. The image of blood dancing in the puddle wouldn't leave Ana's mind. Vesna couldn't have meant for anyone to get hurt, could she? But she hadn't meant for the weaving room to go up in flames, either. She was getting careless with her plans.

If only I'd done as she said, Ana thought, *none of this would have happened*. The hot shame of that realisation crawled on her back like a spider, making her want to curl up and hide. She felt like she was cowering on the floor again as Vesna smashed Tappy beneath her boot heel, wretched and helpless.

And angry.

It wasn't her fault. It had never been her fault. It was Vesna. Ana gripped the keep wall and stared out into the rain, shivering in the cold. Vesna had promised she would leave

Karaline be. Something within her was about to snap again, miserable and furious and far worse than before. She heard the hem of her dress rip as she ran back to the gatehouse. She was on her horse before she knew what she was doing, kicking the beast hard as she urged it down the hill at a reckless gallop.

Her knuckles were white on the reins when she arrived back at the manor. Her boots splashed into the pool of water in the middle of the courtyard, not even bothering to return her horse to the stable after she tumbled out of the saddle. Rain poured from her cloak and hair as she threw open the doors to the great hall. Most of the household was gathered inside for supper, but Ana barely saw them. Her focus narrowed in on her mother, sitting at a table close to the door as if she'd been waiting for her.

"Nastya!" Vesna hissed as her daughter staggered forward, slopping rain and mud over the floor. Ana grabbed her by the shoulders and hauled her upright. A stir of commotion rose around them. Someone tried to put a hand on Ana's arm, but she threw them off with a curse and dragged her mother outside.

"Where are they?" she yelled at Vesna as she tripped down the steps and splashed into the puddle, lapsing unconsciously into her native tongue. "What did you do?!"

"Not here, you stupid girl! You're making a scene!"

Ana could hear the rumble of noise behind them as people came to the door, but for once in her life, she didn't care. She didn't care about any of it. Not her image, her pride, her tapestry, not even the queen's approval. Damn all of it to hell. She was overwrought with emotion, furious with her mother and at herself. With her back against the wall, with her sister missing, an intense rage was finally edging out the years of fear and dependency Vesna had instilled in her. She grabbed her mother by the hair and threw her into the flooded courtyard with a scream. Vesna beat at her with her fists, but Ana was stronger.

"I'll kill you! I'll kill you, you old witch! Where are they? What did you do?!" Ana clawed at Vesna's face, blind with anger as her mother's eyes bulged up at her.

"Stop it! Stop! I sent Sigrad!"

"Why?!"

"I told him to take Calia away till after the trial!"

"What about Karaline?"

"I don't know!" Vesna pleaded, her struggles weakening as she realised she couldn't overpower her daughter. "I didn't know she'd be there!"

"You don't care about her. You never have! All you care about is making me like you!"

Vesna only wheezed in response, and Ana realised she was squeezing her by the throat. She let go in disgust, shoving her down into the muddy water.

"Where did Sigrad go?"

"I don't know," Vesna sobbed, her voice ugly and shrill, so desperate it was almost pitiable. "Stop this, Nastya!"

"Where did you find him? Where did you meet?!"

"In the woods. There's a hunting trail. A clearing with a fallen oak."

Ana knew the place. She and Calia had gone there with Karaline on some of their walks.

She didn't spare another breath on her mother. Footsteps splashed across the courtyard as Lord Oswin's men came out to break up the unsightly scene. Ana ran from them. Her horse had shied away from the fighting, trotting back toward the shelter of the stables, and it whinnied skittishly when she hauled herself into the saddle. She urged the animal back out through the gates with a hard kick, clinging to its neck for dear life as it tried to buck her off. There was still enough light for her to see where she was going. She didn't know how she would find Sigrad in the woods, or if he would even be at the place Vesna had described, but she didn't know what else to do. The knot around her heart had pulled tight and it wouldn't let go. She felt for the knife at her belt and was relieved to find it still there. Sigrad had gone too far once before. She prayed he hadn't done so again.

Her horse barely stayed on the path as the rain lashed down, whinnying and threatening to rear as she urged it up the hunting trail into the gloomy woods. The animal didn't want to be out in this weather, especially not being ridden this hard. Ana feared it might throw her off at any moment, but she didn't slow down. She kept a firm grip on the reins and leaned forward, squeezing tight with her knees as she pressed on through the tree line. With the branches crowding out what little light remained, it almost looked like night had fallen in the woods already. Ana trusted to memory that she was going the right way. It wouldn't be far to the clearing with the fallen tree, not if she rode fast. Clods of wet earth flew from her horse's hooves and rain sprayed from its nostrils. The woods thinned out, and Ana saw the outline of the fallen oak leaning against its upright brother. Her horse tried to rear again when she squeezed the reins to slow down. As wet and cold as she was, her body still felt hot with anger. She barely had the sense to tether her horse to a branch where the fallen tree provided some shelter. Hopefully the beast would calm down before she needed to ride again.

Ana held up a hand to shield her face from the rain and scanned the clearing. All she could see was tall grass, brambly bushes, and the dark woods beyond. Sigrad wouldn't be hiding somewhere so obvious, but perhaps he had a camp nearby.

"Sigrad!" she roared into the rain. Her throat hurt from yelling. She made her way to the edge of the clearing where the patter of rain was muffled by the thick foliage and shouted again. It was too dark to see anything in the woods. Stumbling through snarls of blackberry brambles, she made a circuit of the clearing's edge, yelling until the back of her throat tasted coppery with blood. Her head was throbbing. Exhaustion threatened to overwhelm her strained muscles, but desperation pushed her on. She kept walking in circles, thorns ripping at her legs, rain lashing her back until the light was all but gone.

After what felt like an hour, a voice answered her. She thought she'd imagined it at first, delirious with desperation, but then the grass rustled, and she turned to see a cloaked figure standing between her and the fallen oak.

"Sigrad?"

He nodded. "It's me. Did Vesna send you?"

Ana could only stare at him, struggling to make out his features in the gloom.

"Are Lord Oswin's men coming for me?" he asked nervously.

"Where are Karaline and Calia? Where's Huwel Ward?"

Something in her tone made Sigrad take a step back. "I think I might've killed him. I didn't mean to."

Ana stumbled forward, feeling for the handle of her knife beneath her cloak. "Tell me where they are, you little rat!"

"Why?"

"Don't you dare talk back to me! Where are they?!"

Sigrad continued retreating toward the oak. "You got me in trouble for setting that fire."

"That's not the worst I can do to you. It's no crime to kill an outlaw." Ana wasn't sure if she meant it, but she clutched her knife tight. Sigrad had a long club in his hand.

"Vesna's getting me pardoned. Go away. I'll let them out tomorrow."

"You'll let them out now!" Ana cried, but Sigrad was already turning to run. He made for the fallen tree, where Ana saw that her horse had already been untethered. Sigrad must have slipped behind her and done it while she was distracted. He was as wily as ever. Ana gave chase, but her wet dress slowed her down, tufts of thick grass tangling around her ankles. She tripped and fell, giving Sigrad the distance he needed to leap astride her horse and take hold of the reins. The agitated animal whinnied and reared. For a second, it looked like Sigrad was about to fall, but he managed to hold on and wrestle the beast under control.

Ana's fingertips were an inch from seizing the bridle when he twisted away. The horse kicked back at her, spattering mud over her dress. In sheer desperation, she yanked her knife from its sheath and hurled it at Sigrad. It was a clumsy throw, the blade missing and bouncing off the horse's flank as it fell short. The beast bucked wildly, recoiling from the sting of pain. Sigrad bounced halfway out of the saddle, somehow still managing to hold on, but when the horse bucked a second time the reins tore from his grasp. He sailed through the air, hands clawing at nothing, twisting over sideways in an uncontrollable tumble before he hit the ground on his back.

Ana ran to him as her horse disappeared into the rain. She knelt down and yanked him up by his clothing. He made no attempt to resist. Sigrad's eyes twitched, his mouth opening and closing, but he didn't seem able to move. It looked like he was trying to speak, but there was no breath in him. The only noises he made were a few strange, sickly gurgles from the back of his throat, then his lips stopped moving and his eyes grew dull. Ana dropped him into the grass. His breath was silent, his chest still. He must have broken his back. Ana wanted to weep, but not for Sigrad. For all she knew, he deserved it. What had he done? Where was her sister?!

A dreadful realisation stole up on Anastasia as she stared down at the dead page. If no one else knew where Calia and Karaline were imprisoned, who was going to free them tomorrow? They might be bound somewhere in the woods, freezing and helpless, at the mercy of wild animals and the remorseless elements. Ana looked into the trees, ready to go searching, but the idea sunk to the bottom of her stomach like a stone. It was almost pitch black. There was no hope of finding them in the dark.

Overcome with despair, she buried her face in her hands and wept.

CHAPTER 23

Calia rubbed Karaline's arms to keep her warm as they huddled together on the cellar steps. The rain was incessant, even down here. It echoed from above and below, dribbling from the edges of the board to soak through their clothing before running down the stairs in plips and plops. Nowhere was dry. Nowhere was warm. Calia didn't think she'd ever been so cold in her life. Poor Karaline was shaking like a leaf, her frightened breaths even louder than the trickling water and crashing rain.

The last chink of light had long since faded. Hours must have passed since Sigrad threw them down into the dark. Calia tried not to think about Huw. It made her feel sick to picture him crumpled in the courtyard with blood streaming from his head. But with nothing else to do, the intrusive thoughts wormed their way into her mind, and her shivers worsened.

For the first hour or so, she'd tried in vain to move the board from the top of the stairs, but it was as thick as a door and whatever Sigrad had weighed it down with seemed heavier than a person. Perhaps with a knife she could have cut some of the wood away, but she didn't have one.

After that, she'd thought of wading into the cellar to try and find something that could help, perhaps tools left behind by the builders or a dry spot where Karaline might perch. But after a few steps, the water grew abruptly deeper, and something brushed her hand that felt like a dead animal. She remembered the desiccated corpse she'd seen down here, and her courage was stolen by a sudden fear of dead fingers clawing at her from the pitch-black water.

"How long till morning?" Karaline asked. Her voice was frightfully small, every word stuttered through chattering teeth.

Calia rubbed her arms harder. "It can't be long now."

"I might fall asleep."

"You have to stay awake. Just till someone comes for us. Do you have Blue with you?"

Karaline had sewn a secret pocket inside her dress where she could carry her doll at all times. There was an invisible shifting motion as she drew out the sodden felt creature.

"Why don't we tell Blue a story?" Calia said.

"How will that help?"

"It'll give us something to focus on. Come on. We'll take turns. I'll say one line, then you say the next."

The game occupied them for a while, but Karaline's voice soon trailed off. Calia was struggling to focus as well. She was so terribly cold. At first her body had felt stiff from sitting on the hard stone steps, but that stiffness was going away. She was getting numb. How long would they have to sit here till Sigrad returned? Perhaps someone would notice Huw was missing and start a search. But that wouldn't happen till morning. Would Karaline be able to endure the cold that long? Calia had heard stories about people freezing to death when they slept outside in winter. Her arms closed tight around Karaline, drawing her into the warmth of her body. She felt so small. Her fingers found the wet shape of Blue clutched in the girl's hands. Karaline had made little articles of clothing for the doll in recent weeks, dressing it up in all sorts of different costumes. Sometimes it was a queen with a crown, other times a monk in a black robe, a minstrel with a feathered cap, or a knight with a shield and sword. Calia felt the knight's sword belt looped over Blue's shoulder. It was a thin strip of leather tied to a tiny scabbard. Calia thought the scabbard was a solid wooden stick, but as her fingers probed, she felt something poking out of it. Even half-numb, her fingers recognised the familiar eye of a needle. A nice thick bronze one. The same one she'd given Karaline all those months ago. With a gentle tug, she slid the needle free of the scabbard. A desperate thought crossed her mind of using it to pick splinters from the board overhead, but she knew it was futile. It would take days to pick a hole through a door using a needle, assuming it didn't break in the process.

"How long do you think it would take to open a door with a needle?" she asked Karaline. Several seconds elapsed before she realised she'd received no answer. "Karaline?" She shook the girl abruptly, a jolt of fear going through her.

A quiet groan answered her. Relief washed through Calia, but the fear didn't go away. Karaline wouldn't last much longer. It might be hours yet before dawn broke, and hours more before they were released.

"Come on, let's go to the top of the stairs." Calia tugged Karaline after her as she shuffled up, hoping the movement would warm them a little. She stopped when the board bumped the top of her head. Still clutching Kara close to her body, she propped herself up against the wall and began exploring the wood with her fingertips. It was rough, not smooth and finished. Maybe she couldn't pick a hole in it with a needle, but what if she could break off a splinter or two? Perhaps then she'd be able to squeeze her fingers in and pry open a crack. It still seemed hopeless, but she couldn't sit and do nothing while Kara froze to death.

Finding a splintery notch with her fingernails, she lifted her needle and pushed the tip in. She didn't go too far; the point would bend or the stem would snap if she was anything but delicate. Wiggling as gently as she could, a tiny splinter came away beneath her nails. It was little more than a shaving, but it was something.

For what felt like hours, Calia picked away at the board, talking to Karaline the whole time. The girl stayed with her, but there were moments when she fell silent for a fearfully long time. Calia told her to keep moving her arms and wiggling her toes. She did the same, hoping the dull ache in her muscles was somehow keeping her warm. It was hard to know whether she felt tired when she was this cold. At some point, her fingertips started bleeding, and she was glad their numbness muted the pain to a distant sting. She'd succeeded in scraping a tiny gully in the wood, but every time she tried to push her fingers in and crack off a larger piece, nothing happened. The board was too thick, and she didn't have the leverage to split it open. The futility of her task finally hit her when the first light of dawn filtered in from above. By its faint glow, the crack that had felt appreciably deep to Calia's fingers was revealed to be little more than a scratch. It wasn't going to work.

"Now long now," she whispered to Karaline, hearing tears in her voice. "Look, the sun's coming up. They'll find us soon."

Karaline squirmed against her as if trying to burrow into her warmth. She hadn't spoken for an hour.

"Please say something." Calia felt her desperation overflowing. She couldn't bear the thought of Karaline slowly slipping away as they huddled there in the dark. All night she'd tried to be strong for the girl, but now her resolve was breaking. "Please, Kara," she sobbed. "Don't leave me alone." She wanted her mother, a warm pair of arms to hold her tight and tell her things would be okay. If only she'd stayed at home.

She called for help as the light brightened, but no one answered. Even Karaline's shivers felt weak. Calia wanted to close her eyes and let the cold take her. She felt so bitterly useless. But what else could she do? Her gaze slid down to a chink of light glimmering off the dark water.

She could try the cellar again. Her fears of dead animals and skeletal corpses seemed small now compared to the dread of losing Kara. Stepping back into that freezing pool might steal the last warmth from her body and take her strength along with it. If she went in, she might never come out.

"I'll be back soon," she whispered. "Try and keep moving." It was agony to pry Karaline away from her, knowing she was depriving the girl of the only warmth keeping her alive, but she had to do something. She propped her up with the chink of light shining on her face, then stumbled into the cellar. Her legs were clumsy and unresponsive after sitting on the steps all night, but the bite of the water still made her gasp. Thank God Karaline hadn't been in it for long. As cold as it was on the steps, the water was even worse.

Calia kept one hand on the wall, fearing she would lose her way if she waded blindly into the middle of the room. The water sloshed around her knees as she dragged her feet across the submerged flagstones. She hoped her boots might catch on a hammer or an iron bar—something the builders had left behind. She flinched in fear as something soft brushed against her leg and a flurry of splashes followed. A rat? A big frog? She didn't know how anything could survive down here in this cold. A few paces in, the water deepened. A big chunk of rubble almost tripped her as the water rose to her thighs, but she twisted toward the wall and caught herself at the last moment.

It was horrible, navigating blind like this where anything might strike her feet without warning. Anxiety urged her to go faster, but her good sense told her to slow down. She took each step carefully, probing around on the chamber floor for any shapes that didn't belong.

She judged she was about halfway into the room before

she found something. It wasn't submerged beneath the surface, but affixed to the wall beside her. A hard object caught her hand, jutting out at an angle. She put her fingers in her mouth and sucked them until some of the feeling returned, bringing with it the taste of blood and a sting of pain. With her sense of touch to guide her, she realised that the object was an old bracket mortared directly into the stones. It joined a metal rod that ran upwards to support a conical holder of some kind. Calia had to reach up high to feel what was inside. Something crumbly and waxy, likely an old candle. That part was useless to her, but perhaps she could use the rod as a lever.

She followed the wall down until she found the lower bracket again and gave it a hard tug. The mortar shifted. It had to give way. It had to. She tugged again, then a third time. The bracket loosened a little more with each motion. On the fifth tug, it twisted free. There was a second bracket higher up, but that one was easy to break off with the base hanging loose. With an urgency born of desperation, Calia upended the unwieldy piece of metal and put her boot on the candle holder, twisting the rod to try and tear it loose. It felt like there were decades of rust holding the thing together, but with enough yanking and twisting, it gave just like the mortar. Calia was left clutching a rod a little longer than her forearm. The lower end was still fixed to one of the brackets, too bulky and awkward to do anything with, but the part that had supported the holder was narrow. If only it had been sharp like the end of a claw hammer, then she could have used it to break the board easily. This would just have to do.

She hurried back to the steps as fast as she could, sloshing waves from her thighs as she tried not to trip over any rubble. She wasn't afraid of what lurked in the darkness anymore, but of returning to the stairs and finding Karaline dead. Water poured from her dress as she clambered back up. Kara was where she'd left her, face pale in the chink of light. She was still breathing.

"Not long now," Calia told her, taking the girl in her arms and moving her down the steps so she had room to work. Every second was precious. Feeling the underside of the board again, she found the crack she'd dug with her needle. It hadn't seemed like much at the time, but she was glad she'd made it now. The end of the rod was too blunt to drive into the wood by itself, but it was just barely narrow enough to wedge into the crack. Wiggling it from side to side, she felt the wood give. A burst of hope flared within her, driving back the shivers. She braced the rod with both hands, pushing upwards and to the side as hard as she could. There was a loud crack as the rod juddered an inch deeper. Calia put her shoulder beneath it and pushed again, levering with all the space the stairwell afforded her. A split opened up in the board. Wrenching and twisting, pushing and pulling, she managed to widen it. The crack was about a foot from the edge. When she yanked the rod back and forth, she felt the wood splintering and shifting. If she weakened it enough, she might be able to snap off a piece at the edge. That would open up a gap just big enough for someone as small as her to squeeze through.

She worked feverishly, checking on Karaline every so often to make sure the girl was still with her. It took a painfully long time to work the piece of wood loose. As the morning wore on, she remembered thinking that Karaline wouldn't last the night. These were borrowed hours. Calia had torn two of her nails, and her fingers throbbed like they were about to break, but still she kept working. Once she'd loosened the cracked piece of board as much as she could, she wedged the rod in deep and wiggled her fingers through the crack. Reaching around the edge with her other hand, she lifted herself up and tugged, subjecting the wood to all of her weight.

It didn't shift. She tried again, crying out in frustration, then again, and again, wrenching the unyielding board up and down until she heard something splinter. It shifted a fraction of an inch. One by one, the wooden fibres began to pop, giving her a flex, then a wiggle. Calia's muscles burned as she wrenched on the stubborn piece of wood, trying to tear open the corner of the board like a trapdoor. Inch by agonising inch, it bent further inwards. Light spilt into the stairwell as she wrenched it down one last time and a rectangular hole opened up overhead.

Calia let out a rush of breath, more release than relief. She squashed her body into the narrow opening and squeezed through the gap. The splintered wood dug into her dress and the stone ceiling scraped her scalp. It was a desperately tight fit, but she managed it. The bright light of the courtyard seemed alien after a night underground. The rain had stopped and the sun was out. Calia saw that Sigrad had piled several sacks on the other end of the board to keep it in place. They were painfully heavy, probably full of gravel or mortar, but one by one she managed to drag them away. As soon as the board was free, she pulled it back, picked Karaline up, and lifted her out of the stairwell. Calia stumbled as she walked. Her arms felt like nothing, her legs wobbling like stems of broken grass. It looked like a thousand miles from the keep to Huw's house. She staggered across the courtyard, aching and shivering too much to speak as she cradled Karaline in her arms. She couldn't tell if the girl was breathing or not. If she put her down to check, she might not be able to get back up.

The door to the gatehouse was still flapping open in the wind. When Calia looked in, she found the room empty and the hearth cold. Her first thought was to re-kindle it and get Karaline warm, but it would take hours for the stone room to heat up. They couldn't wait that long. With a groan, Calia turned away and stumbled through the castle gates. She needed to find help. Pete Builder's house was nearby.

She made the agonising walk down the path as fast as she could, fearing she would trip over her feet at any moment. There was no sign of anyone in Pete's yard when she got there. She slumped against his front door, her hand throbbing as she beat her knuckles against the wood until she heard a noise on the other side. The latch rasped back.

"What in Lord's name–" Pete's wife gasped as Calia sagged towards her. She didn't get out a word before collapsing into the woman's arms.

The rest of that morning was a haze. They brought Karaline to the fire and got her out of her damp clothes, then smothered her in blankets and rubbed her arms while feeding her sips of hot tea. Calia was shivering the whole time. She numbly let Pete's wife and the housekeeper change her clothes and wrap her in more blankets. It was a long time before she managed to explain what had happened.

"Should we tell the bailiff?" Pete's wife asked.

Calia couldn't stomach the thought of being interrogated by Lord Oswin right now. She shook her head groggily.

"Please just let Lucy Tailor and Anastasia Fiala know. Wait–oh, poor Huw. Yes, you must tell Lord Oswin. His men need to find Huwel. I don't know where he is. He might be dead." Fresh tears welled in Calia's eyes as Pete's wife comforted her. She sent the housekeeper off to the manor, whereupon Calia fell into a listless doze.

When she opened her eyes again, she was lying on a bed alongside Karaline. Lucy sat to her left, a fraught expression on her face, while Anastasia was on her right with her arms wrapped around her sister.

"How is she?" Calia asked as she sat herself up. A painful stiffness wracked her body. Her arms ached and her fingers stung, but the deep chill that had been sapping her strength was gone.

Karaline answered by turning toward her. She looked exhausted, but the colour was back in her cheeks, and she had the wherewithal to smile. Relief welled up inside Calia, every bit as warm and comforting as the crackle of the hearth. She put a bandaged hand to her mouth and let out a tearful gasp.

Lucy rubbed her shoulders.

"You're alright. You got her here in time."

"Thank you," Anastasia said. She sounded as exhausted as Calia felt. Her hair was tangled, her dress filthy, and she had bramble scratches on her arms.

"What about Huw?" Calia asked.

"They found him," said Lucy. "He'd been dragged halfway down the path behind the castle. He's alive, but not in a good way. The physician says his skull is fractured. He managed to crawl into some bushes to keep the rain off, but he was out there all night."

Calia's momentary happiness faded as a lump came to her throat. "Poor Huw."

"It's in God's hands whether he lives now. The physician says it might be a while before we know for sure. People who get hit in the head like that can drop dead at any moment."

"I'll pray for him." Calia had never been devoutly faithful, but praying was something everyone did when a friend or loved one was deathly ill. It was all you could do.

Anastasia looked to the door, making sure Pete's wife wasn't listening, then said in a low voice: "Sigrad's dead. Vesna had him lock you up so you'd miss your trial. I made her tell me where he was hiding in the woods."

Lucy stared at her in horror. "You didn't."

"I might have. I wanted to. He stole my horse and it threw him off when he tried to get away. I think he broke his back in the fall."

"Have you told anyone?" Calia asked.

Ana gave the pair of them a guarded look. It had taken a lot, Calia realised, for her to divulge such a dangerous secret.

"No. And I'd ask that you keep it to yourselves, too."

"We'd probably better," said Lucy. "Sigrad was an outlaw, but he came from a noble family. They wouldn't be happy if they found out the truth."

Ana gave her an appreciative nod before turning back to Calia. "You missed your hearing."

"I'd forgotten about that." She looked at the door and realised the sun was going down. She must have slept all day. "I suppose they found me guilty when I didn't turn up."

"I haven't heard, but I expect so. I'll speak with the archdeacon tomorrow."

"I should've gone to speak for you," Lucy said. "I was on my way there when Pete's housekeeper told me what had happened. After that, I was too worried about you to think about anything else."

"It's alright. This was more important. Do you think you'll be able to make the archdeacon reverse his verdict, Ana?"

"He's a stubborn man, the sort who doesn't like to admit fault. I expect he'll argue that he should've been informed beforehand if you were indisposed." Ana snorted with derision. "But I'll try. If he won't listen, we'll go to the bishop. It's a farce, holding a trial for someone who can't defend themselves."

"So Vesna got what she wanted after all," Lucy said bitterly.

Ana looked away in shame.

For the first time since the conversation began, Karaline spoke.

"We don't have to go back to her, do we?"

"No," Ana said, taking her sister's hand and squeezing it fiercely. "We're finished with that woman." They were words driven by anger, but Calia sensed that she meant them this time. Karaline had always been Ana's soft spot, the pure little part of her soul that had never been coloured by Vesna's manipulations. If there was one thing in the world that could break her mother's hold over her, it was a threat to Karaline. Vesna had crossed an unforgivable threshold last night.

They ate some supper, then Calia and Karaline went back to bed. Pete and his wife let them stay the night. When Calia closed her eyes, it was with mixed emotions. Karaline was safe, but Huw was at death's door. Ana seemed to have finally accepted the truth about her mother, but Calia now faced a

court verdict that would put her future in jeopardy.
It was a troubled end to the most difficult day of her life.

CHAPTER 24

Despite Lord Oswin's protests, Ana was glad to get away from Ashmount House. She sent servants to collect her things and moved back in with the Goldsmiths. On the few occasions she happened to cross paths with Vesna, she froze the woman out, afraid that she might make another scene if they were forced to exchange words.

The night Karaline had gone missing, she'd wished her mother dead many times over. There were more frightening things in this life than being without Vesna. So many of the lessons she'd learned now seemed meaningless by comparison. Why had she gone back to her? Why had she thought her mother could change? Perhaps she'd genuinely believed she could control her, but you couldn't control someone you were afraid of. Calia had been right. Ana might have been able to endure a lifetime in Vesna's shadow, but Karaline couldn't. She'd almost died because of it.

So she endured Lord Oswin's threats to complain to the queen if she didn't resume her duties with the tapestry. The weavers all knew what they were doing. Most of them had never really needed her oversight in the first place. Hers was a ceremonial position, one Vesna had argued for so that she could claim ownership of the project. The tapestry would have come along just fine without her. Not precisely as she envisioned, perhaps, but Calia's weaving had demonstrated that Ana's artistic style was not the only valid one.

Instead, she busied herself with tidying up the mess that had been left in the wake of her mother's fumbled scheme. Calia was still recovering from her ordeal, and Lucy, while adamant to help, didn't have the tact to navigate a delicate problem like this. Ana went to the archdeacon first. As she'd expected, he was embarrassed by the implication that he'd erred in pronouncing Calia guilty. Instead of reversing his verdict, he doubled down, insisting that it was too late to overturn the ruling now. He was, however, willing to waive Calia's punishment. Most likely it would have been penance and a fine. The church was all too eager to profit from sinful dalliances these days. But the punishment wasn't the real problem; Calia could've paid a fine if she needed to, and penance rarely amounted to more than a slap on the wrist. It was the judgement, which by now was the talk of the town, that would stay around to haunt her. Extenuating circumstances or not, the archdeacon had proclaimed her a blasphemer who fornicated with other women.

Despite Ana's efforts to convince him otherwise, Lord Oswin sent a letter to the queen appraising her of the situation. He'd never been overly fond of Calia, and the ruling—true or not—was enough to raise his ire. For now, Calia would be allowed to stay and finish her tapestry, but the second Oswin received confirmation from the queen, he was sure to throw her out.

Ana hoped to avert that catastrophe before it happened. Enlisting the help of Leander Weaver, the two of them rode across the county to Redland where they met with Bishop Matthew to argue for a pardon. The bishop was surprised to see Ana, and through the tacit hints he dropped over dinner, she deduced that Vesna must have offered him some bribe to put Calia on trial. Having worked that part out, it wasn't difficult to unearth the rest.

"I don't care what my mother may have told you, my lord bishop," Ana told him with a hard stare. "She is not my keeper, and the only promise I make to you is this: I will *never* paint your cathedral if the verdict against Calia Tailor stands."

The bishop deflated after that. He obviously wasn't a man who enjoyed lingering grudges. After a little more wrangling–during which Leander leveraged his own past scandal with the church–the bishop agreed to have Calia pardoned. It had taken longer than Ana would have liked, but she rode back down the road to Ashmount that day with a pleasant lightness in her heart.

It was the first time she'd ever used the song and dance of politics to help another person.

By the time she returned to town, Huwel Ward was back on his feet. Pete Builder's kind wife had agreed to nurse him while he recovered, for he could not stay at the gatehouse all on his own. The old man was still wobbly on his feet and beset by headaches, but the physician was confident that he was on the road to recovery. With a little luck, he might be back to his old self in a few weeks' time. Calia and Karaline were overjoyed with the news.

For a while, life in Ashmount almost returned to normal. Once Calia's fingers healed, she went back to work on her tapestry. Ana resumed her duties overseeing the other weavers, though she kept her visits brief, avoiding Vesna as much as possible. A handful of people gathered at Pete's house every few days to have supper and check in on Huw. Ana felt uncomfortable going, but Karaline insisted, so she begrudgingly took her. It was an atmosphere she was very unused to. Noisy, humble, and full of conversation. But there was cheer to be found in those moments, and while Ana said little, she found herself growing comfortable listening to the others talking while she drank her wine.

Little by little, the wound that had been left by Vesna's

betrayal began healing.

Winter's arrival brought with it a response from the queen. The rains of autumn had eased, making way for still, chilly evenings that left the courtyard glistening with crystals of frost. Anastasia decided not to open the letter when the royal messenger delivered it to the Goldsmiths' door. Instead, she took it to Ashmount House. That afternoon, as the weavers finished up work in the fading light, she went to see Calia at her loom. The tapestry hanging there was complete. The only work that remained was to tidy up some stray threads trailing down the back. Ana smiled when she saw it.

It wasn't a striking piece, not glamorous or breathtaking like hers, but it was the kind of tapestry you could *look* at. There was a comfortable simplicity to it that drew the eye and held your attention, the same way you might spy a squirrel climbing a tree and lose yourself for minutes following its adventures from branch to branch. There were always more details to appreciate, more threads of the visual narrative to follow. Ana wasn't sure whether it was a tapestry fit to show off in a royal hall, but any noblewoman would have been happy to have something so artful adorning her chambers.

"The branches at the top do change the perspective, don't they?" she said to Calia.

"Yes. I'm glad I had your sketch to remind me how they looked. They'll never be the same as the original, but I like to think I've captured some of its spirit."

"You've captured some of your own, too. I like this one more than the squares you wove for me."

"Well, I'm glad you like it," Calia said with a sigh. "It may be the last thing I ever weave."

Ana fingered the letter she was holding behind her back. She took it out, stared down at the royal seal, and offered it to Calia. "I received this today."

"My dismissal."

"I don't know. She'll have heard about the bishop

pardoning you by now."

Calia stared at the letter. She seemed a wiser woman than the one who'd arrived in Ashmount earlier that year, possessed of a quiet strength beneath her humble exterior.

"If you were the queen, would you want an embarrassment like me working for you?"

Ana said nothing. Calia took the letter, broke the seal, and unfolded it. Her expression was dull and acceptant as she scanned the lines.

"She asks that you dismiss me immediately and for Lord Oswin to eject me from the household. She regrets losing a weaver of my talents, but the king is adamant. He will not indulge her personal projects if they bring the crown into association with people of my character."

Ana took the letter and confirmed its contents for herself. The intent was clear. Even if Calia had been pardoned, the king and queen's religious convictions—or perhaps their image—took precedence. Ana crumpled the parchment in anger.

"It's what I expected," Calia said. "Please don't be upset on my behalf."

Ana's first instinct was to argue with her, but she managed to suppress it. She was trying to put that side of herself to more productive use these days.

"You don't need the queen's patronage. A weaver like you can do well enough on her own."

"I suppose so, but I don't really know how. Not unless I stay here in Ashmount and let Leander organise my commissions."

"Would that be so bad?"

Calia smiled and shook her head. "I suppose not. I'm very fond of Lucy and Huw, but my family is in Tannersfield. Once you and Karaline return to the capital, I expect I'll go home. I'd be content being a tailor again."

Ana paced across the chamber, looking at a near-finished square of the Farren Vale that hung from Rovena's loom.

She'd been pondering the future as well. What would she do once the tapestry was finished? Go back to the capital and take more commissions from members of the royal court? Pick up where she'd left off? That idea left a sour taste in her mouth now. It was her mother's life, her mother's dream. It was the life she'd been groomed for, not the one she wanted.

What *did* she want? In truth, she didn't know. Her desires were so tightly intertwined with the ones Vesna had beaten into her that she might never unpick them. She wanted to paint, and she wanted to be with Karaline. Those two things she could at least say with certainty.

She looked back at Calia. "What if you worked for me again?"

"On what?"

"Tapestries. My cartoons and your weaving."

"That didn't go very well before."

Ana walked to Calia's loom and gestured at the large sketch reflected in the mirror. "This one did."

"You'd have to let me do what I wanted. No breathing down my neck."

"I know. It might not be prestigious work. We wouldn't be paid a royal wage. But you could work with the guild here, and there are plenty of wealthy customers who come to Ashmount looking to have fine things made."

"I thought you wanted to be the most famous painter in the kingdom?"

Calia's words stung Anastasia with a familiar pain. Could she stomach a humbler life? A less glamorous one? The people at court would frown and shake their heads when they spoke of Anastasia Fiala, the promising young painter who had failed to live up to her potential.

Her heartbeat quickened, an uncomfortable sweat prickling the back of her neck. Her hand moved instinctively to her upper arm, rubbing an imaginary pinch. She couldn't really do it, could she? She couldn't live with that kind of shame.

"Are you alright?" Calia asked.

Ana took a deep breath and stopped rubbing.

"No, I'm not. I do want to be the greatest painter in the kingdom. I deserve to be." She fell silent for a moment. "But I don't think I should."

"Because you don't want to end up like Vesna."

Ana nodded. "I never thought I could be anything else. But sometimes, when I'm with you and the others, I feel as though I might manage it. That time you told me about your family, how you weren't one of them by birth... I've been thinking about it a lot."

"We don't all have to be what we're born into."

"I'm still not sure about that."

"But you've got a chance to try."

"Yes." Ana's throat grew tight. Calia was one of the few people she'd even spoken to this openly. Perhaps one day she'd be able to say more, like how she didn't want to be the sort of person who could be wounded by her pride, how she was terrified of treating Karaline the way Vesna had treated her, and how ashamed she felt by all the wretched things she'd done. There were a thousand uncomfortable memories in her past, and she didn't want to create any more.

Perhaps, one day, she'd be able to tell her.

Calia stepped forward and took Anastasia's arm. "Alright."

"What?"

"I'll stay if you stay. We can work with the guild and see how it goes."

Ana was frightened. Part of her feared she was making a life-ruining mistake. But to her surprise, a much larger part felt an overwhelming sense of relief. It was as if a yoke that had been around her neck since birth had suddenly come off.

She said goodbye to Vesna a week later. Early in the morning, she strode up the frosty path to the manor and climbed the stairs to the royal solar. Vesna looked up in surprise when she opened the door to greet her.

"Nastya."

"You're leaving tomorrow," Ana said before her mother could get a second word in. "I've paid some gold merchants to take you back to the capital."

Vesna scowled at her. "I am not. I'm staying right here until you come to your senses."

"Then you'll be waiting out in the street. I had a conversation with Lord Oswin last night. I told him I'll stop work on the tapestry immediately if you're allowed to stay here any longer."

Vesna's mouth dropped open in outrage. "Are you trying to destroy what's left of our reputation?!"

Ana felt a familiar anger bubbling up inside her, but she'd been preparing for this moment, and her voice was even when she spoke.

"I don't want to see you again."

"You're being stupid."

"I've made up my mind."

Vesna gaped at her, eyes darting about like a rat caught in a maze. The look of disbelief faded, giving way to one of sorrow.

"How can you do this to your mother? After all I've done for you. I suppose you'll be taking your sister away from me, too. Isn't there any love in your heart, Ana?"

"Stop it."

"After I took you across an ocean? Paid for you to live like a princess? Let you paint every day of your life? You may be angry with me, but I'm still your mother."

Ana gave her a hard look, willing back the sickly feeling that wanted to succumb to Vesna's manipulation.

"Love is something you have to earn."

"I did so much."

"You earned my obligation, not my love. You can keep the house and the money; there's more than enough to see you through the rest of your life. That's what you earned from me. Nothing more."

"You can't throw away everything we've built because of one bad year!" Vesna said with desperation in her voice.

"I'm not!" Ana snapped, her composure finally fracturing. "I'm throwing it away because of a bad lifetime! I hate you! I hate what you are, I hate what you made me, and I hate the thought of ever seeing you again!"

"You'll never amount to anything on your own!"

Ana was afraid she might be right. It was her greatest doubt and her greatest fear. So she poured all of her conviction into her next words, thrusting them out like a shield to push back Vesna's tightening grip.

"I don't care. I'd rather live the rest of my life as a peasant than spend another moment of it with you."

Vesna flinched. For perhaps the first time in her life, she was at a loss for words. She stared at her daughter in disbelief, her lips twitching in search of a protest that refused to come. Anastasia was her masterpiece. Her Farren Vale. She was the work she'd poured her heart and soul into, and it was going up in flames before her eyes.

Now you know what it feels like.

There was nothing else to say. Ana turned on her heel and walked out, feeling stronger with each step.

Vesna left Ashmount the next day.

EPILOGUE

The following May, in the twenty-ninth year of King Fendrel's reign, Calia left Ashmount to attend her brother Wolfram's wedding. She hadn't been back to the manor since her dismissal, but Lucy and Ana kept her abreast of developments in the royal household. Her small Farren Vale now hung in the Fialas' old room, while Ana's vast masterpiece adorned the great hall. Left to their own devices, the weavers had completed their remaining squares more quickly than expected. Ana's hands-off approach seemed to have worked. She'd spent less and less time at the manor as the project neared completion, focusing instead on the house she was having built near the castle path. It was a project that would take the rest of the year. Once complete, it would have workshops for both weaving and painting, a kitchen, hall, and bedchambers. One room would be Calia's. The rest could house more artisans if Ana decided to expand her enterprise. Even without the money she'd left to her mother, she was still a wealthy woman, but they would need work to support them once the building costs of the house had been paid. Ana already had a new job lined up to paint a fresco in Redland Cathedral next month, while Calia had been making do with simple tailoring work. With no pressing commitments tying them down for the next few weeks, Calia had invited Ana and Karaline to accompany her to Wolfram's wedding.

James, the bodyguard who worked for her mother, had come to escort them from Ashmount. It was a few days' ride from Farrenwold County across neighbouring Tannersfield. Wolfram was now the lord of a little village in a place called Elkinshire, but he still lived on the estate of the baron he served. He and his fiancée had been refurbishing a cottage there that was going to be their marital home.

"I've never attended a wedding," Ana said as she rode alongside Calia. There was a clipped aloofness to her words that would have come across as rude to anyone who didn't know her, but Calia had come to recognise it as nervousness. Ana always hid her insecurities behind a mask of superiority.

"And such a humble one at that," Calia teased.

"It won't be that humble, will it? Your brother is a knight, after all."

"Not a very rich one. And his lord's poor. I expect we'll be drinking cider at trestle tables in someone's garden."

"I don't know why I agreed to this."

"Because you're my friend, and you and Karaline are my guests."

Ana shook her head and squinted off into the distance. They were travelling down the main road through Elkinshire, a quiet, rural place peppered with small villages and rolling fields. In the distance, one tall hill rose above the others, its rocky face propping up a crown of fir trees that stretched down the back like a mane of hair. According to Wolfram, that was where they were headed.

James rode ahead as the sun went down while Karaline trotted beside Ana on a pony.

"I've been meaning to tell you," Ana said a little stiffly. "I asked some of my old contacts in the capital to look in on Goldie Weaver."

Calia raised her brow hopefully. "Is she well?"

"As far as I can gather. It seems the rumours about her husband were true. He ran off to marry some woman overseas. But she's taken up with a salt merchant since, and they seem to be doing well for themselves." Ana paused, purposefully avoiding eye contact. "People say he's a kindly man."

"That's a relief. You must help me get a letter to her. We haven't been in contact since she left."

Ana cleared her throat and nodded. She still looked like she was anticipating a rebuke for the part she'd played in Goldie's dismissal, her shoulders tense and her lips thin.

In an effort to lighten the mood, Calia changed the subject back to her brother's wedding.

"Just think, by this time tomorrow you'll have met my whole family."

Ana visibly relaxed. "Are they all like you?"

"No, not at all. You'd find my brother very tiresome. He likes hunting and sports."

"A typical knight, then," Ana said wearily.

"My father gets on well with everyone, though. My mother's a bit eccentric. She likes to speak her mind. And my sister, Livy, she's a flirt, but she's very clever. You could talk to her about business and taxes."

"I've little patience for flirtatious women. They never have their minds on the things that matter. I'm glad you're not like that."

"Do you think you'll ever marry someday?" Calia asked.

Ana thought about it for a moment. "A year ago, I'd have said no. Not to anyone I particularly cared for, at any rate."

"Vesna wouldn't have wanted it, would she?"

"No, she wouldn't. There are a great many things I question whether I should or shouldn't be doing these days. I wonder how much of her advice is still worth listening to." She spoke lightly as if entertaining an idle thought, but she wouldn't have brought it up if she didn't want Calia's opinion.

She rarely spoke of her mother these days.

"I'm sure she had some good advice. You can always talk to me about it. Or Huw, or anyone, really. It's easy to make up your mind when you're only listening to one voice, but I think you end up seeing things more clearly when you listen to lots of people. Life's too complicated for one person to have all the answers."

"You've become insufferably wise, Calia. You're the sort of woman who could look at a sculpture and have no clue how it was made, yet intuit everything the artist was thinking when they made it."

Calia and Karaline giggled in unison.

"You give very funny compliments, Ana."

"I was just making an observation."

"There's a wit to you."

"I've never been one to exercise wit."

"Well, maybe you should try. You'll have plenty of chances at the wedding."

"Hm."

They rode on in silence for a while, the sun sinking steadily lower in the sky. Elkinshire was a peaceful place. It felt earthy and quiet like the woods around Ashmount. Perhaps Calia's family naturally gravitated toward tranquil little corners of the kingdom like this.

With a heavy heart, she realised that she probably wouldn't be going home to live with her parents again. Ashmount had always felt like a temporary adventure to her, something exciting and new but ultimately fleeting. She hadn't really believed she would go on to weave tapestries in the capital afterwards, much less start her own business with someone like Ana. But they *were* going to start a business. The house was being built, the money had been spent, and her heart was set on it. She was going to live in Ashmount, just as her brother was going to live here in Elkinshire. They were all going their separate ways. She put her arms around herself, melancholy for the absence of the past.

It was an odd life, the one she was committing herself to. Most women her age were getting married, starting families, raising children. She still couldn't see the appeal of having a husband, but she did appreciate the sense of belonging that came from family. A family didn't need to be husbands and wives, children and siblings. All it needed was love, and love wasn't guaranteed by the bonds of blood or marriage. Ana's tale was a poignant example of that.

Calia looked at the two women riding beside her and wondered whether, five or ten years from now, they would all still be living together in the house Ana was building. She'd grown to love Karaline, and the more of Anastasia that emerged through her mother's scars, the more she came to care for her, too. Perhaps they could be a little family of their own. Others would come, friends and apprentices, and perhaps some of them would marry, bringing yet more faces into the house. Calia liked the sound of that.

Ana saw her looking at Karaline and said: "She'll be old enough to start an apprenticeship in a couple of years."

"Can I be Lucy's apprentice?" Kara asked.

"You'll have to ask her."

"I'm sure she'd say yes," Calia said. "You're practically her apprentice already. And you wouldn't have to go far."

"I could make dolls in the new house."

Ana wrinkled her nose. "Wouldn't you rather make fine gowns like Lucy?"

"No."

Calia laughed. "Well, I'm sure she'll teach you how to do both."

Ana raised a hand to shield her eyes from the sun as it settled upon the horizon. "You know, I think it'll do us some good to be away from Ashmount after all."

"Why?" Calia asked.

"People still talk about us; the things that happened between me and my mother, you with your trial, how we're building a house together. Perhaps our absence will give the gossip time to cool."

"I hope so, especially if you go to paint that cathedral afterwards. I could stay with my family for a while. I don't know when I'll next have a chance to see them."

"That should give the locals enough time to start scandalising some other prominent figures."

They crested a rise in the road. The path sloped down on the other side toward a village nestled amongst fir trees at the base of the big hill.

"That must be our destination," Calia said.

Busy lights started to flicker in the village as they rode closer. The sun disappeared behind the hills, leaving orange clouds in its wake. Their horses were getting tired, so they dismounted to stretch their legs for the last few hundred yards.

"Do you think of that tapestry as our masterpiece?" Ana asked.

"Which one?"

"The big one."

"Your masterpiece, maybe. Not mine. I only wove a couple of squares."

Ana frowned. "I can't think of it that way. Every time I look at it, all I see is the trouble we went through."

"What about my little tapestry?"

"That one's yours. I only provided the sketch."

"But I wouldn't have wanted to weave it if I hadn't seen your painting. That's what made me fall in love with the Farren Vale. And if you hadn't complained to the queen about my style, she might never have let me weave my own version. So one way or another, you brought my tapestry to life, too."

"You're being whimsical."

"Aren't I just."

Ana made something like a snort of laughter. She swayed in Calia's direction and gave her a bump with her shoulder.

When they reached the village, they found a large public

house heaving with guests. Karaline went to peek in the door with James while Calia and Ana stabled their horses. They paid the groom and gathered up their belongings, but Ana stopped before they went inside.

"Thank you," she said haltingly, "for being my friend, Calia."

Calia put her arms around the taller woman and hugged her.

After a moment, Ana hugged her back.

The next chapter of the Book of Roses saga looks back to the past, following the early days of Sir Roger twenty years before the events of *Elizabeth of Rosepath*.
Mender of Monsters releases on January 5th, 2025. Read on for a preview.

On a storm-torn night, a band of knights stagger through the gates of Wrenvale Abbey, one of their number bleeding from a sword wound to the head. Bound by her oaths as an infirmarer, Sister Hazel is tasked with saving the man's life. But her patient is no ordinary soldier—he is the barbarian known as Red Roger, butcher of peasants, burner of fields, defiler of churches. He is a monster, and Hazel holds his life in her hands. Yet as Hazel nurses Roger back to health, a growing fascination with her savage patient takes hold of her. What drives men to such cruelty, and what, if anything, does it take to bring them back from it?

As Roger's presence drives a growing wedge between Hazel's fellow nuns, challenges from a self-interested bishop and Roger's bloodthirsty comrades rise to threaten the abbey. Roger may be the linchpin holding the future of Wrenvale together, but with so much darkness in his past, how can he be relied upon to do the right thing?
Sister Hazel must find a way to reach him.

Thank you for taking the time to read this book. I write because I hope to give others the same experience I get when I'm curled up with a good novel, lost in a story that grabs hold of me and doesn't let go. If I managed to give you that for even a few moments of your day, it makes it all worthwhile.

If you enjoyed your time in these pages, I'd humbly request that you consider leaving a review on the site you purchased the book from. As an independent author, I rely on word of mouth and community reviews to keep me afloat. It really would make my day!

For notifications on new releases, subscribe to my mailing list: books2read.com/author/kelly-river/subscribe/1/491008

If you would like to follow my social media feeds, read my blog posts, or find out more about upcoming novels in advance, visit my website:
kellyriverbooks.com

Other novels by Kelly River:

The Book of Roses:
Elizabeth of Rosepath
A Heart in the Hills
The Embers of Daylight

Lavender's Wolf
Calia's Needle
Mender of Monsters (Coming January 5th 2025)

Cover art designed by L1graphics:
99designs.com/profiles/l1graphics

MENDER OF MONSTERS PREVIEW

CHAPTER 1

The sound of a man's screams jerked Sister Hazel from her sleep. Her feet slipped from beneath her blanket, hand reaching instinctively for a rushlight before she realised the screams weren't coming from the infirmary next door. They'd barely had any patients in there for a week, let alone someone who would wake her in the night with such ungodly cries.

Hazel's skin prickled beneath her shift as a second cry cut through the sound of rain pattering against her shutters. The noise was echoing up from the cloisters below. Why was there a man in the convent at this hour? Why was he screaming like he'd been stabbed? Had the war finally breached the sacred walls of Wrenvale Abbey? Hazel groped for the rushlights she kept on the table beside her bed, knocking over the ceramic cup she used to hold them in her haste. She heard it shatter on the floor and flinched as a shard of pottery stung her foot. The man screamed again.

Throwing open her door, she hurried into the infirmary. Sister Cora, her assistant, sat on her cot beside the hearth, her shoulders trembling, palms clasped together in fearful prayer.

"Is it soldiers?" Cora whispered.

Seeing the young woman's fear painted in the firelight steeled Hazel's courage. She took Cora's hand and lit a rushlight from the hearth.

"Get dressed and fetch my bag. I'll find the prioress."

Cora nodded and hurried to put on her robe. She was only seventeen, barely out of her novitiate. While Hazel had never pried, she knew her assistant's presence here at Wrenvale was one of many sad consequences of the war. They'd seen more displaced women seeking refuge than they could accept in recent years.

Hazel tried not to tremble as another horrific scream forced its way through the shutters. More male voices accompanied it this time. They sounded angry and desperate. She closed her eyes and whispered a silent prayer. She had to be strong for the others. As the abbey's infirmarer, she would be the one stitching wounds and applying poultices if anyone got hurt.

Not bothering to find her robe, she took her winter cloak from its peg beside the door and threw it over her shoulders. The stone stairs felt like ice beneath her feet. The shouting was getting louder, spilling across the cloisters that separated the south wing from the rest of the abbey. Hazel held up her rushlight, willing her pounding heart still as she hurried down the steps to the ground floor. The infirmary was isolated in the south wing, standing above the guest chambers and their adjoining wash room. Unless Hazel and Cora were hosting travellers or tending patients, they had the building to themselves.

Hazel's breath caught in her throat as torchlight flashed through the guest parlour shutters. They were right outside. The patter of rain eased as the storm passed on, but Hazel feared something far more dangerous awaited her outside.

"Sisters of Wrenvale!" a deep voice boomed. "Where are you hiding?"

The torchlight moved toward the church at the east end of the cloister. If Hazel could slip past them, she might be able to reach the main gate and run to the village for help. But what could farmers do against armed soldiers? No, she wouldn't abandon her sisters. She had to be strong for Cora and the others. Gripping the latch on the parlour door, she lifted it and stepped outside.

Cold drizzle speckled Hazel's brow as she turned to see a dozen men standing at the church door. Those who didn't carry torches had swords and spears in their hands, while two others bore a stretcher between them. The man they were carrying let out another blood-curdling scream.

"Are you in need of a physician?" Hazel called. Her voice sounded thin as the wind rasped in her throat.

The men turned to look at her as one. Guttering torch flames glinted on dirty chain mail, revealing scarred, unshaven faces flecked with droplets of dry blood. As she always did in moments of great fear, Hazel willed her mind away from the present, forcing her ego to drift away until only a shell remained. She was not Hazel, daughter of Enoch; she was Sister Hazel, servant of God. His light filled her, subsuming her fear and stilling her doubts. If it was God's will for her to die at the hands of these soldiers, it was her duty to go willingly.

A tall man with a fur-trimmed cloak and braided hair stepped forward alongside a knight bearing a torch. Hazel recognised both of them. They were Larmond of Saintsmarch and Sir Leo, two young noblemen serving Prince Ralf. The prince had spent the last three years fighting his half-brother for control of the throne. Hazel's fear ebbed, but only a little. Larmond had always been cordial when he visited the abbey before, but the villagers told terrible stories about the cruelty his men had inflicted while rooting out Prince Ralf's enemies.

"I am indeed, Sister," Larmond said, motioning to the stretcher behind him. "I have a wounded man with me."

Hazel's eyes flitted to the figure on the stretcher. She couldn't see him clearly from where she was, but his body was tight with shivers of pain, his screams coming through clenched teeth as he twisted and shook.

Before she could answer, the doors on the other side of the cloister burst open. From the north wing dormitory, half a dozen nuns emerged with lanterns in their hands. Prioress Justinia strode ahead of them into the grassy court, her white robe shining in the lantern light as she approached Larmond. The sure-footed purpose of her movement humbled Hazel, making her feel guilty for having hesitated. At thirty-eight, Justinia was the same age as her. While Hazel's tangled auburn hair fell in a mess from beneath her hood, not a strand of Justinia's straight, dark locks escaped her head covering. She had always been destined to be the abbess's deputy.

"How dare you break into our abbey!" Justinia's voice rang through the cloisters, silencing even the screams of the wounded man as she shouted. "Humble yourselves in the presence of God and beg forgiveness!"

Some of Larmond's men lowered their weapons and made as if to kneel, but the young lord put a hand on his belt and turned toward Justinia with practised ease. He spoke courteously, but Hazel sensed an undercurrent of impatience in his voice.

"Forgive me, Prioress, but your gate was locked and I hadn't the mind to stand outside shouting, so I sent a man over the wall to open it for us."

"You have violated the sanctity of this convent! Prince Ralf shall hear of this."

"He'll hear of it from me first if you stand there yapping while my man bleeds to death," Larmond snapped. "Where's your infirmary?"

"This way," Hazel said, but Justinia spoke over her.

"The sisters of Wrenvale owe nothing to godless barbarians who break in after dark."

Hazel bit her tongue to keep herself from saying anything. Justinia would rather die on Larmond's sword than compromise her principles, but the faces behind her bore none of her uncompromising zeal. The other sisters were afraid. It would do them no good to provoke a prideful young lord's ire.

"Then perhaps you owe something to the man who will soon be your king," Larmond retorted. "The war will be over in a few months, and Ralf will sit on the throne. Would you like me to tell him that your abbey refused aid to his loyal subjects when they threw themselves upon your mercy?"

Hazel gave Justinia an imploring look. "Prioress, it is our duty to help those in need."

Justinia's lips thinned and she strode past Larmond, lifting her lantern so that its light fell upon the face of the wounded man. He shied away as if it hurt his eyes, snarling through a groan of pain. Hazel took a step closer. She'd seen enough battle injuries these past three years to know that there was little she could do for the man. His head was horrifically swollen on the left side where it had been cleaved open from cheek to nose, leaving behind a terrible gash that oozed blood across what remained of his mangled face. Torn linen had been wrapped around his left arm and torso, but it was soaked dark red. Even if his chest injuries weren't life-threatening, Hazel had never seen anyone recover from a head wound delivered with such skull-shattering force.

When Justinia made no objection, Hazel went to the man's side and propped up her rushlight in the grass, bidding the stretcher-bearers lower him down.

"I don't know how much I can do for wounds like this, but we can ease his suffering."

"I need him alive," Sir Leo said. He was a young man like Larmond, but his hair had already receded back to reveal a lined brow that lent him a look of severe authority. Hazel suspected his tough bearing belied his lack of experience.

"This man is one of our most valued soldiers," Larmond

said. "If you require compensation to keep him alive, price is no object."

Hazel shook her head. "It isn't a matter of money, my lords. His skull may be broken. Would two of your men please help me hold him down?"

Leo and one of the others obliged. Hazel looked over her shoulder and saw Cora standing frozen in the guest parlour door with her medical bag clutched to her chest. She motioned her over and took the bag. Fishing out a wooden stick wrapped in leather, she had Larmond's men help her pry open the wounded man's jaw and force it between his teeth. Even the effort of parting his teeth half an inch provoked such a violent response that Leo had to kneel on his arm to keep him from thrashing free.

"Hold still, Roger, you damned fool! She's trying to help you!"

With a third man holding the rod in Roger's mouth, Hazel pushed her fingers between his teeth and felt the flesh inside while her other hand tested the swollen area around the face wound. Applying the gentlest pressure, she probed the flesh from the inside and out as Roger screamed. She was grateful she had three men restraining him, for he was strong enough to have thrown her off with a single arm. She frowned as she felt what she'd been afraid of—the grating shift of bone pieces moving beneath her fingertips. His cheekbone had been destroyed. She could feel it from both the inside and out. Withdrawing her fingers from his mouth, she continued probing the side of his head. It was possible the skull had been fractured further back, but she couldn't find any more pieces of bone moving freely beyond the eye socket.

"It's hard to tell how bad the damage is with so much swelling," she said. "How long ago did this happen?"

"This afternoon," said Sir Leo. "At least, that was when I found him. We were due to meet at that old barn on the road south from here. It seems someone else met him first."

"Was anyone else hurt?"

Leo shook his head. "Half a dozen of Roger's men, but those that weren't already dead died on the way here."

Hazel didn't ask why they'd been meeting in such a clandestine spot miles away from anywhere. She knew who this man was. She'd never seen him before, but the name and the head of curly red hair featured regularly in the villagers' stories. This was the man the people of Wrenhurst called Red Roger. Though her fingers made the motions of a healer, a small part of Hazel was almost grateful that her patient would soon be dead. Last year, she'd heard a tale of Red Roger setting fire to a chapel with women and children locked inside while their crucified priest was forced to watch. That was just one of many horrifying stories. Where Red Roger went, accounts of butchered peasants, defiled churches, and burnt farms followed. Hazel understood all too well the cruelties the chaos of war could unearth, but Red Roger's reputation went beyond the pale. There was no justifying the things this man stood accused of.

Justinia seemed to reach the same conclusion.

"We cannot have this man in the abbey," she said under her breath.

Roger's presence would violate the sanctity of their refuge. He would pose a danger to the nuns. If by some miracle he survived, they would be complicit in the knowledge that they had sent a demon back into the world to spread more strife.

And yet, Hazel disagreed with Justinia.

"It is not our place to judge who is worthy and unworthy of God's kindness," she said, her eyes remaining on Roger as she took off the bloodsoaked linen to examine his chest wounds.

"It is my duty as prioress to ensure the safety of our sisters."

"And it is mine as infirmarer to tend all those God brings before me." Hazel looked up and met Justinia's gaze. For a moment, she saw a twitch of pain in the prioress's eyes, a hint of the old friendship they'd shared when they entered the convent as novices years ago. Then it vanished, replaced by the steely conviction of the woman that girl had become.

"I forbid it. Lord Larmond, you must take this man elsewhere. The physicians in Wrenhurst town will be able to help you."

Larmond's fingers tightened on his belt. "He'll be dead before we're halfway there."

"Then we will pray for his soul."

Sir Leo glared up at her. "If you turn us out, I'll make sure you live to regret it."

Hazel focused her attention back on Roger. The decision was Justinia's to make. Her duty was to lead, just as Hazel's was to heal. Every sister had her role in the abbey, and the precept of obedience bound her to it.

From the back of the group of nuns, a gentle voice spoke.

"Let us not act hastily, my sisters."

The crowd drew apart as a hunched old woman in a white robe limped forward. Though her hand trembled on the handle of her walking stick, her pace did not falter as she approached Larmond's men. Even Justinia's brusque confidence wilted in her presence.

"Mother Superior," Justinia said with a bow.

Though age had shrunken her stature, Mother Mariel's eyes still sparkled with the same intelligence Hazel remembered from the day she entered the abbey. She bore herself with an effortless confidence that inspired courage in the fearful and compassion in the hard-hearted. She had been the abbess of Wrenvale for forty years, and while Justinia oversaw the day-to-day running of the abbey, it was Mother Mariel who had the final say.

"Are your sisters going to waste any more of my time while this man bleeds his life away?" Larmond demanded, though the impatience in his voice betrayed a hint of reservation now.

"This is not a conversation to be had out here in the

cloisters, my son," Mariel replied. "Sister Hazel, Sister Cora, would you bring this man to the infirmary? Lord Larmond's men can take their ease in the guest parlour while I speak with their master in private."

"Of course, Mother Superior." Hazel bowed her head.

Justinia's expression tightened in frustration, but after a moment's turmoil she turned to the others and began ushering them back into the cloisters. Sir Leo and Larmond's other men helped Hazel lift the stretcher while Cora picked up her bag.

Mother Mariel caught her eye before she left. "Take good care of him, Hazel." She looked up at Larmond and rested a hand on his arm when he offered it. "I am sure the young lord's men will show us courtesy while they are here."

"You have my word, Mother Superior," Larmond said.

"If you would accompany me to my house, we can speak on this further."

The group broke apart, leaving the silence of the cloisters to be disturbed only by Roger's intermittent screams. Hazel let out an unsteady breath. She thanked God that the abbess had appeared when she did. She was a diplomatic woman with years of experience handling bishops and noblemen. Whatever she said to Larmond, she was sure to get him and his men out of the abbey with far less commotion than Justinia would have caused.

All Hazel had to do now was ease her patient's suffering as best she could. Perhaps if he died gently rather than screaming and thrashing, Larmond would look more kindly upon them.

Printed in Dunstable, United Kingdom